About the Author

Gail Whitiker is the award-winning author of eighteen historical and contemporary novels. Her books have been distributed in over twenty-eight countries and translated into almost as many languages, though she is still waiting to see one published in her native Welsh! She currently lives on the West Coast of Canada. Visit her website at www.gailwhitiker.com

Regency Scandals

Regency Scandal:

Disreputable Secrets

GAIL WHITIKER

MILLS & BOON

First Published in Great Britain 2020
By Mills & Boon, an imprint of HarperCollins*Publishers*
1 London Bridge Street, London, SE1 9GF

2

REGENCY SCANDAL: DISREPUTABLE SECRETS
© 2020 Harlequin Books S.A.

Brushed by Scandal © 2011 Gail Whitiker
Improper Miss Darling © 2011 Gail Whitiker

978-0-263-29856-7

MIX
Paper from
responsible sources

FSC
www.fsc.org

FSC C007454

This book is produced from independently certified FSC™ paper to ensure responsible forest management.

For more information visit: www.harpercollins.co.uk/green

Printed and bound by
CPI Group (UK) Ltd, Croydon, CR0 4YY

BRUSHED BY SCANDAL

To Mum and Dad, who continue to be an ongoing source of love and support in so many areas of my life. Thank you for always being there.

And to my good friend Lynne Rattray, who inspires me with her joie de vivre and her unflagging sense of humour.

Chapter One

It was a perfect night for sin. The mid-May evening was deliciously warm, the air sweet with the fragrance of rosewater and violets, and the attention of one hundred and forty-nine of the guests moving slowly through the overheated rooms of Lord and Lady Montby's palatial London house was focused on anything *but* the young lady slipping furtively through the French doors and onto the dimly lit balcony beyond.

Fortunately, as the attention of the one hundred and fiftieth guest had been fixed on that silly young woman for some time, the chances of *her* making a clean escape were never very good. Over the course of the evening, Lady Annabelle Durst had watched the exchange of smiles and glances passing between Miss Mercy Banks and a certain red-coated officer, and, given that the gentleman had recently left the room by the same doors through which Miss Banks now passed, Anna had no doubt that a clandestine rendezvous was planned. A rendezvous that could only end in disaster for one or both of them.

'Mrs Wicks, would you please excuse me,' Anna said quietly. 'I've just seen someone I really must speak with.'

'Why, of course, Lady Annabelle, and I do apologise for having taken up so much of your time, but I really didn't know who else to turn to. Cynthia simply refuses to listen and I was at my wits' end, wondering what to do next.'

'I understand perfectly,' Anna said, endeavouring to keep one eye on the French doors. 'Cynthia has always been the most stubborn of your daughters and if you force her to spend a month in Scotland with her grandmother while her sisters are allowed to go to Bath, she *will* rebel. However, I believe the compromise I've suggested should help to alleviate the tension and make everyone feel better.'

'I don't mind saying it's made *me* feel a great deal better,' Mrs Wicks murmured. 'You're an uncommonly wise young woman for your age, Lady Annabelle. Your father must be very proud.'

Aware that her father would have been a great deal more proud had he been sending word of her upcoming engagement to *The Times*, Anna simply inclined her head and moved on. There was no point in telling Mrs Wicks that her unwed state was an ongoing source of consternation to her father or that he had offered to settle not only a handsome dowry, but one of his smaller, unentailed estates on her the moment she announced her engagement. Why bother when there was absolutely no one in her life for whom she felt even the slightest attraction?

As for being deemed a very wise young woman, Anna supposed it could have been worse. She might have been called studious or obliging—agreeable, even—none of which truly described her character. Yes, it was true, she had been dispensing an inordinate amount of advice to wilful young ladies and their frustrated mothers of late, but what was she to do when they kept coming to her for answers? Their problems were relatively easy to understand and comparatively simple to fix, even if the parties involved thought otherwise.

As to the hapless Miss Banks, that was clearly a situation Anna was going to have to deal with personally if she hoped to ward off imminent disaster.

The balcony, illuminated by multiple strands of brightly coloured lanterns strung from one end to the other, ran almost the entire length of the house, but one glance in either direction was enough to show Anna that her quarry had already vanished into the gardens. Foolish girl. Did she really believe that the gardens were empty? That no one else had sought privacy in the shadowy follies and Grecian temples sprinkled throughout the trees?

Obviously not or she wouldn't have allowed herself to be led astray—and Anna had no doubt the girl *had* been led. Mercy Banks was as green as a leprechaun's jacket. Barely seventeen, she was in London for her first Season, so it was only to be expected that, upon meeting a young man who looked at her as though she were Aphrodite reincarnated, she would mistake attraction for something deeper.

Anna had been seventeen once, too. She remembered all too well the excitement of looking up to find a handsome gentleman watching her; the exhilaration of his hand casually brushing hers when they drew close enough to converse, followed by the warmth of his breath as he leaned in close to whisper a compliment.

Oh, yes, she knew well the lure of those forbidden bowers. But *because* she had been prevented from making a mistake by someone who had noticed her infatuation and taken the time to intervene, Anna now recognised the importance in doing the same for others. Unfortunately, as she walked down the stone steps and into the garden proper, she realised she was not the only one intent on locating the wayward Miss Banks. Marching with grim resolve along the gravel path ahead of her was the young lady's mother, determined to find her errant daughter before some dreadful misfortune could befall her.

Obviously, more desperate measures were now called for.

'Mrs Banks,' Anna called in a pleasant but carrying voice. 'What a pleasure to see you again.'

Mrs Banks, a small, rotund lady wearing a dark green gown and a headband adorned with flowers and fruits of an exotic hue, paused to glance over her shoulder; upon seeing Anna, she stopped, her expression of concern changing to one of pleasure. 'Why, Lady Annabelle, how nice to see you again. It must be nearly a month since we last had an opportunity to chat. Lady Falconer's musicale, wasn't it?'

Anna inclined her head. 'I do believe it was.'

'I thought so. Dreadful soprano. I vow my ears rang most painfully for the rest of the night,' Mrs Banks said with a frown. 'But what are you doing out here all on your own?'

'The house was so warm, I thought to enjoy a quiet stroll through the gardens,' Anna said, keeping her voice light and her words casual. 'But where is Mr Banks this evening? I take it he did come with you.'

'Oh, yes, albeit reluctantly. He's not much into these society affairs, but I told him we must make an effort if we hope to settle Mercy in an advantageous marriage.' Mrs Banks sighed. 'For his sake, I hope she finds a husband sooner rather than later. He's that anxious to get back home.'

'I'm sure it will be sooner,' Anna said, heart jumping as she caught sight of a red coat just beyond Mrs Banks's right shoulder. 'But I wonder, Mrs Banks, if you've seen the new fountain Lady Montby recently had installed over by the reflecting pool? It really is quite spectacular.'

'I'm sure it is, but at the moment, I am more concerned with finding Mercy.'

'Really?' Anna affected a look of confusion. 'I am quite sure I saw her inside the house.'

'You did? Where?'

'Heading in the direction of the music room.'

Mrs Banks rolled her eyes, but Anna noticed a definite softening in the lines of tension around her mouth. 'I might have known. Someone told Mercy that Lady Montby had recently acquired a new pianoforte and naturally she was anxious to see it. The child is quite musically gifted,' her mother confided proudly. 'And while I take care not to compliment her too much, I am hopeful it will help in the quest to find her the right kind of husband.'

'I'm sure she will do you both proud,' Anna said, slipping her arm through the older woman's and turning her around. 'But as long as we're heading back inside, why don't we take a peek at the fountain? It will only take a moment, and then you can carry on and look for your daughter.'

Obviously deciding it was a good idea, Mrs Banks made no demur as Anna led her in the direction of the fountain, which was indeed a spectacular affair, and which, more importantly, was located at the opposite end of the garden from where Anna suspected Mercy and her officer were hiding. Once there, she introduced Mrs Banks to Mrs Wicks, who immediately launched into a diatribe about the difficulties of presenting ungrateful daughters to society, whereupon Mrs Banks said how thankful she was that she only had one daughter to marry off, rather than three.

Anna left the two women happily commiserating with one another and quickly retraced her steps. She was almost at the far end of the path when Miss Banks stepped out, her cheeks flushed, her blue eyes wide with apprehension. 'Lady Annabelle!'

'Miss Banks. Enjoying a few minutes *alone* in the garden?' she asked pointedly.

'Yes! That is…no. That is…oh dear.' The girl looked up and the expression on Anna's face turned her cheeks an even brighter shade of red. 'Please tell me Mama didn't know where I was.'

'She did not, but only because I suggested you were still inside the house,' Anna said. 'If she had caught you and your young man out here together, the consequences would have been dire!'

The girl's pretty face fell. 'I know. And I promise I won't do it again. It's just that…'

When she broke off blushing, Anna prayed the silly girl hadn't done anything irredeemably stupid. 'It's just that what?'

Mercy sighed. 'He said it would be all right. He told me… he loved me.'

Of course he had, Anna thought drily. Was a declaration of love not the most common justification for inappropriate behaviour on a young man's part? 'Then I take leave to tell you that he had a very poor way of showing it. Has he secured your father's permission to speak to you?'

Miss Banks looked even more miserable. 'We have not even been formally introduced. We first saw one another in Hyde Park a week ago, then again at a masquerade two nights past.'

'At which time he suggested a rendezvous for this evening,' Anna surmised.

The girl nodded.

'Then you must not see him again until a formal introduction has been made. Whatever his feelings, asking you to meet him alone in a secluded garden demonstrates the worst kind of judgement,' Anna said firmly. 'He must seek a proper introduction and when the time comes to speak of his intentions, he must approach your father and ask permission to call upon you. Please believe me when I say that what he did tonight was *not* an indication of love, Miss Banks, no matter how much you would like to believe otherwise.'

The young girl bit her lip. 'No, I don't suppose it was. But I did so want to see him again…even if only for a few minutes.'

'A few minutes are more than enough to ruin a lifetime,' Anna said more gently. 'You must guard your reputation as fiercely as you would your most precious possession, because right now, it *is* your most precious possession. Once lost it can never be regained and no one will suffer more for its absence than you. So, no matter what *any* gentleman says to you, or how sweetly he says it, do not let yourself be tempted into such an indiscretion again.'

'Yes, Lady Annabelle.'

Anna could see from the expression on Mercy's face that she had learned her lesson and that the episode would not be repeated. Nor did Anna expect that it would. It wasn't that Mercy was bad. She was simply young and impetuous, as were so many girls her age.

As Anna herself had once been.

'And now, we shall return to the house and you will find your mother and endeavour to set her mind at rest,' she said, leading Mercy back along the gravel path. 'As for your young man, you are not to look for him again, and, if he seeks you out, you are to tell him you will not speak to him until the two of you have been properly introduced…which I shall endeavour to do later this evening.'

Miss Banks gasped. 'You would do that for me?'

'I would, but only if you give me your promise that you will never see…' Anna paused. 'What is the officer's name?'

'Lieutenant Giles Blokker.'

'Fine. That you will not see Lieutenant Blokker again without suitable chaperonage. I may not be around to save you the next time.'

'You have my promise, Lady Annabelle. And thank you! Thank you so very much!'

Upon returning to the ballroom, Miss Banks did exactly as she had been told. When Lieutenant Blokker tried to approach her, she treated him to a look that would have done her crusty old grandmother proud and then went in search of her mother. The young man looked understandably crushed, but Anna hoped it had taught him a lesson. If he truly cared for Miss Banks, he would do whatever was necessary in order to further the connection in the manner of which society approved. If not, he wasn't worth having in the first place.

'Do you attempt to save them all from themselves?' asked an amused masculine voice close to her ear. 'Or only the ones who don't know any better?'

Anna turned her head and found herself looking into the face of a stranger. A very handsome stranger, but a stranger none the less. 'Were you speaking to me, sir?'

'I was. And pray forgive my boldness, but I happened to be in the garden when you came upon the young lady, and such was my timing that I was privy to most of your conversation with her just now. She is indeed fortunate to have you as her champion.'

His voice was velvet over steel. Resonant, powerful, the kind of voice that held audiences spellbound and sent impressionable young women swooning. Anna could imagine him reciting Shakespeare on the stage at Drury Lane, or reading love sonnets by Bryon or Wordsworth, those low, sensual tones sparking desire in any young woman's breast.

But was their meeting now entirely coincidental? While she thought him too old for Miss Banks and too casual in his addresses to her, the fact he had been in the garden at the same time as they had, and that he just happened to be standing next to her now, left her wondering.

'I only attempt to save the ones I deem worthy of saving,' she replied carefully. 'The rest I leave to their own devices.'

'Just as well,' the gentleman said. 'Most people sin for the fun of it and wouldn't welcome your intervention, no matter how well intentioned. Unlike Miss Banks, whose romantic heart would likely have got the better of her had you not stepped in to save the day.'

Anna caught an undertone of amusement in his voice and, despite her natural inclination to be wary, found herself smiling back at him. He was certainly an attractive man. His face was long rather than square, his jaw angular, his cheekbones high and well formed. Intelligence gleamed in the depths of those clear grey eyes and his lips, curved upwards in a smile, were firm and disturbingly sensual. His clothes were expensive, his linen impeccable, and while his hair shone black in the light of a thousand candles, the tiny lines at the corners of his eyes put him closer to thirty than twenty.

No, he definitely wasn't after Miss Mercy Banks, Anna decided. He could have eaten the silly little chit for dinner and still gone away hungry. But neither was this a casual conversation, of that she was sure. 'I am undecided as to whether I should be flattered by your comments or offended by them,' she said. 'I had no idea my actions were being so closely observed.'

'A gentleman should never make his attentions too obvious, Lady Annabelle. I pride myself on my ability to observe without *being* observed—a quality necessary to those who involve themselves in the convoluted lives of others. Wouldn't you agree?'

Anna's eyes widened. So, he knew who she was and what she was about. That alone should have put her on her guard, yet all it did was make her more curious. She liked a man who didn't play games; Lord knew, London society was all too full of them. 'I fear you have the advantage of me, sir.

You obviously know a great deal more about me than I do about you.'

'Only because you are more visible in society,' he murmured. 'And as much as I regret the inequity of the situation, we both know it would be ill-mannered of me to introduce myself, so I shall wait for the thing to be done properly as you have so kindly offered to do for Miss Banks.'

His words abruptly called to mind the promise Anna had made earlier and her brows knit in consternation. 'An offer made impetuously at best, I fear. Apart from the officer's name, I know nothing about the man and have no idea if he is even *worthy* of an introduction.'

'Then allow me to set your mind at rest. I happen to know that Lieutenant Giles Blokker is an amiable young man who, despite having behaved with the decorum of a rambunctious puppy, is an excellent catch. His father is Major Sir Gordon Blokker, who distinguished himself with Wellington on the Peninsula, and his mother is the former Lady Margaret Sissely. The boy was educated at Eton, went on to read English and history at Oxford, and, as his father's only son, he is heir to a considerable estate. More importantly, I believe he is the kind of man of whom both Miss Banks's mother and father would approve.'

Surprised by the extent of the man's knowledge and by his willingness to share it, Anna inclined her head. 'I am grateful for your recommendation, sir. How fortunate that you are so well acquainted with the officer.'

'In fact, we've never met. But one hears a great many things during the course of one's social day, and if I feel it is information that may be of use to someone else, I am happy to pass it along. I trust that, in this instance, it serves you well. Good evening, Lady Annabelle.'

With that, he bowed and walked away, leaving Anna with a host of unanswered questions tumbling around in her brain.

Who was he, and why did his sudden appearance at her side not seem as coincidental as he might like her to believe? By telling her all he had about Lieutenant Blokker, he'd put her in the enviable position of being able to make the promised introduction, aware that not only might she be introducing Miss Banks to her future husband, but that he was a gentleman worthy of the role. Had he known more about the predicament in which she'd landed herself than he had chosen to let on?

Not surprisingly, Anna found herself watching the handsome stranger as he moved around the room. She noticed that he did not linger with any one person or group for any length of time, but that his gaze touched on every person there, his expression unreadable as he took note of who they spoke to and with whom they danced. Even when he stopped to speak to an upright older gentleman who was clearly intent on engaging him in a serious conversation, his eyes continued in their restless study. Was he was a private investigator of some kind? He looked too aristocratic for such an occupation, but then, perhaps a man who didn't *look* the part was *exactly* the sort of man who should be doing that kind of work.

He'd certainly made an impression on her. For once she'd actually *enjoyed* having a conversation with a gentleman newly met at a society function. Normally, she was quick to wish them over, knowing all too well what they were really all about.

Is this someone with whom I have anything in common? Do I feel a connection strong enough to spend the rest of my life with him? And, of course, what do we each stand to gain by aligning our families in marriage?

They were all questions Anna had asked herself in the past. And with that one unfortunate exception where the marriage *would* have been a disaster, the answers were always the same.

No, not likely, and nothing.

But this gentleman intrigued her. She found herself watching for him in the crowd, curious to see how he acted with other people, anxious to catch just one more glimpse of him. Wanting to know if he might be looking back at her.

And when he did and Anna felt her gaze trapped in the soft silver glow of his eyes, she knew it was too late to look away. She had carelessly exposed herself, allowing her interest in, and her curiosity about, a stranger to be revealed. Was it any wonder that when he tipped his head and slowly began to smile, she felt the heat rise in her cheeks and the breath catch in her throat?

Goodness, who would have thought that with just one look, he could make her feel as awkward as a schoolgirl, as young and as gauche as Miss Mercy Banks. Surely as a mature woman of twenty-four, she knew better than to encourage the attentions of a man she'd only just met…

Anna dipped her head and boldly returned his smile. No, clearly she did not. But as she opened her fan and reluctantly turned away, the knowledge that a handsome man whose name she didn't know still had the power to make her blush was more than enough to keep the smile on her face for the rest of the evening.

'Parker, have you heard anything I've said?' Colonel Tanner demanded in a harsh whisper.

'Every word, Colonel.' Sir Barrington Parker's expression didn't change, though he was careful to pull his gaze from the face of the exquisite young woman who had just smiled at him across the room. No small feat for a man who appreciated beauty as much as he did. 'You wish me to investigate the disappearance of your mistress—'

'I never said she was my mistress!' the older man blustered.

'There was no need. Avoiding my eyes while you described her told me all I needed to know,' Barrington said smoothly. 'She is approximately twenty years old, slim, with dark brown hair and rather startling green eyes. The last time you saw her she was wearing a pale blue gown with a white shawl and a bonnet with either blue or black ribbons.'

The older man grunted. 'Apologies. Just don't like blathering on to a man who doesn't appear to be listening.'

'I wouldn't accomplish much if I didn't listen, Colonel,' Barrington said, though in truth he hadn't been paying as much attention as he should. Through the mirror on the wall behind Tanner, he had been watching Lady Annabelle Durst attempt to play matchmaker. She had waited until Lieutenant Giles Blokker was in the midst of a small group of people with whom she was obviously acquainted and had sought the necessary introduction. Then, as the other couples had drifted away, she had engaged Lieutenant Blokker in conversation, no doubt with the intent of bringing Miss Banks's name into the discussion.

At that point, Barrington had seen a look of cautious optimism appear on Blokker's face, followed moments later by one of genuine happiness. When Lady Annabelle turned and started in the direction of Miss Banks and her mother, the young pup had fallen into step behind her, clearly delighted that he was on his way to being formally introduced to the young lady who had captured his heart.

'Where did you last see Miss Paisley, Colonel?' Barrington asked, reluctantly dragging his attention back to the matter at hand.

'Hogarth Road. I keep a house there. Nothing elaborate, you understand,' the Colonel said gruffly. 'Just a place for friends to use when they come up to London.'

Barrington nodded. He knew exactly what the house was

used for and it certainly wasn't the convenience of friends. 'I shall make enquiries. Where can I reach you?'

'Best send a note round the club. Wouldn't do to have anything come to the house.'

Barrington inclined his head. Though most wives knew about their husbands' affairs, none wanted proof of them showing up at their front doors. 'As you wish.'

'Look here, Parker, it's not what you think,' the Colonel said, clearing his throat. 'Eliza's not like the rest of them. She worked as a lady's maid in a respectable establishment until the eldest son took a fancy to her. When she was turned off without references, one thing led to another until she ended up in a brothel. That's where I met her,' he said, again not meeting Barrington's eyes. 'She told me her story and naturally I felt sorry for her, so I asked her if she'd like to come and work for me. I knew Constance was looking for a new maid and I thought it might be a way of getting Eliza back into respectable employment.'

Barrington's smile was purposely bland. 'And did your wife agree to take Miss Paisley on?'

'She did, but it wasn't long before she realised there was something going on and I had to let Eliza go,' the Colonel said regretfully. 'Felt so damned guilty, I offered to put her up at the house on Hogarth Road until she was able to find something else.'

With the small stipulation, Barrington surmised, that she become his mistress while she was there. A gentleman's altruism only extended so far. 'It would seem Miss Paisley has much to be grateful to you for, Colonel.'

'I thought so, which was why I was so surprised when she left without telling me,' the Colonel said. 'Bit concerned, if you know what I mean.'

Barrington did know and he wasn't surprised. Tanner was a decent chap, somewhere in his mid-fifties, with four married children and eight grandchildren. His wife had been in poor health for the last five years and, though he was devoted to her in every other way, her ill health had prevented them from enjoying a normal marital relationship. So he had turned, as so many men did, to the ranks of the *demi-monde* and there he had encountered Miss Elizabeth Paisley, the young woman for whom he had developed an unfortunate affection. Now she was missing and the Colonel was worried about her.

Probably with good reason, Barrington thought as he shook the man's hand and walked away. It was a simple fact that women of Miss Paisley's ilk were concerned with one thing and one thing only. Survival. It wasn't easy making a living on the streets of London. A woman never knew if the man who pulled her into a darkened alley and threw up her skirts was going to be a paying customer or the last man she ever saw alive. Being a prostitute was not without its risks. But being the mistress of a wealthy man took away those risks and gave a woman security. It put a roof over her head and kept food on her table. So why would someone like Miss Paisley walk away from all that if she'd had any other choice?

It was a question Barrington couldn't answer. And as he prepared to leave Lady Montby's reception—after deciding it was best that he not stop to engage the delightful Lady Annabelle in conversation again—he realised it was one that would trouble him until he did. To that end, he made a mental note to ask his secretary to make some initial enquiries into Elizabeth Paisley's whereabouts. Sam Jenkins had been with Barrington long enough to know what kind of questions to ask and who to ask them of. Then, depending on what he turned up, Barrington would either call upon one of his extensive network to continue the investigation or delve into the matter himself.

He wasn't sure why, but as he climbed into his carriage for the short ride home, he had a feeling there was more to the disappearance of Miss Elizabeth Paisley than met the eye.

Chapter Two

Anna pulled her dapple-grey mare to a halt by the base of a large oak and waited for Lady Lydia Winston to catch up with her. The two had made a point of riding together on Tuesday and Thursday mornings, and these rousing canters had become one of the highlights of Anna's week. Lady Lydia, daughter of the Marquess of Bailley, was by far one of the most amusing and interesting people Anna had ever met.

'Goodness!' Lydia said as she drew her spirited Arabian bay level with Anna's mare. 'I was sure I had you at the big tree, but you sprinted past me as though I was standing still!'

'I suspect Danby put oats in Ophelia's bucket this morning.' Anna reached down to give the mare's glossy neck an affectionate pat. 'She's not usually that quick off the mark.'

'Nevertheless, I had enough of a lead that it shouldn't have made a difference. Tarik isn't used to being left behind.' Lydia's ready smile flashed. 'I won't be so easily fooled the next time.'

Anna laughed, pleased that her little mare had done so well. She nudged her to a leisurely walk, content to enjoy the glorious morning sunshine and the relative emptiness of the park. During the fashionable hour, the avenue they were now travelling would be crowded with elegant carriages and their equally elegant passengers, but at this time of day it was the perfect place to enjoy a brisk canter.

'By the by, have you heard the news?' Lydia enquired.

'That depends. All I heard at Lady Montby's reception last week was that Cynthia Wicks had threatened to run away if her mother forced her to spend a month with her grandmother in Scotland.'

'Good Lord, so would I,' Lydia declared. 'Lady Shallerton is a cold fish with whom I wouldn't wish to spend an hour, let alone a month. But it wasn't Miss Wick's escapades I was referring to. It was the Baroness Julia von Brohm's.'

'Baroness von Brohm,' Anna repeated slowly. 'Should I know her?'

'La, Anna, where have you been? It is all about town that the Viennese baroness has come to London to find a new husband.'

'Why? What happened to her old one?'

'He died. Almost two years ago now, leaving her a very lonely but extremely wealthy young widow. Apparently, he showered her with the most glorious jewellery and she was heartbroken when he died. Not because he gave her jewellery,' Lydia was quick to say, 'but because they were genuinely in love. But she is finished with her mourning now and has come to London to start a new life. I understand she's taken a very fine house in Mayfair and is in the process of redecorating it from top to bottom.'

'I'm surprised she would have chosen to leave Vienna at such a time,' Anna remarked. 'One would think she would prefer to stay with her family and friends.'

'Friends I'm sure she has, but again, rumour has it that her only brother moved to America when she was quite young and hasn't been heard from since. And both of her parents are dead.'

'How tragic. What about her late husband's family?' Anna asked.

'Apparently, they were never close. Difficulties with the mother-in-law, from what I hear.'

'So Vienna is full of unhappy memories and the arms of her family hold no welcome. No wonder she decided to come to London,' Anna said. 'Has she any close friends here?'

'I don't believe so. Society is wildly curious about her, of course, but it hasn't exactly thrown open its doors in welcome.'

'Then we must be the first to do so,' Anna said without hesitation. 'I suspect once people see the daughters of the Marquess of Bailley and the Earl of Cambermere welcoming her, the rest of the doors will open soon enough. All it takes,' she added with a knowing smile, 'is that first little push.'

Barrington's sword flashed once, cutting a smooth silver arc through the air and echoing down the length of the long gallery. Metal slid along metal as the two men moved through the orchestrated dance of extend, lunge, parry and retreat, and while concentration was etched on the faces of both men, only Barrington's brow was dry. He feinted to the left, drawing his brother-in-law's blade wide and ultimately opening him up to defeat.

'Damn it!' Tom Danvers snapped as the point of Barrington's sword flicked his chest for the fifth time. 'You've beaten me again!'

'And I will continue to do so if you do not apply yourself more keenly to the sport,' Barrington said, drawing back. 'You won't stand a chance if you keep both feet firmly planted on the ground, Tom. You need to keep moving. Dance on the balls of your feet.'

'Oh, yes, that's easy for you to say,' the other man complained good-naturedly. 'I've three stone and five years on you and it's not so easy being nimble when you've more weight below your waist than above it!'

Barrington laughed. 'Then tell that pompous French chef of yours to start preparing less fattening meals.'

'What? And have him quit because *I* had the audacity to tell him what to cook! Jenny would have my head. Monsieur Etienne is the finest French chef in London!' Tom exclaimed.

'Be that as it may, he is not doing *you* any favours by serving all those heavy sauces and rich desserts,' Barrington pointed out. 'If you wish to be quicker on your feet, the weight will have to come off. In fact, I have a solution.'

'I'm not sure I wish to hear it,' Tom muttered.

'Of course you do. I shall take Monsieur Etienne off your hands for a few weeks and you can have Mrs Buckers. I guarantee your clothes will fit better after only three days.'

'Perhaps, but I won't care because Jenny will have left me.'

Barrington clapped his brother-in-law on the back. 'A man must sacrifice for his sport. Ah, there you are, Sam. Has my two o'clock appointment arrived?'

'Not yet, Sir Barrington,' the secretary said, 'but another gentleman has and is asking to see you. I put him in your study.'

Barrington nodded. A visitor in his study meant one of his network had come in with information. Friends he welcomed in the gold salon. Any one else was made to wait in the hall until he had ascertained the nature of their business. He did not purport to be a private investigator, but, because of his past successes, there were those who sought him out regardless.

'Thank you, Sam. Tell the gentleman I shall be there directly.' He turned to smile at his brother-in-law. 'Sorry to cut it short, Tom...'

'No need to apologise. You're a busy man, and, in truth, I've taken all the humiliation I can for one day,' Tom said good-naturedly. 'Before I go, however, Jenny wanted me to find out if you were available for dinner one night this week. She misses you dreadfully and even young George was heard to say it has been a great deal too long since his Uncle Barr came to play with him.'

Barrington's pleasure was unfeigned. 'Tell my sister I shall make a point of coming one evening this week, and then inform my nephew that I shall be sure to arrive early enough to play two games of hide and seek with him.'

'He will not sleep for the knowledge,' Tom said, starting for the door. 'By the by, I should warn you that you won't be the only guest.'

Barrington groaned. 'Don't tell me Jenny's matchmaking again?'

'I'm afraid so.'

'Who is it this time?' He sighed.

'Lady Alice Stokes.'

Barrington dug into his memory. 'Lady Alice—?'

'Stokes. Eldest daughter of the Earl of Grummond,' Tom supplied helpfully. 'Beautiful, cultured and an heiress in her own right. Jenny thinks she would be perfect for you.'

'That's what she said about the last three ladies she introduced me to and they were all unmitigated disasters.'

'True, but at least you wouldn't have to worry about Lady Alice marrying you for your money. Or for your title,' Tom pointed out.

True enough, Barrington conceded. An earl's daughter could do much better than a baronet, and if she had her own money, his wouldn't be as much of an attraction. 'Very well, you may tell my sister I shall come on Friday. That should give her ample time to put everything in place.'

'You're a brick, Barrington,' Tom said in relief. 'I was afraid you'd bow out if I told you the truth, but I didn't like the idea of you being caught off guard.'

'Rest assured, I shall be the perfect guest,' Barrington said. 'And you need not fear retribution from my sister. I shall act suitably surprised when the beautiful Lady Alice and I are introduced.'

'You are a gentleman in every sense of the word.'

'Just don't let me hear any mention of the words *engagement* or *marriage* or I shall be forced to renege on my promise,' he warned.

Tom grinned. 'I shall do my utmost to make sure you do not.'

They parted on the best of terms; Tom to return to his happy home, Barrington to return to his study to find out what new information had come to light. While there might be more comfort in the former, he was not of a mind to complicate his life by taking a wife. Investigating the underhanded dealings of others was hardly conducive to forming intimate relations with gently reared young ladies. It was neither the occupation of a gentleman nor what he'd planned on doing when he'd returned to London after his father's death.

However, when an unfortunate set of circumstances involving two of his father's friends and a large sum of money had forced him into the role, Barrington had discovered a unique talent for uncovering the hidden bits of information others could not. His carefully cultivated network of acquaintances, many of whom held positions of power and even more who held positions of knowledge, made it easy for him to find out what he needed to know and, over time, he had established himself as a man who was able to find solutions for people's problems.

Naturally, as word of his reputation had spread, so had his list of enemies, many of them the very men he had helped to expose. Beneath society's elegant and sophisticated façade lurked a far more dangerous element—one comprised of men to whom honour and truth meant nothing. Men who were motivated by greed and who routinely committed crimes against their fellow man.

Hence Barrington's wish to remain single. While he could be reasonably assured of his own safety, he knew that if his enemies tried to get to him through the woman he loved, he would have no choice but to comply with their demands. The unscrupulous did not trouble themselves with morals when it came to getting what they wanted.

That's why he had taken to avoiding situations that might place him in such an awkward situation. He existed on the fringes of society, close enough to be aware of what was going on, but far enough away that he wasn't seen as potential husband material. So far it had worked out well, much to the annoyance of his happily married sister. He was able to assist the people who came to him with problems, while avoiding the complications that came with marriage.

Now, as he headed to his study, Barrington wondered which of the sins was about to be revealed and who would be thrown out of Eden as a result. Paradise was sometimes a very difficult place in which to live.

'Ah, Richard,' he said, opening the door to see his good friend, Lord Richard Crew, standing at the far end of the room, his attention focused on a particularly fine painting by

Stubbs that covered a large part of the end wall. 'Still hoping I'll sell it to you?'

'Hope has nothing to do with it,' Crew murmured. 'Eventually, I'll name a price you won't be able to refuse.'

'Don't be too sure. I've rejected every offer you've put forward so far.'

'Fine. I'll make you another before I leave today.'

Barrington smiled as he moved towards his desk. Lord Richard Crew was an ardent lover of horse flesh and owned more paintings by Stubbs, Tillemans and Seymour than any other gentleman in London. Quietly picking them up as they came available for sale, he had amassed an impressive collection—with the exception of *Whistlejacket*, a magnificent painting of a prancing Arabian thoroughbred commissioned by the Marquess of Rockingham and acknowledged by many to be one of Stubbs's finest. *That* was the piece of work currently hanging in Barrington's study, and the fact that he owned the *one* painting his friend wanted more than any other was a constant source of amusement to him and an ongoing source of irritation to Crew.

'Did it ever occur to you,' Barrington asked now, 'that money doesn't enter into it?'

'Not for a moment,' Crew said, finally turning away from the canvas. 'Every man has his price and it's only a matter of time until I find yours. But rest assured, I *will* find it. And I know exactly where I'm going to put *Whistlejacket* once I finally wrest it from your iron grip.'

Barrington smiled. 'And where might that be?'

'In my study, opposite my desk. That way I'll see it when I'm working.'

'I would have thought you'd want it in your bedroom.' Barrington moved to the credenza and poured brandy into two glasses. 'That way, you'd see it most of the time.'

'True, but I would only be paying it half as much attention.' Crew's smile widened into a grin. 'After all, there are so many *other* pleasurable things to occupy oneself with in the bedroom, wouldn't you agree?'

The question was rhetorical. Lord Richard Crew's reputation as a lady's man was honestly come by because, in point of fact, Crew adored women. He had ever since a buxom dairy maid had introduced him to the pleasures of Venus in the loft of his father's barn, followed in quick succession by three of the housemaids, two of the village shop girls, and a married woman Crew had steadfastly refused to name.

As he'd grown into a man, his appreciation for the fairer sex had not waned, but out of respect for his parents, he'd left off tupping the household servants and moved on to ballet dancers and actresses. He had steadfastly avoided marriage and refused to trifle with virgins or débutantes, saying it was a matter of pride that he had never deflowered an innocent or given false hope to a well-born lady. And once it became known that he preferred his women uncomplicated and experienced, the list of married ladies willing to accommodate his voracious appetite grew.

Hence Barrington's surprise when, during the investigation of the Marchioness of Yew's infidelity, he'd learned that his good friend was finally in honest pursuit of the lady's very respectable and exceedingly lovely nineteen-year-old daughter, Rebecca.

'Sexual conquests aside, dare I hope you've come with news about the identity of Lady Yew's alleged lover?' Barrington enquired.

'Nothing alleged about it.' Crew strolled towards the desk and picked up a glass in his long, slender fingers. 'I happened to be in the lady's house on the occasion of the young man's last visit and saw them acting very lover-like towards one another.'

'How convenient. Were you there in hopes of seeing the lovely Lady Rebecca or to question the mother?'

'Most definitely the former.' Crew raised the glass to his nose and sniffed appreciatively. 'Unlike our young Romeo, I have no interest in romancing ladies over the age of thirty. The bloom has long since gone from that rose.'

'But with maturity comes experience,' Barrington said, reaching for his own glass. 'A gently reared miss of nineteen will know nothing of that.'

'Fortunately, I am more than willing to teach her all she needs to know.' Crew swallowed a mouthful of brandy, pausing a moment to savour its flavour before sinking into a chair and resting his booted feet on the edge of the desk. 'However, returning to the matter at hand, the gentleman in question is not our typical Lothario. I've never heard his name mentioned in association with lady *or* ladybird; in truth, I'd never heard of *him* until his arrival in London just over a month ago. So the fact he has chosen to dally with a marquess's wife is somewhat unusual.'

'Are you sure they *are* lovers?'

Crew shrugged. 'Lady Rebecca confided her belief that they are. She told me she's seen the gentleman enter her mother's private quarters on more than one occasion, and, as I was leaving, I saw them myself going upstairs together hand in hand.'

'Damning evidence indeed,' Barrington said. 'And reckless behaviour for a man newly arrived in London. Does he suffer from a case of misplaced affection or unbridled lust?'

'Knowing the marchioness, I suspect the latter,' Crew said in a dry voice. 'It's well known she favours younger men because her husband is a crusty old stick twenty-five years older than she is.'

'Still, she has charmed a legion of men both younger *and* older than herself, and, up to this point, her husband has always been willing to turn a blind eye,' Barrington said. 'For whatever reason, he is not inclined to do so this time.'

Crew shrugged. 'Perhaps he fears a genuine attachment. It's all very well for a woman to take a lover to her bed, but it is extremely bad taste to fall in love with him. People have been known to do abysmally stupid things in the name of love.'

'Too true. So, who is the poor boy Lord Yew is going to flay?'

'His full name is Peregrine Tipton Rand.'

'Good Lord. *Peregrine Tipton*?'

'A trifle whimsical, I admit, but he's a country lad visiting London for the first time. Apparently, his father owns a farm in Devon. Rand's the oldest of four brothers and sisters but he hasn't shown much interest in taking over from his father. Seems he's more interested in books than in bovines, so when the mother died, the father shipped him up here to stay with his godfather in the hopes of the boy acquiring some town polish. Unfortunately, all he acquired was an affection for Lady Yew.'

Barrington frowned. 'How did a country boy come to be introduced to a marchioness?'

'Through the auspices of Lord Hayle, Viscount Hayle.'

'Hayle?' Barrington's eyebrows rose in surprise. The beautiful Lady Annabelle's *brother*? 'I wouldn't have thought the Earl of Cambermere's heir the type to associate with a country gentleman of no consequence.'

'I dare say you're right, but as it happens, he has no choice.

Rand is *staying* with the family. Cambermere is the man reputed to be his godfather.'

'Reputed?'

'There are those who say the lad bears a stronger resemblance to the earl than might be expected.'

'Ah, I see.' Barrington rapped his fingers on the desk. 'Wrong side of the blanket.'

'Possible, though no one's come right out and said it.'

'Of course not. Cambermere's a powerful man. If he did father an illegitimate child years ago and now chooses to have the boy come live with him, no one's going to tell him he can't. Especially given that his own wife died last year.'

'But there are other children living in the house,' Crew pointed out. 'Legitimate children who won't take kindly to their father foisting one of his by-blows on them.'

Especially the son and heir, Barrington reflected grimly. Viscount Hayle was not the kind of man to suffer such a slight to his family name. If he came to suspect the true nature of Rand's paternity, he could make things very difficult for all concerned. So difficult, in fact, that Rand might hightail it back to the country, and that was something Barrington had to avoid. He needed to find out as much as possible about the young man *before* news of his liaison with Lady Yew went public—because there was no doubt in Barrington's mind that it would. The marchioness wasn't known for being discreet. Her list of lovers was a popular topic of conversation at parties, and the fact that *this* time, her husband had chosen to make an example of the young man would definitely make for scintillating conversation over wine and cards.

'You've gone quiet,' Crew said. 'Mulling over how best to break the news to dear Peregrine's unsuspecting family?'

'As a matter of fact, I was.' Barrington got to his feet and walked slowly towards the long window. 'I met Lady

Annabelle Durst at Lady Montby's reception the other week.'

'Ah, the beautiful Anna,' Crew murmured appreciatively. 'Truly one of society's diamonds. I cannot imagine why she's still single.'

Barrington snorted. 'Likely because she's too busy trying to prevent silly young women from ruining themselves.'

'An admirable undertaking, though knowing how many silly young women there are in London, I don't imagine it leaves much time for looking after her own future.'

'Virtually none,' Barrington said, his thoughts returning to the lady whose existence he had first learned about during an investigation he'd undertaken the previous year. It had not involved Lady Annabelle directly, but had focused instead on the uncle of one of the girls she had been trying to help. As a result of that investigation, however, Barrington had become familiar with her name and with her propensity for helping naïve young girls navigate their way through the choppy waters of first love.

Always from a distance, of course. Given his own self-imposed boundaries, Barrington knew better than to risk getting too close to her, but he was strongly aware of her appeal and smart enough to know that she could be dangerous for that reason alone. He'd met a lot of women in his life, but there was something about Lady Annabelle Durst that set her apart from all the rest. Something rare. Something precious. Something indefinable...

'Well, if you're going to sit there all afternoon and stare into space, I'm leaving.' Crew drained his glass and set it on the desk. 'I am expected for tea with Lady Yew and her daughter; if you have nothing more to tell me, I may as well be on my way.'

'Fine. But while you're sipping tea and whispering endear-

ments in Lady Rebecca's ear, see if you can find out anything
else about her mother's relationship with Rand,' Barrington
said. 'The more I know about the situation, the better off I'll
be when it comes time to confront him with it.'

Crew unhurriedly rose. 'I'll ask, but, given the extent of
the marquess's displeasure, I doubt you'll hear Rebecca *or*
her mother mention the name Peregrine Rand with favour
again.'

Anna was reading Shakespeare when the door to the
drawing room opened. Leaving Hamlet on the page, she
looked up to see their butler standing in the doorway. 'Yes,
Milford?'

'Excuse me, my lady, but a gentleman has called and is
asking to see Mr Rand.'

Anna glanced at the clock on the mantel. Half past eight.
Somewhat late for a social call. 'Did you tell him Mr Rand
was from home?'

'I did, but he said it was a matter of some urgency and
wondered if you knew what time he might be home.'

'Lord knows, I certainly don't.' With a sigh, Anna set her
book aside. 'Did the gentleman leave his card?'

Milford bowed and silently proffered the tray. Anna took
the card and read the name. *Sir Barrington Parker.* How
strange. She knew the man by reputation rather than by sight.
A wealthy baronet with an impressive home, he was, by all
accounts, a cultured, educated and exceedingly charming
man who was also reputed to be one of London's finest
swordsmen. The story went that he'd spent several years in
Paris training under a legendary French master; when his
father's death had compelled him to return to England, Sir
Barrington had been besieged by the pinks of society asking

him to teach them his skills. With very few exceptions, he had refused every request.

Why, then, would he be here now, asking after a man with whom he was unlikely to have even the slightest acquaintance? 'Ask him to come in, Milford. Then inform my father that we have a visitor.'

The butler bowed. 'Very good, my lady.'

The wait was not long. Moments later, the door opened again and Milford announced, 'Sir Barrington Parker.'

Anna rose as the butler withdrew, but the moment the baronet arrived she stopped dead, totally unprepared for the sight of the man standing in her doorway. *'You!'*

'Good evening, Lady Annabelle.' Sir Barrington Parker strolled into the room, as impeccably turned out as he had been the night of Lady Montby's reception. His dark jacket fit superbly across a pair of broad shoulders, his buff-coloured breeches outlined strong, muscular thighs and his cravat was simply yet elegantly tied. 'I told you an occasion would present itself whereby our introduction could be made in a more acceptable manner.'

'You did indeed,' Anna said, struggling to recover from her surprise. She'd thought about him several times since meeting him at Lady Montby's, and, while she'd found him a powerful presence there, he was, in the small confines of the drawing room, even more compelling. 'I simply did not think it would be in my own home or that the illustrious Sir Barrington Parker would turn out to be the gentleman with whom I exchanged opinions the other night.'

'Illustrious?' His beautiful mouth lifted in a disturbingly sensual smile. 'I fear you are confusing me with someone else.'

'On the contrary, rumour has it that you are an excellent fencer and an unparalleled shot. *And* that you've uncovered more than your fair share of secrets about those who move in the upper reaches of society.'

His smile was indulgent, much like that of a teacher addressing an errant pupil. 'You and I both know how foolish it is to put stock in rumours, Lady Annabelle. One never knows how or why they start and most often they are proven to be wrong.'

'Do you deny that it was you who exposed Lord Bosker as an embezzler?' Anna said. 'Or that you just *happened* upon that letter naming his fine, upstanding cousin, Mr Teetham, as his accomplice?'

'I tend to think the timing was, for the most part, coincidental,' Sir Barrington said, careful to avoid a direct answer. 'Their crimes would have come to light soon enough. They grew careless, too confident in their own ability to deceive.'

'But *you* were the one who drew attention to what they were doing,' Anna persisted. 'Had you not, they would most likely have continued in their games and who knows what other crimes they would have perpetrated. But forgive my manners, Sir Barrington. Pray be seated.'

'Thank you. And while your confidence in my ability is flattering, I should tell you it is entirely misplaced.' He glanced at the chairs arranged in front of the fireplace and settled into the wingback chair opposite the one upon which her book lay open. 'There were other people involved in their arrest and to a far greater extent than myself. But, as we are talking about other people's affairs, how did matters proceed between Miss Banks and Lieutenant Blokker after you and I parted company the other night?'

Surprised he would even remember the conversation, Anna managed a smile. 'Remarkably well, all things considered. Lieutenant Blokker turned out to be a delightful young man and I realized, after speaking with him, that while the manner of his approach to Miss Banks left much to be desired, his intentions were strictly honourable.'

'Ah yes, the ill-fated rendezvous in the garden,' Sir Barrington mused. 'Not the best thought out of plans, but thanks to you no harm came of it.'

'And thanks to you, the two are now formally introduced and eager to begin a courtship,' Anna said. 'But I don't suppose Miss Banks's romantic escapades have anything to do with your reason for being here this evening.'

'Regrettably, they do not. I was actually hoping to speak to your house guest, Mr Rand, but I understand he is from home.'

'Yes, he is.' Anna gazed at him, surprised to feel her heart beating a little faster than usual. Obviously she wasn't used to being alone with such a disturbingly handsome man. 'I wasn't aware the two of you were acquainted.'

His dark brows arched ever so slightly. 'Are you acquainted with *all* of Mr Rand's friends and associates, Lady Annabelle?'

'As a matter of fact, I am. Peregrine has only recently come to stay with us, and, given how anxious my father was that he become known in society, I took the liberty of including him in all of *my* social activities,' Anna said. 'That being the case, I think I can safely say that I *do* know with whom he is and is not acquainted. I have never heard him speak of you.'

Briefly, the gentleman smiled, but while it softened the lines of his face, it did nothing to lessen the intensity of the expression in his eyes. 'I am not acquainted with Mr Rand, Lady Annabelle, nor is he with me,' he said quietly. 'I've come here at the behest of another, on a matter of extreme urgency to both.'

'An urgent matter?'

'Yes. One I would prefer to discuss in private with the gentleman. Or, failing that, with your father, if he is at home.'

'He is, Sir Barrington,' Lord Cambermere said, walking into the room. 'But if Edward has done something that warrants discussion—'

'It is not Edward Sir Barrington wishes to speak to you about, Papa,' Anna said calmly. 'It is Peregrine. And there is no point in my giving you privacy since we both know Peregrine will tell me everything the three of you say the moment Sir Barrington leaves.'

'He may not wish to tell you this,' Sir Barrington said, slowly getting to his feet. 'And I would prefer to speak to you about it in private, my Lord.'

Cambermere frowned. He was a tall, solidly built man with warm brown eyes, a ruddy complexion and dark hair that was just beginning to show signs of grey at the temples. His clothes were more suited to a country gentleman than a man about town, but now that his year of mourning was over, Anna was hopeful he might once again take up an interest in socialising, and, by necessity, his appearance.

'Yes, I'm sure you would,' the earl said. 'But I have no doubt Anna speaks the truth about the boy's repeating everything we say. He's my godson, you see, and the two have become as thick as thieves in the short time they've been together. I'm surprised he's gone out without her tonight. Still, he's a quiet enough lad. I can't imagine him doing anything that would be inappropriate for Anna to hear about.'

Anna could tell from the look on the baronet's face that he was less than pleased with her father's decision. Equally aware that trying to force the earl into a private interview was not the conduct of a gentleman, Sir Barrington merely shrugged those broad shoulders and said, 'Very well, though you may wish to change your mind once I begin to relate the details of the situation. You see, not long ago, a titled gentleman came to see me with regards to a personal matter concerning his wife.'

'His wife?' The earl looked decidedly confused. 'What has this to do with Peregrine?'

'The gentleman suspected his wife of having an affair,' Sir Barrington continued. 'Naturally, he asked me to make enquiries as discreetly as possible and to keep the results similarly confidential. He knew I'd had some success in this area and I agreed to look into the matter for him and see what I could learn. Now, having discovered the identity of the gentleman, I felt it behoved me to hear his side of the story. That's why I'm here. I regret to inform you, Lord Cambermere,' Sir Barrington said quietly, 'that the gentleman guilty of having an affair with the wife of a highly placed nobleman is none other than your godson, Mr Peregrine Rand.'

Chapter Three

'Peregrine!' Anna said on a gas. 'You think *Peregrine* is having an affair with a married woman? But that's impossible!'

'The facts would indicate otherwise,' Sir Barrington said. 'But perhaps you would care to explain why you believe it to be so unlikely?'

'Because he isn't the type to get involved in something like that. In fact, I don't think he's ever even been involved with a woman. He is…a student of history,' Anna said, needing to make him understand why his accusation was so totally misplaced. 'Old bones and ancient ruins hold far more appeal for Peregrine than would the charms of the most practised seductress.'

At that, Sir Barrington's mouth lifted in a smile. 'I doubt Lord Yew would appreciate his wife being referred to as a practised seductress, but—'

'Lord Yew!' Cambermere interrupted. 'Dear God, don't tell me you're talking about the marchioness?'

'I am.'

'Damn!' The earl muttered something under his breath,

then abruptly turned to his daughter. 'I think under the circumstances it would be best if Sir Barrington and I were to continue this conversation in private, Anna. There's nothing here you need to be involved with.'

'But why not? I already know the worst,' Anna said. 'And I stand by my claim that Peregrine is innocent of the charge.'

'Unfortunately, I have evidence to the contrary,' Sir Barrington put in. 'And I do not intend to reveal *that* in front of you, no matter what your father says.'

'Of course not,' Cambermere mumbled. 'Not fit for a lady's ears, I'm sure. But I will have the details of it before the lad comes home.'

'But, Papa—'

'No, my dear. Sir Barrington and I will discuss this alone,' her father said firmly. 'When Peregrine gets home, have Milford send him straight to my study. And you are *not* to speak with him beforehand.'

Anna said nothing as the two men left the room because, in truth, she didn't know what *to* say. Peregrine involved in a scandalous affair with a married marchioness? Impossible! Even if he were to lift his head out of his books long enough to look at a woman, it certainly wouldn't be to one married to another man. He had a stronger moral code than that, of that she was sure.

And yet Sir Barrington Parker claimed to have proof of the affair. What kind of proof could he have, and how had Peregrine come to be accused of this wretched undertaking in the first place? Had Lord Yew a grudge against him? Perhaps as the result of a card game or a wager? Had they had words over some political issue, or a difference of opinion over the current government's handling of some matter of concern to both of them?

There had to be *something*. Anna refused to believe that

Peregrine would ever stoop to something as shoddy as an affair. He might have been raised in the country, but everything about his behaviour thus far convinced her that his parents had instilled good moral values in him.

Why should that change simply because he was visiting London for the first time?

'And you are quite sure of your facts?' Cambermere said unhappily.

'Quite.' Barrington walked unhurriedly around the earl's study. It was a comfortable room—masculine yet not oppressively so, with large leather chairs, several glass-fronted bookcases and a large mahogany desk, the surface of which was covered with papers and estate ledgers. Tall windows bracketed a portrait of the fifth Earl of Cambermere, the present earl's father, and on the wall opposite hung one of a lady Barrington suspected of being the late Lady Cambermere.

Obviously, the earl liked looking at his wife's portrait. Perhaps she'd spent time with him here, keeping him company while he worked on the complexities of estate business. Certainly there was evidence of a woman's touch in the room: the brass candlesticks on the side table; the throw cushions that picked up the dark blue of the curtains; the warmth of the Axminster carpet. All the small, homely things that turned a house into a home. All the things his own house was so noticeably lacking.

'I never lay charges without being sure, my Lord,' Barrington said. 'It wastes time and inflicts unnecessary pain on the innocent. Mr Rand's activities were confirmed by a family member who saw the two enter Lady Yew's chamber and by a friend of mine who happened to be in the house at the same time as Rand. He was quite specific about the details of Mr Rand's visit, right up until the time he and the lady went upstairs arm in arm.' Barrington turned to face the older man. 'And regardless of whether or not what took place upstairs was of an intimate nature, you know as well as I do that his being alone with the marchioness is more than enough to convict him.'

'Damn!' the earl swore again. 'I never expected behaviour like this from Peregrine. Edward's always been one for the ladies. God knows how many have lost their hearts to him. But he's a good-looking lad and as charming as they come.'

'Has he shown no interest in marrying?'

'No, and at almost twenty-six, he's of an age where that's exactly what he *should* be turning his mind to,' the earl said testily. 'I've told him as much, but he doesn't pay heed to me. Says he'll marry when he's good and ready and not a moment before.'

'So he likes to play the field,' Barrington said.

'Always has. But Rand isn't inclined that way. In the time he's been here, I don't think I've ever heard him *talk* about a woman, let alone embroil himself in a sordid affair with one. My daughter was right in that regard.'

Barrington didn't bother to offer a reply. Family dynamics were neither of importance nor of interest to him. Emotion had to be kept separate from fact or everything risked drowning in sentimentality. Some might consider him cold for harbouring such a belief, but as far as he was concerned, it was the only way to do business. 'My Lord, I trust you appreciate the gravity of the situation,' he said bluntly. 'Lord Yew is understandably angry that his wife entered into an intimate relationship with another man; while it is correct to say that the lady is equally to blame, it is the gentleman the marquess intends to punish.'

'Of course,' Cambermere agreed. 'Men are always at fault in these situations. Well, what do you propose we do about it?'

Barrington was about to answer when the door to the room burst open and Lady Annabelle swept in, all blazing eyes and righteous indignation. 'Forgive me, Papa, but I simply *cannot* stand by and allow Sir Barrington's accusation to go unchallenged. Peregrine would *never* do something like this. It runs contrary to everything he stands for—which leads me to believe that it must be Sir Barrington's information that is in error.'

Barrington stared at the woman standing just inside the door, aware that she truly was magnificent. The candlelight deepened her hair to a rich, burnished gold and, in the dim light, her eyes shone a clear, deep blue. She was like a golden lioness protecting her cub. He almost hated having to be the one to prove her wrong. 'I have someone ready to swear that Mr Rand spent time alone with the marchioness in her private rooms, Lady Annabelle,' he said quietly. 'I need not tell you how damaging such a disclosure would be.'

He saw her eyes widen and knew that she did indeed appreciate the gravity of what he'd just said. But it was equally clear that she still didn't believe him. 'How do you know your witness was telling the truth, Sir Barrington? You have only his word that what he claims to have happened really did. I know Peregrine and I can assure you that he is not the type of man—'

'Anna, please,' her father interrupted. 'If Sir Barrington says he has proof of Peregrine's guilt, we must believe him.'

'But why? If he only took the time to speak with Peregrine, he would know that what he is suggesting is quite impossible.'

Cambermere sighed. 'You must forgive my daughter, Sir Barrington. She has grown uncommonly fond of my godson in the short time he's been here and is clearly reluctant to hear ill spoken of him.'

'I understand,' Barrington said, wondering if the closeness between the lady and Mr Rand had anything to do with the fact that they might well *be* brother and sister. 'Is Mr Rand spending the rest of the Season with you?'

The earl nodded. 'That was the plan. His father and I are… old friends. We were…at school together,' he said, glancing at a file on his desk. 'Haven't seen him in years, of course, but I was at his wedding and agreed to stand as godfather to his firstborn.' He turned towards the window, his face half in shadow. 'A few months ago, I received a letter from him, telling me that his wife had died and asking if I'd be willing to take Peregrine for a few months. Show him the sights of London, that sort of thing.'

'And you agreed.'

'I thought it the right thing to do.' The earl swallowed hard, his voice when he spoke gruff. 'He is my godson, after all.'

Barrington nodded, not sure whether it was grief or regret that shadowed the earl's voice. 'Are *you* aware of the company your godson keeps, Lord Cambermere?'

'Can't say that I am. His interests run vastly different to mine. He doesn't ride, he prefers not to hunt and I don't believe he's all that partial to moving in society. As my daughter said, he would rather spend his evenings with a book.'

Or in the marchioness's bed. 'Do you know where he is this evening?' Barrington enquired.

He saw the look that passed between Cambermere and his daughter, but wasn't surprised when the earl said, 'No. As I said, I don't make a study of the boy's comings and goings.'

'Yet you said Lady Annabelle usually goes with him to social engagements.'

'Yes.'

'Then why is she not with him tonight?' Barrington asked.

Barrington glanced at Lady Annabelle as he waited for a response. What little he knew of her encouraged him to believe that she would give him an honest answer. But when he saw her colour rise and her golden brows knit together, he suspected she already had. 'I see.'

'No, you don't see!' Lady Annabelle said quickly. 'Peregrine didn't ask me to accompany him because he was going to visit someone with whom he was already acquainted. It wasn't necessary that I go along.'

'Were you not surprised that you did not also receive an invitation to the reception?'

'Not at all. There are often events to which I am invited that other members of my family are not,' she explained. 'We may move in the same circles, Sir Barrington, but we do not have all the same friends.'

Barrington knew there was nothing to be gained in challenging the remark. Lady Annabelle was trying to defend Mr Rand—and failing badly in the attempt. 'Lord Cambermere,' he said finally, 'my client has made it clear that he intends to make an example of the man involved with his wife. However, for the sake of you and your family, I would prefer to see this matter settled quietly and with as little scandal as possible. If I could get Lord Yew to agree to it, would Mr Rand be willing to break off his association with Lady Yew and swear that he would never see her again? Perhaps be willing to write a letter to that effect?'

Cambermere nodded. 'I don't see why he would not—'

'But why *should* he write such a letter, Papa!' Lady Annabelle demanded. 'If he has done nothing wrong, surely there is no—!'

'*Enough*, Anna! If you cannot keep silent, I *will* ask you to leave,' her father said, displaying signs of impatience for the first time that evening. 'I don't know if you appreciate how serious a matter this is. In years gone by, Peregrine would have been called out for such an offence. In fact, I'm sure the thought crossed Yew's mind. He is not a man to be trifled with.'

'But you are condemning him without trial,' she persisted. 'Pronouncing him guilty without even giving him a chance to prove his innocence. All on the strength of *this* man's say so!' she added, her voice suddenly growing cold.

Barrington's eyes narrowed. So, the fair Lady Annabelle would defend her visitor to the last, blindly ignoring the evidence that he had put forward. Pity. While her loyalty did her credit, all it meant was that the outcome of the situation would be that much more painful for her in the end.

'If I may suggest,' he said slowly, 'I am well aware of how shocking this must sound and agree that Mr Rand must have his hearing and be given a chance to explain. But I do have an appointment with Lord Yew tomorrow afternoon and he will be looking for answers. So I would ask that you speak to Mr Rand as soon as possible and get back to me at the earliest opportunity.'

'I shall speak to him the moment he returns home this evening,' the earl said, 'and send word to you first thing in the morning.'

'Thank you. You have my card.' Barrington glanced at Annabelle, but wasn't surprised that she refused to meet his eyes. 'I regret, Lady Annabelle, that our introduction should have taken this form. It is not how I wished we might have started out.'

'Nor I, Sir Barrington.' She did look at him then and Barrington saw how deeply she was torn. 'If you knew Peregrine as I do, you would understand why I say that he is incapable of such a deceit.'

'Sadly, it is not possible for me to be intimately acquainted with everyone I am asked to investigate. Nor would it do me any good to encourage that kind of relationship. I must judge what I see without emotion clouding my vision. I trust the word of those who provide me with information and trust my own skills when it comes to assessing the value of what they've told me. I have no reason to doubt the source of this particular piece of information.'

'Yet who is to say that your source is any more honest than Peregrine?' she parried. 'He is as much a stranger to you as your source is to us. Does he even *know* Mr Rand?'

'By sight, and that is all that matters,' Barrington said. 'I deal in facts, Lady Annabelle. Not emotion. One dilutes the other to such an extent that the truth is often unrecognisable.'

She shook her head. 'I'm not sure I like your truths, Sir Barrington. You presume a great deal without being personally involved.'

'It is *because* I am not personally involved that I am able to reach the conclusions I do.'

'Then I sincerely hope that when we come to you with proof of Peregrine's innocence, you will offer him as sincere an apology as he deserves,' she said.

Barrington inclined his head. 'I will be happy to offer an apology if such is warranted. But if he is guilty, I expect the same courtesy from you. I'm good at what I do, Lady Annabelle—and I haven't been wrong yet.'

Her chin rose and he saw a flash of defiance in her eyes. 'There is a first time for everything, Sir Barrington. And in this instance, I will enjoy being the one who points it out to you.'

Barrington stared down at her, aware that while she frustrated him to the point of distraction, she also aroused in him feelings of an entirely different nature. In fact, he was finding it harder and harder to look at her and not imagine how she would feel in his arms. How the softness of her body would fit into the hard angles of his and how sweet the taste of her lips would be.

And that was the problem. While he admired her more than any woman he'd ever met, the fact that he wanted her in his bed was an unforeseen and unwelcome complication.

'I expect time will provide the answer to that,' he said, offering her a bow. 'My lord,' he said, turning to her father, 'I look forward to your visit on the morrow.'

'I will be there, Sir Barrington.' The earl's face was set in grim lines. 'Of that you can be sure.'

In the weighted silence that followed, Anna restlessly began to pace.

'You don't like Sir Barrington,' her father said flatly.

'It is not so much the man I dislike as his attitude,' Anna muttered, her eyes on the faded pattern of the carpet. 'I am as deeply convinced of his error as he is of mine, yet he is intractable.'

'And you are not?' her father retorted. When she said nothing, he continued, 'What of his claim that he has never been wrong?'

'A man may make whatever claim he likes, but we have only his word that it is the truth. And regardless of what he says, I will *not* believe Peregrine guilty of this.' Anna stopped and looked at her father. 'You know what kind of man he is, Papa. You've spent time with him. Talked with him at length.'

'Yes, I have, but women can make fools of us all. And sometimes circumstances compel us to do things…to *be* things…we would not normally do or be,' her father said.

Anna shook her head. 'That may hold true for some men, but *not* Peregrine. He is a good and honest man. I would stake everything I own on that.'

'Then I would advise you to be careful, my dear. Sometimes what we believe in our hearts is as far from the truth as it is possible to be. And that which we say will *never* happen, happens with alarming regularity.'

'You're speaking in generalities,' Anna said. 'I'm talking about Peregrine, and I know him a damned sight better than—'

'Annabelle!'

Anna sighed. 'A great deal better than does Sir Barrington Parker. Besides, if Lady Yew *is* having an affair, it is only what her husband deserves, cold, unfeeling man that he is.'

'Nevertheless, she is his wife and it is her duty to remain faithful to him,' the earl said.

'Even though he has kept a score of mistresses since the day they were married?'

The earl's face flushed. 'You should not be speaking of such things!'

'Why not? It isn't as though Lord Yew makes an effort to conceal his activities. He is constantly seen at the theatre with one or other of his mistresses. I'm surprised he hasn't invited them home to dine—'

'Enough! I will not hear you speak of such things, Anna,' the earl said harshly. 'Go back to the drawing room and continue with your needlework. I shall deal with Peregrine when he comes home and then we will settle this matter once and for all!'

It was well past midnight by the time Peregrine finally came home. Lying awake in bed, Anna heard the front door open, followed by the sound of muffled conversation. No doubt Milford telling Peregrine that the earl wished to see him. She heard footsteps, the sound of another door opening and closing, and then silence.

How long would the interview take? Would her father give

Peregrine a chance to explain himself? Or would he assume, as Sir Barrington had, that Peregrine was guilty and demand that he make amends at once?

It did not make for pleasant contemplation and, irrationally, Anna wished it had been anyone *but* Sir Barrington Parker who had brought forward the accusation. Because despite what she'd said to him tonight, she *was* attracted to him, more than to any man she'd ever met. She felt surprisingly at ease in his company, even though the sight of him set her pulse racing and her thoughts whirling. She enjoyed his sense of humour, admired his intellect and sensed that beneath that cool and controlled exterior beat the heart of a strong and passionate man.

But how could she be attracted to *any* man who wilfully intended to persecute a man whom she considered as practically a member of her family? Their formal introduction had been made as the result of his coming here to investigate Peregrine's behaviour. An *erroneous* investigation, Anna assured herself. Because if she allowed herself to believe that Peregrine would indulge in such a pastime, it could only mean that she didn't know him as well as she'd thought—and she liked to believe that being able to read people on an intuitive level was something she did well.

It was what enabled her to offer advice to confused young women who came to her, and to their equally confused mothers. By cutting through the layers of emotion, she was able to see down to the bones of the situation. And yet, was that not the very justification Sir Barrington Parker had used for his conduct tonight?

'...*I deal in facts, Lady Annabelle. Not emotion. One diluting the other to such a degree that the truth is often unrecognisable...*'

Perhaps, but in this case, emotion was all Anna had to go on. Emotion and trust. She had to believe in the integrity of

her family and all they stood for. For where would she be—
indeed, where would *any* of them be—if she could not?

Anna awoke to the first rays of sunshine slanting in
through her bedroom window and realised that she had fallen
asleep without ever having heard Peregrine come upstairs.
Bother! Now she had no way of knowing what the result of
his conversation with her father had been. Nor could she just
barge into Peregrine's room and ask him. He might be her
father's godson, but he was still a young, single male and it
would be inappropriate for her to go to his room alone, even
under circumstances like these.

With that in mind, Anna quickly rang for her maid and set
about getting dressed. Peregrine was normally an early riser,
but if she could catch him before he set off, she might have
a chance of finding out what she needed to know. Unfortunately, though she hurried her maid through her preparations,
it wasn't timely enough. By the time she reached Peregrine's
room and knocked on the door, there was no answer and she
could hear nothing from inside. He must have already gone
down for breakfast. Perhaps he'd passed a poor night after
the interview with her father.

Given how angry her father had been, Anna knew that to
be a definite possibility.

In the breakfast room, however, she was disappointed to
find only her brother seated at the long table. Edward looked
up at her entrance, his greeting somewhat reserved. 'Good
morning, Anna.'

Anna inclined her head as she made her way to the sideboard. 'Edward.' Though only two years separated them in
age, they had never enjoyed a close relationship. Edward
tended to belittle her efforts at helping others, while she
couldn't understand his cavalier treatment of friends and
servants alike. She had once seen him cut a good friend

dead when word of the fellow's marriage to a lady of lesser standing had reached him, saying that anyone who associated with rubbish was like to be tainted by the smell. And when his valet had come down with a fever, Edward had dismissed him, saying he couldn't abide to be in the same house as a sick man. Her father had offered to reassign the poor man to the stable, but not surprisingly, the valet had chosen to leave.

Now, as Anna helped herself to a slice of ham, a piece of toast and a boiled egg, she was thankful the rest of the staff were in such excellent health. 'Have you seen Peregrine this morning?' she asked, sitting down across from her brother.

Edward didn't look up from his newspaper. 'No.'

'What about Papa?'

'Out.' He turned the smoothly ironed page. 'Said he would be back in an hour.' He glanced at the clock. 'That was half an hour ago.'

So, her father had already left to meet with Sir Barrington Parker. That meant she *had* to speak to Peregrine as soon as possible. But where was he? And if he'd gone out, when might he be back? If she could talk to him, find out what had really happened, she might be able to speak to Sir Barrington on his behalf.

Leaving her plate untouched, she got up and headed for the door.

'What, no breakfast?' Edward enquired. 'Cook will be displeased.'

'I haven't time. I have to find Peregrine.'

'He's probably still in his room,' Edward said, turning another page. 'I understand he was drinking quite heavily at the Grundings' soirée last night.'

Anna stilled. 'Where did you hear that?'

'From someone who was there.' He finally looked up and smiled. 'It seems our country guest is finding London very much to his liking.'

Pursing her lips, Anna left the room. Edward hadn't meant the remark kindly. For whatever reason, he'd taken an instant dislike to Peregrine and had taken to making snide comments about his appearance, his manner of dress, even his accent. Anna had taken him to task about it several times, but it hadn't made any difference. The sniping continued and Edward made no attempt to hide his feelings when Peregrine was around.

Fortunately, Peregrine knew how Edward felt about him, but he refused to make an issue of it, saying it likely stemmed from the difference in their upbringings. Edward had been raised in a nobleman's house and was heir to an earldom, whereas Peregrine had been raised on a farm with parents who, though comfortable, were neither titled nor gentry.

Still, he was a guest in their home and he deserved better. Anna liked him very much. Despite his obvious lack of sophistication, he was good natured and quick to laugh and didn't belittle her efforts the way Edward did. He admired her for caring enough about the welfare of others to get involved and he also liked many of the same things she did, so they frequently found themselves laughing together at the various social events they went to.

Edward, on the other hand, was never to be found in the same room as Peregrine. Supremely conscious of his own position in society, he sought the company of those equal to him or blessed with a higher status. If there was a snob in the Durst family, it was definitely her brother.

Reaching Peregrine's door, Anna raised her hand and knocked. 'Peregrine?' When she heard no response, she waited a moment and then tentatively pushed it open.

He wasn't there. Worse, his bed hadn't been slept in.

Anna felt a knot form in the pit of her stomach. *Where had he spent the night and where was he now?* Equally important, what kind of mood was he in? Peregrine was an uncommonly sensitive man. If her father had falsely accused him of having an affair with Lady Yew, Peregrine might well have left the house angry and embarrassed that his godfather would believe such shameful lies about him. But where could he have gone?

There was only one way to find out. Heading to her bedroom, Anna fetched her bonnet and gloves. Returning to the hall, she rang for Milford and asked to be told where Sir Barrington Parker lived.

'Lady Annabelle Durst, Sir Barrington,' Sam said quietly.

Barrington looked up from the deed of land he had been perusing and saw the lady standing in his doorway. She looked like a breath of summer in a gown of pale yellow silk trimmed with deeper yellow ribbons, an elegant wide-brimmed bonnet perched atop her golden hair. Her lips were a soft dusky rose, but her blue eyes appeared unusually bright against the pallor of her skin. She was distraught and, recognising that, he rose at once. 'Lady Annabelle.'

'I hope my timing is not inconvenient, Sir Barrington.'

'Not at all. Pray come in. Bring your maid, if you wish.'

'No, I would rather speak to you privately.' Lady Annabelle waved the girl into a chair outside his study. 'I cannot bear not knowing.'

So, it was curiosity that had compelled her to come. Obviously, she hadn't spoken to her father yet. Barrington indicated the high-back chair in front of the fireplace. 'Won't you sit down?'

She did not. Visibly upset, she began to pace. Barrington understood the compulsion. He had been a pacer once himself. 'May I ring for tea?'

'Thank you.' This time, she did look at him. 'That would be most welcome.'

He glanced at Sam, who nodded and quietly withdrew.

For a moment Barrington said nothing, more interested in studying her than he was in initiating a conversation. She was as beautiful as ever, but this morning she looked to be drawn as tight as a finely strung bow. He had a feeling that if he pulled too hard, she would snap. 'What did you wish to ask me, Lady Annabelle?' he said softly.

Her head turned towards him, her blue eyes filled with misgivings. 'Have you seen my father this morning?'

'I have.'

'And? Did he speak to you about Peregrine?'

Barrington nodded, aware that he was far more in control of his emotions than she was of hers. 'Are you sure you won't sit down?'

'Please…just tell me,' she implored. 'I wanted to ask Peregrine myself, but he wasn't in his room this morning; by the looks of his bed, he hadn't slept there at all.'

'I suspect he did not,' Barrington agreed. 'Lord Cambermere informed me that after his conversation with Mr Rand last night, the young man left the house without any indication as to where he was going or when he might return. Apparently he was in a state of considerable distress.'

He saw her eyes briefly close. 'Did he admit to…what you accused him of?'

Barrington wished he could have said otherwise, but he wouldn't lie. Not even when he knew the boy had. 'No.'

With a soft cry, Lady Annabelle sank into a chair. 'I knew it! I *knew* he was innocent.' When Barrington made no response, she raised her head, her eyes narrowing at the expression on his face. 'You don't believe him.'

'It takes more than a man *saying* he didn't do something for me to believe him innocent when the evidence speaks so clearly of his guilt.'

'But why would he lie?' she protested.

Barrington gave a non-committal shrug. 'Why does anyone

lie? To protect themselves or to protect someone else. I'm sure you've had dealings with young women who told you one thing, yet did another.'

'Yes, because they had no wish for their misdemeanours to become public.'

'Exactly. Mr Rand is likely embarrassed by what he's done and hopes to convince others that he is not at fault.'

He saw her stiffen. 'Peregrine has *never* lied to me.'

'Perhaps there has not been enough at stake for him to do so,' Barrington said quietly. 'Now there is.'

The door opened again and Sam walked in, carrying a silver tea service. At a nod from his employer, he set the tray on the small table beside the desk and then quietly withdrew. Barrington crossed to the table and picked up the milk jug. 'Milk and sugar?'

'Just milk, thank you.'

He poured a drop into one of the cups, then filled both cups with hot tea. Accepting hers, Lady Annabelle said, 'I still think you're wrong, Sir Barrington. If Peregrine said he is not involved with Lady Yew, he is not. Why can you not accept that as truth?'

'Because the rest of his behaviour leads me to believe otherwise. How do you explain the fact that he chose not to stay home last night?'

'I suspect he was deeply embarrassed by my father believing him capable of such reprehensible conduct. Would *you* not wish to avoid someone who had accused you of doing something you had not?'

'Maybe. But I also like to think I would be mature enough to admit my mistakes, if I were so foolish as to make them.'

'And I repeat, I do not believe Peregrine has made a mistake.'

He heard the quiet certainty in her voice and was moved to

smile. He, too, had once been so trusting; so willing to believe in the goodness of others. When had he lost that *naïveté*?

'The attraction between a man and a woman is one of the most powerful forces on earth, Lady Annabelle,' he said. 'You have no idea how many crimes are committed, and how many lies are told, in the name of that attraction.'

'Not perhaps as well as you do,' Lady Annabelle agreed, 'but we are talking about Peregrine's character and of that I believe I *can* speak with authority. If he told my father he is not having an affair with Lady Yew, he is not.'

'Then it would seem we have reached an impasse,' Barrington said. 'There is nothing more to say.'

She looked somewhat taken aback by his easy acceptance of her statement, but, equally willing to accept it at face value, she finished her tea and then set the china cup and saucer back on the table. 'What will you tell Lord Yew?'

'I don't know,' Barrington said honestly. 'But I have between now and two o'clock to work it out.'

'Then I shall leave you to your deliberations.' She stood up and offered him her hand. 'Thank you for seeing me, Sir Barrington.'

'My pleasure.' Barrington felt the softness of the glove in his hand, the slenderness of the fingers within. 'I'm sorry that circumstances are such that you leave believing the worst of me. Again.'

'Actually, I don't. We each have our own ways of involving ourselves in other people's lives, Sir Barrington,' Lady Annabelle said. 'I tend to think the best and assume people innocent until proven guilty, whereas you believe the exact opposite.'

'Not at all. I simply strive to uncover the truth,' Barrington said. 'That is why people come to me. And experience has taught me that if the truth is not immediately discernible, it *will* come out in the end.'

'Then at least you and I are able to part knowing that the truth of *this* matter has already been established,' she replied. 'Goodbye, Sir Barrington.'

Barrington inclined his head, but said nothing as she left the room. He stood by his desk until he heard the sound of the front door close before letting his head fall back and breathing a long, deep sigh.

So, the lovely Anna thought the matter closed. Wrong. Peregrine Rand *was* guilty. The fact he had chosen not to *confess* his sin meant absolutely nothing. In his heart, he knew what he'd done and, if Peregrine was as noble as Lady Annabelle made him out to be, guilt would eat away at him until he had no choice but to make a clean breast of it. Either way, the young man was doomed to failure.

As it seemed was he, Barrington reflected, when it came to securing the good opinion of the lovely Lady Annabelle Durst. If it turned out that his accusations were correct and Rand was guilty of having an affair with Lady Yew, she would resent him for having proven her wrong. On the other hand, if Rand was telling the truth, she would resent him for having doubted his integrity in the first place. In short, they had reached a stalemate. And contrary to what either of them might wish to believe, in a situation like this, there was simply no way one or the other of them was going to win.

Chapter Four

Anna finally caught up with Peregrine later that afternoon. She had been resting in her room, nursing the megrim she'd had for the better part of the day, when she heard the heavy thump of footsteps in the hall and realised he was finally home. Pushing the lavender eye pads aside, she quickly got up and went to the door. 'Peregrine!'

He clearly wasn't in the mood for conversation. Dressed in boots, hacking jacket and breeches, he didn't stop when she hailed him and was almost at the bottom of the stairs before she finally caught up with him. 'Peregrine, wait! I need to talk to you.'

'I haven't time.' His voice was unusually brusque. 'I'm going riding with friends and I'm already late.'

'Then you'll just have to be a few minutes later,' Anna said, putting her hand on his arm and turning him around. 'Where were you last night? I was worried about you.'

'You had no reason to be. I simply went out.'

'But not until *after* you spoke to Papa. Why did you leave again? And why didn't you come home?'

He flicked the hard leather crop against the top of his

boot. 'I lost track of time. When I realised how late it was, I decided it was best I just stay out.'

'Why? Because of something Papa said?'

Peregrine was a good-looking young man with a shock of thick, black hair, deep brown eyes and a wide, generous mouth. A mouth that suddenly narrowed in anger. 'I don't care to talk about it.'

'But you don't have a choice, Peregrine. There's a rumour going around town that you are having an affair with Lady Yew,' Anna said, needing him to understand the gravity of the situation. '*I* know it isn't true, but you can't simply pretend the rumour doesn't exist.'

'As a matter of fact, I can. I told your father as much when he questioned me about it last night and I certainly don't intend to stand here and justify my behaviour to you!'

Stung by the vehemence of his reply, Anna said, 'I'm not asking for justification. I just told you I don't believe what people are saying. But a meeting is being held this afternoon between Lord Yew and the man he asked to investigate his wife's infidelity and your name is going to come up—'

'Damn it, Anna, did I not just say that I don't want to talk about it?'

'But you must! Your reputation as a gentleman is at stake, don't you understand?'

'What I understand is that a man's private business is not his own,' he snapped. 'Do you know why I jumped at the chance to come to London? Because I was tired of having to listen to my father's sanctimonious preaching. Of being told what I could and could not do. I thought that by coming here, I would finally be able to lead my own life. Yet now I find that every move I make is watched and criticised by people I don't know, and that even you and your father have no qualms about intruding into something that is none of your business.'

'None of our business?' Anna repeated in astonishment. 'How can you say that? You are my father's godson. We *care* about you.'

He had the grace to look embarrassed. 'I'm not saying you don't.'

'Then why are you being so defensive? I know you didn't have an affair with Lady Yew,' Anna said. 'For one thing, she's already married. For another, she must be at least fifteen years older than you.'

'Since when did either of those things matter to the fine, upstanding members of society?' Peregrine shot back. 'Half of London seems to be involved with people other than their wives or husbands. Why should Susan and I be any different?'

'*Susan?*' Anna interrupted, shocked. 'You call her *Susan*?'

'Yes.' He raised his chin in defiance. 'What else would one call a good friend?'

'Given that she happens to be someone else's *wife*, I would have thought Lady Yew the more appropriate form of address,' Anna said, concern lending an edge to her voice.

'You're being stuffy, Anna. I didn't do anything wrong,' Peregrine said. 'She gave me leave to speak to her in such a manner.'

'Really? And what else did she give you leave to do?'

The tips of Peregrine's ears flamed red. 'Nothing.' But when he refused to meet her eyes and began fidgeting with his crop, Anna knew he was lying to her—and she felt the foundations of her world tremble.

So, it *was* all a lie. Peregrine *was* involved with Lady Yew. Worse, he was *in love* with her. He'd given himself away when he'd spoken her name. His mouth had quivered and his eyes had softened, the way a person's always did when they referred to the man or the woman they cared about deeply.

And she, stupidly, had believed him. She had defended him to both her father *and* to Sir Barrington Parker, a man she had charged with making a false accusation, when all the while it was Peregrine who had been telling lies.

Needing to regain a measure of calm, Anna turned her back on him, clenching her fists at her side. 'Since you obviously did not see fit to inform my father of the truth last night, I will have it now,' she said, fighting to keep her voice steady. '*Are* you having an affair with the Marchioness of Yew?'

'Anna, *please*!'

'Don't Anna me! I want the truth, Peregrine. People's reputations are at stake here. Mine included.'

'Nonsense! This doesn't concern you!'

She whirled to face him. 'Of course it concerns me! I spoke up on your behalf,' she cried. 'I defended you to someone who was ready to think the worst of you. And I refused to believe them when they told me what you were supposedly guilty of.'

Footsteps on the stairs alerted Anna to the fact that they were standing in a place where anyone might hear them, prompting her to grab Peregrine's arm and pull him into the drawing room. 'Furthermore,' she said, closing the door behind them, 'I assured Father and this...other gentleman that you couldn't possibly have been guilty of having an affair with Lady Yew because you didn't even *know* her.'

'But I did know her,' Peregrine admitted.

'How? *I* didn't introduce the two of you.'

'No. Edward did.'

'Edward?' Anna repeated, confused. 'But...when were the two of you ever at a society function together?'

'It wasn't at a society function we met.' Peregrine ran his fingers through his hair, hopelessly dishevelling it. 'Edward had been on at me, saying that if I had any hopes of becoming a gentleman, I needed to educate myself in gentlemanly ways.

That meant knowing how to shoot, how to ride and how to fence. Since I'm already a good rider and I can handle a gun, that only left fencing, a sport to which I've had absolutely no exposure. Edward offered to take me to Angelo's and I met the Marquess of Yew there.'

'That doesn't explain how you met his wife,' Anna pointed out.

'She was waiting for him outside in their carriage,' Peregrine said. 'Edward pointed her out to me when we arrived. When I commented on how beautiful she was, he kindly offered to introduce us.'

Kindly? Anna doubted her brother had *ever* had a kind thought in his head when it came to Peregrine. 'All right, so you were introduced. If you knew Lady Yew was married, why did you pursue her?'

'Because on the way home after the match, Edward told me about their marriage. He said it was a loveless union and that Lady Yew was desperately unhappy because Yew paraded his mistresses right under her nose and didn't give a damn as to what she thought.'

'Be that as it may, she *is* his wife and you were wrong to interfere.'

'But she doesn't *love* him!' Peregrine said, his voice rising. 'She told me that what she feels for me is the most wonderful, the most exciting feeling she's ever experienced, and that when we finally are able to be together—'

'Together?' Anna interrupted incredulously. 'Are you telling me that Lady Yew said she was going to *leave* her husband?'

'Not in so many words, but—'

'Don't play games with me, Peregrine. Did she or did she not *say* that she was going to leave her husband?'

'Not exactly, but—'

'So she made you no promises that she would run away with you,' she said flatly.

'Well, no, but—'

'There are no buts, Peregrine. Lady Yew has been playing with you.'

'She wouldn't do that!' he said hotly. 'You don't understand how it is between us! She *loves* me!'

'Love? I doubt the woman knows the meaning of the word,' Anna said dismissively. 'In fact, I can give you the names of at least ten other young men with whom she claims to be in love. Men with whom she has flirted and danced and driven nearly insane with jealousy. It's what she does.'

'I don't believe you,' Peregrine said, stubbornly clinging to his beliefs. 'She said nothing to me about other men. And even if there were, it doesn't signify. What she felt for them could be nothing compared to what she feels for me. She said she's never met anyone like me before.'

Anna sat down, aware that Peregrine was no more educated in the ways of love than poor Mercy Banks. 'I'm sorry, Peregrine, but Lady Yew is *not* going to run away with you. Her husband is one of the richest men in England. He owns properties in four counties and his personal worth is staggering. As his wife, Lady Yew is one of the most influential women in society. If you think she would risk throwing that all away to run off with the penniless godson of the Earl of Cambermere, I would advise you to think again.'

'But Edward said—'

'I don't care what Edward said,' Anna said, though she damn well did care and she intended to talk to her brother at the first opportunity. 'Tradition is the foundation upon which society is built. Noble families marry into noble families, thereby ensuring that the tradition carries on. Casting discretion to the wind and haring off because you believe yourself in love with someone else's husband or wife is destructive to the fabric of society—and nobody knows that better than those who occupy its uppermost rungs. I'm sorry, Peregrine, but the kindest thing you can do for yourself is to get over this as quickly as possible and then move on with your life.'

Anna knew it was a sobering speech, but she also knew it was one Peregrine needed to hear. He had to understand that his hopes were futile, that whatever dreams he harboured were as insubstantial as fairy dust.

'But I *love* her,' he whispered, misery inflecting every word. 'How am I supposed to get over that? I've never felt this way about a woman before.'

'You get over it by waking up each day and telling yourself that she is married to a man who will *never* divorce her… even if she wished him to.'

Anna said the words as gently as she could, but she still saw Peregrine wince and felt her heart go out to him. It was never easy hearing that the person you loved didn't love you in return. In fact, finding out that you were little more than a source of amusement, whether it be for an hour or a day, or even a year, was the most devastating thing imaginable. It destroyed your confidence and tore at the very foundation of who you were.

Having been through it, Anna knew exactly how injurious it was to one's sense of well-being.

For a few minutes, Peregrine just sat there, his brow furrowed, his eyes bleak with despair as he struggled to come to terms with everything she had told him. It was hard waking up from a dream, but he had been indulging in an impossible fantasy; for his own good, Anna knew he had to come back to reality.

He finally stood up and slowly began to walk around the room. 'Part of my reason for staying out last night,' he said slowly, 'was because I was embarrassed. I never expected your father to find out what was going on. I thought it was just between Sus—between Lady Yew and myself.'

'Yes, I'm sure you did,' Anna said. 'But while London might seem like a big city, never forget that there are eyes and ears everywhere. When you play with fire, you will eventually get burned.'

'I know, but you never really believe that. It's as though you're living in a bubble. You can see out, but no one can see in. But, of course, everyone can.' Peregrine dropped his head and breathed a long, deep sigh. 'Your father thought it would be a good idea if I were to…write a letter to Lord Yew, apologising for my behaviour. He said that if I promised not to see Lady Yew again, it might…smooth things over with him.' He raised his head. 'Do you think he's right?'

Aware that it was Sir Barrington Parker who had suggested writing the letter, Anna simply inclined her head. 'I think the letter a good idea, yes. With luck, it will set the marquess's mind to rest and persuade him to let the matter go. Because if he takes it into his head to persecute you, Peregrine, there will be no future for you in London.'

Peregrine nodded, and for a full five minutes he was silent, reviewing his options. Then, as if realising he had none, he said finally, 'Very well. I shall write the letter. But I'll give it to you, rather than to your father. I don't think he ever wants to see me again.'

'Don't be a goose, of course he wants to see you.'

'You weren't there,' Peregrine said ruefully. 'You didn't see the look on his face. Why do you think I lied to him, Anna? God knows I didn't want to. But when I saw how disappointed he was at even having to *ask* me if I was involved with Lady Yew, I knew I couldn't tell him the truth. So I lied. That's why I couldn't stay here last night,' Peregrine admitted. 'I was too ashamed to sleep under the same roof as him. He's been so good to me. I couldn't bear to repay him like this.'

'Oh, Peregrine,' Anna whispered. 'If Father was disappointed, it was only because he cares about you and wants you to do well in London. He knows how harsh society can be towards those who flaunt its rules.'

'Then society is a hypocrite!' Peregrine cried. 'I'm not the only man involved with a married woman. There are countless other such affairs going on and everyone knows it!'

'Yes, and they are tolerated as long as they are conducted discreetly and with neither party voicing an objection,' Anna told him. 'But for whatever reason, Lord Yew has chosen to object to the liaison and, as a gentleman, you have no choice but to withdraw.'

The gravity of her words must have penetrated his romantic haze, because for the first time Peregrine seemed to appreciate the magnitude of what he had done. He glanced down at his boots, his mouth working. 'Very well. I shall go for my ride as planned and while I am out I shall think about what I wish to say. Then, I shall come back and write a letter of apology to Lord Yew.'

Anna did a quick mental calculation. Sir Barrington had said he was meeting with the marquess at two. There wasn't a hope Peregrine would be back from his ride in time to have the letter finished and delivered by then, which meant she had no choice but to send word to Sir Barrington herself.

'Peregrine. Have I your word that you will stop seeing Lady Yew, that you will say as much in your letter to Lord Yew?'

Peregrine frowned. 'Have I not just said I would?'

'Yes, but I need to be very clear as to your intentions.'

'From where I stand, I don't think I have any choice.'

'Fine. Then off you go on your ride,' Anna said. 'I'll see you at dinner.'

'Not tonight.' Peregrine got up and slowly walked towards the door. 'Edward said he would be dining at home this evening and I have no intention of sitting at the same table and letting him humiliate me any further in front of your father.'

'Why would he do that?'

'Because I was foolish enough to confide my feelings for Lady Yew to him.' Peregrine looked at her and sighed. 'He knew exactly how I felt—and he said nothing at all about it being a hopeless quest.'

Anna needed no further explanation. How could she explain that it was just her brother being himself? 'I'm sorry, Peregrine. Really, I am. And I know how hard it is not to be with the person you love, but there will be others. You have only to open your heart and let love find you.'

His mouth twisted. 'I've been open to love a long time, Anna, but this is the first time it's come anywhere close to finding me. Infatuation is one thing, but true love doesn't come along every day.'

No, it did not, Anna reflected as she sat down to write the letter to Sir Barrington. True love was elusive: as fragile as a sigh, as mysterious as the night. It inspired placid gentlemen to write romantic poetry and sensible young women to lose themselves in dreams. For those lucky enough to find it, love could be a life-altering experience.

But falling in love could also be a painful and humiliating experience, one that shattered a person's belief in their own self-worth and that was best forgotten as quickly as possible. Her brief, ill-fated liaison with the Honourable Anthony Colder was a prime example of that, as was poor Peregrine's misplaced affection for Lady Yew. If anyone needed proof of the *destructive* power of love, they need look no further than that.

Lady Annabelle's note arrived well in advance of Lord Yew's visit and while Barrington was relieved that a solution had been found, her words did not make him feel better. Not when he knew what it had cost her to write them.

Sir Barrington,
As time is of the essence and Mr Rand is otherwise occupied, I thought it best to send word of his intentions as quickly as possible. I have been informed that he is indeed guilty of having an affair with the lady in question; however, he has assured me that he intends to end the relationship and that he is willing to confirm the same in a letter addressed to her husband. I hope you will convey these sentiments to the gentleman and that he will find it a satisfactory resolution to the problem.

    Neither my father nor Mr Rand has been made aware of this correspondence and I would prefer that it remain that way. As one who has been accused of 'involving herself in the convoluted lives of others', I think it the wisest course of action.

It was simply signed 'Annabelle Durst' in a clear and legible hand.

So, Mr Peregrine Rand had been unable to maintain his lies in the face of the lady's questioning. Good—because there was no doubt in Barrington's mind that Annabelle *had* questioned him. Profess to believe him she might, but she had still needed to hear from his own lips that he was innocent of the charge and that the rumours were not true.

How devastated she must have been to find out that they were…and how difficult for her to write this note. She had believed wholeheartedly in the young man's innocence, put trust in her intuition when it came to what he would and would not do—only to discover that her intuition was not strong enough to stand up against the wishes and desires of his own heart. Disillusionment was always a bitter pill to swallow.

He glanced again at the parchment in his hand. Closing his eyes, he raised it to his nose and gently inhaled. Yes, it was still there…a lingering trace of her fragrance, the scent sweet but sensually provocative. An echo of the lady herself. He set the parchment down and walked slowly towards the long window, his mind filled with thoughts of Anna.

It was a long time since a woman had affected him to this degree. Indeed, he wasn't sure one ever had. For the most part, he'd always believed aristocratic ladies to be like exotic birds: lovely to look at, but troublesome to own. They strutted around society's stage like the fragile, inconsequential creatures they were, generally offering nothing of substance beyond the ability to play the piano or paint pretty pictures. It was the reason he had found commitment so easy to avoid.

But Lady Annabelle was neither fragile nor inconsequential. She was intelligent. Passionate. The quintessential lady and beautiful beyond all. But beauty without soul had never appealed to him, and it was because she cared so much about other people that Barrington found himself so strongly attracted to her. She cared about Mercy Banks and the host of other silly young women who needed her help in extricating themselves from situations that could have ruined them. She cared about her country visitor, who might well be her half-brother, and about her father, who, with typical male arrogance, was ready to dismiss everything she said. Yes, admirable indeed was the Lady Annabelle Durst. A lady worth getting to know.

And yet, as a result of what had passed between them, Barrington doubted a deeper acquaintance was possible. In his hand, he held her acknowledgement that she had been wrong, and he right. That was the first strike against him. He had proven everything she had most desperately wanted not to believe. She had stood up for a man who hadn't deserved her loyalty, and she had been let down. Matters would never be easy between them now.

Still, now that he knew the truth about Rand, he would do everything he could to mitigate Lord Yew's anger and to settle the matter as humanely as possible. As for Rand, if he truly believed himself in love with Lady Yew, he was already suffering enough by having found out what she was really like. No point making it worse by dragging his name through the mud, and by association, the beautiful Lady Anna's.

The note Anna received from Sir Barrington later that afternoon was brief, but reassuring.

Your note was well timed. I met with Lord Yew, and after being assured of Mr Rand's willingness to see the error of his ways, the marquess is willing to let the matter go. He will settle for a letter and a promise of restraint on Mr Rand's part and shall consider the matter closed. I have not written to your father. I leave it to you to inform him of the outcome, and Mr Rand. I remain,
Your most humble servant
B.

Anna folded the letter and tapped it against her chin. So, the matter was resolved. The Marquess of Yew had been informed as to the identity of the guilty party and had been willing to accept an olive branch in the form of a promise and a written apology. Sir Barrington had handled the matter admirably. As long as the marquess honoured his word, Peregrine would be free to go about London without the finger of blame being pointed at him at every turn.

Just as well, since Anna was quite sure he would have bolted had such been the case.

Unfortunately, as she set out for her afternoon visit to the Baroness von Brohm, Anna realised that the entire affair had left a bad taste in her mouth. Not only were her feelings towards Peregrine affected by what she had learned, but her brief acquaintance with Sir Barrington Parker had been tainted by the events they had both unwittingly been drawn into. She had insinuated that he hadn't known his business, accused him of misjudgement and gloated when she'd believed him wrong. She owed him an apology.

But was he the type of man to whom apologising was easy? She remembered the way he had teased her over her steadfast belief in Peregrine's innocence, mocking her belief in the man's inability to tell lies. Would he be condescending of her apology now? Had he been waiting for just such a moment to say, 'I told you so'? Anna hated to think of him as being deliberately cruel, but, not knowing the nature of the man, she had little else to go on.

She was not at all surprised that thoughts of him occupied her fully during the carriage ride to Mayfair.

Julia von Brohm was not what Anna had been expecting. Thinking to see a pale, unhappy woman in her mid-forties wearing the unrelieved black of a widow still in mourning for her husband, Anna was surprised to be greeted by a slender and very attractive woman of no more than thirty, garbed in a stunning gown of rich burgundy satin. Her honey-brown hair was arranged in a simple but elegant chignon at the nape of her neck, and her eyes were a clear, bright blue that appeared even brighter against the translucent whiteness of her skin.

'Lady Annabelle,' the baroness said, extending both hands in greeting. 'I cannot tell you how pleased I was to receive your note.'

'And likewise, how pleased I was to receive your acceptance,' Anna said. 'I regret that my good friend, Lady Lydia Winston, was unable to come, but her mother was taken to bed with a terrible head pain and required her assistance.'

The baroness's pretty face softened in sympathy. 'Poor lady. Having had a mother-in-law who suffered with megrims, I know the role a daughter must play. But I am so pleased that you were brave enough to come on your own.'

Anna tilted her head to one side. 'Brave?'

'Come now, Lady Annabella. You must surely have heard the rumours—that I am a lonely widow who cannot stop crying for her late husband. That I am a beautiful woman whose company must be endured, but not enjoyed.'

The smile came easily to Anna's lips. 'I knew you were a widow, Baroness, and I assumed that you would be lonely. But I certainly did not hear that you were dismal company or someone to be avoided. And even if I had, I would have come anyway and drawn my own conclusions.'

'I am very glad to hear it,' the baroness said in her charmingly accented voice. 'And I think that you and I are going to become good friends. Ah, Smith,' she said to the young maid who appeared in the doorway. 'We shall have tea and a plate of pastries. Cook would be most upset if we did not offer our guest a sampling of her wares.'

As the maid curtsied and withdrew, the baroness turned back to Anna. 'I hired most of the staff upon my arrival, but dear Frau Hildenbaum has been with my family since I was a girl. She insisted on coming to London with me and when she heard I was having an English lady to tea, she set to work. She has been baking since early this morning.'

'How delightful, for I confess to a definite weakness for pastries,' Anna said as she sat down on a comfortable sofa across from the baroness. The room was quite beautiful, the walls papered in pale blue and gold silk, the shades of which were reflected in the carpet and furnishings. An exquisite medieval tapestry was suspended from a brass rod between the two long windows that gave view over the square below, and numerous other works of art adorned the walls. The baroness either had exceptional taste or the good fortune to have ancestors who did.

Even more stunning was her jewellery. Anna's eyes were repeatedly drawn to the brooch pinned to the bodice of her gown. It was shaped like a flower, with a single piece of amber in the centre and with petals made up of diamonds and rubies.

'You are admiring my brooch?' the baroness asked during a lull in the conversation.

Anna looked up, embarrassed to have been caught staring. 'Yes. Forgive me, but it is so beautiful.'

'My late husband gave it to me for my twenty-first birthday.' The baroness's face glowed. 'Ulrich spent a lot of time travelling and often came home with little trinkets like this. He had exceptional taste.'

'Baroness—'

'Please, won't you call me Julia?' she interrupted gently. 'I have no wish to be so formal with you.'

'Then you must call me Anna. And I was about to say that your husband must have loved you very much to have given you such an exquisite gift.'

As soon as the words left her lips, Anna regretted having uttered them. She had no wish to invoke unhappy memories for Julia and she feared that mentioning her late husband in such a way might be all that was required to bring them on. But apart from a delicate flush, Julia remained admirably in control of her emotions. 'He did love me. Ours was a true love match. Not common in our world, I suppose, but I was more fortunate than most.'

'So it wasn't an arranged marriage.'

'Oh, yes, but Ulrich and I fell in love shortly after we were introduced. That probably sounds ridiculous, but it is the truth.'

'I think you were indeed incredibly fortunate,' Anna said. 'I know of so many marriages that are arranged for the benefit of the parties involved and end up being the most dismal of relationships. That is why I always prefer to see marriages based on love. Have you any children, Bar—Julia?'

Where the mention of her husband had not brought tears to her eyes, the mention of children did. 'Sadly, no. Ulrich and I were not able to conceive a child together. Perhaps if we'd had more time—'

When Julia broke off, Anna leaned over to place her hand over the other woman's. 'I am so sorry for your loss, Julia,' she said gently, 'but you are young enough to marry again and to bear many healthy children.'

Julia nodded, her eyes glistening with unshed tears. 'I would like to think so, but if the difficulty in conceiving lies with me, it will not matter who I marry. I know that will serve as a deterrent to certain gentlemen.'

'Only those looking to set up a nursery,' Anna said, seeing no point in not stating the obvious. 'If we are being practical, there are many older gentlemen who would be happy to offer you marriage without children being a condition.'

'You are kind to say so, Anna, but, in truth, I do not long for a husband. The memory of Ulrich is enough.'

'But memories won't keep you warm at night and you are far too beautiful to spend the rest of your life alone,' Anna pointed out. 'You must get out in society and start mingling again.'

'I would like that,' Julia admitted, 'but in the three weeks I've been here, I have not received a single invitation.'

'Then we must start the ball rolling.' Anna smiled, convinced more than ever that she had done the right thing in coming to visit the baroness. She pulled an invitation from her reticule and handed it to Julia. 'This is from the Countess of Bessmel. It is an invitation to a soirée at her home the evening after next.'

'An invitation!' Barely managing to conceal her delight, Julia broke the seal and unfolded the invitation. 'But we have never met.'

'I know, but I chanced to be at a breakfast with the countess the other morning and told her I intended paying a call on you. She said she was planning to do the same, but that the pain in her legs was preventing her from getting around. That's when she asked if I would be good enough to deliver the invitation to you and to say how much she hopes you will attend.'

Julia read the invitation again and her smile brightened immeasurably. 'This is…so very good of you, Anna. And of Lady Bessmel, of course. I will write at once to accept.'

'Excellent, because she is looking forward to meeting you,' Anna said. 'Lady Lydia will also be there, and with three such highly placed ladies at your side, you can be assured that the rest of society will take notice.'

Julia's smile was as radiant as the diamonds pinned to her breast. 'Thank you, Anna. I feel better simply for having met you. And perhaps before you leave, you would like to see some of my other jewellery? I can assure you that a few of the pieces make this brooch look quite plain.'

Chapter Five

Though Barrington did not make a habit of attending all of the society functions to which he was invited, he recognised the wisdom of dropping in on certain, select events. Dark alleys and gentlemen's clubs were all very well, but he had learned long ago that most of the truly useful gossip was to be overheard in the drawings rooms and ballrooms of society. And given that Lady Bessmel was acknowledged to be one of the finest gossips in London, the thought of missing an event at her magnificent Park Lane mansion was tantamount to professional suicide. Now, as Barrington stood opposite the entrance to the grand ballroom, watching the parade of swirling dancers make their way around the room, he wondered how many darkly held secrets would be exposed tonight.

A quick sweep of the room revealed the usual attendees: blue-blooded aristocrats with their equally blue-blooded wives, a smattering of officers and politicians, some in the present government, some casualties of the last, as well as the miscellaneous collection of ladies and gentlemen who, though not titled, were well born enough to receive the much-coveted invitations. Colonel Tanner was standing at the far side of the room with his pale little wife, but, other than a brief nod in Barrington's direction, betrayed no sign of having seen him.

Barrington allowed his gaze to move on. He was used to being ignored by those for whom he worked, if one wished to call it that. It was a hazard—or a blessing—of the job, depending on how one looked at it.

Then, suddenly, there was a commotion as three ladies entered together. Lady Annabelle Durst, magnificent in lilac silk, Lady Lydia Winston, lovely in shimmering green, and a third, slightly older but equally striking woman with whom Barrington was not acquainted. She wore an elegant silver-grey gown, long white gloves and a diamond necklace that could have fed London's poor for a year. And when he heard whispers in the crowd and realised that most of Lady Bessmel's guests didn't know who the lady was, he put the pieces together. This must surely be the mysterious Baroness Julia von Brohm.

More importantly, however, it was also the first time he had seen Anna since the arrival of her note acknowledging Peregrine's guilt. How would she receive him? With haughty indifference or grudging acceptance?

Knowing that the question had to be asked, he crossed the room to where she stood and bowed in front of the three ladies. 'Good evening, Lady Lydia. Lady Annabelle.'

'Why, good evening, Sir Barrington,' Lady Lydia said with unaffected pleasure. 'How nice to see you again. I thought perhaps you had been in hiding, we have seen so little of you.'

'Alas, I have been kept busy with work,' Barrington said, conscious of Anna's eyes on him.

'Yes, so I understand,' Lady Lydia's eyes sparkled with mischief. 'I happened to bump into your sister at Hatchard's the other day. She said you haven't been round for a visit since the occasion of her last dinner party.'

Barrington's mouth twisted, remembering his less-than-memorable meeting with Lady Alice Stokes, a pleasant woman with whom he'd had absolutely nothing in common. 'I will go round and see Jenny this week. And apologise,' he added with a rueful smile. Then, bowing towards Anna, said, 'I trust all is well at home, Lady Annabelle?'

'Yes, thank you, Sir Barrington.' Her expression was tranquil, but Barrington thought he detected a quiver in her voice. Surely she wasn't nervous about seeing him again?

'And Mr Rand?' he asked.

'He is doing as well as can be expected, under the circumstances,' she said quietly. Her hair was drawn softly off her face and caught up with a cluster of deep pink roses. Barrington thought she had never looked lovelier. 'Are you acquainted with Baroness von Brohm?' she asked, adroitly changing the subject.

'I am not,' Barrington said, turning towards the third lady, who was watching him with undisguised interest. 'I was hoping I might prevail upon one of you to make the introduction?'

'With pleasure. Baroness, may I present Sir Barrington Parker,' Anna said smoothly. 'Sir Barrington—Baroness Julia von Brohm.'

The lady regally inclined her head. 'Sir Barrington.'

'Baroness.' Barrington bowed over her hand. 'I'm surprised it has taken this long for us to meet, given that word of your arrival has been swirling for weeks.'

'There has been a great deal to do and I have kept much to myself,' the baroness admitted. 'But Lady Annabelle felt it was time to make my appearance in society and I am grateful to her and Lady Bessmel for their kindness in making it happen.'

'We decided to take Julia under our wing,' Anna explained. 'I'm sure you won't find that surprising, given what you know of me.'

Barrington wasn't sure if she was taking him to task, but when he saw the twinkle in her eye, he allowed himself to hope that the remark intended nothing of the sort. 'Yet another convoluted life exercise?' he ventured.

He was relieved to see her smile, and for the first time since the arrival of her note, he felt himself breathe properly again.

'Ah, Parker, good evening,' Lord Cambermere said, joining them. 'Might have known I'd find you hoarding the three most beautiful women in the room.'

'On the contrary, having only just made the baroness's acquaintance, I cannot be accused of hoarding. Especially since the other two ladies are as well known to you as they are to me.'

'Julia, allow me to introduce my father, Lord Cambermere,' Anna said with a smile. 'Papa, Baroness von Brohm.'

The earl's gaze sharpened, a man appreciating the beauty of a woman. 'I had heard of your arrival, Baroness, and am compelled to say that Vienna's loss is our gain. I trust you are enjoying life in London?'

'To be honest, I have experienced very little of it, Lord Cambermere,' the baroness replied. 'As I told your daughter, I have been busy setting up my household. There has not been much time for sightseeing or socialising.'

'But now that Julia is finished with all that, I have assured her that we shall be seeing a great deal more of her in society,' Anna said. 'Tonight is her début, if you will.'

'And a splendid début it is,' the earl said quietly. 'Would you allow me to introduce you to a few of my friends, Baroness? Having seen me in conversation with you, they will not forgive me if I neglect to do so.'

Barrington saw the look of pleasure that warmed the baroness's face, but also noticed the look of startled surprise on Anna's. Obviously she wasn't used to her widowed father paying court to a beautiful woman, especially one who was also so recently widowed. But, true to form, she recovered with swiftness and grace. 'Yes, do go, Julia. Papa knows everyone and he is perfectly respectable. Just don't start him talking about horses.'

'Oh, but I love horses!' the Baroness was quick to say. 'My late husband's stable was one of the finest in Vienna.'

'Good Lord,' the earl said, leaning forwards. 'Never tell me that your late husband was Captain Baron Ulrich von Brohm?'

A soft gasp escaped the baroness. 'Yes. Did you know him?'

'I most certainly knew *of* him. I read several of his papers on early equine development and thought his ideas were nothing short of brilliant.' The earl offered the lady his arm. 'I would be honoured to have a chance to speak to you about him.'

As an opening gambit, it couldn't have been better. Barrington watched the baroness place her gloved hand on Cambermere's sleeve, aware that her eyes were bright with interest as they rested on his face. They were already talking about horses as he led her away, prompting Barrington to wonder how many of the earl's friends were likely to be introduced to the beautiful baroness that evening.

'I think you have a success on your hands, Anna,' Lady Lydia whispered. 'If everyone else is as taken with the baroness as your father, we will surely see her married before the end of the Season!'

Barrington tended to echo Lady Lydia's assessment, though he wondered how Anna felt at having her father's affection for the woman so bluntly stated. It wasn't always easy for daughters to accept a new woman into their father's life, especially daughters who still lived at home. The arrival of a stepmother could make their lives hellish. Still, given the friendship that seemed to exist between Anna and the baroness, Barrington doubted that would be the case here.

'Sir Barrington,' she said suddenly, breaking into his thoughts, 'I wonder if I might have a word with you? In private.'

He turned to find her sapphire gaze fixed on him. 'By all means.'

'Then I shall go and speak to Lady Bessmel,' Lady Lydia said promptly. 'She mentioned having received news of her son in Scotland and I have been longing to hear how Thomas goes on. I shall catch up with you later, Anna. Good evening, Sir Barrington.'

Barrington inclined his head, but he noticed that Anna waited until her friend was far enough away so as not to hear their conversation before turning to him and saying, 'I hoped I would have a chance to speak to you this evening, Sir Barrington. I'm sure we both recognise that I owe you an apology with regard to Peregrine.'

Barrington studied the face upturned to his, aware that it exposed far more than she realised. 'You owe me nothing, Lady Annabelle. I took no pleasure in being the bearer of bad news.'

'Nevertheless, I accused you of dealing in false information and that was a criticism of your professional conduct. For that, an apology must be offered.'

'*Must* be?' he repeated. 'Am I to conclude that you do not *wish* to apologise?'

Her gaze clouded over, a tiny frown appearing between her brows. 'Please don't misunderstand. If I appear reluctant to admit my error, it is only because it has caused me to question things about myself that I've not had reason to question before. I thought I knew Peregrine better than anyone. Certainly better than you. And I believed I was right in defending him when you first charged him with the affair. But, as it turns out, I really didn't know him at all. I was convinced he would never do something so foolish as to engage in an affair, yet that's exactly what he did.'

'But you and I both know that Mr Rand is not the first man to catch Lady Yew's eye, nor will he be the last,' Barrington said. 'She is the type of a woman who needs constant attention. Sadly, he is just the latest on a very long list of conquests.'

'I know, but that doesn't make it any better,' Anna said ruefully. 'And it certainly doesn't excuse what he did.'

'Love makes its own excuses. It has ever been thus.'

'Perhaps, but what disturbs me the most is that he truly *believed* she loved him.'

'He will get over it,' Barrington said with a smile. 'He is a young man and all young men must fall in love with at least one unsuitable woman in their life. It is a rite of passage. Useful in teaching us what to watch out for when we *do* finally go looking for a wife.'

Her smile was a reluctant twisting of her lips. 'I wish I could be as convinced of that as you, but when I see him suffering…'

'Women pine for love not found while men suffer from love already lost. It is our Achilles' heel, if you will. And for what it's worth, I suspect Rand was more in love with the idea of *being* in love than he was with the actual act of loving,' Barrington said, hoping to ease her guilt. 'By all accounts, he liked to read to her and she enjoyed listening to him.'

He saw a tiny smile lift the corners of her mouth. 'Peregrine has a lovely speaking voice. Not as mellifluous as yours, of course, but I expect he would have done well on the stage.'

She liked his voice. There was really no reason the compliment should have meant anything to him, but it did. Strange the things a man clung to. 'Regardless, I think it little more than a case of boyish infatuation. Lady Yew is a beautiful woman. She was probably flattered that a good-looking man so much younger than she would find her attractive and offered more encouragement than she should.'

'For all the good it did either of them,' Anna said with an edge to her voice. 'But I *am* sorry, Sir Barrington. You told me that collecting information was what you did and you obviously do it very well. I will not be so foolish as to doubt you again.'

Barrington inclined his head, wondering why he felt as though she was saying goodbye. 'With luck, there will be no occasion for us to find ourselves in a situation like this again.'

Then she smiled and, with her very next words, confirmed his suspicions. 'I suppose not. In fact, given what we know of each other, I doubt our paths will have any reason to cross again.'

As expected, the baroness's introduction to London society was a complete success and doors that had been closed to her in the past were suddenly thrown open with abandon. Society embraced her with the fervour of a shepherd welcoming home a long-lost lamb and gentlemen flocked to her side, eager to secure favour.

Because she was seen to be such good friends with Lady Bessmel and the daughters of the Earl of Cambermere and the Marquess of Bailley, her name constantly appeared high on the list of society events, both intimate and grand. Not surprisingly, Anna's brother and father were frequent visitors to Julia's afternoon salons, though the earl was very careful not to do anything that might result in scandal being attached to her name. He never stayed longer than was appropriate, or tried to take up too much of her time. But it was noted and remarked upon, after several society gatherings where both were in attendance, that the widowed Earl of Cambermere was evidencing a marked partiality for the company of the beautiful Baroness von Brohm.

Naturally, Julia was delighted with all the attention, but Anna noticed that she, too, was careful not to indicate a preference for any one gentleman over another, perhaps because she was still clinging to the memory of her late husband. But she was a gracious and entertaining guest, and though her list of contacts grew by the day, she never forgot that it was Anna's kindness that had originally launched her into society.

As such, she decided to hold a dinner party in Anna's honour, inviting, along with the rest of her family, twenty other guests including Lord and Lady Bessmel and Lady Lydia Winston. Knowing the company would be very smart, Anna decided to wear one of her newest gowns, an elegant creation in pale gold silk, a colour that was exceedingly flattering to her fair complexion. Her hair was arranged in a loose cluster of curls with a few wisps hanging free to frame her face. Elbow-length gloves, her mother's pearls and a light sweep of colour across her cheeks were all that were required to complete the ensemble.

Half an hour later, she stepped out of the carriage in front of Julia's house, with her father and Edward close behind. Both looked very elegant in their black-and-white evening attire, her father especially so. Peregrine, who was still reluctant to show his face in society, had decided to remain at home.

'Good thing, too,' Edward said in the disparaging tone he always used when Peregrine's name came up. 'No point the boy thinking he's entitled to move in good society when it's obvious he belongs in the country.' He plucked a strand of hair from the sleeve of his jacket. 'Besides, he'd likely just embarrass us in front of the baroness. He does, after all, have an eye for older women.'

'That was unkind,' Anna said flatly. 'You are as much to blame for Peregrine's fall from grace as he is.'

'I don't see how. I wasn't the one who jumped into bed with Lady Yew.'

'Don't be coarse, Edward, and please keep your voice down,' Anna said in a fierce whisper. 'You shouldn't have told him about the state of their marriage.'

'My dear Anna, there isn't a soul in London who doesn't know the state of the Yews' marriage,' Edward said blandly. 'Why should I have left Rand in ignorance? He would have found out sooner or later. And just because I told him Lady Yew was open to lovers didn't mean he had to go sniffing after her as though she were a bitch in season. And you needn't look at me like that,' he said when she turned a chilling glance on him. 'You're too old to pretend an ignorance of what goes on between a man and a woman. I know how besotted you were over Anthony Colder.'

Anna winced, the mere sound of the man's name causing her pain. 'I would thank you not to mention him in my presence again.'

'Why not? Surely you're not still pining over the fellow. He wasn't worth it, you know. The stories I could tell—'

'This conversation is over,' Anna said coldly. 'Please keep your opinions to yourself and refrain from making damaging comments about Peregrine in public, lest you find yourself defending rumours about your own less than sterling behaviour.'

'*My* behaviour?' Her brother's eyes widened in a credible imitation of innocence. 'What possible concern could you have about that?'

'I see no need to explain myself. We are both aware of your reputation with women.'

He slowly began to smile, clearly enjoying himself. 'And what have you heard about my reputation, pray tell?'

'Amongst other things, that you are fickle and heartless,' Anna said, boldly meeting his gaze. 'We've gone through three maids in the last year and I suspect your unwelcome attentions towards them had much to do with the reasons they all left. If you must indulge yourself, kindly do so in a manner that does not disrupt the household or result in frightened young girls being sent back to the country in tears.'

His eyes narrowed and for a long moment he stared at her in silence. 'Well, well, so the pretty bird has sharp talons,' he murmured finally. 'Who would have guessed?'

'Guessed what?' their father asked, joining them.

'Nothing.' Anna turned her back on Edward, shutting out his obnoxious comments and his condescending gaze. She knew he enjoyed goading her and most of the time she was able to rise above his petty teasing, to treat his remarks with the chilly disdain they deserved. But tonight he'd touched a nerve and, despite her best intentions, she had lashed out at him, a reaction she would no doubt come to regret. 'We should go in. I have no desire to keep the Baroness waiting.'

They were escorted by the butler into an elegant drawing room where most of the guests had already assembled. Anna saw Lydia talking to Lord and Lady Bessmel and smiled in acknowledgement of her friend's wave. She left her father and brother and went to join them.

'Good evening, Lord Bessmel, Lady Bessmel,' she greeted the older couple. 'And, Lydia, I'm so pleased to see you. How is your mother this evening?'

'Much better, thank heavens,' the girl said, clearly relieved. 'This last megrim has been very difficult for her, but the doctor gave her something that seems to be helping. But what an exquisite gown, Anna. Surely one of Madame Delors's?'

'I thought the occasion demanded something suitably festive.' Anna took a deep breath and glanced around the room. She had no idea if Sir Barrington had been invited, but she found herself looking for him regardless. 'Have you seen our hostess yet?'

'No, but I expect she will be down shortly.'

'Not the thing for a lady to be late for her own dinner party,' Lord Bessmel remarked.

'Patience, Harry,' Lady Bessmel said, patting her husband's arm. 'I'm sure the baroness is simply waiting for the right moment to make her appearance. Most Europeans have a flair for the dramatic. But what lovely pearls, Annabelle. Your mother's, if I'm not mistaken.'

'Yes,' Anna said, surprised that the countess would recognise them. 'How did you know?'

'I remember her wearing them. White or pink pearls are relatively common, but that shade of gold is quite rare.'

'They were a gift to her from Papa,' Anna said fondly. 'He always said Mama had the perfect complexion for them.'

'She did. Fortunately, so do you and they go perfectly with your gown, which I must tell you is absolutely exquisite. But look, I do believe the baroness comes.'

As expected, all eyes turned towards the door where the baroness, resplendent in sapphire satin, stood for a moment framed in the doorway. Her lovely face was wreathed in smiles, but Anna was quite sure it wasn't her smile or her gown that caused the collective gasp of astonishment that echoed around the room, but the magnificent diamond-and-sapphire necklace that was draped around her throat.

'Forgive me, dear friends, but a minor crisis upstairs

delayed my arrival,' she announced to her assembled guests. 'I trust you have been attended to in my absence.'

'We have been very well treated,' Lord Bessmel said as the baroness joined them. 'The important thing is that you are here now and looking quite spectacular, if you don't mind my saying so.'

'I don't mind you saying so at all, Lord Bessmel,' Julia said with a soft gurgle of laughter. 'In fact, I am convinced it is the one thing a lady *never* tires of hearing. Anna, my dear,' she said, pressing her cheek to Anna's. 'How beautiful you look tonight. You will most certainly rob the gentlemen of their senses. And, Lady Lydia, how delightful to see you again. I trust your mother is feeling better?'

'She is, Julia, thank you; she is so sorry she couldn't be here this evening. Unfortunately, noise tends to aggravate her condition.'

'I understand,' Julia said with a sympathetic nod. 'Megrims are such tiresome things. You are lucky not to be afflicted.'

'Good evening, Baroness.'

Julia turned and her smile brightened. 'Lord Cambermere, Lord Hayle, I am so pleased you were both able to attend.'

'An opportunity to spend time in the company of a beautiful woman should never be missed,' Cambermere said as he brushed his lips over her hand in a courtly, old-world gesture. 'And may I say you look magnificent this evening.'

A becoming flush rose in her cheeks. 'You are very kind to say so.'

'Kindness has nothing to do with it,' the earl assured her. 'I'm sure there isn't a gentleman in the room who doesn't agree with me.'

'Fortunately, most of them come with wives,' Edward cut in smoothly. 'Those of us who are single definitely have the advantage this evening.'

His smile was charismatic and his words flattering. Anna

saw her father's expression falter as Edward neatly inserted himself between them, but Julia's attention was already diverted, her head turned towards the door. 'And here is yet another handsome gentleman come to join our group. Good evening, Sir Barrington.'

Anna hadn't needed to hear Barrington's name to know that he was in the room. She'd felt the atmosphere change, a subtle quickening of interest as he crossed the floor like a sleek black panther moving through the forest. She saw heads turn, watched eyes widen and flirtatious smiles disappear behind discreetly raised fans. Obviously she wasn't the only one impressed by the width of his shoulders and the unfathomable depths of those cool grey eyes—

'Anna!'

Hearing Lydia's voice, Anna turned, but it wasn't until she saw the slight widening of her friend's eyes that she realised she had been staring. Botheration! The last thing she needed was Sir Barrington Parker mistakenly thinking she was interested in him. Or worse, infatuated by him.

Fortunately, the gentleman seemed completely unaware of her preoccupation, his attention now focused solely on his hostess. 'Good evening, Baroness,' he greeted her in that distinctively low, seductive voice. 'Forgive my late arrival. I was unavoidably detained.'

'You owe us no apologies, Sir Barrington,' Julia said easily. 'You are here now and that is all that matters. I believe you know everyone?'

Sir Barrington nodded, his gaze touching briefly on each of them as he paid his respects. Finally, he turned to Anna, his mouth curving in that maddeningly provocative smile. 'Lady Annabelle.'

'Sir Barrington,' she said, wishing she possessed even a fraction of his composure. 'We have not seen much of you this past while.'

'I was out of London for a few days on business, but made sure to return in time for this evening's gathering.'

'And for the fencing demonstration,' Lord Bessmel said with a wink.

Sir Barrington turned to stare at him. 'I beg your pardon?'

'The fencing demonstration. The one Lord Yew asked you to put on.'

'Forgive me, Lord Bessmel, but I am not aware I was giving a fencing demonstration. Where did you hear news of it?'

'From Lord Hadley,' the older man replied. 'He said he'd heard you speaking to Lord Yew, and that you had agreed to a series of open engagements at Angelo's.'

'Open engagements?' Anna repeated. 'What does that mean?'

'It means that every red-blooded male capable of lifting a sword will be there looking to take Parker on,' Bessmel explained with a smile. 'Should make for a damn good show!'

Anna glanced at Sir Barrington in bewilderment. Surely Lord Bessmel was mistaken. Sir Barrington Parker didn't give demonstrations. Everyone knew that. And if he did choose to spar, it would be with someone of his own choosing.

Could this be the Marquess of Yew's doing? she wondered. Had he demanded this of Sir Barrington as well as everything he had already asked of Peregrine? 'Is this true, Sir Barrington?' she asked in a low voice. 'Is this what you agreed to do?'

'Not exactly,' he murmured. 'What I agreed to was a private lesson with Yew's son, pointing out areas where he might improve. I certainly said nothing about a series of engagements with anyone who felt up to sparring with me.'

'But I fear that is what everyone is expecting,' Bessmel said, adding hesitantly, 'are you going to back out?'

'Surely it cannot be called backing out when one never agreed to it in the first place,' Lydia objected.

'I wouldn't have thought so,' Sir Barrington agreed, 'but I shall speak to Lord Yew about it when next I see him.' Then, seemingly unconcerned, he turned his attention to their hostess again. 'Baroness, that is an exceptionally beautiful necklace.'

'Why, thank you, Sir Barrington.' Julia caressed the deep blue stones with loving fingers. 'My late husband bought it for me. He knew my partiality for sapphires.'

'It is a remarkable piece of workmanship,' Cambermere agreed. 'I hope you keep it safely locked away.'

'I haven't thus far.' Julia's eyes widened. 'Is London such a dangerous place that one need fear being robbed in one's own home?'

'Not as a rule, but I regret to say there have been a series of jewel thefts in London of late,' Sir Barrington informed her. 'I understand Lord Houghton's home was broken into two nights ago and a number of valuable items taken.'

'You should be on guard yourself, Cambermere,' Bessmel said. 'I dare say your daughter's pearls are worth a pretty penny.'

'They are, but I suspect to Anna, like myself, their value is far more sentimental.' The earl turned to smile at her. 'My wife loved pearls. She always said they drew their warmth from the one who wore them. I gave her that necklace on our wedding day.'

'Was your wife born in June, my lord?' Julia enquired.

Cambermere looked surprised by the question. 'She was.'

'Then she was fortunate to be able to wear them without

tears. It is considered bad luck to give a bride pearls unless they are her birthstone.'

'Then you must also have been born in June, Lady Annabelle,' Sir Barrington said quietly, 'for the pearls to glow so richly against your skin.'

Anna felt her cheeks grow warm at the subtle caress in his voice. 'On the contrary, my birthday is in September.'

'Then, like the baroness, you should be wearing sapphires.'

'I say, Cambermere, these women could bankrupt us if they were of a mind to!' Lord Bessmel said with a hearty laugh. 'Now you will have to go out and buy your daughter a string of sapphires, just to appease the superstitious amongst us.'

'I think not,' Anna said quickly. 'Sapphires are beautiful stones, but, like Mama, I prefer the warmth of pearls.'

'I can understand why,' Sir Barrington said as the others turned away to chat amongst themselves. 'They are exceptional, as is the lady wearing them.'

Anna slowly raised her eyes to his face, aware of the fire in his eyes as his gaze lingered on her necklace. The low *décolleté* of the gown exposed far more skin than she was used to and she could almost feel the heat of his eyes burning her. When he finally raised his eyes to meet hers, the desire in them was plain. Was it any wonder her heart was beating double time?

Thankfully, Julia, catching the eye of her butler, said, 'Dear guests, shall we proceed to the dining room? I do believe dinner is served.'

Chapter Six

At the conclusion of an exceptional meal, the baroness led the ladies into the drawing room, leaving the gentlemen to enjoy masculine conversation, good cigars and several fine bottles of port. Barrington, who enjoyed these sessions more for the information they provided than for the chance to socialise, accepted the offer of a light from Viscount Hayle, who settled into the chair next to his. Noticing the man's obvious boredom, Barrington said, 'Is the evening not to your liking, Hayle?'

Hayle slanted him a mocking glance. 'I get tired of listening to men like Bessmel and Richards bickering over political situations about which they know nothing. It's a waste of everyone's time and, frankly, I'd rather spend the night gambling or in the arms of a mistress.'

Barrington drew on his cigar, taking a moment to study the other man through the rising curl of smoke. 'I'm surprised Mr Rand didn't come with you tonight. I thought he usually accompanied your sister to these kinds of events.'

'He was invited but, thankfully, he declined,' Hayle said

tersely. 'It's bad enough having him around the house all the time, let alone being forced into society with him.'

'You do not care for Mr Rand?'

'Would you?' Hayle fired back.

Barrington was startled by the flash of raw emotion he saw in the other man's eyes and wondered if Hayle knew how much of himself he had given away. 'I'm not sure I know what you mean.'

'Then you're the only one who doesn't,' Hayle muttered. 'All you have to do is *look* at Rand to know he's no more my father's *godson* than he is the bloody Prince of Wales's.'

So, that was it. The son suspected the connection and wasn't in the least happy about it. Barrington tapped ash from the end of his cigar. 'I'd be lying if I said I hadn't heard rumours, but I don't believe anything's been substantiated.'

'Of course not. My father's the only one who can substantiate rumours like that and you can be damn sure he's not going to. Not now that he's met the baroness.' Hayle's eyes narrowed as he glared at his father sitting farther up the table. 'It's embarrassing the way he carries on with her. God knows, he's old enough to be her father.'

'I take it you do not care for the fact that the earl and the baroness seem to like one another?'

'I do not. It's unseemly the way he follows her around, hanging on every word she says. He might just as well come out and ask her to go to bed with him.'

Barrington reached for his glass of port, intrigued by the depth of vitriol pouring from the other man. 'I think you judge them too harshly. Your father is an amiable gentleman and the baroness is an exceedingly gracious woman. And as they are both widowed, why should they not enjoy one another's company?'

'There *is* a considerable difference in their ages.'

Barrington shrugged. 'The baroness can't be any more

than twenty-nine or thirty, and your father is, what…in his late forties? There are far wider gaps in age between husbands and wives in society.'

Hayle slowly began to smile. 'Yes. Like Lord Yew and his wife. But then, I suspect you already know all about that.'

Barrington inhaled deeply on his cigar. Hayle was bound to know about Peregrine's folly, but he was damned if he'd be the one to shed any light on the matter. When it came to secrets, he was as adept at keeping them as he was at prying them out of others.

Fortunately, Hayle didn't appear to be in need of an answer. 'How much do you think that sapphire necklace is worth?' he asked instead.

Barrington's shrug was carefully non-committal. 'I'm no expert, but, given the size and quality of the stones, I should think it considerable.'

'Enough to keep a man in brandy and cigars for the rest of his life, I'll wager.'

'Probably. How fortunate that you and I need not worry about such things.'

Hayle snorted. 'Speak for yourself.'

Barrington's gaze sharpened. 'You are your father's heir.'

'Oh, yes. But as he's still in his forties and hale and hearty, I'm not likely to inherit any time soon,' Hayle said sourly. 'So, what's your connection with the baroness?'

'We have no connection, *per se*,' Barrington said, aware that the man changed subjects more often than a lady changed her mind. 'We were introduced by your sister at Lady Bessmel's reception and have seen each other at a few society gatherings since, but nothing beyond that.' He gazed at the earl's son through a fine wisp of smoke. 'I understand it was your sister's idea to launch the baroness into society.'

'Of course it was. Anna loves to manage other people's lives. Personally, I think her time would be better spent smoothing her way into some man's bed,' Hayle said in a disagreeable tone, adding when he saw Barrington's stern look, '*After* she marries him, of course. Anna would never do anything as irresponsible as compromise herself. But it's long past time she was wed. Father's too soft. He won't force her into an arranged marriage, even though he knows it would be best for all concerned.'

'I'm sure your sister would have no problem finding a husband if that was something she truly wanted,' Barrington said, careful to keep the annoyance from his voice. 'She is an exceedingly beautiful woman.'

'But meddlesome and outspoken,' Hayle remarked. 'Men don't like that in a wife. They want quiet, biddable women who know their place. Anna is neither biddable nor accommodating, as I'm sure you know from the brief time you've spent with her. Mind, I've heard her mention *your* name more than once and that's saying something. Better watch yourself, Parker, or she'll have you in the parson's mousetrap before you can turn around.' He drained the contents of his glass, then signalled the waiter for a refill. 'So, I hear you're giving a fencing demonstration at Angelo's this week.'

Barrington's hand tightened on his glass. 'No. I am giving Lord Yew's son a lesson. In private.'

'I heard you were going to fight.'

'You heard wrong.'

'But why wouldn't you fight?' Hayle asked. 'You're reputed to be the finest swordsman in London. Why not show everyone that you are?'

'Because that's not what I do.'

'Then why are you giving Yew's boy a lesson?'

'I agreed to it as a favour to the marquess. I also happen to like Lord Gerald. He shows a great deal of promise with the foil and he is anxious to better himself.'

'Maybe, but you'll never make a fighter of him. He's too

soft,' Hayle said. 'He hasn't the heart for it. You'd do far better sparring with me. At least I'd give you a run for your money. So what do you say? Are you up for it?'

Barrington's expression was deceptively benign. He was used to cocky young men challenging him. At one time, he'd encouraged it, fond of pitting his skills against all comers. But that game had lost its appeal years ago.

He was about to say as much when the door to the dining room opened and one of the younger maids walked in. He hadn't noticed her earlier in the evening, which meant she likely hadn't been in the room. He would certainly have remembered her if she had. She was somewhere in her early twenties, with dark brown hair and rather startling green eyes—

Barrington stiffened. Green eyes and dark brown hair. Was it possible he'd found Colonel Tanner's elusive Miss Paisley? If so, he wasn't surprised that the Colonel had asked him to look for her. Though petite, she had a lush, curving figure that was nicely displayed in the black gown and white apron. Her face was heart shaped and delicate and she had a truly lovely smile. But equally aware of having drawn the attention of nearly every man in the room, her cheeks turned bright pink as she made her way towards the butler, who was standing in the corner overseeing the proceedings.

A whispered conversation followed, during which the butler's heavy eyebrows drew together in annoyance. Then, with a flick of his hand, he dismissed her.

As she headed back in their direction, Barrington noticed Hayle doing a leisurely appraisal of her charms. Then, slowly raising his glass, he watched her over the rim and when she was no more than five feet away, coughed. Not discreetly, as a gentleman might, but in a manner that was guaranteed to draw attention.

The girl glanced in their direction—and her step faltered.

Barrington heard her breath catch and saw her eyes widen as they met those of the man sitting next to him. Beside him, Hayle just smiled. Coldly. Like a spider watching a fly, knowing it was doomed.

The butler, noticing her standing in the middle of the room, said sharply, 'Be off with you, girl!'

She went, all but running to the door. Hayle turned away, seemingly uninterested. 'Bloody endless evening,' he muttered into his glass.

But the girl didn't leave. Barrington saw her hesitate by the door, saw her turn around to take one last look at Hayle, and the expression in her eyes said it all.

'Oh, I don't know,' Barrington remarked, drawing deeply on his cigar. 'Seems to me it's all in how you look at it.'

Anna was seated at the pianoforte playing an air by Bach when the drawing-room door opened and the gentlemen filed in. She knew the piece well enough not to be flustered by their arrival and kept on playing, watching with interest as they took their various seats and settled into conversation with the ladies. Her father stopped to chat with Lady Bessmel, but eventually ended up at Julia's side. His face was flushed and he was smiling. No doubt the result of an extra glass of port after dinner.

Edward spoke briefly to Lady Lydia Winston, but, judging from the expression on her face, the conversation was not at all to her liking. She stiffly got up and walked away. Edward just laughed.

'I was going to ask if I might turn the pages for you,' Sir Barrington said, quietly appearing at her side. 'But since it's obvious you play from memory, I doubt you are in need of my help.'

The glow of his smile warmed her. 'Nevertheless, it is kind of you to offer, Sir Barrington.'

'Kindness had nothing to do with it. I was looking for an excuse to talk to you.'

Anna was tempted to ask why he felt the need of an excuse, but the teasing quip died on her lips when she saw the way he was looking down at her. 'About something in particular?'

'Of course.' He stared a moment longer, before turning his attention back to the room.

Anna kept her eyes on the keyboard, waiting for her breathing to settle. Would it always be like this? Was she destined to feel this trembling excitement every time Barrington drew near? She certainly hoped not. It wouldn't bode well for their friendship if she did.

She cast a sideways glance at him and knew he was taking it all in. Making mental lists about the people and situations that intrigued him. Watching. Always watching.

'It must get tiresome,' she said at length. 'Always having to watch the behaviour of others.'

He turned back to smile at her, one eyebrow raised in amusement. 'That depends on your point of view. Some people spend their entire lives studying the behaviour of others. Wanting to know what their friends and acquaintances are doing. It's called being nosy and society suffers from it excessively.'

Her lips twitched. 'That's quite true, but what you do is entirely different.'

'Why would you say so?'

'Because you don't watch people with the intention of catching them doing something wrong. You watch with a view to catalogue it all for future reference. You notice who they speak to and who they ignore, if they drink too much or not at all, and if they dance with that person and not this one.'

'You make me sound rather devious,' he observed.

'No. Just observant. Something that probably serves you well given the nature of your...occupation.'

The piece of music came to an end and Anna rose to the polite applause of the guests. Miss Constantine was to play next, and as that young lady moved forwards to take her place at the piano, Anna dropped back and fell in beside Barrington.

'Did I detect a note of censure in your voice just then?' he asked as they slowly walked away from the instrument.

Did he? Anna didn't like to think she was revealing too much of herself, but with him, it wasn't always easy to know. 'I have the feeling, Sir Barrington, that one is never entirely safe around you. You see a great deal without ever giving the appearance of actually looking. That makes you dangerous.'

'Only to those with something to hide. The innocent have no reason to fear me.' His eyes found hers and held them captive. 'I trust *you* do not find me dangerous, Lady Annabelle?'

'Danger comes in many forms. I suspect knowing a man like you does not come without risks.'

'*Life* does not come without risks,' he said softly. 'But you're right. A man like myself is always more of a target, as are the people who associate with me.'

Thinking he was being overly dramatic, Anna smiled and said, 'In that case, you'd best warn Miss Erickson to keep her distance.'

'Miss Erickson?'

'Miss Sofia Erickson. I happen to know she is very fond of you.'

Barrington said, 'I'm not sure I know her.'

'Of course you do. Eldest daughter of Viscount Oswell and recently returned from visiting her aunt in Edinburgh. She made her come out this Season and has already been acknowledged as one of its greatest successes. She speaks French and Italian fluently, is an accomplished rider, and an exceptional singer.'

A smile ruffled his mouth. 'And have you had occasion to save the young lady from herself?'

'Good Lord, no.' The sensual curve of his lips brought a series of highly inappropriate thoughts to mind, but Anna forced herself to ignore them. 'She is one of the most intelligent young women I've ever met. She is mindful of the proprieties and quite capable of telling a gentleman to watch his manners if she feels he is out of line.'

'Tell me, how do you come to be so involved in the lives of all these young women?' Barrington asked curiously as they sat down together on the velvet settee. 'Surely your father would wish you to pay more attention to your own future than chasing around after everyone else's?'

Anna felt the familiar warmth creep into her cheeks—an annoyingly common occurrence since meeting this man. 'One can do both at the same time. Helping someone else navigate the path towards marriage does not mean I cannot walk the path myself.'

'But if you are too busy looking out for the welfare of others, how can you see to your own?'

'I hardly think I am doing one to the exclusion of the other,' Anna said defensively. 'Besides, what I do for these girls is important. All too often they find themselves swept up in the emotion of the moment and don't stop to think about the repercussions.'

'And so you step in,' he said softly. 'Like you did with Mercy Banks and Fiona Whitfield, and God knows how many others, in an attempt to save them from themselves.'

'It is all very well for you to mock me, Sir Barrington, but you cannot deny that—' Anna broke off to stare at him. 'How did you know I was involved with Fiona Whitfield?'

'Do you really need ask?'

'Yes, I fear I must. Fiona's mother and father were adamant that word of what happened to Fiona not leak out. I gave them my word that I would say nothing and, since the young man was sent abroad, I don't see how you could possibly be aware of what took place.'

'As it happens, I was making enquiries into the activities of Miss Whitfield's uncle,' Barrington told her. 'I learned of your association with the family at that time. And though I did not delve into the particulars of Miss Whitfield's situation, I did learn of *your* involvement with her whilst speaking to another family member.'

Anna gasped. 'Someone else knew what happened to Fiona?'

'I'm afraid so. But, like you, they were sworn to secrecy. And it worked out well enough in the end. She married Lord Priestley's son earlier this year and I understand they are very happy together.'

'Yes, thank goodness. It could have turned out so badly for her, and all because of that despicable man.' Anna sighed. 'It really isn't fair, you know. A man may tempt a woman with honeyed words and longing looks, yet *she* is the one who must behave with propriety at all times. If he manages to steal a kiss, he is not thought of any the less, whereas she is deemed to have loose morals.'

'Sadly, it has always been thus,' Barrington remarked. 'Society makes the rules and we must obey.'

'No. *Men* make the rules and then demand that women follow them. It is no wonder we sometimes falter.'

She saw the surprise in his face. 'Am I to assume from your comment, Lady Annabelle, that you yourself have faltered in the past?'

'That is none of your business!' she exclaimed.

'No, I don't suppose it is.' He laughed softly, the sound

sending shivers up her spine. 'But your reputation doesn't suggest a woman who would be easily led astray. I find my curiosity piqued at the thought of you having ever done anything wrong.'

'Then you will just have to live with piqued curiosity,' Anna said, abruptly standing up.

'Anna, wait, I meant no offence,' he said, likewise getting to his feet. 'If I've inadvertently touched a nerve, I apologise. It was never my intention to hurt you.'

Anna shook her head, too distracted by unpleasant memories of the past to notice his lapse into familiarity. 'And I did not mean to be abrupt, Sir Barrington, but I have no wish to talk about what happened in my past.'

'I understand. We've all made mistakes, some worse than others. But given your untarnished reputation and excellent standing in society, it's obvious your mistake, if that's what it was, did not serve as your undoing.'

'It could have,' Anna whispered, 'had a friend not come along when she had.'

And that was the tragic truth of her brief flirtation with the Honourable Anthony Colder. As a naïve seventeen-year-old, Anna had all but thrown herself at the god-like creature, believing the smiles he had bestowed upon her were the result of a genuine and mutual affection. Little had she known that his interest had more to do with her father being the Earl of Cambermere than it did with any charms she might possess herself. Anthony had been an avid social climber, as well as the most handsome man she had ever met. With those laughing blue eyes and a smile that set butterflies dancing in her stomach, she would have given him anything he'd asked for. And if he'd had his chance, he would have taken it.

Mrs Mary Fielding had known that, too. A twice-married woman wise to the ways of men like Anthony Colder, Mrs Fielding had seen the growing infatuation between the two young people and had guessed at its source, being more familiar with Anthony's background than most. She had known of his gambling debts, his easy way with women, and his devil-may-care attitude. And on that evening when Anthony, having drunk too much brandy and feeling far too sure of himself, had caught Anna alone in the gazebo by the lake and torn her gown in a boorish attempt at seduction, Mrs Fielding had appeared and promptly sent him packing. She had stayed with Anna until the worst of her grief had passed, and then, after drying Anna's tears, she had lent her a shawl to cover the tear and had sent her regrets back to their hostess, explaining that Lady Annabelle was unwell and that she was seeing her home in her own carriage.

It had been a painful lesson, but one Anna had learned well. She had gone home that evening and made no mention of the event to anyone. She regretted having told her parents and her brother of her affection for Anthony, but after that night she never mentioned his name again. Nor, thankfully, did she see him. Mrs Fielding informed her not long after that he had left the country.

Anna had never been so glad to see the back of anyone in her life. And though she thought it was impossible for her to blush any deeper, she was wrong. Even after all this time, her face burned at the memory of her stupid, stupid mistake…

'Tell me what happened, Lady Annabelle,' Barrington said in a low voice. 'Your secrets are safe with me. I know, better than most, the value of discretion.'

'Yes, I'm sure you do,' Anna said quietly. 'But the only way to completely ensure one's secrets is by keeping them entirely to oneself.'

'I'm sorry you cannot bring yourself to trust me.'

She looked up at him, surprised that he would mention trust in such a situation. 'I do not know you, Sir Barrington.

And the trust of which you speak is generally reserved for relationships between husbands and wives.'

'I've always thought that bonds of trust can exist between friends as well as lovers.'

'Perhaps, but it takes time to establish that kind of bond,' she said, sounding flustered even to her own ears. 'You are a single gentleman and I a single lady. It isn't the thing for us to…share secrets of an intimate nature. But if you were looking for a wife, you would do well to consider Miss Erickson. Apart from her many other attributes, she is a genuinely nice young woman.'

'What makes you think I'm looking for a wife?' he asked.

'Why would you not be? You just told me that we must abide by society's rules, and society dictates that men and women should marry. Is that not the purpose of these gatherings? To place one in the path of the other?'

'I suppose it is.' He hesitated a moment before adding, 'But I think it only right to tell you that Miss Erickson would not be of interest to me, even if I were of a mind to marry.'

If he were of a *mind* to marry? 'Are you telling me you intend to remain single?' Anna asked, eyebrows lifting in shock.

'That was my plan, yes.'

'But what of your obligation to your family?'

'I fear the task of continuing the Parker name will fall to a distant cousin with whom I am not acquainted,' Barrington said blandly. 'As to the obligation owed, I am more concerned with the welfare of the lady with whom I might wish to spend my life than I am to the furthering of my ancestral line.'

'Then I would have to say you are unique in your thinking,' Anna said. 'Most society gentlemen are concerned with their family name and marry to beget an heir.'

'Yes, but you should know by now that my life is not that

of a typical society gentleman. My reputation is such that people come to me when they wish to learn things about others. And because I ask questions people have no wish to be asked, I continuously put myself at risk.'

'Surely you exaggerate the danger.'

'I do not.' His smile held secrets she could not begin to imagine. 'The people I usually investigate are not the honourable men you meet in society, Lady Annabelle. They are scoundrels and blackmailers, men who operate beyond the boundaries of the law and who are completely without conscience. When I get too close, they get nervous. And when I convict them, they look for retribution.'

'But surely not of a life-threatening kind!'

He shrugged, as though trying to make light of it. 'There have been attempts on my life in the past and I have no reason to believe there will not be attempts in the future. The easiest way to ensure my silence is to eliminate the possibility of my saying anything at all. That said, I will not knowingly put anyone else in danger.'

'But if these men have issues with you, why should you fear for the safety of those close to you?'

'Because there *is* no better way to strike back at me than to hurt someone I care about.' They had walked, by tacit agreement, onto the balcony. Barrington rested his arms against the stone balustrade and stared down into the garden. 'And who could be dearer to me than the woman to whom I would give my name…and my heart.'

Anna felt her mouth go dry. Strange that the breeze should suddenly feel so cool. Was her body overly warm? They were standing quite close; close enough that she could feel the heat radiating from his body. 'So you would choose to live… without a woman to share your life,' she whispered, 'rather than expose your wife to possible harm?'

'In a heartbeat.' He turned his head so that his eyes bored

into hers. 'How could I say I loved someone if I didn't care about their safety? If the thought of something happening to them didn't tear me apart?'

Anna shivered. 'You could give up what you're doing. You are a gentleman. You have no need to work.'

'And what would I do with myself then?' He reached out and took her hand in his. 'I have servants to run my estate and stewards and secretaries to see to my affairs. But a man must have something of his own or what reason has he for getting up each day?'

As he spoke, his fingers caressed the palm of her hand, smoothing the tender skin at the base of her wrist. His touch was light, non-threatening—and it turned Anna's world upside down.

She closed her eyes, the sounds of the room beyond fading into the distance. She knew she should pull her hand free, but she was neither willing nor anxious to do so. His thumb was painting circles on her skin, lulling her with a touch.

'We get up because…that is what the world expects of us,' she said huskily. Dear Lord, what was he doing? Not content with massaging her palm and wrist, his thumb was continuing its treacherous voyage along the inside of her arm, causing disturbing quakes in her sanity. 'Surely there is…a kind of security, perhaps even of comfort, in the carrying out of our daily task?'

'Ah, but there are far sweeter pleasures to be enjoyed than that, my lady,' Barrington murmured as he brushed the back of his free hand against her cheek. 'The smoothness of a woman's skin, the softness of her hair.' He gently twined a lock around his finger and held it to his face, inhaling the delicate fragrance. 'Finer than silk and more precious than gold.' Then, releasing it, he gently grasped her chin between thumb and forefinger and tilted her face up. 'Last but not least, the sweetness of her lips…'

Anna had been kissed before…but never like this. Never by a man whose touch was enough to make her long to release her tenuous hold on respectability. His mouth moved over hers slowly, thoughtfully, shattering her resolve and filling her with a desperate need to be loved. Surely she deserved this. Surely, after everything she'd been through, she was entitled to some small measure of love and affection for herself?

As he deepened the kiss, Anna raised her arms, twining them around his neck, wanting to be close and then closer still. His tongue teased her lips apart and heat poured through her body, flowing like molten fire through her veins. She moaned, feeling desire rise and want settle low in her belly. Ah, the sweet, sweet pleasure…

But the pleasure was bittersweet. Even as his arms tightened around her, Anna knew it could come to nothing. Barrington had no intention of marrying. He'd just told her as much. And if he wasn't willing to offer marriage, what they were doing now was not only wrong, it was self-destructive. She wanted more from him. Much more than he was willing to give. And in the end, she would be the one who walked away with her heart in ruins. And therein lay the true sadness of the situation. The one man with whom she could have foreseen a future was the one man with whom it would never be.

'Stupid, stupid, *stupid*!' she whispered, breaking free of his arms.

'Anna, what's wrong?' he asked huskily.

'What's wrong? *I'm* wrong,' she whispered. '*This* is wrong. Because right now, I'm no better than the foolish young women whose reputations I fight to protect.'

'That's ridiculous!'

'Is it? You just told me you have no intention of marrying, yet I allowed myself to be held in your arms and kissed like any cheap whore. What is that if not the height of stupidity?'

Anna flung at him. 'At least Mercy Banks was hopeful of a marriage resulting from her liaison with Lieutenant Blokker! You've made it clear there is no such happy ending in sight.'

His face darkened, his breathing heavy and uneven. 'I said that because I don't want you harbouring false hope. But it doesn't change the way I feel about you.'

'And is that supposed to make me feel *better*? Am I supposed to be comforted by the knowledge that you desire me, yet have no intention of offering marriage?' Anna shook her head. 'There is a word for that kind of relationship, Sir Barrington, and it is not flattering.'

'It was never my intention to compromise you, Anna,' he said quietly. 'I care too much for you.'

'My name is Lady Annabelle. And if you care so much for me, leave me alone!'

Without waiting for his answer, Anna picked up her skirts and fled. Angry tears blurred her vision as she ran down the length of the balcony. *Idiot!* She'd made a fool of herself again, allowing herself to be held and kissed as though she were a naïve young schoolgirl. She, who prided herself on knowing all the games and all the excuses, had let herself be taken in. And by doing so, Barrington had undermined everything she believed in. When she had allowed him to kiss her, she had wanted to believe that it meant something. But it was obvious to anyone with an iota of sense that it meant absolutely nothing. Sophisticated Barrington might be, but he was still a man, and when it came right down to it, he wanted the same thing as every other man. Pleasure without commitment. Love without obligation. The very things she kept warning her young ladies to avoid.

The breeze came up and, once again, Anna felt chilled. She hadn't stopped to fetch her wrap before venturing outside, but neither was she about to run back into the drawing room now.

Observant eyes would see the evidence of her tears, recognise the flush in her cheeks and put their own interpretation on the events—and nothing on earth was going to persuade her to tell anyone what had really happened.

She glanced back over her shoulder, wondering if Barrington had followed her. She didn't know whether to be relieved or disappointed when she saw that he hadn't. All right, so she'd made a mistake. It wasn't the first time she'd done so, but at least this time she was old enough to recognise it for herself. Barrington had made his feelings for her clear. The episode would not be repeated. From now on, she would treat him exactly the same way he treated everyone else. Coolly. Professionally. Without emotion. He would never make her cry again.

It was a good ten minutes before Anna felt calm enough to venture back into the house. Not by the drawing room through which she'd left. That would be far too embarrassing, especially knowing that Barrington had gone back in only a short time ago. Instead, she walked to the end of the balcony and, finding another set of glass doors, tried the handle. Thankfully, it was unlocked and pushing it open, she walked into a small study—only to stop and gasp in shock.

Her brother and Julia's maid were standing by the door, locked together in a passionate embrace. *'Edward!'*

At once, the pair sprang apart, but it was too late to disguise what they had been doing. The maid's dark hair had come down around her shoulders, her gown was in disarray and her lips were red and swollen.

Embarrassed, Anna looked away. Obviously, her brother wasn't above seducing pretty housemaids, whether they be his own or someone else's. Refusing to meet his eyes, she murmured, 'Excuse me', and then immediately made her way to the door. Edward said nothing, but she heard his mocking laughter following her through the door. She supposed she shouldn't have been surprised. Her brother had once again proven himself the immoral creature she believed him to be.

And what about you? the little voice nagged. *Are you so much better? So much more virtuous?*

Anna felt her face burn with humiliation. No, perhaps she wasn't. She kept remembering the passionate encounter she'd just shared with Barrington, the shameless manner in which she had allowed him to kiss her. Oh, yes, she'd *let* him kiss her. She wasn't about to lay the blame for what had happened entirely at his door. He was gentleman enough that if she had asked him to stop, he would have—but she hadn't done that. She'd wanted to know how it would feel to kiss him. To watch his head bend slowly towards her, and to feel his mouth close intimately over hers.

It had been everything she'd expected—and more.

But Barrington was no more likely to become her husband than Julia's maid was to become Edward's wife. They had both been indulging in impossible fantasies.

'Let he who is without sin cast the first stone…'

A sobering thought. As Anna made her way back to the drawing room, she realised that the proverbial stone would never find its way to her hand.

Chapter Seven

For the next few days, Barrington went around like a bear with a sore head. Unable to forget what had happened between Anna and himself at the baroness's dinner party, he was quick to anger and slow to unwind, because he knew he'd hurt her. And hurting her was the last thing he'd ever wanted to do.

He'd still been in the drawing room when Anna had finally returned, but she hadn't approached him again. She had remained coldly aloof, treating him as though he wasn't there. He wasn't surprised that she had left shortly after.

He'd left early as well, all pleasure in the evening gone. Upon returning home, he'd made for his study and downed a stiff glass of brandy, followed in quick succession by two more. But the potent liquor had done nothing to assuage his guilt, or to help him find escape in sleep. When the morning had come, he'd been as tired and as irritable as when he'd gone to bed.

Much as he was this morning, three days later, as he made his way to Angelo's Haymarket rooms for his ten o'clock appointment with the Marquess of Yew's son.

Barrington deeply regretted having made the appointment.

The last thing he felt like doing was teaching the finer points of fencing to the gangly nineteen-year-old son of a man he neither liked nor respected. However, he had given Yew his promise that he would show the boy a few things and he was a man who kept his word. All he could do now was hope the hour passed quickly and that he didn't do the boy an unintentional injury.

Unfortunately, Lord Bessmel was right when he'd said that word of the lesson—or demonstration—had spread. By the time Barrington arrived, the room was filled to overflowing with gentlemen of all ages, some carrying swords, some just there to observe. It was worse than he'd expected.

'Ah, Parker,' Lord Yew greeted him with a smile. 'Good to see you. Quite the turnout, eh? I vow you draw a larger crowd than Prinnie.'

'Perhaps because you put it about that this was to be a demonstration, rather than the private lesson we agreed to,' Barrington said.

'Really?' the marquess said lazily. 'I don't recall saying this was to be a lesson. But never mind, now you and Gerald have a suitable audience.'

'An audience that comes armed and ready to spar?'

The marquess smiled. 'You should be thanking me, Parker. You have your pick of opponents and since we both know there's not a man in the room who can best you, you're guaranteed to come out on top. Why not just have fun with it?'

'Because that's not what I do.' Barrington's jaw tightened. Unfortunately, they both knew this was something of a command performance. A 'small additional favour' in exchange for the marquess's silence over Peregrine Rand's affair with his wife. And while Barrington would normally have refused to play a part, all it took was the memory of the look on Anna's face when she had spoken of Rand's guilt to make him change his mind. He didn't particularly care about the other man's feelings, but he would have done almost anything to prevent hers being further injured.

'I've lived up to my side of the bargain, Yew. I trust you intend to do the same.'

'Are you questioning my integrity?' the marquess asked, peering down his long, patrician nose.

'No. But I know how angry you were with Rand and I don't want to think that all of this has been for naught.'

The marquess chuckled. 'I can assure you it has not. In point of fact, I wasn't really angry at all.'

Barrington's mouth tightened. 'I beg your pardon?'

The marquess's expression was remote as he gazed at the milling crowd. 'Rand is not the first man to make love to my wife, and, God knows, he won't be the last. Susan is voracious in that regard and while I enjoy sex as much as the next man, I am not inclined to engage in it as often as she might wish. So I turn a blind eye to her affairs. It flatters me to know that she is still beautiful enough to attract other men; it flatters her to know that she is desired by men younger than herself.'

No stranger to the unusual, Barrington was none the less bewildered by Yew's unexpected admission. 'Then why did you go to the trouble of persecuting him?'

The marquess's gaze narrowed. 'You really don't know?' When Barrington shook his head, Yew said in amusement, 'Because I was asked to.'

Having casually dropped his bomb, the marquess strolled away. Barrington, aware that the eyes of the room were on him, allowed nothing of his anger to show, knowing it would incite too many questions he wasn't prepared to answer. But he *was* angry. Furiously so. Someone had been playing with Peregrine Rand—and, by association, with him.

'Good m-morning, Sir B-Barrington,' Lord Gerald Fitzhenry said, coming up to him. 'It's v-very good of you to d-do this for me.'

Lord Yew's youngest son was a quiet, unassuming young man, who, though raised in an atmosphere of wealth and privilege, had managed to lose none of his good nature as a result. Perhaps the stutter kept him from becoming too arrogant, Barrington reflected. It wasn't a fashionable affectation, but a lifelong affliction, one the boy had desperately tried to overcome. But it was exacerbated by nerves and, given the unexpected turnout in the room, Barrington knew this morning's performance would be more difficult for Lord Gerald than usual. As such, he turned to face the lad with a reassuring smile. 'You show a great deal of promise, Lord Gerald. Perhaps I can point out a few things that will help you become an even better fencer.'

The boy's face shone. 'I would l-like that, very much.'

'Good. Then shall we take our positions?'

As Barrington led the way onto the floor, he was conscious of every eye in the room following him. He was acquainted with many of the gentlemen present and knew that some of them were decent fencers and were here for that reason alone. Having been taught by one of the finest swordsmen in France, Barrington possessed skills few others did and the chance to watch him spar today was an opportunity too good to miss.

But not all the gentlemen in the room had come simply to observe his technique. A movement at the far end of the room drew Barrington's attention. Looking up, he saw Hayle leaning against the wall, sword in hand. He had come to fight. He'd made that very clear.

Barrington had no intention of indulging him. Men like Hayle only wanted to prove their superiority over others. It was likely one of the reasons Hayle resented Rand's presence in the house. Though Rand offered no tangible threat, he was a competitor for the earl's attention, perhaps even for his affection. And if Hayle believed that Rand was his half-brother, he would naturally assume there was an affinity between his father and the other man he couldn't affect or control.

He wouldn't like that. Hayle needed to be seen as the only cock of the roost, and, so far, he had. Lord only knew what would happen if and when he found out otherwise.

An hour later, it was all over.

'You did well,' Barrington said, removing his mask and walking towards Lord Gerald. 'But you would do better if you kept your arm straight and the weight of your body on the front of your feet. You need to be able to move quickly around your opponent. Try to catch him off balance.'

'Yes, Sir B-Barrington,' said the grateful but sweating youth.

'And don't forget what I said about practising your double and triple feints. They'll stand you in good stead when you find yourself pushed to defend yourself. If you like, come round to the house and I'll lend you a couple of books that helped me when I was where you are.'

The boy's face shone as though he'd been given the keys to the kingdom. 'Thank you so much, Sir B-Barrington. I will t-try to d-do that.'

Barrington smiled and clapped the lad on the shoulder. He was glad now that he'd agreed to the lesson. Lord Gerald had turned out to be a surprisingly good swordsman and he was appreciative of the time he'd been given. He would benefit by what he'd learned today.

'Who's next then, Sir Barrington?' someone called out from the crowd.

Despite the cheers that greeted the man's words, Barrington shook his head. 'Sorry, gentlemen, the show's over. You can all go home now.'

Amidst the rumble of disappointment, another voice said,

'But this was to be a demonstration. Surely you wouldn't send everyone away without giving them what they really came here to see.'

Barrington's mouth compressed into a thin line. So, Hayle would challenge him publicly. A foolish thing to do. 'I'm sure there are others who would favour you with a match, Lord Hayle.'

'But it is with you I wish to engage, Sir Barrington,' Hayle said softly. 'Will you not stand and face me? I have been acknowledged a better than average fencer and would welcome an opportunity to go up against the best.'

Hearing the room suddenly fall silent, Barrington sighed. 'My purpose this morning was to instruct Lord Yew's son. It was not a general invitation to spar.'

'But surely there can be no harm in engaging in a friendly match,' Hayle said, advancing on to the floor. 'You are acknowledged the finest swordsman in England. Every one of us here could benefit by watching and learning, and I am willing to put myself forward as your student. If nothing else, I promise you a better match than the one you just concluded.'

'I was not engaged in a match,' Barrington reminded him. 'I was giving a lesson.'

'Then consider me your student and this an opportunity to improve *my* skills,' Hayle said with a grin.

Hearing murmurs in the crowd that were pushing for the match, Barrington sighed. Hayle obviously wasn't going to back down, especially if he felt he had the backing of his friends. And while he needed a lesson, Barrington knew it was in humility rather than sword play. 'Very well.' He walked back into the room and donned his mask. 'Prepare to engage.'

An excited murmur rolled through the crowd. Men who were halfway to the door quickly turned around and ran back into the room, aware that a far more entertaining show was about to get underway. Triumph and anticipation suffused Hayle's face as he stripped off his jacket and donned a mask.

In silence the two men made their way to the centre of the floor. After offering the traditional salute, they both took their opening stance.

It didn't take long for Barrington to assess his opponent's level of skill. Hayle was a showy fencer and quick on his feet, but there was no strategy to his play; at times, his technique was downright sloppy. Barrington easily scored five hits in a matter of minutes—and watched his opponent's face grow redder with each one.

'I think that's enough for one morning,' he said, starting to remove his mask.

'Stand your ground, sir!' Hayle shouted. *'I* will say when this is finished.' He took up his stance again. *'En guarde!'*

Barrington saw the anger in the other man's eyes and knew this could only end badly. He had no wish to humiliate Hayle in front of a room full of his friends and acquaintances, but neither was he about to throw the game in order to appease his vanity. 'Very well. We shall play one more bout and then call a halt. Does that meet with your approval?'

Hayle gave a terse nod and resumed his position.

The match recommenced. Barrington tried not to make the other man look bad, but the more desperate Hayle became, the more careless his play. He was caught flat footed several times and as the bout went on his moves became more and more erratic. After receiving his fourth hit, he shouted, 'Damn you, Parker!', then, abandoning sportsmanlike conduct altogether, he lunged, aiming the point of his sword directly at Barrington's throat.

Barrington heard the gasp from the crowd, but was already out of range. He stepped lithely to one side and quickly raised his own foil, deflecting the blow. Hayle spun around and was about to charge again when a voice rang out, 'Enough, Edward! Put down your sword! This engagement is at an end!'

The command vibrated with anger, but Hayle was oblivious, his attention riveted on his adversary. Barrington held his position, too, unwilling to trust his opponent. He risked a quick glance across the room and saw the Earl of Cambermere standing by the edge of the crowd. His face was red and he was shaking with barely suppressed fury. 'Did you not hear me, sir?' he called again. 'I said put down your sword!'

'I will not, sir!' His son's face was equally flushed. 'How dare you ask me to!'

'How dare *I*?' his father exploded, marching on to the floor. 'You impugn our family's honour by behaving in such a way and then have the audacity to question me? No, sir, I *will* not have it! If you cannot control your temper, find another sport in which to indulge.' He ripped the foil from his son's hand and threw it on the floor. 'This is a gentleman's game. You will apologise to Sir Barrington at once or I'll know the reason why!'

Barrington slowly lowered his sword, but remained in a ready position, prepared to fight if Hayle picked up his sword and re-engaged him. He had no idea what the man was going to do, but it was evident to everyone in the place that Hayle was beyond furious. In that moment, Barrington wasn't sure the man wouldn't turn on his own father and run him through.

Thankfully, the moment passed. As if realising he couldn't win and that his reputation would only suffer further by prolonging the encounter, Hayle took a step back, then bent to pick up his sword. 'I will not apologise to you this day or any other, Sir Barrington,' he said coldly. 'But I do regret

that we were unable to finish our match. I look forward to
the opportunity of doing so in the future.' Then, without so
much as a second glance at his father, he snatched up his
jacket and left.

Barely had the door closed before the level of conversation swelled to fill the silence. Barrington heard snippets of
conversations, some questioning, many derogatory. Overall,
none were particularly complimentary of Hayle's behaviour
on the floor. Fencing was, after all, a gentleman's sport and
what the audience had just witnessed was a display of anything but.

It was a few minutes before the earl was calm enough to
speak. When he did, Barrington could see it was with considerable effort. 'Sir Barrington, pray accept my apologies
on behalf of my son. His behaviour was unforgivable and I
am truly sorry.'

'Apology accepted, but I suggest you do not take this
too much to heart, Cambermere,' Barrington said. 'It is not
uncommon for a young man to wish to win, especially in
front of his peers.'

'If a man cannot win fairly or lose graciously, he should
not play the game,' Cambermere snapped. 'I'm sorry you
had to see that side of Edward's nature. He's always been a
competitive lad, but of late, he has become even more so. I
suspect it has much to do with Peregrine's arrival.' The earl
sighed. 'They have not become the friends I'd hoped.'

'Was it realistic to believe they would?'

The earl glanced up, his sharp eyes meeting Barrington's.
But Barrington's didn't waver, and, not surprisingly, the earl
was the first to look away. 'Perhaps not. But they had to meet
at some time.'

'Did they? I would have thought it possible for their paths
never to have crossed. But it's a moot point now. You made

the decision to invite Rand to London and must now deal with the consequences,' Barrington said.

'I know. But I was asked if I would have him,' the earl said quietly. 'And I wanted him to come.'

Used to gleaning meanings from things that were left unsaid, Barrington inclined his head. 'Then it really is none of anyone else's business.'

'Yet people choose to make it so,' Cambermere said fiercely.

Barrington's smile was tight. 'People like to pass judgement on matters that do not concern them. Some do it with the best of intentions, others do it without any care for the consequences at all. But as we said, the matter is private and one that concerns you and your family alone.'

Even has he said it, however, Barrington realised he had been given another glimpse into the complicated workings of Lord Cambermere's family, and it was evident from the morning's events that all was far from harmonious. There were simmering resentments, unsettled grievances, and barely restrained tempers. Instead of warming to the fact that his father had brought his godson to London, Hayle intended to do whatever he could to make Rand feel unwelcome—even to the point of humiliating him in front of his peers.

That much had become patently clear. As Barrington left the club and climbed into his carriage for the drive home, he *knew* who had asked the Marquess of Yew to make an example of Peregrine Rand. And, sadly, he also knew the reason why.

A full week passed during which Anna neither saw nor heard from Barrington. She told herself she didn't care, but as she lay awake in the dark hours of the night, she knew she was lying to herself. She *did* care. And it troubled her deeply that they had parted on such bad terms.

Try as she might, she couldn't forget the feeling of Barrington's arms closing warm and strong around her. She kept remembering the tenderness of his mouth as it moved with deliberate slowness over hers, sending shivers of delight up and down her spine.

It still made her quiver when she thought about it.

Still, longing for something you couldn't have was a complete waste of one's time, and there wasn't a doubt in Anna's mind that she would never have a life with Barrington. He'd made it perfectly clear that he had no intention of getting married, and it certainly wasn't her place to get him to change his mind. *She* was the foolish one if she thought there was any merit in that.

'Ah, Anna, there you are,' her father said, walking into the drawing room. 'Not going out this evening?'

'I'm not, but it would seem you are,' she said, rousing herself. 'Is that a new coat?'

To her amusement, her father's cheeks took on a ruddy hue. 'I decided it was time to spruce up my wardrobe. Doesn't do for a gentleman to let himself go and I haven't paid much attention to things like that since your mother died.' His voice softened. 'I had no reason to.'

'And have you a reason now?'

He glanced at her, suddenly looking boyish. 'Would it disturb you if I said I had?'

'Not at all. I like Julia very much.' Anna hesitated. 'I take it we are referring to Julia?'

'Of course!'

'Good. Then if she makes you happy, why should I object?'

'Oh, I don't know,' the earl grumbled. 'Some people say I'm past such things. That I'm too old for her. I am nearly twenty years her senior, after all.'

'If the lady does not mind, why should you? You don't

look your age, and she *is* past thirty, Papa. Old enough to make her own decisions.'

Her father glanced down at the floor. 'Your brother is not pleased by the association.'

Anna sighed. 'My brother is not pleased with anything at the moment so I shouldn't worry about it. Do what I do. Ignore him.'

'Can you not try to get along, Anna? He is your brother, after all.'

'Yes, he is, but I cannot bring myself to like the way he treats people; his attitude towards Peregrine is abysmal. He demonstrates a resentment that is neither warranted nor deserved. I've tried to tell him as much, but he refuses to listen.'

Her father looked as though he wanted to say something, but then he sighed, and shook his head. 'I blame myself for the distance between the two of you. Perhaps had I paid more attention to Edward when he was younger—'

'The fault is not yours, Papa,' Anna interrupted firmly. 'Edward has been given every opportunity to show himself the better man. He has wealth and position—there is absolutely no reason for him to be so harsh and judgemental towards others.'

'Perhaps he will change when he meets the right woman. It is my sincere wish that you both find suitable marriage partners and leave this house to start your own lives.' Her father regarded her hopefully. 'Is there no one for whom you feel even the slightest affection, my dear?'

Sadly, there was. But while Anna would have liked to give her father the reassurance he so desperately craved, there was no point in raising his hopes. Or hers. 'I fear not. But am I such a trouble to you that you would try to make me leave?'

'Far from it. You're a good girl, Anna. And though I don't

say it often, I am very proud of you. A week doesn't go by that some grateful mother doesn't tell me how helpful you've been in smoothing the troubled waters between her and her daughter. Most of them credit you with having saved their sanity!'

Surprised by the admission, Anna said, 'I can assure you they were exaggerating. None of the situations was that dire. It is simply easier for a stranger to see what needs to be done than someone who is intimately involved.'

'Nevertheless, they all told me how helpful you were and that I should be very proud to have such an admirable young woman for a daughter. And I told them all they were right.'

Her father was not normally an affectionate man, so when he suddenly bent down and pressed his lips to her forehead, Anna was deeply moved. 'Oh, Papa.' She got up and hugged him, aware that it had been a long time since she'd done so. If this was Julia's doing, she could only hope that the romance continued.

'Yes, well, I'd best be off,' the earl said gruffly. He stepped back and smoothed his jacket. 'Jul—that is, the baroness and I are having dinner together and then going on to the theatre.'

'Sounds lovely. Have a good time.'

'Yes, I expect we will.'

Anna smiled as she watched him go. It was strange to suddenly find herself in the role of the parent. She was well aware that she was the one who should have been going out for the evening and her father the one wishing her well. But there was only one man with whom Anna wished to spend time and the chances of that happening were getting slimmer all the time.

Troubled as he was by his feelings for Anna, Barrington knew he couldn't afford to ignore his other commissions. In particular, the locating of Miss Elizabeth Paisley. His belief that he'd found her at Baroness von Brohm's house had turned out to be false. He had gone back a few days later to question her, but the moment she'd walked into the drawing room, he'd known he was mistaken. The maid's name was Justine Smith, and though she was the right age, the right height, and had the right colour hair, her eyes were all wrong. Hers had actually been a pale misty blue where the Colonel had specifically told him that Elizabeth Paisley's were a deep, clear green. Barrington thought that in the candlelit room the night of the baroness's dinner party, he must have been mistaken when he'd thought the maid's eyes were green.

And so, at eleven o'clock that morning, Barrington resumed his investigation by visiting the premises of one Madame Delors, fashionable modiste. Dressmakers were privy to a great deal of gossip about wives and mistresses, and if someone had taken over the protection of Miss Elizabeth Paisley, there was a good chance Madame Delors would know about it.

Barrington stopped inside the door and glanced around the compact little shop. It was years since he'd had reason to frequent such an establishment, but it was evident they hadn't changed. Bolts of richly coloured fabric of every type and shade filled the shelves; dress patterns were tacked to the walls; and in the centre of the room stood a raised podium surrounded on three sides by mirrors.

'*Bonjour, monsieur,*' called a charmingly accented French voice. '*Puis-je vous aidez?*'

The owner of the establishment was small and compact, with dark inquisitive eyes and a head of flaming red hair that surely owed more to artifice than it did to nature. Still, it suited her well and Barrington doffed his hat. '*Bonjour, madame.* My name is Sir Barrington Parker. I would like to ask you a few questions, if you have a moment to spare.'

The woman's eyes narrowed, his comment obviously having put her on guard. 'What kind of questions, *monsieur*?'

'About a woman.' He purposely didn't use the term lady. 'One I believe you dressed in the not-too-distant past.'

'I dress many women, *monsieur*. You will 'ave to give me 'er name.'

'Miss Elizabeth Paisley. Petite, lovely, with dark brown hair and uncommonly pretty green eyes.'

The modiste evidenced neither surprise nor recognition. 'I do not think I know the lady.'

'Really? I was told you'd made clothes for her. Perhaps you dealt with the gentleman who bought them. A Colonel Tanner?'

Madame Delors obviously knew a thing or two about what one did and didn't say to gentlemen asking questions about other gentlemen's ladies. 'I 'ave many gentlemen coming to buy clothes for their ladies, *monsieur*. But they do not always give me the names of the ladies they are buying for.'

'No, I suppose not. And perhaps I should explain my interest in her.' Barrington walked farther into the store, cataloguing a thousand details in a single glance. 'Miss Paisley has recently come under my protection and it is my desire that she wear…a particular type of clothing when we are together. But because her taste and mine do not coincide, I am not willing to allow her to come in and order her own garments. Hence my reason for coming to see you today.'

'Ah, *je comprends*,' Madame Delors said. 'You would like me to make 'er a new wardrobe suitable only for you.'

'Precisely. Naturally, money is not a concern.'

'*D'accord*. What type of clothes do you wish to see 'er in, *monsieur*?'

'Intimate evening gowns, white and silver only, with simple but elegant lines. Semi-transparent. No heavy swatches of lace. No artificial birds or flowers. Nothing that will detract from the tantalising lines of her body.'

Madame Delors slowly began to smile. 'So the lady will not be wearing these gowns in public?'

'Definitely not,' Barrington said, resting both hands on the carved head of his ebony cane. 'They are for my eyes only. But I cannot tell you what size to make her garments because I do not have her measurements.'

Madame Delors smiled and nodded. 'I think I know the lady you speak of, *monsieur*.'

'Excellent. I trust it hasn't been too long since you last saw her? Women's figures do tend to change,' Barrington said, adding with a wink, 'a little more weight this week, a little less the following.'

Madame Delors's smile was reassuring. 'I saw 'er not all that long ago and 'er figure 'as not changed.'

'Good. Did she seem happy?'

The modiste gave a snort. 'The ladies come to me for clothes, *monsieur*. It is up to you gentlemen to make them 'appy!'

Barrington carefully hid a smile. Oh, yes, Madame Delors was definitely a shrewd business woman. He pulled three coins from his pocket. 'Do you happen to remember, on the occasion of her last visit,' he said, dropping one into her palm, 'if she collected the clothes herself or if you sent them somewhere else?'

The modiste's eyes locked on the shimmer of gold in her hand. 'I'm not sure...'

Barrington dropped another coin. 'Perhaps now?'

'The lady picked up the clothes,' the modiste said slowly, 'but I sent the bill to the gentleman.'

'To Colonel Tanner?'

When the modiste shook her head, Barrington dropped

the last of the coins into her palm. 'Then to whom did you send the bill?'

The modiste smiled and pocketed all three. 'Viscount Hayle.'

Anna was on her way to visit Julia when she remembered that Madame Delors had sent her a note asking her if she might be able to come in for a fitting. Anna had ordered two new morning dresses and a ball gown the previous week; although most fashionable modistes made house calls to their better clients, Madame Delors preferred to have her ladies come to her, saying it was easier to work in her showroom where she had everything necessary for making the required alternations.

Anna didn't mind. It was an excuse to get out of the house and it wasn't that much out of her way. But as she walked up to the front of the shop and went to open the door, it was suddenly opened from within and by none other than the man who had been uppermost in her mind for the last several days. 'Sir Barrington!'

'Good morning, Lady Annabelle. Lovely morning, isn't it?' He spoke without concern, as though it was the most natural thing in the world for her to find him coming out of a dressmaker's shop.

'Indeed. I feared it might come on to rain, but the skies have cleared up nicely.' Anna said, striving to match the casualness of his tone. There was only one reason a single gentleman frequented a shop like this, and it wasn't to keep abreast of the latest fashions. 'I've not seen much of you about town of late.'

'I have been otherwise occupied,' he said, drawing her aside as a mother and her three giggling daughters made to enter the shop. 'This is a very busy place.'

'Madame Delors is London's darling when it comes to

fashion,' Anna said. 'She boasts an illustrious clientele, most recently the Duchess of Briscombe.'

Barrington smiled. Given that Madame Delors also dressed the Duke of Briscombe's latest mistress, he knew better than to place too high a value on her level of exclusivity. 'Speaking of not being visible around town, how is Mr Rand going on?'

Anna sighed. 'Not at all well. He misses Lady Yew dreadfully; though I have told him she is not worthy of the heartache, I cannot dissuade him from his feelings.'

'Of course not. Love isn't logical,' Barrington said. 'It finds warmth in the most inhospitable of environments and draws comfort from the most uncomfortable of people. It demands neither explanation nor excuse. It is content merely to be.'

Anna stared at him in surprise. Such sentiments from a man like this? 'How is it you know so much about love, Sir Barrington, when, by your own admission, you have chosen to banish it from your life?'

'Who better than a man who has chosen to live without love when it comes to knowing how easily it takes root?' His grey eyes impaled her. 'I am not immune to the emotion, Lady Annabelle. I simply cannot give it a home. As I tried to explain to you the other night and failed so miserably.'

It was an olive branch, and Anna recognised it as such. But she knew she had to be cautious. The wounds from their last encounter were not yet healed. 'You didn't fail. It was simply not something I wished to hear. I do not believe any man or woman is truly happier spending their life alone.'

'It is not the natural order,' he agreed. 'God intended that man and woman should live together. It was the reason He gave them a home in Eden.'

'Until the serpent tempted Eve and they were cast out.'

Barrington smiled. 'As I recall, it was Adam's willingness

to eat the forbidden fruit that incurred God's wrath. Temptation has always been there. It is simply a man's ability to resist that sets him apart from others.'

'A philosopher,' Anna mused. 'I would not have thought it of you.'

'When you have learned as much about your fellow man as I have, you tend to become either jaded or philosophical. I choose the latter.'

Of course he would, Anna reflected, because he was that type of man. 'Well, I mustn't keep you here.' She gave him a falsely bright smile, aware that she was still no wiser as to why he was coming out of a busy modiste's shop now than she had been a few minutes earlier. 'I'm sure you have business elsewhere.'

'I do, my lady,' he murmured. 'But none, I can assure you, as pleasurable as this.'

As soon as she finished her business with Madame Delors, Anna headed for Julia's house and was pleasantly surprised to find Lady Lydia already there. She and Julia were partaking of tea and cakes and no doubt sharing the latest *on-dits* that were enlivening the drawing rooms of society. Her pleasure soon evaporated, however, when she discovered that it was not society's goings on that were keeping her two friends so occupied, but an unexpected crime.

'Your sapphire-and-diamond necklace has been *stolen*?' Anna said when Lydia informed her of it. 'But how? And when?'

'I have no idea how *or* when,' Julia admitted forlornly. 'I was dressing for the Buckerfields' reception last night and asked Smith to bring my jewellery case. When she did, I unlocked it to find the necklace gone.'

'But surely it has not been stolen,' Anna said. 'Perhaps just misplaced?'

Julia shook her head. 'I am very careful with my jewellery, Anna. I always take it off and put it immediately into the case. Then I lock it and put it away.'

'Is it possible someone took the key?'

'I keep the key on a ribbon around my neck. I only take it off to bathe and, sometimes, when I go to bed.'

'Have you questioned the servants about the matter?' Lydia asked. 'Your maid, for example. She would be in a perfect position to steal it.'

'I have spoken to all of them and to a person they denied knowing anything about it,' Julia said. 'And given how horrified they looked at the idea of something of mine being stolen, I can't imagine any of them actually *doing* it.'

'So what are you going to do?' Anna asked.

'I suppose I shall have to report it, but I don't like what I am going to have to tell whoever comes to take down the details.'

Lydia frowned. 'Why not?'

'Because the only people who knew about that necklace were the ones who came to my dinner party. I haven't worn it on any other occasion.' Julia bit her lip. 'What if one of my guests took it?'

'I don't believe that for a moment,' Anna said flatly. 'The people you invited were friends. They would never steal from you.'

'And if a thief did break into your house,' Lydia said, 'he would naturally go for the most valuable piece of jewellery he could find, don't you think?'

'So you believe this the work of a random criminal?' Julia asked doubtfully.

'I think it must have been,' Anna said. 'For one thing, what would any of your friends, or even other members of society, gain by taking the necklace? They would never be able to wear it in public.'

'But they could break it up and sell the stones individually,' Julia said. 'They might even be able to have some of the larger diamonds cut into smaller pieces.'

Anna didn't know what to say. It seemed impossible to imagine a thief breaking into Julia's house and stealing her favourite piece of jewellery, but it was even more incredible to think that someone she knew might have done it. 'I honestly don't know what to say, Julia,' she said at length. 'Other than that I am so very sorry this has happened.'

'Your father did warn me about keeping my jewels in a safe,' Julia said. 'But I truly did not think it would be necessary.'

'Have you hired any new servants?' Lydia asked. 'Or had people in the house who wouldn't normally be here. Chimney sweeps, for example, or trades people coming and going?'

'There have certainly been trades people in and out,' Julia admitted. 'The entire house is being redecorated and there has been a steady stream of paper hangers and plasterers coming through on a daily basis. But I instructed my maid to make sure they were never alone in my room and I have no reason to believe my orders were not followed. No, I shall have to hire a private investigator and ask him to look into it.'

'I say,' Lydia said, glancing at Anna. 'Why don't you get in touch with Sir Barrington Parker?'

'Sir Barrington?' Julia frowned. 'What would he know about matters like this?'

'You'd be surprised,' Anna murmured. 'However, he is very good at finding things out and I agree with Lydia that he is probably the best person to contact about this. He is nothing if not discreet.'

'Well, if you think that highly of him, I will certainly speak to him,' Julia said. 'I would very much like to have my necklace back. It has sentimental value far beyond any monetary value I could ever put upon it.'

'I don't think you will be disappointed with Sir Barrington's methods,' Lydia said, adding with a sly look at her friend, 'he has made quite an impression on Anna.'

'Lydia!'

But Julia was beaming. 'Has he really? How wonderful! I thought I detected something between the two of you at my dinner party, but when things became rather chilly later in the evening, I didn't want to appear rude by asking personal questions.'

'There is nothing between myself and Sir Barrington Parker,' Anna said quickly. 'I will not deny that he is…an attractive and engaging man—'

'Exceptionally so,' Lydia added.

'But we do not see eye to eye on several important matters and I doubt we will do so in the future,' Anna concluded. She reached for an iced *petit four*, hoping to distract the attention of the other two. 'However, I do stand by my assertion that he can be of help in this situation.'

Julia got up and crossed to the bell pull. 'Well, I am grateful for the recommendation, Anna, though I am sorry to hear there is nothing of a more romantic nature going on between the two of you. Sir Barrington really is such a handsome man. And that *voice*! I could listen to him all night. However, it is the heart that dictates these matters and, if you are not in love with him, there is nothing more to say. Ah, there you are, Smith. We'd like some fresh tea, please. This has gone cold.'

'Yes, ma'am.' The maid bobbed a curtsy, but something in the way she bent to pick up the tray drew Anna's attention. On her previous visits, the maid had served tea with both skill and efficiency. This time, however, she seemed slightly ill at ease. She also seemed thinner than she had on those earlier occasions, her black gown hanging loose around her shoulders. Anna thought it might have been a different girl, but upon closer inspection, she realised she was mistaken. The girl had the same heart-shaped face and the same dark brown hair pulled back in a tight chignon.

Perhaps she had things on her mind, Anna reflected as she reached for a macaroon. Servants had problems just like their employers. Maybe she'd recently fallen out with her gentleman friend, or a member of her family wasn't well. There were any number of reasons she might be looking poorly.

Still, it was none of her business, and as they waited for fresh tea to arrive, the conversation veered back to more congenial topics. Anna was simply thankful they had moved away from the subject of Sir Barrington Parker. His name was coming up far too often in conversation for her liking, and she wasn't at all happy at hearing that Julia thought there was something going on between them. She'd even been tempted to correct Julia's phrasing of her recommendation of Barrington, by saying it wasn't Sir Barrington of whom she thought so highly, but, rather, his skills as an investigator.

Unfortunately, that wasn't true either and when it came right down to it, Anna preferred not to lie to Julia. But she had to stand firm when it came to her feelings for him. She had to accept his reasons for keeping her at arm's length and move on. She had every intention of marrying one day; while she hoped it would be for love, she was intelligent enough to know that the luxury of feelings did not always accompany a proposal of marriage.

As to whether or not Sir Barrington Parker ever married, that was really no concern of hers.

Chapter Eight

Barrington received a visit from Baroness von Brohm at half past ten the following morning. She was shown into the gold salon, whereupon she briefly told him about the theft of her necklace and of her sincere hopes for its recovery. He then asked a series of pointed questions, which she answered to the best of her ability. An hour later, he stood by the window and reviewed everything she had told him. He didn't have a lot to go on, but he had already concluded that there were four possible answers to the question of who might have stolen her necklace.

The first was that the jewel thief who had been plaguing London for the past three months had returned and struck again. He would have had a relatively easy time getting into the baroness's house. During his questioning, Barrington discovered that she often slept with her window open and that her bedroom was located at the rear of the house on the second floor, close to a small clump of trees. It was possible that someone had climbed a tree to the second floor, gained access through the open window and, after taking the baroness's necklace, had managed to escape the same way.

The stumbling block was that in order to get into the baroness's jewellery box, the thief would have had to get at the key the baroness kept on a ribbon around her throat. Barrington doubted any thief would have been able to remove the ribbon, steal the necklace, and make his escape, all without disturbing the baroness's slumber.

The second option was that a servant had taken it. This was certainly the more logical answer. The baroness employed a butler, a housekeeper, three maids, and a parlour maid, all of whom would have had access to her room at times when she was not present. But again, they would have needed the key to open the locked box, and, according to the baroness, the box showed no signs of a forced entry. It had been neatly opened and closed.

The third possibility was that a visitor to the house had taken the necklace. Barrington thought this the least likely of the four, but experience had taught him that it was often the *least* likely suspect who actually committed the crime. In this case, it meant that one of the many people who had paid calls on the baroness had gone up to her room and taken the necklace. But again, there was the matter of the key.

Which left the fourth and most likely possibility—that the baroness had simply misplaced the necklace. That kind of thing happened all the time. It explained why the jewellery case hadn't been tampered with and why the key hadn't gone missing. It also cleared any visitors to the house of the theft.

Unfortunately, the baroness had stated most emphatically that she had *not* misplaced the necklace and that she was in the habit of locking her jewellery away immediately after taking it off. The practice had been instilled in her by her late husband.

So where did that leave him? What was he missing with regard to the stolen necklace?

'Excuse me, Sir Barrington,' Sam said from the doorway. 'Lord Richard Crew is here.'

'Thank you, Sam. Be so good as to show him in.'

Barrington was relieved to have caught Crew at home. He'd sent a note to him immediately following the baroness's departure, but given his friend's sexual proclivities, one never knew where he was or what state he might be in. A fact confirmed when Crew walked into the room, looking slightly dishevelled and none too bright-eyed.

'You'd better have a damned good excuse for this, Parker,' he said testily. 'I was enjoying a rather delicious breakfast in bed when your note arrived.'

'Forgive me,' Barrington said, grinning, 'but I'm sure the lady won't mind drinking champagne alone.'

'Probably not, but I'm not sure I *want* her drinking it alone. I was rather enjoying what she was doing *before* your letter arrived, demanding that I present myself at your door.'

'It was not a demand. And I did say at *your* convenience.'

'Hah!' Crew said, collapsing into a chair. 'We both know that at *my* convenience really means at *yours*. So what was so urgent that it couldn't wait until later in the day?'

'Two things. I need you to make some discreet inquiries on behalf of a lady.'

'A lady?' He brightened. 'Always ready to be of service. Do I know her?'

'Baroness Julia von Brohm.'

'Ah, the merry widow. Yes, we were introduced at some gathering, though the name of my host and hostess escapes me at the moment. What has happened to the poor lady that she requires your services?'

'A rather magnificent sapphire-and-diamond necklace was stolen from her home a few days ago. I want you to keep your ear to the ground for any information that might come to light about it.'

'Do you think it's our jewel thief again?' Crew asked.

'It's possible, but I need to check out all avenues. I'll be questioning the baroness's staff over the next few days, but if someone's stolen the necklace with a view to selling it, you might catch wind of it before I do.'

'Wouldn't be the first time,' Crew agreed, putting his hands behind his head. 'I'll drop in at a few of the clubs and see if anyone's suddenly turned up flush.'

'You might want to check the hells as well. A necklace like that would go a long way towards settling a man's debts,' Barrington suggested.

'No doubt. What's the second request?'

Barrington opened the top drawer of the desk and took out an envelope. 'I need you to do some digging into an old family tree. The specifics are in the letter. Read it at your leisure—'

'But report back to you as soon as possible,' Crew said in a dry voice.

'Expedience is always the order of the day. By the by, how did your meeting go with the lovely Rebecca?' Barrington enquired as his friend got up to leave. 'Has she agreed to marry you yet?'

'No, though I expect an acceptance very soon. As I was leaving, Lady Yew brushed her hand against a rather sensitive part of my anatomy—and I'm quite sure it wasn't by accident.'

Barrington burst out laughing. 'I *beg* your pardon?'

'You needn't sound so shocked; I am more or less the right age; given that she is looking for a replacement for Peregrine Rand, she obviously thought to see if I was interested.'

'Even though you have been paying court to her daughter?'

'Perhaps she wants to bed me before her daughter gets the chance.' Crew's eyes flashed wickedly. 'Make sure I have all the necessary equipment.'

'As if your reputation would leave anyone in doubt,' Barrington said cynically. 'How did Lady Rebecca take to her mother's interest in you?'

Crew slowly began to smile. 'If I don't miss my guess, the next time I call, the dear girl will be pushing the butler aside in her haste to throw open the front door and give me her answer—which I have every expectation of being yes. After all, if she doesn't, she knows damn well whose bedroom I *could* be spending my nights in!'

Anna trotted Ophelia through Hyde Park, alert for the gentleman to whom she had sent a hastily scrawled note, asking that he meet her. It had been a bold gesture, and secretly she feared Barrington might soon tire of these imperious messages. But she had to know if Julia had been to see him and, if so, what he thought the chances of recovering the stolen necklace were. While she might not approve of or agree with his marital aspirations or lack thereof, Anna did believe that if anyone could find the missing necklace it was he.

Thankfully, he appeared within moments, sitting tall and easy in the saddle, his coat as black as that of the spirited thoroughbred he so easily controlled. His hands were strong and steady on the reins; in spite of her best intentions, Anna felt a quiver of anticipation at the thought of being close to him again. She'd told herself over and over that there was no hope of anything developing between them, but that didn't take away from the strength of her attraction for him. The way he looked at her, without the lewdness or speculation she saw so often in other men's eyes, made her feel as though she mattered, both as a woman and as a person. And the memory of the one kiss they had shared still caused her heart to quicken…

She really had to get over this. It was bad enough that thoughts of him kept filling her mind, but this silly racing of her pulse every time she saw him was ridiculous! It was imperative that she appear as cool as he was. As impervious to his charm as he so obviously was to hers.

He raised his hand and then put his horse to a brisk trot in her direction. Anna used the time to bring her breathing under control.

'Lady Annabelle,' he greeted her, drawing to a halt.

'Good afternoon, Sir Barrington. Thank you for agreeing to meet with me.'

'To quote your father, the opportunity to spend time with a beautiful woman should never be missed.'

And now she was blushing again. *So much for being impervious.* 'Forgive me for being so inquisitive, but I was anxious to know if Julia had been to see you?'

'As a matter of fact, we spent time together this morning.'

'And? Do you think you will be able to help her?'

'I will do what I can, of course, but there are many questions that need to be asked and several possible leads to follow. It will take time.'

'But there may not *be* that much time!' Anna cried. 'Given the size of the stones, Julia said the thief might decide to take the necklace apart, or to have the gems cut smaller.'

'That possibility does exist,' Barrington acknowledged. 'The jewels are too large to sell as they are, unless whoever took the necklace intends to sell it outside London. If they have contacts on the Continent, it could easily be sold intact in Paris or Brussels.'

Anna bit her lip. 'Julia will be heartbroken. That necklace means the world to her.'

'I know and am making inquiries. But whoever took the necklace isn't going to make it easy for us to find him.'

Anna ran her gloved hand over the smoothness of the mare's neck. 'Nevertheless, I'm glad you're involved. I know you'll find who did this and bring him or her to justice.'

He raised an eyebrow. 'Her?'

'Why not? Desperation knows no gender. A woman who needs money to feed her family is just as likely to steal as a man.'

'But it is more often a man who will take that kind of risk. A woman on her own is more likely to avail herself of…other avenues.'

'Such as prostitution?' she said quietly.

He met her regard evenly. 'Yes. Or, if she is attractive enough, becoming the mistress of a wealthy man. However, I would caution you not to let your thoughts dwell on this, Lady Annabelle. It will not result in the culprit being brought to justice any faster and will only serve to cause you needless worry. I will advise you of whatever results I am able to find as soon as I have them.'

'Thank you.' Anna wished she could think of something else to say, but she didn't know how or where to start. She usually found conversation so easy, but with him it was always a challenge. 'Well, I suppose I had best be—'

'Lady Annabelle!'

Hearing the shrill feminine hail, Anna turned to see a carriage approaching and smiled when she recognised the mother and daughter sitting within. 'Mrs Banks, Miss Banks, good afternoon,' she said.

'Lady Annabelle, I thought it was you and I simply had to come and tell you the news,' Mercy Banks said, jumping up as the carriage drew to a halt.

'Mercy, for goodness' sake, sit down!' her mother admonished. 'A lady does not bounce up and down like a hoyden!

You must forgive my daughter, Lady Annabelle. She has become quite uncontrollable of late.'

'Because I am so happy, Mama,' Miss Banks said, and though she promptly sat down, her joy could not be contained. 'I am to be married, Lady Annabelle, and it is all thanks to *you*!'

Aware of Barrington's eyes on her, Anna laughed and said, 'On the contrary, I think you played a considerable part in the production. I take it your intended is Lieutenant Blokker?'

'Of course.' Mercy's face assumed that dreamy aspect Anna had come to associate with young men and women in love. 'There could never be anyone else. He proposed to me at home in the garden yesterday and naturally I said yes.'

'Then I am very happy for you. When is the wedding to be?'

'The date has not yet been set,' Mrs Banks said proudly. 'We have been invited to dine with the young man's parents in Hanover Square to go over the details.'

'Hanover Square,' Barrington murmured so that only Anna could hear. 'Very nice.'

Anna only just refrained from rolling her eyes. 'Mrs Banks, Miss Banks, may I introduce Sir Barrington Parker.'

The gentleman gallantly doffed his beaver. 'Ladies.'

'Sir Barrington,' Mrs Banks said graciously. 'I believe I saw you in conversation with Lady Annabelle at Lady Montby's reception.'

'You did, though it was only in passing since we had not been formally introduced at that time,' Sir Barrington said smoothly. 'Unlike your daughter, I was not fortunate enough to have someone make the introduction for me.'

'Happily, it seems to have been made in the interim. And we will, of course, be sending Lady Annabelle an invitation. We are happy to see her bring an escort,' Mrs Banks said. 'I expect the affair to be quite grand.'

This time, Anna knew better than to look at the man beside her. 'Thank you, Mrs Banks. That would be very nice.'

'Well, we must be off. There is so much to do between now and the wedding, whenever it turns out to be. Good afternoon, Lady Annabelle, Sir Barrington.'

'Goodbye, dear Lady Annabelle!' Mercy called as the carriage pulled away. 'And thank you again!'

In the silence that followed, Anna heard Barrington chuckle—and felt her cheeks burn. 'I would have preferred that you not be a witness to that.'

'Why not? I found it highly diverting,' the odious man said. 'And you should be proud. You managed to get Miss Mercy Banks engaged, though in truth I'm not sure who is the more pleased: the mother or the daughter.'

'I venture to say they are equally delighted for entirely different reasons.'

'True. Hanover Square does have a very nice ring,' Barrington murmured. 'But I've no doubt it *will* be a splendid affair.' He turned to her and smiled. 'The wedding breakfast alone will be reason enough to attend.'

'Good. Since you *will* be attending, at least you can be assured of a good meal.'

'I beg your pardon?'

'Well, you didn't think I was going to this on my own, did you?' Anna enquired innocently. 'You are as much to blame for their engagement as I, so it seems only fair that you should accompany me to the celebration.'

It was an audacious statement and Anna held her breath as she waited for him to answer. What had got into her? A lady *never* asked a gentleman—it simply wasn't done. Fortunately, Barrington didn't seem to mind. Ever so slowly, he began to smile. 'It would be my honour to escort you, Lady Annabelle. Assuming, of course, that I am not engaged in resolving the convoluted lives of others on that particular day.'

Suppressing a ridiculous desire to laugh, Anna gathered the reins in her hands and lightly flicked her crop against the mare's withers. 'I trust, Sir Barrington, that on this most auspicious occasion, the convoluted lives of others will just have to go on without you.'

As well as involving Lord Richard Crew in the investigation of the baroness's necklace, Barrington made his own enquiries in a part of town the gentry seldom frequented. He wore clothes specifically chosen for the occasion: a hacking jacket a few years out of date, an old pair of topboots, scuffed and in need of a polish, and a beaver, too wide at the brim and looking decidedly worn. The effect was the appearance of a man down on his luck. One who was right at home with the patrons of the Rose and Thistle. Only the elegance of the ebony cane hinted at the presence of wealth, but Barrington wasn't about to venture into London's seedier neighbourhoods without it. The specially constructed walking stick had saved his life on more than one occasion.

He strolled into the inn at a few minutes past midnight and caught the eye of the landlord standing behind the bar. Jack Drummond nodded, drew two shots of whisky and, after a brief whisper in the barmaid's ear, led the way into a quiet back room. Barrington kept a watchful eye on the bar's patrons, but no one paid any attention to them as they passed. When they reached the small room at the end of the hall, Jack closed and locked the door behind them.

'Been a while, Sir Barrington,' the burly man said. He set the glasses down on a table and pulled up a couple of chairs. 'Everything all right with you?'

'Can't complain, Jack, can't complain.' Barrington leaned his cane against the back of the chair and sat down. 'You?'

'Never been better. Had a baby since last I saw yer and a

right little beauty she is. Don't know how with an ugly mug like me for a father.'

Barrington grinned. 'I suspect Molly had a lot to do with it. Is she well?'

'Aye, sir, she's fit as a fiddle.' Jack's face lit up like a child's on Christmas morning. 'Still happy to put up with me and that's saying something. Best day's work I ever did marrying that woman and it was only thanks to you I got the chance.'

Barrington shook his head. 'If you hadn't knocked the knife out of that Irishman's hand, I wouldn't be sitting here tonight.'

'And if *you* hadn't come running round that corner, shouting to wake the dead, that knife would have been buried in my chest clear up to the hilt.' Jack glanced at the ebony cane and smiled. 'Still carrying it, I see.'

'Never go out without it.' Barrington smiled. 'Some things are best not left to chance.'

'Can't argue with that. But you didn't come all the way down here to reminisce about the old days. What can I do for you?'

'I need you to keep an eye out,' Barrington said without preamble. 'A rather spectacular necklace was recently stolen from a lady's house and it's possible that over the next while, whispers about the necklace, or the necklace itself, may make its way into your inn. I want to know who's doing the talking and what they're saying.'

'I can do that,' Jack said with a nod. 'What kind of jewels are we talking about?'

'Sapphires and diamonds. Fairly large stones, so the thief may try to sell it by the piece. Or, if he leaves it whole, he may try to smuggle it out of the country. I'd appreciate you letting me know if you hear anything.'

'You've got my word on that, Sir Barrington,' Jack assured him.

Barrington pulled an envelope from his pocket. 'Use this if you think it will help. Otherwise, spend it on Molly and that new baby.'

Jack took the envelope, but didn't open it. 'You're a good man, Sir Barrington. I'll let you know if I hear anything. Chances are, if something that valuable's making its way around London, I'll hear about it sooner or later. Shall I contact you in the usual way?'

Barrington nodded as he tossed back his brandy. 'It's worked well in the past.' He stood up and held out his hand. 'Thanks, Jack.'

'A pleasure doing business, Sir Barrington,' Jack said, likewise getting to his feet. 'You can be sure if that necklace or any of its parts makes it down this neck of the woods, you'll be the first to know.'

Anna had intended to tell her father about Julia's necklace as soon as she'd heard about its theft, but one thing led to another and the days passed without her having a chance. Consequently, when she and her father finally sat together in the breakfast parlour a few days later, Anna wasn't surprised to find out that he already knew.

'Julia informed me of it over supper at the Hastings' last night,' the earl said, cutting into a slice of ham. 'Shocking turn of events. I told her to contact the authorities, but she informed me she had already engaged Sir Barrington Parker to look into the matter and that she'd done so on your recommendation.' He sent Anna a speculative glance. 'I thought you didn't like the man.'

'I do not like or dislike him. In truth, it was Lady Lydia's suggestion that Julia get in touch with him,' Anna said. 'I merely agreed that he would be a good choice because he was bound to be more discreet than most. He also seems to be privy to a great deal of information not known to the general public.'

'And how have *you* come to know that?'

Aware that her father was watching her a little too intently, Anna said casually, 'During my dealings with one of the young ladies whose life I was endeavouring to fix, I met Sir Barrington and he was able to provide me with information that was extremely valuable in securing the lady's happiness.'

'I see. So you've spent considerable time talking with him, then?'

'Not considerable, no.' Anna set her knife down. 'We met at Lady Montby's, spoke briefly at Julia's dinner party, then chanced to encounter one another in the park the other day.' She decided not to tell her father about the visit she had paid to the baronet's house over Peregrine's affair with Lady Yew. That would spark far too many awkward questions. 'It was then he informed me of his meeting with Julia.'

'I see.'

Anna sighed. 'Why is it gentlemen say that all the time, when I am quite convinced none of you see anything at all!'

'Oh, I don't know.' She was annoyed to see her father smile in that knowing kind of way. 'I think I'm beginning to see *some* things very clearly indeed.'

Disappointingly, very little information surfaced about the stolen necklace. London's underworld kept to itself, and those who were foolish enough to divulge what they knew suffered a noticeably shortened life. Consequently, neither Jack Drummond nor Lord Richard Crew were able to provide Barrington with the information he needed.

Closer to home, he questioned each member of the

baroness's personal staff, but turned up nothing of use. They were all extremely upset by the nature of the theft, but none were able to offer anything that pointed him in the right direction.

It was discouraging to say the least, but he still had one more avenue to explore. Knowing that gentlemen who imbibed too freely often tended to say far more than was wise, Barrington paid a late-night visit to one of his old haunts. The hell was known for high stakes' play and the young bucks who flocked to it were willing to risk all on the turn of a card.

Barrington knew many of them personally. Heirs to great estates who frittered away the years engaged in various debaucheries while waiting for their fathers to die. Restless second sons with little expectation of inheriting anything, but with allowances generous enough to allow them to gamble or drink their way into serious trouble. And the inevitable hangers-on. Those who clung to the coat-tails of the wealthy with either enough money or enough charm to make them tolerable.

Barrington knew them all. He had watched both his father and his grandfather drink themselves into oblivion and had sworn as a young man that he would never follow in their footsteps. As a result, for the first time in over two hundred years, the Parker name bore not a trace of scandal. And while his own line of work had not made him the most popular man in London, at least he knew he was doing what he could to make life better for those who were deserving of it.

But at what cost to yourself?

The question was unsettling. As was the fact that of late, he'd been asking it of himself more and more often. At one time, he had been able to ignore it because he had honestly believed there was nothing he would rather be doing, that there was no cost to exposing the dregs of London society.

But that wasn't true any more. His happiness was the cost. The warmth of a woman's love was the cost.

Anna was the cost—and the realisation hit him hard. Until recently, he hadn't allowed himself to say it. Even to think it. But ever since that night on the balcony, he realised that his feelings had begun to change. The idea of spending his life alone wasn't so appealing any more—and it was all because of Anna. He wanted to go to sleep with her curled up next to him, then to wake up and see her smiling at him. He wanted to lose himself in the lush warmth of her body and to experience the passion he knew he would find in her arms. Passion a few short minutes on a balcony had given him a tantalising glimpse of.

But, out of habit, he had put her off, telling her that he had no intention of marrying and using what he did as an excuse to keep her at a distance.

For the first time in his life, he wished he hadn't needed to.

Around one o'clock in the morning, after three hours of hard play, Barrington was getting ready to call it a night when one of the doxies came over to him and sat down in his lap. Her faded gown left little to the imagination and, as she draped her arm around his neck, Barrington was treated to a glimpse of full, rounded breasts and a long, slim neck. 'Sir Barrington Parker?' she whispered.

He looked up into a face that was still pretty and nodded. 'Yes.'

'Then somebody wants to see you.'

Surprised at not being propositioned, he said, 'What makes you think I want to see him?'

'Beats me, love, but he said he'd wait for you in the garden and not to be long about it. Said he had something to tell you.'

As she slowly straightened, she ran her hand up his chest, her fingers lingering for a moment at his throat. His shirt was open, his cravat long since having been shed. As she stroked the warm bare skin, she watched his face for signs that her attempts at seduction were succeeding. When she saw none, she sighed and moved away, obviously on the prowl for more lucrative business.

Barrington collected his winnings, picked up his cane and slowly got to his feet. It never paid to appear anxious in a place like this. Though most of the patrons were either drunk or unconscious, one never knew when watchful eyes might be following one's movements. Instead, he sauntered past the other tables, stopping to pretend an interest in one of the games, before heading towards the door.

The light grew dim as the corridor narrowed and the sounds of conversation and laughter faded away. Barrington concentrated on moving carefully now, senses alert for danger. Someone had gone to the trouble of following him here and of trying to make contact. He had no idea whether it was friend or foe, but experience had taught him well. The last thing he needed was an ambush by someone hiding in a darkened doorway.

Fortunately, no such attack came to pass and when he finally reached the unlocked back door, he stepped out into a small patch of heavily overgrown garden and looked around. For a moment, he saw nothing. Then, as his eyes adjusted to the gloom, he saw the faint outline of a man standing against the stone wall at the far end of the garden.

'Sir Barrington Parker?' The man's voice was coarse, the accent more north country than London.

'Yes.' Barrington slowly walked forwards. 'Who are you and how did you know to find me here?'

'Who I am doesn't matter. What I've got to say does. I understand you're looking for a necklace.'

Barrington stopped dead. So, the rats were finally making their way to the surface. He wished the light was such that he could put a face to the voice, but the man had positioned himself in such a way that his features remained in complete obscurity. 'What do you know about that?'

'Just what I was told to pass along.'

Barrington raised one eyebrow in surprise. So, the man was merely a conduit, a lackey of the person in possession of the necessary information. 'Does your master require payment for his information?'

'No. Said it was enough that the guilty party be exposed for what he'd done. A settling of an old score, if you will.'

Barrington smiled. A vendetta. How Italian. 'Very well,' he said slowly. 'What can you tell me?'

It took three minutes. Three minutes and Barrington had his name. A name he would have spent an eternity looking for and never found. After that, his informant slipped quietly into the night, the creaking of the back gate the only indication he'd ever been there.

Barrington stood alone in the silence of the neglected garden. He was used to hearing lies and rumours. Used to sifting through mounds of trivial information until he stumbled upon that one piece that might be of value. And he could honestly say there were only a handful of times in his entire life when he had truly been surprised by the nature of a revelation. This was one of those times.

But as he turned and slowly headed back into the house, he realised he wasn't only surprised, he was deeply apprehensive. The line he walked now was one of the finest he ever would. More than the reputation of a gentleman was at stake. Personal boundaries were about to be crossed. Feelings would be trammelled into the dust, beliefs battered, and impressions irrevocably altered.

He had the name of his thief. And, if his identity proved true, Barrington knew he risked losing everything that had come to matter in his life.

Chapter Nine

Having just returned from a drive in the park, Anna was about to enter the house when she heard the clatter of carriage wheels in the street behind her. Aware that it was slowing down, she turned in time to see a matched pair of greys pulling an elegant black cabriolet draw to a halt in front of the house. Moments later, Sir Barrington stepped out, ebony cane in hand, his black beaver glistening in the afternoon sun.

'Sir Barrington,' Anna said, cursing the tiny catch in her voice. 'This is a surprise.'

He looked as startled as she, but there was something else in his expression she couldn't quite define. 'Lady Annabelle. I thought you would be out paying calls.'

'In fact, Lord Andrews has just returned me home from a drive in the park.'

'Andrews!' His countenance darkened. 'You allowed him to take you driving?'

'I did,' Anna said, caught off guard by the sudden intensity in his voice. 'He has been after me for weeks to allow him to show me his new pair of blacks, so when the weather turned fine this morning, I decided I would allow him to do so.'

'And did you enjoy your drive?'

Remembering several rather alarming moments when the horses had been going too fast for safety, Anna was tempted to tell him no, but pride demanded a different answer. 'It was…invigorating.'

He snorted. 'Invigorating. Andrews is a mediocre whip at best and notorious for buying troublesome animals. He has an inflated opinion of his ability to train them, so when a seller tells him a horse is bad tempered, Andrews tells them they're not using the right methods of control. But most of the time, he ends up selling the horses back to whoever he bought them from and always at a loss.'

'I admit, they were a touch wild,' Anna conceded, 'but for the most part, he seemed able to keep them under control.'

'Nevertheless, I would ask you not to drive out with him again. He is not a man I would encourage you or any other young woman to spend time with.'

Anna bristled. Having already made up her mind not to see Lord Andrews again, the warning was unnecessary, but she resented Barrington's belief that he had the right to tell her who she should and should not see. 'I think you are too hard on the gentleman, Sir Barrington. He was very pleasant to me. Attentive to my wishes and interested in what I had to say.'

'What do you know about the viscount, Lady Annabelle?' Barrington asked softly.

'Not a great deal,' she was forced to confess. 'He told me his wife died two years ago and that he has three married sisters he seldom sees.'

'He also has four children ranging in ages from six to thirteen and he is looking for a new wife to take care of them.'

'He cannot be looking very hard,' Anna said. 'I've spoken to several young ladies who told me of their desire to become the next Lady Andrews, but apparently, he offered them no encouragement whatsoever.'

'Yet he seemed interested in you?'

'Actually, no. During the course of our drive, he asked me a great many questions about Miss Dora Preston.'

'Miss Preston?' Barrington said quietly. 'Of course. A painfully shy young woman of nine and twenty, who now finds herself in a precarious financial situation as a result of her parents' death. She is neither pretty nor accomplished and has received no offers of marriage. Furthermore, as an only child, she has no brothers or sisters to whom she can apply for help.'

'Then why, given all that, should you not be pleased to hear that Lord Andrews is interested in her?' Anna asked, thinking it a logical question—until she saw the look on his face. 'Don't tell me you know something about him as well?'

'I'm afraid I do. And it is not the kind of information that recommends him to *any* woman, let alone one who is alone in the world and so terribly naïve.'

'Dare I ask why not?'

'Because Lord Andrews can be…unstable.'

'Unstable.'

'He has been known to suffer from hallucinations and bouts of paranoia.'

'The poor man. Is he not well?'

'Not when under the influence of opium, no.'

'Opium! *Lord Andrews?*'

'For obvious reasons, it is not something the man publicises,' Barrington said. 'It started out as a medical treatment for some unspecified condition several years ago, but over time, he grew addicted to its more…pleasurable aspects. It is the reason he has no communication with his sisters. They are afraid for the welfare of his children when he is under the influence. I know for a fact that the eldest sister has tried to remove the children from his care, but has been unsuccessful in her attempts. Marrying someone like Miss Preston leads me to believe he is looking for the kind of wife who will not ask questions. One who will be grateful just to have been asked and who has no family to worry about her. With such a wife in place, Andrews's sisters won't have a hope of taking the children away from him.'

Dear Lord, it was enough to make her feel ill. Anna couldn't believe that the man with whom she had just parted company would be the type to take opium, but neither could she dismiss it out of hand. Not when it was Barrington who had made her aware of it.

'If what you say is true, I must warn Miss Preston not to entertain his suit,' Anna said quickly. 'Though for the life of me, I cannot imagine what reason I am going to give her. She knows what her chances of marrying are. She'll never have another opportunity like this.'

'I have every confidence you will find a convincing explanation. If not, you can always tell her the truth. For her sake, she must not consider his offer. Nor must any other young lady for that matter.'

'I cannot protect them all!'

'I know. Fortunately, Andrews will likely retire to the country before the end of the Season, especially if he meets with no success in London. He will probably marry a woman from the local village. He does not look to marry well, only quickly.'

Anna nodded, aware that once again she was in his debt. 'Thank you for the information, Sir Barrington. Though I do not feel better for having learned of it, I know it will help Miss Preston in the long run.'

'There are, unfortunately, many men like Andrews in

society. Hallucinatory drugs will always hold an appeal for that sort of man.'

Aware that they were still standing on her front step, Anna said, 'Forgive me, I have rudely kept you out here talking. Would you like to come in?'

'Only if your father is at home.'

'I don't believe he is,' Anna said, wondering at the nature of his call. Surely the Marquess of Yew hadn't some further issue with Peregrine. 'He informed me when I left with Lord Andrews that he would be out until later this evening.'

'Then perhaps I will try again later.' He touched the brim of his beaver, then turned to go.

'Sir Barrington?' When he stopped and turned back, Anna said, 'Have you had any luck finding Julia's necklace?'

His expression didn't change, but something in his eyes hardened. 'No, though I have recently been made aware of information pertaining to the theft. But it is nothing I am at liberty to share at this time. Good afternoon, Lady Annabelle.'

With that he walked back down the path and climbed into his waiting carriage. The driver flicked the whip and the horses set off.

Anna walked into the house, unable to shake a feeling of gloom. Finding out the truth about Lord Andrews had not been pleasant and she made a promise to herself to send a note to Miss Preston that very afternoon. But it wasn't only that. Barrington had called to see her father and in finding him absent had made it perfectly clear that he had no desire to spend time in *her* company. Contrary to what she'd believed, it was obvious that the breach between them wasn't healed at all.

The rest of the day passed uneventfully, though Anna was aware of feeling strangely on edge. Even in the carriage en route to an evening engagement, the conversation she'd had with Barrington lingered in her mind. Was there anything the man *didn't* know? He seemed to be in possession of the most disturbing information about almost everyone she knew. Even unassuming Lord Andrews, whom she found herself observing during the course of the evening, harboured secrets that were both dark and disturbing. Watching him speak quietly to an elderly lady, Anna found it difficult to equate the seemingly upright gentleman with a man who indulged in a substance whose prolonged use was known to affect the mind and body in terrible ways.

'Are you sure you did not misunderstand Sir Barrington?' Lydia asked after Anna had acquainted her with Lord Andrew's unsavoury pastime.

'I can assure you I did not,' Anna said, keeping her voice down. 'Sir Barrington was very convincing in his description of the man's activities; given that I've no reason to doubt him, I took the liberty of writing to Miss Preston and advising her not to encourage Lord Andrews's suit. I told her Mr. Atlander would be a far better choice.'

'Until you speak to Sir Barrington about *him*,' Lydia murmured. 'And find out that *he* is not all he seems to be either. Faith, it must be disturbing to know so much about so many people. Only think of the kind of secrets Sir Barrington is forced to keep. He could utterly destroy people if he was of a mind to.'

'Only if they did something foolish. If one is innocent of all crimes, people have nothing to fear from him.'

'And what about you, Anna?' Lydia asked quietly. 'Have you anything to fear from Sir Barrington Parker?'

Anna took a sip of champagne. That was the problem with close friends. They saw far too much. 'I have no idea what you mean.'

'I think you do. You speak of him quite often, you know,' Lydia said, 'and in a tone of voice that leads me to believe you are not entirely indifferent to him.'

'Be that as it may, we both know exactly where we stand.'

'You may know where you stand, Anna, but are you happy about it?'

Anna raised her glass to her lips instead of replying. *That* was a different question altogether.

The house was quiet when Anna got home. Milford met her at the door and took her evening cape. 'Thank you, Milford. Is my father still up?'

'He is, my lady, but he went to his room and said he was not to be disturbed.'

Anna paused in the act of removing her gloves. 'Did Sir Barrington Parker call this evening?'

'He most certainly did,' Edward said, coming down the stairs. 'That will be all, Milford.'

Anna wasn't surprised by her brother's curt dismissal of the servant, but she was surprised to find him still at home. 'You're not usually here this time of evening,' she said as the butler withdrew.

'I had planned on going out, but when Parker arrived, I decided to stay. I'm glad I did, though you won't be.'

Anna flinched at his tone of voice. 'I assume he came to speak to Papa about Peregrine?'

'On the contrary, he came to speak to Father about the baroness's necklace. It seems the thief has been found.'

Something in his face set Anna's heart racing. 'Who is it?' she whispered.

'Can you not guess?'

Dear God, it was someone she knew? 'Stop playing games, Edward. Just *tell* me and be done with it!'

'Oh, I'll tell you, but you won't so easily be done with it. Because the thief is someone you know. A man you were raised to love and respect.' Her brother donned his hat and started for the door. 'A man who has lied and deceived us all. Our much loved and revered father!'

Her father had stolen the baroness's necklace?

Impossible! In fact, it was more than impossible. It was ludicrous! Her father was a wealthy man. He had no reason to steal anything—and he certainly wouldn't have stolen something from Julia. So why on earth had Barrington come here and accused him of having done so?

Woodenly, Anna made her way to the drawing room. There had to be a mistake. Barrington had been given the wrong information. One of his informants had followed the wrong lead. Tracked down the wrong man. Her father was *not* a thief. She was willing to stake her life on that.

She closed the door behind her and walked on unwilling feet towards the fireplace. She was cold, chilled from the inside out, her mind struggling to come to grips with what she had just learned. What kind of man was Barrington that he could do this to her family? He had *spoken* to her father. Socialised with him. Yet he had still come here and accused him of this heinous crime.

'How could you, Barrington?' she whispered. 'How *could* you do this unspeakable thing to my father?' She bit her lip, fighting back tears. 'To *me*.'

Barrington stood in his study, gazing into the fire, his conscience burning as hot as the flames in the grate. How long would it be? How long before she arrived on his doorstep demanding an explanation to the accusations he had laid at her father's feet?

It couldn't be long. She might even come tonight…straight from having spoken to her father. Unless she didn't get a chance to speak to him. The earl might well have gone out, or refused to speak to her. No doubt he needed time to come to grips with the fact that someone had supposedly seen him stealing the baroness's necklace while she lay sleeping in her bed.

Certainly Barrington had needed time. When the shadowy figure had first mentioned the earl's name, Barrington was sure he must have heard wrong. The Earl of Cambermere a thief? It was laughable! The man was a peer of the realm. An aristocrat. Such conduct would be anathema to him.

Yet, the man had repeated the earl's name several times over the course of the next few minutes, though never once had he vouchsafed the name of the person who was the apparent source of the information.

Not that it mattered, Barrington reflected grimly. He had been given the Earl of Cambermere's name as the person who had committed the crime. And, as his first and only suspect, he was obliged to follow it through. For Anna's sake, he prayed God it wasn't the only name he received.

Anna had no idea how she had passed the hours of that terrible night. It certainly wasn't in sleep. She had lain awake through the long midnight hours, getting up several times to pace the length of the room. At one point, she had opened the curtains and stared at the moon, but it gave her no comfort and eventually she had staggered back to bed. But she hadn't been able to sleep and still lay awake when the first fingers of light began to creep into her room. She watched the blackness of the night sky give way to a dark indigo hue, then to lighter blue as the sun climbed higher in the sky. She heard the sounds of the servants moving about in the house below. Laying fires. Dusting furniture. Setting out breakfast. And still she thought about Edward's words.

A man you were raised to love and respect...a man who has lied and deceived us all...

No, she *wouldn't* believe it. Nor would she wait any longer to have it shown up as the lie she knew it to be. She got up and dressed even before her maid arrived to help her, then went down to the library where she knew her father spent most of his early morning hours. He would be off to his club for lunch, but Anna had no intention of seeing him leave *before* she'd had a chance to speak with him. Not today.

She knocked on the library door, but waited until she heard his voice before pushing it open. 'May I come in, Papa?'

'Anna.' He rose as she entered, surprise and uncertainty reflected in his eyes. His complexion was grey and he looked as though he hadn't slept. 'What are you doing here?'

'I came to see you.' Swallowing hard, Anna closed the door and took a step towards him. 'I needed to hear it from your lips that this is all an abominable lie.'

He knew what she was talking about. Anna saw it in the way his eyes closed ever so briefly. The way his shoulders sagged. 'Did Parker tell you?'

'No. Edward did.'

'Ah.' Making no move to deny it, the earl sighed and sank back into his chair.

'I don't believe it, Papa,' Anna said. 'Someone has told a hurtful and outrageous lie!'

'Yes, they have,' he agreed. 'But they have also offered damning evidence to back up their claim.'

'What kind of evidence?'

'Someone told Parker that I was seen taking Julia's necklace.'

'*Seen…?*' Anna gasped. 'But…by whom?'

'He wouldn't tell me.'

'Why not?'

'He said it was an anonymous source.'

'Then how do you know he's telling the truth?'

Her father looked up. 'Because we're talking about Sir Barrington Parker and he doesn't lie.'

'I wasn't referring to Sir Barrington telling a lie,' Anna said tersely. 'I was talking about his anonymous source. How do we know *he* is telling the truth?'

'We don't. Right now, it's my word against his, whoever he is.'

'Then there can be no contest. You are the Earl of Cambermere!' she exclaimed.

'Which means nothing since the person who saw me was apparently *in* the house the night it happened,' her father said wearily.

'But that doesn't make sense. You've never been alone with Julia in her house,' Anna said. 'And how could you steal the necklace if she was there with you?'

She was surprised to see her father's cheeks darken as he turned away. 'Suffice it to say, that *is* what I stand accused of.'

'Well, it's ridiculous and I don't care what the gossip mill is saying. You are innocent and we are going to make sure everyone knows it!'

'Ah, Anna, have you forgotten how society works? It doesn't matter what people believe. It is enough that someone put it about that I stole the necklace for society to cry scandal.'

'But they have no proof!' Anna cried. 'So far, it is one

man's word against another's—and we don't even know who the other man is! Surely people are intelligent enough to know that, without proof, it is only lies and speculation.'

'One would hope so.'

Anna began to pace. 'Why would Sir Barrington not tell you the name of the person who claims to have seen you take it?'

'He told me he couldn't until further investigation was carried out.'

'Then for all we know, it could be someone deliberately making mischief,' Anna said, grasping at straws. Grasping at anything that might banish the wretchedness from her father's eyes. 'Someone who wishes to hurt you for some unknown reason.'

'I did think of that,' her father said. 'But who have I slighted to such an extent that they would wish to destroy my reputation like this?'

Anna bit her lip. 'You don't think Peregrine…?'

'Peregrine?' Anna was relieved to see a look of genuine shock appear on her father's face. 'Why on earth would he turn on me in such a manner?'

'Perhaps because of the situation with Lady Yew. He was angry and hurt that you didn't believe him when Sir Barrington accused him of having an affair.'

'Rightly so, given that it turned out Parker was correct.'

Reminded of the man who had brought this terrible news into the house, Anna felt a red-hot wave of anger. How dare he disrupt her family's life like this? She had been willing to believe him up until now, but not this time. He and he alone was the cause of her father's humiliation and unhappiness.

'Then I shall go to Sir Barrington myself. I will *demand* that he tell me who his source is and have him explain why he would believe such a ridiculous lie.'

'You're bringing emotion into it,' her father warned. 'Parker doesn't deal in emotion. He deals in facts.'

'Not any more,' Anna said tersely. 'This time, he is dealing with emotions. Yours and mine and Julia's. And by the time I'm through with him, he is going to know *exactly* how challenging dealing with an emotional woman can be!'

Barrington was in the long gallery sparring with his brother-in-law when his secretary arrived to tell him that Lady Annabelle Durst had called and was waiting below.

'Shall I inform her that you are engaged, Sir Barrington?' Sam asked.

'No.' Barrington slowly lowered his foil. 'Ask her to wait in the salon. I shall be there directly.'

'Lady Annabelle Durst,' Tom repeated after the secretary left. 'The Earl of Cambermere's daughter?'

'Yes.'

'Interesting. Is she calling on a business matter or may I have the pleasure of telling your sister that a lady has finally caught her brother's eye?'

'You may definitely *not* tell her that because this is not a social call,' Barrington muttered. 'Lady Annabelle is here with regards to an investigation.'

'Pity. A liaison with Cambermere's daughter would do much to lessen Jenny's disappointment over what happened with Lady Alice,' Tom remarked.

'Duly noted,' Barrington said, ushering his brother-in-law towards the door. He wasn't about to tell Tom that appeasing his sister was the least of his worries right now. 'I trust you can see yourself out.'

Without waiting for an answer, Barrington hurried to his bedroom to change into more appropriate attire. The coming confrontation was not going to be easy and he needed to be prepared. A fact proven true when he opened the door to the salon five minutes later and Anna flew at him like a tigress on the attack. 'How could you do this?' she demanded.

'Do what?'

'Accuse my father of stealing the baroness's necklace. You know he would never do such a thing!'

Barrington slowly closed the door behind him. 'I did what I had to after receiving information from a credible source—'

'Damn your credible sources!' Anna cried. 'We're talking about *my father*. And you know as well as I do that he would never steal anything from anyone! *Especially* Julia!'

'Calm yourself, Anna. I didn't say that I *believed* what I had been told, nor did I charge your father with any crime. But I was given a piece of information and it was my duty to follow it up. So I asked him a few questions.'

'What kind of questions?'

'That is between your father and myself,' he replied evasively.

'But I don't understand. If you don't believe him guilty, why are you putting him through all this?'

'Because there are procedures that must be followed.' Barrington linked his hands behind his back and slowly walked towards the window. 'When did he tell you of my visit?'

'He didn't,' Anna said tightly. 'Edward did.'

'Edward?' Barrington's head came up. 'When?'

'Last night. He waited until I arrived home to tell me that you had called to see Father. I assumed it had something to do with Peregrine, but Edward said you had come to see Papa about the theft of Julia's necklace.'

Barrington didn't trouble to hide his surprise. 'I wonder

how he knew? Your brother wasn't in the room when I spoke to your father.'

'He must have been standing outside in the corridor listening to your conversation,' Anna said. 'Edward is not above doing such things, especially if he thought you'd come to see my father about Peregrine.'

'I see,' Barrington said quietly. He was beginning to have his own suspicions about Viscount Hayle, but knew it was best he keep them to himself for the time being. 'What did your father say when you spoke to him?'

'He told me what *you* had accused him of, but said that you would not name the person who had made this foul accusation against him,' Anna said in a low voice. 'How could you not tell him, Barrington? Surely my father has a right to know who is bringing these charges against him.'

'He will. But for now, I thought it best not to reveal too much. To say something out of turn won't do anyone any good,' he advised.

'But you must know what this will do to his reputation,' she said, 'whether it turns out to be true or not. Why can't you just *say* that the other person is lying and proclaim my father innocent?'

'Because until I am convinced of the part that *everyone* has played in this, I'm not willing to say who is guilty and who is not.'

'But you just said my father didn't do it—and why would he? He likes Julia,' Anna said. 'Why on earth would he jeopardise a possible future with her by stealing something so precious to her?'

'Trust me when I tell you that thought has already occurred to me.' Barrington hesitated a moment before saying, 'You said Edward spoke to you about your father?'

'Yes.'

'It hasn't escaped my notice that there is a certain amount of tension between your father and your brother at the moment,' he said.

'It's hardly surprising,' Anna said in a voice of resignation. 'Papa is pressuring Edward to marry Lady Harriet Green and Edward wants nothing to do with it.'

'Why? Is he opposed to the idea of marriage or just the lady your father wishes him to wed?'

'A bit of both, I think,' Anna admitted. 'Papa thinks very highly of Lady Harriet and he's told Edward so any number of times. He says she possesses all the qualities necessary to be the next Countess of Cambermere.'

'And your brother doesn't share his opinion.'

'Edward says that who he marries is no one's business but his own. I suppose he's right, but Papa is concerned about the future of the family. He says Edward has lived the life of the gentleman about town long enough and that it's time he settled down to his obligations.'

'Which means marrying and producing an heir,' Barrington said.

'Precisely.'

'Are there no other members of the family capable of doing so?' Barrington asked. 'I believe your father has several brothers and sisters?'

'Two brothers, one sister,' Anna said. 'Aunt Hestia is married to a Scottish laird and lives in Edinburgh. I remember meeting her when I was about six and not liking her very much. She has two girls. Father's youngest brother, Cyril, went away to France and was eventually killed in battle, and his next eldest brother sailed off to China and never came back. I suspect he knew he wouldn't have much of a life, given that Papa was heir.'

'So it *is* up to Edward to continue the family name,' Barrington said thoughtfully.

'Yes, and given that he is showing absolutely no inclination to do so, it is only to be expected that relations between him and my father are strained,' Anna sighed.

'Yes, I can see why they would be,' Barrington said. 'Anna, I cannot share with you what I was told, but I promise I will do everything I can to get to the truth of the matter.'

'There is only one truth: that is that my father is innocent of this vile charge,' Anna said, raising her chin in defiance. 'I don't care what manner of evidence has been brought against him. He is a good man. An honourable man. And if you don't believe that, we have absolutely nothing more to say to one another.'

Chapter Ten

The evidence against her father *was* damning, Barrington reflected in the silence after Anna left. It was part of the reason he hadn't been willing to share it with her. He was loathe to provide her with details of a circumstance that would put the blame for the theft squarely on her father's shoulders *and* give her undeniable proof that the earl and the baroness engaged in an intimate relationship. But that was what the messenger had told him and what he was obligated to follow up on.

A servant in the baroness's household had seen Lord Cambermere take the necklace after leaving the baroness sleeping peacefully in her bed. Apparently, the maid had gone into her mistress's bedroom, expecting her lady to be alone, and had discovered the earl in the act of taking the necklace from the jewellery case. She claimed that Lord Cambermere hadn't seen her, but that from where she had been standing, she'd had a clear view of the proceedings. After locking the jewellery box, the earl had slipped the necklace into the pocket of his coat, and then returned to the baroness's bed.

The baroness had not woken and, shocked beyond words, the maid had backed quietly out of the room.

Barrington sighed. It might be only the word of a servant against that of an earl, but the messenger had provided details too specific to be dismissed as fabrication or hoax. Details of the room's interior. A description of the jewellery box. Even where the dressing table was located in relation to the bed, what colour the curtains were, and what manner of knick-knacks had adorned the top of the bedside table. Only a maid, with unrestricted access to the baroness's bedroom, would have been able to provide details like that.

Besides, what reason had she to lie? She claimed to have no prior knowledge of the earl. She hadn't worked in his household and had no reason to hold a grudge against him. All she cared about was her mistress and how upset she had been when she'd found out the necklace was missing. It was that grief, combined with a sense of loyalty, that had prompted Miss Smith to tell *someone* what she had seen that night. And, in turn, for that person to tell the man who'd met with Barrington in the darkened garden.

If it *was* true, it meant Cambermere had certainly had the opportunity to commit the crime. But he still lacked a motive and Barrington didn't believe anything was done without motive. Dogs barked because they were frightened. Beggars stole because they were starving. Prostitutes sold their bodies because they needed a roof over their heads.

What reason had Cambermere for stealing?

Barrington idly picked up a piece of Venetian glass, turning it over in his fingers as his mind went back over his various encounters with the earl. Was it possible the man had serious debts? His home was quite grand, but there had been an air of genteel shabbiness about the place. Small signs of neglect a less observant person might have overlooked. Worn patches on the arms of the chairs. The burgundy velvet curtains faded, their bottom edges frayed. Even the mahogany desk had been in need of a good polish.

Barrington had originally put it down to a lack of interest on the earl's part, a sad consequence of Lady Cambermere's death. But now he wondered if it might be an indication of something more. Even the earl's appearance had been wanting, now that Barrington thought about it. Signs of wear at the man's cuffs. The style of the coat slightly out of date. Boots that had seen better days.

Still, if the earl was having financial difficulties, he wouldn't be the first peer to fall on hard times. Cambermere owned a house in town and several smaller estates in the English countryside. The upkeep of such establishments commanded a huge outlay of money. It was the reason many cash-strapped peers resorted to marrying heiresses. It was either that or risk sacrificing their family's land and holdings. But was the earl really in such dire financial straits?

Surprisingly, it was Lady Bessmel who provided some insight into the situation as the two of them stood chatting over lobster pâté the following evening.

'Yes, Cambermere has a lovely estate in Kent,' she told him. 'I used to visit him and Isabel there quite often.'

'What was Lady Cambermere like?' Barrington enquired.

'Quiet. And thoughtful. She enjoyed London, but she was far happier in the country. She loved her garden and her horses. And her books, of course. She would read for hours on end, saying she found precious little time for it in London.' Lady Bessmel sighed. 'I was very sorry when Isabel died. She was…a gentle person. The kind who gave of herself. I believe her death hit Peter quite hard.'

'Were they in love?'

The countess smiled. 'As much as anyone in our circle can be, I suppose. It was an arranged marriage, but it turned out quite well. Peter was a good husband. I never heard stories about him keeping a mistress or visiting the brothels. He seemed content with his life, at least until Isabel died. Then he seemed to lose focus. He couldn't settle to anything. That's why it's so nice to see him finally making an effort again.'

'Making an effort?' Barrington asked.

'With the baroness. It can't have escaped your notice that he is very much taken with her.'

'Yes, I had noticed.' Barrington smiled. 'Can you tell me anything more about the earl? Has he vices?'

'What man doesn't? He gambles at cards, but not a great deal, and he drinks no more or less than anyone else. I suppose his greatest weakness is horses.'

'Horses,' Barrington repeated. 'Is he a frequent visitor to the track?'

'More now than he used to be. I never remember him gambling while Isabel was alive, but a woman's death can change a man. In the beginning, I think it was simply a diversion,' Lady Bessmel said. 'Something to think about other than the fact that his wife wasn't there any more. But over time it gets into a man's blood.'

'Does he win more than he loses?' he asked idly.

'Who knows? Dame Fortune can turn either way. One day she smiles on you, the next she spits in your face. I'm sure Peter's had his share of both, but he's a private man so I doubt anyone knows the true extent of his winnings. Or of his losses.'

It was a conversation that stayed with Barrington the rest of the night—because if the earl *was* in serious debt, Barrington had his motive. The baroness's necklace was worth a small fortune, enough to cover most any man's debts. And given Cambermere's position in society, it was unlikely he would have to take the necklace apart. Connections here and abroad would allow him to dispose of the piece without the sale being traced back to him.

But if the earl was hopeful of marrying the baroness, why bother to steal her jewellery? Julia von Brohm was an exceedingly wealthy young woman with more than enough money for the two of them to live on. Of course, being a widow, her money was her own, and, if she chose, she could have a lawyer draw up papers to ensure it stayed that way. If Cambermere needed funds to pay off his gambling debts, he could apply to her, but given that his debts *were* the result of gambling, she might not wish to put any of her money to them. Barrington remembered a remark she'd once made about gentlemen foolish enough to squander their money on the roll of a dice not being worth the time or the trouble to know. That being the case, he doubted she would willingly give any of her money to a man who had bankrupted himself at the tables or the track.

However, if it was Cambermere's intention to pay off his debts *before* he married her so that he could go into the marriage free and clear, he would then be able to use her money to look after the maintenance of his estates. And surely she wouldn't object to that, given that she would be mistress of them all. So it really came down to two questions.

How deeply in debt had Cambermere landed himself? And how far was he willing to go to dig himself out?

The next morning Anna called for her horse to be saddled and went for a much-needed ride. She feared she might explode if she stayed at home any longer. Trying to read, or doing any one of a hundred and one other things that would normally have distracted her, would be of no use today. She needed to get out of the house and away from her thoughts.

Her father had already done so. Having been offered an invitation to a shooting party, he had left for the weekend gathering at a house about ten miles outside London. It was only to be a small gathering of gentlemen, but Anna knew her father would find comfort in their company. But it did leave her at loose ends. Peregrine was still quiet and withdrawn as he struggled through his own emotional healing and Edward was scarcely at home.

And Barrington didn't call.

Anna told herself she was glad of that. After all, they had nothing to say to one another. She'd made it quite plain that to take a stand against her father was to take a stand against her, and Barrington had made his own position perfectly clear. He intended to pursue the investigation against her father; in the absence of any other, her father was still the main suspect.

Well, loyalty and emotion might mean nothing to him, but they meant everything to Anna. She believed unequivocally that her father was innocent. Barrington was trying to prove him not guilty. There was a subtle but distinct difference.

Unfortunately, as much as Anna had hoped that fresh air and brisk exercise might distract her, neither served to ease her mind. She felt no more relaxed when she arrived home than when she'd left. And when Peregrine emerged from the drawing room, white-faced and shaken, her spirits plummeted even further. 'Goodness, Peregrine, what's wrong? You look positively ill.'

'Thank God you're back! Come in here!' he said urgently. 'And close the door.'

Anna did, wearily hoping his agitation had nothing to do with Lady Yew. She wasn't sure she could cope with one more piece of bad news—or with the mention of that woman's name again. 'What's this all about? If you tell me you've seen the marchioness—'

'This has nothing to do with her,' Peregrine assured her quickly. 'This is worse. Much worse!'

Worse? Anna didn't like the sound of that. And when

Peregrine began to pace up and down the length of the room, looking as though he might burst into tears at any time, she knew there was trouble in earnest. 'What's going on, Per? If it's bad news, just tell me and get it over with.'

He stopped pacing, but didn't look at her. 'I don't know *how* to tell you. I'm hardly able to believe it myself!'

'Believe what?'

He looked ready to say something, then squeezed his eyes shut and took a deep breath. 'No. It's best I show you. You won't believe me otherwise.' With that, he took her hand and led her out of the room and towards the staircase.

'Where are we going?'

'You'll see,' was all he would say. At the top of the stairs, he stopped and cocked his head, listening. Then, with a brief nod, he carried on until they were standing outside the last door in the hall.

'This is Papa's room,' Anna said unnecessarily.

'I know.' Peregrine took another quick glance in either direction, then, to Anna's astonishment, opened the door and dragged her in.

'Peregrine, what on earth are you doing?'

'I have to show you something.' Closing the door, he turned the key in the lock. Then, walking over to the door that connected the earl's room to his valet's, he locked that one as well.

'Peregrine, you're beginning to make me very nervous,' Anna said, unconsciously lowering her voice.

'I'm sorry, but I found something in your father's things that you really must see.'

'You were going through his things?' Anna said, shocked.

'I was looking for his watch.'

'His watch?' The story was getting more bizarre by the minute. 'Why?'

'Because Edward asked me to,' Peregrine admitted.

'I don't understand.'

'Edward was supposed to take your father's watch to Mr Munts for repair,' Peregrine explained, 'but he told me he was late for an appointment and asked me if I would take it instead. I said I would and asked him where the watch was. He told me the earl usually kept it in one of two places. I checked the first place and it wasn't there. But when I looked in the second...'

He stopped, prompting Anna to say, 'You found it?'

Peregrine nodded. 'But I found something else as well.' He led her to the large corner wardrobe and, pulling open the doors, pointed to a small drawer. 'Open it.'

Not sure why, Anna did—and saw a leather bag with a drawstring opening lying on a pile of neatly folded handkerchiefs. 'Is that what you want me to see?'

He nodded. 'Take it out.'

The bag was heavier than expected, and Anna felt the contents shift as she picked it up.

'Open it,' he whispered.

'We really shouldn't be going through Papa's things,' Anna whispered. 'This could be something personal.'

'Open it, Anna.'

There was an edge of fatalism in his voice, and reluctantly, she loosened the drawstring and tipped the contents of the bag into the palm of her hand.

The baroness's diamond-and-sapphire necklace twinkled up at her.

'Oh, dear God!' Anna said—and promptly dropped it. 'What on earth is *that* doing here?'

'I have no idea.' Peregrine reached down and plucked the necklace from the depths of the boot into which it had fallen. 'But we both know it's not supposed to be here.'

The discovery left Anna speechless. How could the necklace be here—in her father's room? In his wardrobe? He had professed his innocence and she had believed him. Then she had gone to Barrington and told him that her father was innocent of the charge and that if he didn't believe her, they had nothing further to say to one another. Yet now she found the baroness's necklace nestled amongst her father's things.

'It's impossible,' she whispered. 'Why would he do this?'

'I've been asking myself that all afternoon,' Peregrine said miserably. 'And coming up with nothing.'

Anna stared at the necklace. It didn't make sense. The necklace shouldn't be here. In fact, this was the last place in the world it should be…

'All right, let's not jump to conclusions,' she said, knowing there had to be a logical explanation. 'Just because we found the necklace here, doesn't mean Papa took it.'

'Then how did it come to be in his things?' Peregrine asked.

'Obviously, someone *put* it here.'

'Who? No one else comes into his room,' he said.

'*You* did!' she reminded him.

'Only because Edward asked me to. And I certainly didn't put *this* here.' He was silent for a moment. 'What about the servants? They come and go all the time.'

'But none of them would have an opportunity to steal a diamond necklace from the baroness,' Anna pointed out.

'And we *did*?' Peregrine demanded.

'Of course not! But at least we move in the same circles. We have access to her house.'

'But none of us would have taken it.'

Yet, the necklace was here. In her father's wardrobe. Peregrine was holding it in his hands.

'It really is fabulous, isn't it?' he said, staring down at it in fascination.

Anna didn't want to look, but it was almost impossible not to. She had never seen such amazing stones. Even in the dim light, the sapphires seemed to glow with brilliant blue fire and the diamonds were as white as any she'd ever seen. Truly, it was a necklace fit for a queen.

'A man would never have to work again if he owned something like that,' Peregrine whispered. 'He could buy anything he wanted. Go wherever he wanted. He'd never have to worry about money—'

'Stop talking like that!' Anna admonished, finally taking the necklace away from him. 'This is going back to the baroness where it belongs.'

'*Back* to the baroness? But…aren't you going to tell anyone you found it?'

She stared at him as though he'd suddenly sprouted a second head. 'Are you *mad*? And have Papa implicated in a crime he didn't commit? Not on your life! Whoever put this necklace here clearly intended to make trouble for Papa and I'm not about to see that happen,' Anna said. 'We have been unbelievably fortunate in finding the necklace before he got home. And I am going to return it to Julia at the first opportunity.'

'I see.' Peregrine crossed his arms in front of his chest. 'And where, pray tell, are you going to tell her you *found* it?'

The question stopped Anna in her tracks. 'Oh.'

'Exactly. If you can't come up with a logical explanation, you're better off not giving it back to her at all. It will just make her suspicious.'

'But the longer the necklace is missing, the more time someone has to spread lies about Papa's having taken it,' Anna said.

Peregrine glanced at the necklace and shook his head. 'I

think you should tell Sir Barrington Parker. Isn't he the one the baroness asked to look into the matter?'

'Yes, and I'll tell you right now, he is the very *last* person I intend to tell about this!' Anna said fiercely. 'Can you imagine what he would say if he were to learn that we found it here? He would think Papa took it.'

'I hate to say this, but…' Peregrine looked distinctly uncomfortable. 'Are you absolutely sure your father *didn't* take it?'

Anna's mouth fell open in disbelief. 'Peregrine, how *could* you?'

'I'm not saying he did! It's just that—'

'I don't want to hear it,' Anna said, cutting him off. 'There isn't a doubt in my mind that my father is innocent. He would never do something like this. *Never!*'

'Then what are you going to do?'

'I'll tell you.' Anna slipped the necklace into the pocket of her riding skirt, a plan already forming in her mind. 'First off, *you* are going to take Papa's watch to Mr Munts and make sure you get a receipt for it.'

'A receipt,' Peregrine repeated in bewilderment.

'Yes. Then, upon returning home, you will give the receipt to Milford and make sure you tell him that Edward instructed you to take Papa's watch in for repair, and that either Milford or James can pick it up when it's ready.'

Peregrine's heavy brows drew together. 'Why am I doing all that?'

'Because I want the reasons for your *being* in Papa's wardrobe to be very clear. It's possible that whoever put the necklace here intended that someone other than Papa should find it. Most likely a servant. And knowing how servants gossip, the culprit hoped news of the necklace's discovery *in* Papa's wardrobe would start making its way through society.

Fortunately, *we* found it and can make sure no such rumours leak out,' Anna said.

Peregrine frowned. 'I don't understand the reason for all the secrecy. We certainly aren't going to say we saw the necklace.'

'Of course not. And before this day is out, the necklace will be safely back in Julia's hands. But if, for some bizarre reason, this does fall back on us, I want it made very clear that you went into the wardrobe looking for Papa's watch because it needed to go to Mr Munts for repair, and that you did *not* see anything untoward while you were there.'

'So if anyone asks, we're going to lie,' Peregrine said simply.

'Precisely. It's the *only* way we can protect Papa. Now if you'll excuse me, I have to get dressed. I have a very important call to make!'

There was only one thought on Anna's mind as she turned her phaeton into Mayfair a short time later. She *had* to get the necklace back into Julia's house—and she had to do it without anyone seeing her!

It should be relatively simple. Once in Julia's parlour, she would pass some pleasant time with tea and conversation before making an excuse to leave the room. A visit to the convenience would probably be the best. That would give her time to slip upstairs and make her way to Julia's bedchamber.

Once inside, she would place the necklace on the floor beneath Julia's bedside table, or better yet, under her dressing table, and then return to the drawing room to resume her visit. In the next few minutes, she would bring the conversation round to the necklace and casually ask if Julia had looked *under* the furniture in her room since jewellery could so easily slip off a night table or a dresser and become lost. If

Julia replied that she or the servants had already looked in such places, Anna would simply advise her to look again and casually change the subject; then, after a suitable amount of time, she would bid Julia a good day and leave.

Really, it was so simple. Julia would find the necklace exactly where Anna said it might be, laugh at herself for not having been more careful—and that would be an end of it. There would be no more stories about the necklace having been stolen. No more rumours about her father's possible involvement. And no need to involve Sir Barrington Parker at all.

Anna almost felt like laughing as she walked up to Julia's front door.

Unfortunately, her neatly laid plans began to fall apart the moment she walked into the house. As the butler opened the drawing room door and announced her, Anna was horrified to see Sir Barrington Parker sitting comfortably at Julia's side.

'Sir Barrington!' she gasped, completely ignoring her hostess.

'Lady Annabelle.' He rose to greet her, his voice decidedly amused. 'You look as though you've seen a ghost.'

'Do I?' *Calm.* Above all, she had to remain calm. No one must know this was anything but a routine visit in the course of her social day. Easier said than done given the weight in the bottom of her reticule. 'Perhaps just my…surprise at finding you here. I didn't see your carriage in the street.'

'It being such a lovely day, I decided to walk,' Barrington told her. 'A brisk walk is always good for clearing the mind.'

'So I've heard,' Anna murmured, wishing desperately for something that might clear hers. 'Julia, how rude you must think me. I greeted Sir Barrington without even acknowledging you.'

'No apologies are necessary, my dear,' Julia assured her with a smile. 'You probably came, hoping to have a cosy chat, and were surprised at encountering our mutual friend. I would have been similarly nonplussed.'

'You are too kind in your forgiveness. But how well you look today.' Anna flicked a cautious glance in Barrington's direction. 'Am I to hope you've had news concerning your necklace?'

'In fact, Sir Barrington and I were just talking about it.'

'Really?' Anna felt her heart skip a beat. 'What did he say?'

'I was about to inform the baroness,' Barrington said smoothly, 'that I am following up on several leads and hope to have an answer for her very soon.'

Anna pasted a smile on her lips. 'How encouraging.'

'Yes, isn't it?' Julia said happily. 'At this point, the only thing that matters is recovering the necklace. I really don't care who took it—'

'You don't? I mean…it's important that we know who *did* take it, of course,' Anna said as two pairs of eyes turned to stare at her. 'But surely its safe return is the more important issue.'

'It is to me,' Julia said. 'I was going to tell Sir Barrington that I won't press charges if he feels that might encourage the thief to return the necklace to me intact.'

'Oh, but that is exceedingly generous of you,' Anna said, aware that matters were improving by the minute.

Or were until Barrington said, 'It *is* generous of you, Baroness, but I doubt the authorities will agree. A law has been broken. Someone must be made to pay.'

'But surely if Julia does not wish to press charges, there is no need for the authorities to be involved,' Anna said, annoyed at his interference.

'As I said, a crime has been committed and retribution must

be made. I suspect the baroness's wishes will be taken into account, but I cannot guarantee they will be honoured.'

Anna abruptly stood up, her stomach twisting. 'Julia, will you excuse me for a moment?'

'Of course, Anna, but are you feeling all right? You've gone dreadfully pale.'

'Have I?' Anna clutched at her reticule. 'Perhaps it's the heat. I am feeling a bit faint.'

'Then you must lie down.' Julia immediately got to her feet. 'I would suggest my room—'

'Oh, yes, that would be perfect!'

'Except that I have workmen repapering all the bedrooms,' Julia finished. 'I fear you would have no solitude at all.'

'No, really, that would be fine,' Anna assured her. 'I just need to lie down for a moment—'

'Then you must lie here on the sofa,' Barrington interrupted, getting to his feet. 'And I shall leave the two of you to some quiet conversation.'

'No, please, that isn't necessary,' Anna said, seeing her carefully thought-out plan disintegrating. With workmen in the bedrooms and people coming and going, she wouldn't have a hope of secreting the necklace in Julia's bedroom without being seen. 'I hate to see you leave on my account.'

'Rest assured, I was preparing to depart when you arrived,' Barrington said with a smile. 'I only dropped by to apprise the baroness of my progress. But I do hope the next time we meet you are feeling more like your old self.'

Wondering if she would ever feel like her old self again, Anna murmured, 'Yes, I'm quite sure I shall be fully recovered by then.'

'If you will wait for me at the front door, Sir Barrington,' Julia said, 'I'll fetch that list of names you asked for. Anna, will you be all right on your own for a few minutes?'

'Yes, of course,' Anna said, fighting back disappointment

as she sank down on the sofa. 'I shall just…lie here and wait for you.'

She was aware of Barrington lingering in the doorway, but didn't have the courage to look back at him. The man was too observant by half. Anna was terrified of what he might read in her eyes. As it was, she felt the necklace glowing like a beacon in her hands. But what was she to do with it now? She couldn't take it away again. Not with the clock ticking on her father's exposure. She had to make sure Julia found the necklace today. And if she couldn't safely get upstairs, she would just have to leave the necklace somewhere in here. But where?

The moment the door closed, Anna sprang to her feet and started searching for a likely place. It couldn't be somewhere immediately visible or Julia would wonder why she hadn't seen it before. But if it was too well hidden, she wouldn't find the necklace at all and the point of the exercise was to put it somewhere that it *would* be found.

Then, Anna spotted it—a large palm standing by the half-open French door. If the necklace was found in the branches, it could be suggested that during his escape, the thief had clumsily dropped it and it had landed in the tree. It was feeble, Anna admitted, but at the moment she had nothing better. And she was fast running out of time. She *had* to make sure the necklace was found in Julia's house *today*.

With that in mind she moved towards the palm, scanning for a likely branch. The necklace was too heavy to be supported by the uppermost branches, but it would be obscured if it was dropped directly into the base. She could, of course, put the bulk of it in the base and leave part of it trailing out…

Risking another glance at the door, Anna unfastened her reticule and reached in for the necklace. She would try it in several places and leave it in the one that looked best. Unfortunately, one of the claws holding the centre diamond was tangled in the fabric, causing her to waste precious seconds extricating it. Finally, it came free and, with infinite care, Anna leaned forwards to place it amongst the thicker branches lower down on the trunk. She tried to arrange it in a manner that made it look as though it had fallen, but the dashed thing kept bending the branches and falling into the base.

And then, the unthinkable happened. Hearing a movement behind her, Anna turned—and blanched.

Sir Barrington Parker was standing by the door, watching her.

Chapter Eleven

Damnation! Caught red-handed—and by the last person on earth she could afford to be caught by!

Seconds dragged by like treacle in winter. Barrington didn't say a word, but she could tell from the look on his face that this wasn't going to be good.

Then Julia's voice, saying, 'Sir Barrington, where are you?'

Anna gasped—and in that split second, Barrington moved. Launching himself across the room, he pushed her aside and scooped the necklace out of the palm, dropping it into an inside pocket of his coat. Barely had it disappeared than the drawing-room door opened and Julia walked in. 'Ah, there you are, Sir Barrington,' she said in surprise. 'I thought you were going to wait for me by the front door.'

'I was until I suddenly remembered there was something I wished to ask Lady Annabelle,' Barrington said, as calmly as though he had been sitting in one of the chairs reading a magazine. 'So I came back and found her up and moving around.'

Julia glanced at her friend. 'Are you feeling better, Anna? Your colour certainly seems to have returned.'

In point of fact, Anna's face felt like it was on fire. 'I am, thank you, Julia. It must have been…the tea.'

'I'm so glad. I've always sworn by it as a restorative. Here is the information you wanted, Sir Barrington,' Julia said, handing him a folded piece of parchment. 'I hope it helps.'

'I have a feeling it will go a long way towards solving the case,' Barrington said, remarkably composed in light of what had just happened. He turned and gave Anna a bow, nothing on his face to indicate that he had just found her depositing a stolen necklace into the heart of an ornamental palm. 'I'm quite sure I will be seeing you again very soon, Lady Annabelle.'

Far too soon, Anna reflected after he left. She had botched the job as badly as it was possible to botch it. She could only imagine what was going through Sir Barrington's head at that moment.

In point of fact, Barrington had so many thoughts running through his head he hardly knew where to begin. Lady Annabelle Durst had come into the baroness's house in possession of the missing sapphire-and-diamond necklace. She had been attempting to hide it in the base of the palm tree when he had unexpectedly walked back into the room and caught her.

Who was she trying to protect? An unusual question given what he had just seen, but in truth, the possibility of *her* having stolen the necklace had never crossed his mind. She had absolutely no motive and likewise no opportunity. It was also highly unlikely that she had simply stumbled upon the necklace and gone to the baroness's house intending to return it to its rightful owner. If that had been the case, she would have given it to the baroness the moment she'd walked into the room.

But she hadn't. She had held on to the necklace; upon finding herself alone, she had taken it out of her reticule and tried to conceal it in the base of the palm. A place the baroness *would* eventually have found it, though not, perhaps, today.

Obviously Anna hadn't wanted the baroness to discover that *she* was the one returning it. That would have necessitated a series of explanations that would have been awkward to say the least. But having been caught red-handed, what kind of explanation would she offer *him*?

Barrington found himself looking forward to that discussion.

The next question was where to conduct the interrogation? He couldn't do it at her home. Her brother or Peregrine Rand might be present, and possibly her father as well. Nor could he do it at his own house. If he invited her to call on a matter of business, it might raise questions in other people's minds. But if she wasn't calling on business, it was morally inappropriate for her to be there at all.

For that reason, as soon as Barrington got home, he wrote Anna a note, asking if he might take her for a drive in the park that afternoon. Being a lovely day, he suggested using the open carriage and assured her that, if she wished, his secretary could come along as chaperon. He doubted she would elect to speak in front of her maid, given the delicate nature of what they would be discussing.

Her response came back with equal promptness. Yes, she was available for a drive, and, no, she would not bring her maid. If chaperonage was required, she was happy to have it provided by his secretary, who had been very pleasant to her on the occasion of their last meeting.

Barrington smiled. Obviously the lady had already considered her options. If she was going to speak in front of anyone, she clearly preferred that it be his servant rather than hers.

He called for her at half past four and was not at all surprised to find her waiting for him. She had changed into a carriage gown of rose-coloured silk, the lace bodice threaded with deeper pink ribbons. Her hair was tucked up under another of her wide-brimmed bonnets and she carried a white parasol trimmed with deep pink ribbons. She looked absolutely enchanting—and completely innocent.

Surprising for a woman who had stepped so easily into the role of accomplice to a thief.

'Good afternoon, Sir Barrington,' she said as she walked down the steps to meet him.

'Lady Annabelle.' He smiled as he handed her into the barouche, 'Thank you for agreeing to meet with me.'

'I assumed there was no point in putting it off.'

'None whatsoever.' Barrington climbed in and sat down in the seat opposite. She waited until Sam flicked the whip and set the horses moving, the clatter of their hooves making it difficult for the conversation to be overheard, before she began to speak.

'I suspect you wish to ask me about what happened at Julia's this morning without my family being present for the interrogation. Just as well, since I suspect you intend to ask some rather problematic questions,' she said.

Problematic. An understatement to say the least. 'Shall we start with how you came to be in possession of the baroness's necklace?' he suggested.

'Ah, but I was not in possession of it,' she told him. 'I was walking by the French doors and chanced to look down and there it was! Lodged in the base of the palm.'

'Really. And how do you suppose it came to be there?'

The look she gave him was comprised of equal parts

surprise and disappointment. 'Really, Sir Barrington, is the answer to that not obvious?'

'Not to me.'

'Clearly, the thief dropped it as he was attempting to make his getaway.'

'His...getaway,' he repeated blankly.

'Yes. After he took the necklace from Julia's bedroom,' she said helpfully.

'So he did not make his escape through her bedroom window, but came downstairs to the drawing room and slipped out through the French doors.'

'Precisely.'

'An interesting theory,' Barrington said slowly. 'And plausible, I suppose, had my timing not been such that I opened the door in time to see *you* removing the necklace from your reticule and carefully inserting it *into* the palm.'

'Ah,' Anna said, sitting back. 'How unfortunate. Then it would probably be safe to say that you would find any attempt on my part to make you believe that I found the necklace quite by chance equally unbelievable.'

'No. I believe you *did* find the necklace and probably by chance, but the question of import now is *where* did you find it?' He sat forwards. 'In your brother's room—or your father's?'

He watched her cheeks turn bright red as her mouth dropped open in an exclamation of surprise. 'I cannot imagine why you would say such a thing—'

'For what it's worth,' he interrupted, '*I* think you found it in your father's room.'

She went rigid. 'Why would you say that?'

'Because Rand is still getting over his affair with Lady Yew and hasn't the clarity of mind to plan something like this. Likewise, if your brother had taken the necklace, I suspect he would either have held on to it until things cooled down, or he would have arranged to have it cut into smaller pieces that he could sell more easily. That leaves your father. Who, as it turns out, had both the motive and the opportunity to take it.'

'Motive?' Anna snorted. 'What possible motive could my father have had for stealing Julia's necklace?'

'The same as claimed by so many gentlemen of the *ton*,' Barrington said softly. 'Debt. In your father's case, through losses incurred at the racetrack.'

'How dare you! My father does not bet on horses!'

'Ah, but he does, dear lady. And though he wins more than he loses, he did suffer an unfortunate streak of bad luck last year from which he has been struggling to recover. A necklace like the baroness's would go a long way towards taking him—indeed, your entire family—out of dun territory.'

He knew immediately that what he'd told her had come as a complete shock. She'd obviously had no idea that her father had amassed such staggering debts, so the thought of him stealing a priceless necklace in an effort to clear himself had never occurred to her.

'If what you say is true—and I am not saying for a moment that I believe it is,' Anna said, 'my father would surely have had other ways of raising the money necessary to cover his obligations.'

'If he has, he has not availed himself of them. But let us not deviate from what we are here to discuss,' Barrington said firmly. 'The fact is, *you* came into the baroness's house with her necklace in your reticule, therefore, I have no choice but to ask you *where* you found it and *how* it came to be there. Unless you also wish to be viewed as a suspect.'

He saw the indecision on her face and knew she was debating as to how much to reveal. To say too much was to condemn someone else. To say too little was to condemn herself.

'Sir Barrington, if I tell you where I found the necklace, would you be willing to let it go?'

'In all honesty, I don't see how I can.'

'But you heard what Julia said. She is willing to drop all charges as long as the necklace is returned.'

'I understand that. But without a logical explanation as to *why* it was taken, we cannot know what the thief had in mind. At the very least, someone is getting away with a crime.' Barrington leaned forwards so that his face was close to hers. 'Someone took that necklace out of the baroness's house, Anna. I need to know who it was and why they did it. Because if their intent was to incriminate the person in whose room it was found, it's possible they may try again when they realise their first attempt has failed.'

'Incriminate!' Barrington saw the brief but unmistakable flash of hope in her eyes. 'Then you're open to the possibility that the person who *took* the necklace may not be the same person in whose room the necklace ended up.'

'I am open to the possibility, yes,' he admitted.

'And to the idea that…foul play may have been involved.'

'Oh, foul play has most definitely been involved, but who was the target? The baroness—or your father?'

His words fell into a strained silence. Barrington didn't have to be a mind reader to know that Anna was waging a silent battle with herself, struggling with how much she should say. Once she told him where the necklace had been found, there was no going back. The guilty party would be exposed and she would have been the one to expose them.

But did she trust him enough to know that he was only interested in finding out the truth? Or would her natural inclination to protect the people she loved stop her from giving him the answers he needed?

'Anna, I'm not out to condemn anyone,' he said softly.

'And what you tell me today will stay between you and me. No one else need know.'

'But you told Julia you would have to contact the authorities—'

'I said that because I couldn't allow her to believe that the perpetrator of the crime would be allowed to go free. Not until I have more information. But if you know something that can put me on the right path, I beg you to make it known.'

He held his breath while she made her decision. It was within her power to compromise the entire investigation. If she refused to tell him where she'd found the necklace, he would have no choice but to make accusations that would ultimately force her hand. And in doing so, he risked sacrificing any chance of ever gaining her good opinion.

Fortunately, something in what he'd said must have got through to her. With a heavy sigh, she said, 'The necklace was in Papa's room. Peregrine found it when he went to retrieve one of my father's watches. The necklace was lying next to it.'

Barrington wasn't sure whether to feel relief or remorse. 'Was it hidden away?'

'No. It was inside a small leather bag, but the bag was in plain sight.'

'So the thief intended that it be found easily,' Barrington said, his mind working. 'Does your father know you found it?'

Anna shook her head. 'Papa went to the country three days ago. He knows nothing about any of this.'

'Then we have no choice but to wait for his return to ask him about it. Either way, you must prepare yourself for the fact that word may leak out about the necklace having been found in his possession.'

'But it can't!' Anna said urgently. 'Papa would be disgraced!'

'I will do whatever I can to keep this quiet, Anna, but other people are involved and we have no control over what they might say. If the necklace was planted in your father's things, someone obviously wished to make trouble for him. The only way they can do that is by spreading rumours about where it was found. All *we* can do is work at uncovering the truth as quickly as possible,' Barrington said.

'But if you *believe* him innocent—'

'What *I* believe has nothing to do with it. Opinions are just that. To unerringly affix blame, I must have proof.'

'Then *find* the proof, Barrington,' Anna urged. 'Do whatever you have to, but find it. There is no question that my father is innocent.'

'May I point out that you were equally convinced of Mr Rand's innocence when it came to the charges levelled against him?' he said gently.

Anna sucked in her breath. 'That was unfair! Peregrine lied to me because he believed himself in love with that wretched woman. The situation with my father is entirely different. He has no reason to lie.'

'From my perspective, no one ever does,' Barrington said softly. 'However, I shall call upon your father when he returns and ask him what he knows about the necklace. His answers will go a long way towards determining where we go from here.'

She was silent for a moment, considering, perhaps, what he had said. 'I want to be there,' she said unexpectedly.

'I beg your pardon?'

'I want to be there when you interview my father. I want to hear what he has to say.'

Foreseeing difficulties she couldn't imagine, he said, 'I strongly advise against it.'

'Why?'

'Because questions will be asked that will be...uncomfortable.'

'For whom?'

'For both of you.'

Anna's face twisted. 'But if they help to uncover the truth, they must be asked. And I wish to be there to bear witness to my father's innocence.'

'Anna—'

'It's settled,' she said. 'I shall send you a note upon his return. And when you reply to it, I want you to make it known that I am to be included. Will you do that for me, Barrington?'

He knew from the stubborn set of her mouth that she wasn't going to back down. She intended to be there to witness her father's absolution. Well, he'd warned her. He could do no more than that. 'I will do this, as long as you know that I do it under duress.'

She smiled, confident of having won the argument. 'I don't need your approval, Barrington. Only your agreement. Besides, I doubt there's anything you can say to my father in my presence that will embarrass me any more than you finding me secreting a stolen necklace in the base of Julia's palm.'

Barrington sat back and sighed. 'I wouldn't be so sure about that.'

Anna was as good as her word. The day after her father's return, she sent Barrington a note advising him that her father was home, and of his agreement to the interview regarding the baroness's necklace. As such, when Barrington called at the house the following evening, Anna met him at the door, saying she had already advised her father of her intention to be present at the interview, given that she was as much involved in the matter as anyone else.

Thankfully, both Hayle and Peregrine were out, though Barrington thought he saw Hayle's carriage pull away just as he arrived. What he might make of it, Barrington didn't know or care. He was far more concerned with what he was about to find out from the earl.

In the drawing room, Anna sat down in the chair by the fireplace and clasped her hands together in her lap. Her expression was composed, but her eyes betrayed the nervousness she was feeling over what was to come.

By comparison, her father's face was untroubled, the result of his being completely unaware of what had transpired in his absence. 'Evening, Parker,' he said as Barrington walked into the room. 'May I offer you something in the way of refreshment?'

'Thank you. I'll have a brandy.'

'I'll join you. Sherry, Anna?'

'Thank you, Papa.'

As Cambermere crossed to the credenza to pour the drinks, Barrington moved closer to where Anna sat. 'This is your last chance,' he said, leaning down to speak quietly in her ear. 'Things are going to be said that *will* be difficult for you to hear. Are you quite sure you wish to stay?'

'Quite sure,' she said, though the slight quiver of her bottom lip told a different story.

Unaccountably annoyed, Barrington turned away. He hated seeing her like this. Hated knowing that the next few minutes were going to be even more difficult than what she had already endured. But there was no easy way of asking the earl what he must; while he wished there was some way of comforting Anna, he realised it was neither his place nor his right to do so. A fiancé or a husband could offer comfort. Not a man charged with finding out the truth about a crime in which her father might or might not be implicated.

'So, Anna tells me you've news about the baroness's

necklace,' the earl said, handing Barrington his brandy. 'Is it good news or bad?'

'A bit of both, I'm afraid. Your good health, my Lord,' Barrington said, raising his glass. 'Lady Annabelle.'

He saw the delicate colour in her cheeks as she tipped back her glass and wondered if it was the potency of the sherry or the unwitting caress in his voice when he'd spoken her name. He'd have to be more careful about that in the future.

Thankfully, the earl seemed oblivious. 'Well, what have you to tell us?'

'The good news,' Barrington began, 'is that the necklace has been found.'

'Has it, by Jove! Excellent!' There was no mistaking the relief in the earl's voice. 'Jul—that is, the baroness will be very pleased. Where did you find it?'

'That, I'm afraid, is the bad news.' Barrington felt Anna's eyes on him, but purposely kept his gaze on her father. 'The necklace was found in your bedroom.'

'My *bedroom*?' There was a moment of stunned silence as Cambermere's smile gave way to a look of utter confusion. 'You found Julia's necklace in this house…in *my* room?'

'Actually, Peregrine found it,' Anna said unhappily.

Her father turned to stare at her in bewilderment. 'And would you care to tell me what Peregrine was doing in my room?'

'He was looking for your watch.'

'My watch.'

'Yes. Edward said you had asked him to take it in for repair.'

'Yes, I did. But I asked Edward, not Peregrine.'

'But Edward had to go out, so he asked Peregrine to take it instead,' Anna said quickly. 'Edward told him where the watch was and when Peregrine went to get it, he found…the necklace.'

'The necklace was in my *wardrobe*?'

Unhappily, Anna nodded. 'In a leather bag next to your watch.'

'But that's impossible!' Cambermere said. 'The last time I saw that necklace, it was around Julia's throat. You were both there, at the dinner party.'

'Then you have no idea how the necklace came to be in your room?' Barrington asked slowly.

'I no more know how it came to be in *my* house than how it came to be taken from the baroness's.' The earl's expression hardened. 'I understood that was *your* job, Parker.'

The note of accusation was unmistakable, but Barrington merely inclined his head. Now came the hard part. 'It was reported to me that someone saw you take the necklace from the baroness's bedroom while she lay sleeping.'

Anna's complexion paled. *'Wh-what?'*

The earl was furious. 'How dare you, sir!'

'Sorry, Cambermere. I'm only repeating what I was told,' Barrington said calmly.

'I don't care what you were told! It's a damned lie!'

'Do you deny being alone with the baroness in her bedroom?' Barrington pressed.

Upon hearing Anna's muffled exclamation, the earl hissed, 'Damn it, man! *Must* we talk about this in front of my daughter?'

Barrington glanced at Anna, aware that her face had gone as red as the glass globes over the lamps. He'd known it would, but it was too late to do anything about it now. 'She asked to be present for the interview and since this is a critical point in the investigation, discussion of it cannot be avoided. If you wish to leave, Lady Annabelle, you are welcome to do so. I will call you back at a more appropriate time.'

'Can't imagine there *being* a more appropriate time

for something like this,' Cambermere muttered under his breath.

But Anna shook her head, struggling to overcome her embarrassment. 'No, I'll stay. And I am sorry, Papa. It isn't Sir Barrington's fault that I'm here. I insisted on being present during his questioning and I am truly sorry if my being here causes you embarrassment. But it is necessary that we get to the truth of the matter.'

'Lady Annabelle isn't mistaken, my Lord,' Barrington said. 'And I regret that the nature of the question had to be so indelicate. But while what you and Baroness von Brohm do behind closed doors is your own business, you would do well to remember that servants talk.'

'Servants!' Cambermere barked. 'Are you telling me it was a servant who claimed to have seen me take the necklace?' At Barrington's brief nod, the earl's face darkened ominously. 'Give me his name, Parker. Give me his name and I'll get to the bottom of this myself. I'm damned if I'll have my name dragged through the mud like some three-legged dog dragging a stick. Whoever told you they saw me take Julia's necklace was telling a lie. An out-and-out lie!'

'Be that as it may, it isn't a lie that you've spent time alone with the baroness.'

The earl coloured. 'No.'

'Then it's possible a servant may have seen you in her bedroom—'

'Perhaps it *is* best I leave.' Anna abruptly stood up, glancing apologetically at Barrington. 'I'm sure it would be easier for my father to talk about this if I weren't here—'

'No, wait,' the earl said. 'Wait.' He cleared his throat, then reached for his glass. After downing the contents, he set the empty glass on the table. 'This isn't the kind of thing one normally discusses in front of…one's children. Especially one's unmarried daughter. But it would be naïve of me to think that…word of this might not leak out and that you wouldn't eventually come to hear of it.' He glanced at his daughter and sighed. 'Yes, I've spent time alone with Julia. We've come to care for one another. I haven't tried to hide that from you, Anna. And given that we are both widowed, we felt there was no harm in…moving forward with our relationship. Can you understand that, my dear?'

Anna nodded, and though Barrington could see that she was still having a hard time meeting her father's eyes, her voice was steady when she said, 'I understand. And I don't blame you, Papa. But it doesn't make things any easier.'

'No, it doesn't,' Barrington agreed. 'Because the question remains, why would a servant make up a story about having seen you take the necklace if there was no truth to it? What would they stand to gain by such a lie? And how do you explain the necklace turning up in your room?'

'I can't explain it.' The earl shook his head, his anger spent. 'I have no answer for any of your questions, Parker. I sincerely wish I did.'

'I think it's someone trying to stir up mischief,' Anna said. 'Someone who holds a grudge against you. The maid, perhaps?'

'I questioned the young lady at length,' Barrington said. 'But she said she doesn't know you and I believe that she's telling the truth, so I doubt a grudge enters into it. Might it be someone to whom you owe money wanting to make things… unpleasant for you?'

The earl's head snapped up. 'What do you know about that?'

'Only that you had a run of bad luck at the track last year,' Barrington said quietly, 'and that you have vowels outstanding to Lords Greening, Featherstone and Blakeley. Your son has also amassed rather staggering debts thanks to losses incurred at the faro table. Debts you have also been endeavouring to pay off.'

He heard Anna's sharp intake of breath. 'Is this true, Papa? Do you and Edward truly owe so much?' When he reluctantly nodded, Anna said, 'Why didn't you tell me?'

'Because it doesn't concern you,' Cambermere growled, though not unkindly. He glanced at Barrington and sighed. 'I can't deny that there are those to whom I owe money, but the debts are not so large that someone need go to these lengths. I assured Greening and Featherstone they would have their money by the end of the month, and Blakely a month or two after.'

'And your son's debts?'

'With luck, they'll be paid off by the end of the year.'

'But what have debts to do with the baroness's necklace being found in Papa's room?' Anna asked.

'They provide a reasonable motive for theft,' Barrington explained. 'A gentleman's debts are seldom a well-kept secret. One has only to read the morning papers. I found out without any difficulty that your father's and brother's combined debts tally to well over sixty thousand pounds.'

Anna blanched. 'Dear God, so *much*!'

'You needn't sound so horrified, it isn't as large as that,' her father muttered. 'I've managed to pay off thirty thousand of it already.'

'Unfortunately, your son accumulated another twenty this past week,' Barrington said quietly.

The earl was aghast. 'Twenty thousand pounds—in *five days*?'

'I'm sorry to be the one to break the bad news to you, Cambermere, but you would have found out soon enough. And I suspect that whoever took the necklace knew of those debts and planned on using them as the justification behind your stealing the necklace.'

The earl seemed to age ten years as he stood there. 'I can't believe that someone would go to these lengths to incriminate me. But I stand by what I said. I did *not* steal Julia's necklace. I wouldn't dream of doing such a cowardly, selfish thing. To think how it would hurt her...' He transferred his gaze to Barrington. 'I don't suppose you have any idea who *is* behind this?'

'Not yet,' Barrington said, 'but I will find out.'

'And until you do, I'm the guilty party,' the earl said heavily.

'You are *not*, Papa!' Anna cried. 'We all know you didn't take the necklace.'

'You and I know that, my dear, but I'll wager Parker has his doubts. And so he should. Right now, the finger of blame is pointing squarely at me.'

'Only as a result of circumstantial evidence.'

'No. As a result of the fact that I was supposedly seen taking the necklace by a member of Julia's staff, and that the said necklace was found in my room by a member of my own family,' her father said bluntly. 'The proof could hardly be less circumstantial.' He clasped his hands behind his back and glanced at the man standing opposite. 'Well, what do you intend to do?'

'For now, I shall tell the baroness that I know where the necklace is, but that I am not at liberty to say where, or to reveal the identity of the person who took it.'

'She's bound to ask,' Anna said.

'Yes, but I am not required to give her an answer. I'll tell her it may compromise the integrity of the investigation.'

'Decent of you, Parker,' the earl said gruffly. 'I'd hate having Julia think she couldn't trust me.'

It was that more than anything else that convinced Barrington of Cambermere's innocence. If a man was that worried about what a woman thought of him, he wouldn't knowingly do something that would destroy his chances of having a relationship with her.

And yet, as he walked home after the interview, Barrington thought about his feelings for Anna and realised he was guilty of doing just that. He was conducting an investigation into the theft of an extremely valuable necklace and, given the lack of any other viable culprit, was still holding her father up as the leading suspect—and earning Anna's resentment as a result.

But *was* Cambermere guilty? Barrington's gut told him no, but he'd met skilful liars before. Men who swore on their children's heads that they were good family men who never lied, cheated, or stole so much as a crust of bread. All the while they were beating their wives half-senseless and mugging old men for brass buttons.

Oh, yes, he knew all about the complexities of deceit. Lies rolled off the tongues of the rich as easily as they did off the tongues of the poor. He'd even come across men he'd *wanted* to believe. Upright, likeable men whom he had respected until he'd found out what they were beneath the polished manners and charming smiles.

Good men turned bad, Barrington called them. Whether by chance or inclination, somewhere along the line they'd made the wrong choices. Some were driven by greed, others by desperation. And once a man faltered, it was only a matter of time until he did so again; the crime becoming a little darker, the stakes a little higher.

Had the earl faltered? Or was it all a carefully constructed plot to make it look as though he had? That was the ultimate question. And until Barrington ascertained who stood to gain by the earl's downfall, the final answer would remain just beyond his grasp. Tantalisingly close, yet agonisingly far.

Chapter Twelve

Anna had no particular desire to pay a call on Julia the following day. Given what she knew about the necklace—*and* about her father's relationship with Julia—she feared it would be both embarrassing and awkward. But when she received Julia's beautifully written note asking her to visit, Anna knew it would be churlish to refuse. The woman's spirits were desperately low as it was. How could she possibly be so cruel as to avoid her now, simply because she had no idea how to act?

And so she went, determined to appear as positive as possible. After all, there was really no reason for Julia to talk about the necklace. She knew the investigation was ongoing and that Barrington would inform her of any new leads the moment they became available. And she certainly wouldn't bring up her relationship with Anna's father. Married or widowed ladies did not talk to single ladies about matters pertaining to the bedroom, so there was no reason to think she would bring that up.

No, Anna was quite sure she was making a mountain out of a molehill. She and Julia would pass their time talking about the new books they were reading, or the poetry recital at Mrs McInley's, or what they planned to wear to Lady Schuster's masquerade a week from Friday. Safe, comfortable topics all.

Unfortunately, all thoughts of comfort fled when Anna walked into the drawing room and found, not just Julia seated on the blue velvet settee, but her brother, Edward, as well.

'Edward! What are you doing here?' Anna exclaimed.

'Am I not allowed to pay morning calls the same as everyone else?'

'I thought you did not care for the custom,' she said bluntly.

Her brother's handsome face curved into an angelic smile. 'A man's likes and dislikes can change given the right motivation.'

'Pray do not take him to task him, Anna,' Julia said quickly. 'He has been most diverting company. He bade me speak about Vienna and I was amazed at how homesick I became. Then, we started talking about you—'

'Me?' Anna levelled a sardonic glance at her brother. 'I can't imagine what the two of you would have to say about me.'

'Can you not?' Edward said innocently. 'I would have thought the possibilities endless. However, in this instance, we were talking about Sir Barrington Parker and the fact that he seems rather taken with you. He calls frequently at the house and I understand you have driven with him in the park. Although,' Edward added with a smile, 'I think he calls as much to see Father and Peregrine as he does Anna, so I suppose I could be mistaken as to which member of the family he is the most interested in.'

'Perhaps it would be safe to say that Sir Barrington has become a good friend of the family,' Julia said, obviously sensing an edge of conflict in the air.

'You could say that.' Edward turned to smile at his sister. 'As you already know, Parker is something of an expert when it comes to investigating the dark doings of others. And unfortunately, my family is no stranger to infamy. Peregrine, for example, was foolish enough to involve himself in a sordid affair with the Marchioness of Yew—'

'I'm sure the baroness has no desire to hear about that, Edward,' Anna said coldly.

'Why not? I found it extremely amusing,' her brother replied unrepentantly. 'Can you imagine, Baroness, an unsophisticated country boy coming to London for the first time and believing himself of interest to the beautiful Lady Yew? In fact, he even went so far as to claim that she was in love with him and that she had every intention of leaving her husband to be with him.'

'Really?' Julia flicked an uncertain glance in Anna's direction. 'I had not heard.'

'It happened before you arrived in London,' Anna said tightly. 'And my brother has no business speaking of it. Apologies have been offered and given that the marquess is agreeable to putting the matter behind him, I see no reason why my brother should not do the same.'

It was an awkward moment and Anna could practically feel the tension vibrating in the air. But she was damned if she was going to let Edward embarrass her in front of Julia with sly remarks about Barrington or inflammatory ones about Peregrine.

Unfortunately, her brother was a master at turning the other cheek. 'How unfortunate it is that social calls must be of such limited duration, Baroness. I fear my time is up. But I did enjoy talking to you about Vienna. As you say, it is a beautiful city and I look forward to seeing it again, now that travel around Europe is so much easier.'

'You must be sure to visit Schonbrunn Palace,' Julia said,

happy for the change of subject. 'It is one of the loveliest places on earth.'

'If you recommend it, I will be sure to include it in my travels. Perhaps we might even visit it together one day.' Edward rose and bowed over her hand. 'Until tomorrow.' Then, straightening, he nodded at his sister. 'Anna.'

Anna inclined her head, not quite in dismissal, but not far off—and Edward knew it. His eyes cooled as he smiled down at her. 'You may be interested in knowing that just before you arrived, I was telling the baroness that I had stumbled upon some information with regards to her necklace. I expect to have more news very soon.'

He left the room with an elegant bow, but in the silence that followed, Anna felt as though a hand was closing around her throat. *He knew about the necklace. And he was going to tell Julia her father was the one who'd taken it.* There could be no other explanation for what he'd just said. And in exposing their father as the thief, Anna knew it would destroy any chance he might have had for a future with Julia. Worse, it would go a long way towards establishing Edward in a more favourable position with her—which meant she had to convince Barrington not only to tell Julia about the necklace, but to return it to her as soon as possible. Before any more harm could be done…

'Anna, are you all right?' Julia enquired softly.

Anna looked up, aware that her worries must have been reflected on her face. 'Fine. It's just that Edward and I are not on the best of terms these days.'

'No, I thought not. Never mind, I'm told it often happens between siblings,' Julia said, making an attempt at light-heartedness. 'But I am surprised Lord Hayle and Mr Rand are not on better terms. I would have thought they'd be good company for one another, being so close in age.'

'I believe that was my father's hope as well, but it is not to be,' Anna admitted with a sigh. 'They are two very different men and they do not see eye to eye on anything.'

'How unfortunate,' Julia murmured. 'Your brother has been so kind to me. He's called several times this week to see how I was faring and to ask if there was anything I needed. When I enquired as to how your father went on, he said it was unlikely he would call, given the nature of the investigation surrounding my necklace. I didn't know what he meant by that.' Julia chewed thoughtfully on her lower lip. 'Or what he meant when he said he was following up on some leads of his own.'

'I don't know either,' Anna said, hoping she sounded convincing. So, Edward was paying regular calls on Julia and dropping hints as to his father's involvement in the theft. What a dutiful son, she thought cynically.

She *had* to talk to Barrington. If Julia was to hear from Edward that their father had taken the necklace—

'Ah, Jones, there you are,' Julia said as a maid came in with the tea tray. 'I was just about to ring.'

'Beg pardon for the delay, ma'am,' the girl said. 'Cook wasn't able to find the right jam.' She put the tray down hard and one of the sandwiches fell to the floor. 'Oh, I'm ever so sorry.'

'That's all right,' Julia said as the girl bent to retrieve it. 'That will be all.'

The girl's cheeks went as bright as cherries, and hastily stuffing the fallen sandwich into her apron pocket, she bobbed a curtsy and left.

'My apologies, Anna,' Julia said. 'The girl is new and sadly in need of training.'

'What happened to your other maid?'

'Unfortunately, Miss Smith left to attend to her sick mother. At least, that's what she told me, though I wonder if there might not be a man involved,' Julia confided. 'I noticed a definite change in her over the last little while, both in manner and in appearance. She lost weight and didn't seem as competent at her job. When I asked her if she was all right, she assured me she was, but given that I wasn't about to pry into her personal life, I left it at that. But I was sorry to lose her. It's not easy finding good staff.'

No, it wasn't, Anna reflected, but neither was finding a good position. Were Miss Smith's reasons for leaving as simple as Julia made them out to be? Anna hadn't forgotten the sight of her brother and the maid locked in a passionate embrace. Had Miss Smith been caught in the arms of another guest and the discovery forced Julia's hand? If the maid had allowed Edward to kiss her, who was to say that she hadn't allowed other men to do the same—or worse?

Still, Anna knew it was none of her concern. Servants no more appreciated their affairs being discussed by their betters, than those above stairs liked thinking their problems were being discussed by those below. As such, she wasn't at all sorry when the conversation veered back to the upcoming masquerade and to the elaborate costume Julia was planning to wear. They spent the next half-hour happily discussing hairstyles, with neither Edward nor the missing necklace being mentioned again.

It wasn't often that Barrington found himself in a quandary. His nature was such that when he was given a task, he set about resolving it as efficiently as possible. That was the manner in which he had approached the Marquess of Yew's request that he find his wife's latest lover, and the manner in which he had expected to solve the case of the baroness's missing necklace.

But when faced with the daughter of the prime suspect *insisting* that he return the necklace *before* the identity of the thief could be confirmed, Barrington realised that resolution was going to be neither quick nor easy.

That was his dilemma as he stood beside her at the Billinghams' soirée two nights later and the reason for his preoccupation. Because by doing what Anna asked, he risked compromising the entire investigation. There were always a series of steps that needed to be followed. Questions that had to be asked. Leads that had to be investigated. Following the steps in order helped ensure that he didn't miss a vital piece of information.

Doing what Anna suggested threatened to throw everything off. It was like closing the barn door after the horse had bolted. Granted, he was relieved to have the necklace back in one piece, but it wasn't just a simple matter of handing it back to the baroness now and calling the case closed. He had to find out what had prompted the theft in the first place. He'd meant what he'd said when he'd told Anna that if the thief found out his first attempt to discredit the earl had failed, he might well try again.

But how could he not try to accommodate her when doing so would make her so happy—

'Barrington?'

Her voice, gently insistent, recalled him to the moment. Guiltily, he looked down to find her watching him. 'Forgive me, Anna, I was following a train of thought.' They had slipped into the comfortable habit of calling each other by their first names when they were alone and Barrington was glad of it. Somehow, it lessened the distance between them. Now, as he gazed down at her, he tried not to notice how glorious she looked in the beautiful cream-coloured gown, the soft swell of her breasts rising provocatively above the edging of fine lace. 'You were saying something about your brother?'

'I was saying that I'm afraid he's going to expose my father in front of Julia,' Anna whispered. 'Why else would he have said what he did?'

'I don't know.' Barrington tried focusing his attention on her face, but that didn't work either. Her smile captivated him, her mouth entranced him. And her lips…her lips were an invitation to seduction—

'Barrington, are you even listening to me?' she accused.

'Yes, of course.' He dragged his mind back with considerable effort. 'What makes you think your brother would turn on your father in such a way?'

'I'm not saying he would. But you said yourself, there's been tension between them of late and that's why I need you to return the necklace to Julia as soon as possible. If she has it in her hands, she won't believe that my father had anything to do with its theft, no matter what kind of rumours she hears.'

'Why would she believe your father guilty of having taken the necklace if she *didn't* have it in her hands?' Barrington asked logically. 'Has she any reason to doubt your father's integrity?'

'No, but Edward can be very persuasive when he wants to be. If he wished to put my father in a bad light with Julia, he is entirely capable of doing so. And I didn't like the way he was looking at her. It was far too…familiar. And Julia admitted that he had been to see her several times since the theft of the necklace.'

Barrington let his gaze travel around the room, his thoughts occupied with what she had just said. So, the son was paying court to the woman his father was in love with and making no attempt to hide it. It wasn't a pleasant situation for anyone and it had the potential to cause considerable harm. 'Anna, I understand your concern—'

'No, I don't think you do. You don't know my brother the way I do. You don't how vindictive he can be.'

Having born witness to Hayle's temper during the fencing match, Barrington was strongly tempted to disagree, but, equally aware that voicing an opinion would only stir up another hornet's nest, he said, 'Very well. If it means that much to you, I will return the necklace to the baroness tomorrow.'

'You will?'

'Yes, but you are to tell no one that I've done so, and I shall counsel the baroness to do the same. The integrity of the investigation *must* be maintained—as much as it is now possible to do so.'

Anna glanced down at the floor, but when she raised her head and smiled at him, Barrington caught his breath. He had been the recipient of a thousand smiles, but none had ever affected him to the degree hers did. 'Thank you, Barrington. I am now and for ever in your debt.'

And you are now and for ever in my heart.

The sentiment came unbidden, and Barrington stood motionless, the realisation having caught him totally unawares. *He was in love with her.* He had no idea when it had happened. All he knew was that he wanted to pull her into his arms and whisper a thousand secret longings in her ear. To take her to his bed and make love to her until they were both weak and trembling. To obliterate every thought from her mind that didn't involve him.

But he couldn't do any of those things because nothing had really changed. Anna was still who she was and he was still who he was. Their situations hadn't altered. Only the way he thought of her…

'Parker! A word in private, if you don't mind.'

The crisp, imperious voice had Barrington turning around in surprise. 'Good evening, Colonel.' Curious. Tanner never spoke to him when other people were around. He wondered what could have prompted the change. 'I was just finishing speaking to Lady Annabelle.' He turned back and bowed over her hand. 'Would you excuse me?'

'Of course. But we will speak again soon?'

He saw the glimmer of hope in her eyes and felt it echoed within his heart, though for entirely different reasons. 'You may be sure of it.'

She departed in a whisper of silk, the sweet scent of gardenias lingering in the air. Barrington didn't follow her progress across the room because he knew better than to display an interest in her here, where all the world could see. But he felt her absence keenly. 'You wished to speak to me, Colonel?'

'Damn right I wished to speak to you. I want to know if you've found Elizabeth!'

'I have, but I fear you will not be happy with what I am about to tell you.'

'Why not?'

'Because it turns out that Miss Paisley has come under someone else's protection.'

'The devil you say!' The Colonel's bushy white eyebrows drew together. 'You mean…she's left me?'

'I'm afraid so,' Barrington replied gently.

'But why? I gave her everything she asked for: gowns, trinkets, pretty ribbons for her hair.'

'Can you think of any other reason she might have left?'

The Colonel's cheeks coloured. 'I never asked her to do anything disrespectful, if that's what you're suggesting. Wouldn't consider such a thing.'

Barrington studied the face of the man before him and felt a genuine stab of pity. Tanner obviously had feelings of affection for Miss Paisley, but if *she* didn't care about him in return…

'I have no answers as to why she left, Colonel,' he said quietly. 'I can only tell you that she did.'

'Who is he?'

'I'd rather not say.'

'Why not? That's why I engaged you, isn't it?' Tanner said gruffly.

'No, you engaged me to find out where Miss Paisley was and if she was safe. That's what I've done. There's really no value in my telling you anything more than that.' Besides, he would no doubt find out soon enough on his own, Barrington reflected. The movement of mistresses between society gentlemen was not a closely guarded secret.

The Colonel knew it, too. He gazed across the room, disappointment evident on his face. 'So you don't think she will come back?'

'I have no reason to believe she will, no.'

The older man nodded. 'Right. Well then, I suppose that's an end to it. At least I know she's all right.' He cleared his throat, rocked back and forth on the balls of his feet. 'Appreciate you taking it on, Parker.'

'I'm sorry the news wasn't better, Colonel.'

Tanner nodded, but walked away before Barrington had a chance to say anything more. It was clear that Miss Paisley's defection had hurt him and Barrington was again moved to wonder what had prompted her to leave. The Colonel had taken her off the streets and given her a place to live, paid for the clothes on her back and made sure there was food on her table—yet she had still walked away.

Why? What prompted a woman like that to leave a man who had been so good to her? The arrival of a wealthier lover? One with a loftier title? Surely that could be of no consequence to a woman like Elizabeth Paisley. She was a lady's maid turned prostitute, not a blushing débutante looking for a husband. And while Hayle was certainly the younger man, Barrington doubted he would have given her more in the way of jewels or clothes than the Colonel. It was quite possible he'd given her less, believing that mistresses were twenty to the dozen. Tanner, being older and wiser, knew more about life and love…

Love. Oh, dear God, surely that wasn't what had lured Elizabeth Paisley away? The misplaced belief that Hayle might offer her more than just a bed? That he had genuine feelings for her?

As unlikely as it seemed, Barrington knew it wasn't an impossibility. If Miss Paisley had any degree of education, she would know more of the world than the hardened doxies who made their livings on the streets and might well believe that such things happened. According to Tanner, she *had* come from a decent family, only to fall on hard times when her parents had died. She had tried making a living as a lady's maid, but had fallen victim, as so many women did, to the wandering hands of the master and, without the references necessary to obtain another post, had ended up on the streets.

Yes, it was entirely possible that Eliza's move had been prompted by unattainable dreams, Barrington reflected sadly. He'd rather think it was that than something more disturbing. Something that bordered on the devious. Something that was in all ways far less admirable…

Anna stood by the edge of the dance floor and listened to the lilting strains of a waltz. The dance was far less scandalous than when it had first made its appearance in the ballrooms of society, but it was still one of the few that could raise eyebrows. Gentlemen sometimes moved a little too close and, if a mother's watchful eye was turned, a hand might draw a slender waist nearer or hold a lady's hand tighter than was acceptable.

Anna had spent a good deal of time watching the actions of couples on the floor. While it was not advisable for single girls to dance the waltz, there were always those who did and who had required Anna's services not long after. Tonight, however, her thoughts were not on the dancers, but on the situation with her father and her brother, and even more so with the uncomfortable predicament in which she found herself with Barrington.

She knew that by asking him to give the necklace back to Julia, she was asking him to do something that went against his principles, but she was so afraid for her father's reputation that it was more than she could do to withdraw the request. But what damage had it done to her relationship with Barrington? It felt as though they had not been easy with one another for an age. And though she knew they would not have a future together, why, oh, why couldn't she just put him from her mind altogether? This constant thinking about him was wearing her down. Why couldn't she just accept that he was beyond her reach and move on?

Because you want to be the one, whispered the voice inside her head. *The woman he turns to in the darkness of the night. The one who smoothes the lines of worry from his brow, and who makes him forget everything but the sweetness of the moment...*

'Anna, where have you been?' Lydia said, coming up to her. 'I've been looking for you all evening!'

'Why?' Anna said, lingering in dreams. 'Is something wrong?'

'I've just heard the most dreadful thing.' Lydia glanced around, lowered her voice. 'About your father.'

The dreams vanished, destroyed in the rush of returning reality. 'Tell me!'

'Not here.' Taking her arm, Lydia led Anna to a far corner of the room. When she was sure they were beyond anyone's hearing, she said, 'There's a rumour going around that—' she broke off, blushing furiously. 'Oh dear, this isn't at all easy.'

'Please, Lydia. I must know!'

'Yes, of course you must. It's just that…I can't believe he would do something like this.'

'He?'

'Mr Rand.'

'Peregrine?' Anna frowned in confusion. 'I thought you said you'd heard something about my father?'

'I have.' Lydia took a deep breath and said, 'Apparently, someone overheard Mr Rand say that…he'd found the baroness's necklace amongst your father's things.'

'What?' Anna didn't realise how loud she'd spoken until she saw heads begin to turn in their direction. Quickly forcing a smile, she waited for them to look away again before leaning in closer to Lydia. 'There must be some mistake. Peregrine thinks the world of my father. He would *never* do something like this.'

'That's what I thought, too, but I'm just repeating what I heard. And there's more,' Lydia said unhappily. 'Rumour has it that your brother's debts have been paid off and people are wondering where the money came from.'

Anna's first thought was that they had not acted quickly enough. Her second was to wonder how to stem the damage before matters got any worse. 'Who started the rumour?'

'No one seems to know. But it isn't a secret that your father and brother were having trouble meeting their debts. So when word leaked out that the baroness's necklace had been stolen and that she and your father were…well, involved, it was suggested that your father might have seen an easy way out of his financial difficulties. Then when Mr Rand said he'd found the necklace in your father's things, followed by word of your brother's debts being cleared, it only added fuel to the fire.' She broke off, sick at heart. 'I'm so sorry, Anna, but I thought you should know.'

Anna muttered something unrepeatable, apologised to

Lydia, then quickly left the room. She was seldom moved to profanity, but what else could she say when matters kept going so terribly wrong? Peregrine had been discovered in an illicit affair with Lady Yew. Everyone seemed to know that her father and brother were mired in debt. And now rumours were flying that her father was a thief and that a member of his own family had given him up.

It was enough to make a saint turn to the devil!

But even as anger and disbelief swelled at the thought of Peregrine having betrayed her father's secret, common sense told her it couldn't be true. Peregrine would *never* reveal what he had seen. She had been there with him the day he'd found the necklace. She had seen the anguish on his face and known that he'd suffered over that discovery as much as she had.

No, Peregrine wasn't the one who'd started the rumour. Barrington was right; the person who wished her father harm was definitely the one behind all this. The lie was just one more piece in a carefully devised plot to incriminate her father, and whoever had laid the groundwork for this unspeakable crime had done their job well. Her father's reputation couldn't *hope* to survive a constant barrage of rumours and innuendos. He would be destroyed, given the cut direct by those who mattered in society. Even those who might have the courage to defend him risked being cut, and those who believed him guilty would never speak to him again. But there had to be a way of finding out who it was and of exposing him for what he'd done.

Anna thought back over everything Barrington had said. *...a maid in the baroness's house...gone in to check on her mistress....saw him take the necklace...*

So, a maid had seen her father take the necklace. Which maid? The same one Anna had seen kissing her brother in the darkness of the deserted study? A very pretty maid who'd left the baroness's employ shortly after the necklace disappeared—

Anna gasped. Was it possible? She'd seen Edward and the maid together *before* the necklace had disappeared. Then the maid had left and a few days later Anna had discovered that Edward had acquired a new mistress. She'd overheard him talking to one of his friends about a girl named Eliza.

Coincidence—or something more calculated?

Unlike many of his friends, Edward didn't keep his mistresses close at hand. He preferred to put them up in a house on a quiet street south of Regent's Park. Fortunately, Anna had stumbled upon the address one day whilst cleaning out a desk drawer and committed it to memory.

Now, as she stepped out of the carriage onto what was a clearly less than affluent street, she was glad she'd thought to do so. She scanned the row of plates and found Number Nineteen second to last in the row—an unprepossessing brick townhouse with dark shutters and blackened chimney pots.

Paying the driver a guinea to wait, Anna took a deep breath and started towards the door. Her heart was pounding and though part of her wanted to turn around and get back in the cab, curiosity and a need to discover the truth drove her forwards. She raised her hand to the knocker and brought it down sharply, three times.

An older woman wearing a white apron over a stiff black gown opened the door. Her face was hard and unforgiving as she stared down at her caller. 'Yes?'

'Is Miss Smith in?' Anna enquired.

Watching the woman run a critical eye over her appearance, Anna was glad she'd thought to wear the clothes she had. Dressed in a plain gown and pelisse in a nondescript shade of brown, a straw bonnet the style of which was a few years out of date, and leather gloves that were far from new, she resembled nothing so much as a governess or a servant, an assessment clearly shared by the housekeeper. 'What would you be wanting with Eliza?'

'I'd like to talk to her, if I may. We used to work together at Baroness von Brohm's and I was wondering—'

'Justine, is that you?' a voice floated down from the landing. 'How did you get—oh!'

Eliza Smith was halfway down the stairs before she realised that her visitor wasn't who she thought. Her pretty face fell and her smile disappeared. But when she looked at Anna again and recognition dawned, her expression of disappointment changed to one of fear. With a muffled cry, she bolted back up the stairs.

'Miss Smith, wait!' Anna cried. 'I need to talk to you!' She went to move past the housekeeper, but found her way blocked. 'Kindly step aside.'

'I don't think the girl wants to see you,' the woman said.

'Well, I'd like to see her,' Anna said. 'If you'll just let me through…'

It was like trying to move a mountain. The woman wouldn't budge and, given that the doorway wasn't wide enough for Anna to go around her, she was stuck. 'Why won't you let me see her?'

'Because the master said I wasn't to let anyone in and I know better than to disobey,' the woman said. 'He'd have my job, and I've six mouths at home to feed.'

Recognising desperation, Anna stepped back, her eyes narrowing even as her stance straightened. 'How much does your master pay you?'

The woman's cheeks flushed, both as a result of the autocratic tone and by Anna's sudden change in stature. 'That's none of your business.'

'It could be.' Anna opened her reticule and taking out a

coin, held it in front of the woman's face. 'This would feed your family for a month.'

'That's a guinea!'

'It is. And if you let me pass, it's yours.'

'Who are you?' the housekeeper asked, staring at the coin like a hungry dog eyeing a bone. 'Maids and governesses don't carry that kind of blunt.'

'I am neither a lady's maid nor a governess. And I have plenty more of these.'

It was shameless blackmail, but Anna suspected it was the only way she was going to get what she wanted. She needed the woman's co-operation and, if necessary, she was prepared to buy her way into the house. Fortunately, she didn't have long to wait. The housekeeper grabbed the coin and jerked her head in the direction of the stairs.

'Go on then, but be quick about it. Gold won't keep me safe if he comes round and finds I've let you in. Five minutes is all you get!'

Deciding it would have to be enough, Anna ran up the darkened stairway, her soft-soled boots making no sound on the threadbare carpet. Turning right at the landing, she found herself standing in front of a closed door. 'Miss Smith?' she called, trying the handle and finding it locked.

'Go away!'

'Eliza, please! I need to talk to you!'

'I've got nothing to say!'

'That's not true. You can help a lot of people by talking to me,' Anna insisted.

'I don't care about other people,' came the girl's muffled reply. 'Nobody cares about *me*.'

'*I* care,' Anna said. 'And if you'll let me, I'll get you out of here.'

Silence followed her rashly offered promise, leaving Anna to wonder if she'd said the right thing. If this was the girl's only home, she might not be all that anxious to leave. But looking at the water stains in the ceiling, the faded and peeling wallpaper, and the warped floorboards beneath her feet, Anna couldn't help thinking how lowering it must be to come home to this every night.

'Eliza, please!' Seconds were ticking by. Any minute, the housekeeper would appear at the bottom of the stairs, demanding that she leave, and Anna wasn't so naïve as to think she would get a second chance at getting back inside. 'I promise you won't come to any harm. Just open the door.'

Out on the street, Anna heard a vendor raucously hawking his wares. She heard the sounds of children laughing and the clatter of carriage wheels as they rattled past the front door. Normal, everyday sounds—and still the door remained closed. Which meant Anna had no choice. She only had time for one last desperate attempt.

'You won't get away with it, Eliza,' she said quietly against the door. 'I know you took the necklace. And I *will* go to the authorities if you refuse to talk to me.'

Chapter Thirteen

That was all she said. Fear or anger would compel the girl to open the door now because it didn't matter whether the accusations were true or not. A servant accused of stealing from her employer couldn't hope to win her case.

Eliza Smith was obviously smart enough to know that. Moments later, the door opened and she stood silently in the doorway.

Anna caught her breath. The girl facing her now wasn't the same pretty maid who had served her tea at Julia's house. Her once-shining hair hung lank around her small face, her complexion was ashen and there were faint purple shadows on her cheeks and around her beautiful green eyes. Dear God, what had Edward done to her? 'Are you all right?'

'Fine.' The girl lifted her chin, but Anna saw the way her lips trembled. 'What do you want?'

'To ask you a few questions.' Anna made no attempt to move forwards. 'I think you know about what.'

The girl didn't say a word. She simply turned and walked back into the room, every step a reflection of her state of mind. Anna followed, mutely taking in the details of her surroundings. The walls were papered in the same faded maroon silk as in the hallway, the curtains were pale grey and frayed at the edges, and the bed and dressing table… well, she'd seen better furnishings in a boarding school. Her brother obviously hadn't expended any time or money on the upkeep of this house.

'How did you get past Betty?' Eliza asked in a flat voice. 'She was told not to let anyone in.'

'I bribed her,' Anna said, closing the door. 'I wasn't going to leave without seeing you.' She took a few steps into the room, and then stopped. 'What happened to you, Eliza? Those bruises on your face—'

'I fell,' the girl said, abruptly turning away. 'And hit my head on the door.'

'Eliza—'

'It was foolish you coming here,' Eliza said, an element of fear in her voice. 'My gentleman could be back at any time.'

'I know who owns this house, Eliza,' Anna said gently. 'And judging from those bruises, you would do well to get away from him as soon as possible.'

'I can't,' Eliza said, shaking her head. 'He'll kill me.'

'No, he won't,' Anna said. Her brother might be many things, but a murderer wasn't one of them. 'But I need you to tell me the truth about your relationship with Edward and about the baroness's necklace.'

The girl collapsed on to the bed, her dark hair falling forwards. 'I can't!'

'Yes, you can,' Anna sat down beside her. 'If you did nothing wrong, you have nothing to be afraid of.'

'But I *did* do something wrong.' The girl looked up and Anna saw tears forming in the huge green eyes. 'I didn't want to, but he told me it would be all right. That I wouldn't get caught.'

'He being my brother,' Anna clarified.

The girl nodded. 'He told me the baroness had so many other lovely bits of jewellery that she'd never miss that one piece. And he told me he'd protect me if anyone came along asking questions.'

'But if you knew that what you were doing was wrong, why did you do it?'

Eliza stared at the dirty bedcover. 'Because he asked me to. He said that…if he had the necklace, he could sell it and then we'd have the money we needed to run away together.'

The cruelty of the lie stabbed at Anna's heart. 'And you believed him.'

'I loved him,' Eliza said, dragging the back of her hand across her eyes. 'I did from the very first time I saw him. I would have done anything to make him happy. *Anything.*'

'But you must have known it couldn't work between you. What about the difference in your situations?'

'Edward assured me that it didn't matter.' Eliza looked at her and Anna saw the naked hope shining in her eyes even now. 'He said that because I spoke properly and carried myself well, no one would know I wasn't a lady. Especially when I was all dressed up. And I did have nice clothes when I met him.'

Suspecting that the clothes were cast-offs from a previous employer, Anna said, 'You were lucky that your former mistress was so generous.'

Eliza bit her lip, guilt adding to the misery on her face. 'They weren't from an employer, my lady. They were from a gentleman. I did work as a lady's maid, but when the mistress found her son trying to break into my room, she said I'd have to leave and that she wouldn't provide me with references. So I left, and when I couldn't find decent work, I ended up in a brothel.'

Anna sighed. It wasn't an unusual story. Girls in Eliza's

position had very few avenues open to them, even those who, like her, were fortunate enough to have some degree of education or training. 'That must have been very difficult for you.'

'It was horrible,' Eliza said bluntly. 'But, it could have been worse. Mrs Brown, the woman who kept the place, made sure we had good food and there was always medical care if any of the girls needed it. She told me her clients were very particular about that kind of thing and that she couldn't afford to have any of her girls getting sick.'

Anna nodded, knowing how miserable the lives of girls forced into prostitution could be. Even for those who had the good luck to find an establishment where the abbess cared about their welfare, a girl's worth diminished with every year that passed. As her looks faded, so did her value. 'Were you there long?'

'No. I met the Colonel…the gentleman I mentioned…on my first night. He was a kind man. I think he knew how frightened I was and he was…very gentle with me,' Eliza said, avoiding Anna's eyes, though two bright spots of colour stood out on her cheeks. 'Afterwards, he asked me about myself, where I'd come from and if I had any family. I told him I'd been born in Leeds, but that I'd moved to London after my parents died. I explained that I'd been a lady's maid and told him why I'd had to leave. He was quiet for a bit, then he asked me if I might consider working for his wife. Apparently she needed a maid; when I reminded him that I didn't have any references, he said it wouldn't be necessary and that I was to present myself at his house at ten o'clock the following morning.'

'And you were given the position?' At Eliza's nod, Anna said, 'You were exceedingly fortunate.'

'Yes, I was. Of course, there was one small…additional requirement,' Eliza added, again avoiding Anna's eyes.

'That you become his mistress?'

Eliza nodded. 'He said he and his wife hadn't shared a bed in years due to her being so poorly. He asked if he could see me, and when I said I didn't like the idea of him coming to me in the attic, he told me he'd be careful. It was all right for a while, but I think his wife saw the way he looked at me and knew what was going on, so she asked me to leave. She wasn't mean about it. She said she knew her husband kept mistresses, but that she wasn't willing to live with one in her own home.'

That was fair enough, Anna thought. She couldn't imagine *any* woman being happy about seeing the face of her husband's mistress in the mirror every morning as she brushed out her hair or fastened her gown. 'What happened after that?'

'The Colonel felt so bad about my having to leave that he said if I was willing to…continue with the arrangement, he'd put me up in a nice little house and buy me clothes and make sure I had everything I needed. Since I liked him well enough and thought it would be an easy life, I agreed.'

'Yet you left him.'

Eliza began fidgeting with the edge of the bedsheet. 'It was never my intention to be somebody's mistress, my lady. Even though the Colonel wasn't demanding, I didn't feel right about…what I was doing. So one day, I looked through a newspaper he'd left on the dining room table and happened to see an advertisement for a lady's maid. I thought I didn't have much of a chance, but I desperately wanted the position, so I put on the nicest of the gowns he'd given me and wore new gloves and a bonnet so I would look respectable.'

'And you went to see the baroness?' Anna said.

Eliza nodded. 'She was ever so nice. She didn't seem to care that I had no references. She said she liked the way I looked and that I had a nice way about me. She told me what the wages were and said I could start right away. And I did, as Miss Eliza Smith. I thought it would be best to start with a clean slate. I left the Colonel's house that very day.'

'Did you tell him about the position?'

Eliza shook her head. 'I didn't have the heart to. But I only took one of the dresses he bought me, apart from the one I wore to the interview.'

'So you didn't leave the Colonel because of my brother?'

'Oh, no, my lady!' Eliza said quickly. 'The first time I saw Edward was just before the baroness's dinner party. I was on Bond Street, picking up some things for her ladyship when I saw him walking towards me. I remember thinking I'd never seen a more handsome man in my life. I saw him twice more after that, and each time I did, my knees would go weak and I'd feel all quivery inside, as if I was filled with feathers. I'd never felt that way about a man before. Then when he turned up at the baroness's dinner party and I saw him with that other gentleman, I thought I was going to faint dead away.'

'But you didn't,' Anna said drily.

'No. Mr Hansen told me to be off and I had to go. But I was that upset, I couldn't settle to anything, so I went into the study to tidy up. Edward must have seen me and followed me. Then when you came in—' Eliza broke off, her face turning bright red. 'Well, you know what happened.'

Anna did, aware that the sight of her brother and Miss Smith locked in a passionate embrace would stay with her for the rest of her life. 'So you became Edward's mistress,' she prompted.

The girl nodded 'I lived for those moments, my lady. They were the only thing that kept me going. Please don't misunderstand, it wasn't just about *being* with him. Or about the fact he was a gentleman. It was just that…no one had ever made me feel the way he did. No one had ever said…they loved me before.'

Anna felt her heart go out to the girl. Poor Eliza. She was no different than Mercy Banks or Cynthia Wicks…or herself when faced with a man who made her bones melt. Reason and logic flew out the window when rational thought was banished by irrational desire.

Because love wasn't logical. The mistake was in trying to make it so.

'When did things begin to change?' Anna asked, her gaze touching on the bruises.

'After I took the necklace,' Eliza said in a dull, flat voice. 'That's when he stopped talking about us being together. He stopped treating me like a lover—and started treating me like a whore.' She looked up and Anna saw the hopelessness in her expression. 'That's when I saw him for what he really was.'

Anna nodded and resolutely got to her feet. 'You can't stay here any longer, Eliza. It will be safest if you come away with me now.'

'I can't!'

'Yes, you can. Obviously the relationship isn't going to continue if this is how he treats you. Besides, I need you to tell someone the truth about the necklace.'

Eliza's lips were pressed tightly together, her head going from side to side.

'Listen to me,' Anna said firmly. 'There's a rumour going around that my father stole the baroness's necklace. A rumour I have every reason to believe my brother started. And if nothing is done to correct it, my father's reputation *will* be destroyed.'

'I know,' Eliza said miserably. 'I felt terrible when I heard that. I asked Edward about it, but that's when he turned on me. He said it was none of my business and that I wasn't to talk to anyone about what really happened. He said if I did, he'd hurt Justine.'

Anna frowned. 'Justine?'

'My sister,' Eliza said, her eyes filling with fresh tears. 'Edward said he'd…make it worse for her if I stepped out of line. That's why he told Betty I wasn't to have any visitors—or to be let out.'

Anna stared. 'You're not allowed to go out at all?'

'Not unless he's with me,' Eliza said. 'I have to do as he says or he'll hurt her. And I couldn't bear that, my lady. Justine's younger than me and she's never been as strong. I've spent the last two years looking after her. That's why I was willing to do whatever I had to in order to get money. I promised our mother I'd take care of her.'

Anna sat back, struggling to come to terms with this disquieting piece of news. Her brother was keeping one girl a prisoner and threatening another with physical harm? What kind of monster was he? He obviously had no conscience at all…

'…and Justine's been so happy working for the baroness.'

'I beg your pardon?' Jerked from her thoughts, Anna said, 'Your *sister* works for the baroness, too? But you were the one I saw—'

And then the penny dropped. Of *course*. Eliza was the girl Anna had *first* seen at Julia's house, but she wasn't the *same* girl who had served her tea on several occasions after that. *That* had been Justine. And if you didn't look closely, it would be all too easy to mistake one for the other. Both girls had the same dark hair and the same elfin face, but where Eliza's eyes were a deep, clear green, Justine's were a pale misty blue.

'Eliza, did Sir Barrington question *you* about the theft of the baroness's necklace, or your sister?' Anna asked shrewdly.

'That was Justine,' Eliza said sheepishly. 'She didn't

know anything about the necklace, so when the butler told us someone was coming to ask questions about its theft, I asked Justine to work in my place. And because she knew nothing, she was able to be convincing when the gentleman questioned her.'

'So you and your sister have been sharing the job without the baroness knowing?'

A guilty flush suffused Eliza's cheeks. 'I didn't think she'd mind, my lady. I was nervous the first time Justine stood in for me, but she said everything went well and the baroness didn't question me about it when I went in next, so we carried on.'

'And none of the baroness's other servants questioned the arrangement?'

'None of them knew. There was only myself and the tweenie on that floor and she wouldn't say boo to a goose. Cook had quarters downstairs and Mr Hansen's room was on a separate floor. And Justine and I were very careful about our comings and goings.'

'But why did you do it?'

'To give Justine the training she needs to become a maid,' Eliza explained. 'I realised I wouldn't be able to look after her all the time, or make enough money to support the two of us, so we decided she would learn the skills necessary to go into service. I gave her as much time as I could when we lived with the Colonel—'

'Justine *lived* with you in the Colonel's house?' Anna interrupted. 'Did he *know* that?

'I made sure he didn't,' Eliza said. 'I had no choice, my lady. Justine had been working as a nanny to a man who worked at a bank. When he started trying to get her alone, I knew I had to get her out of there before it was too late. So I told her to leave and had her come live with me. The Colonel never knew,' Eliza assured her. 'I was the only one who went to him. Justine stayed in the kitchen whenever he came round. She knew what I was doing and she wasn't happy about it, but neither of us was in a position to complain.'

'Where is Justine living now?' Anna asked.

Eliza blushed deeply. 'At Mrs Brown's.'

Anna gasped. 'Your sister's staying at a *brothel*?'

'Only until I can make other arrangements,' Eliza said quickly. 'I couldn't leave her at the Colonel's, but I didn't want to bring her here either, so I let her use my room at the baroness's house until I gave notice. Then both of us had to leave. I couldn't afford to have Edward know where she was.'

'But to arrange for her to stay at a brothel—'

'It's the only place I could afford, my lady, and she's not working,' Eliza said. 'Mrs Brown promised me that. She's letting Justine have a small room in the basement, well away from the other girls. But I have to get her out as soon as I can.'

'Then we shall do so this very afternoon.' Anna abruptly got to her feet. 'You and your sister need to disappear until this situation can be satisfactorily resolved.'

'But Edward will come after me,' Eliza whispered. 'And Justine, too, if he finds out where she is!'

'He won't get the chance,' Anna said resolutely. 'I'm going to take you to the home of a good friend, then go back for Justine. Together we'll work out how to keep both of you safe until someone I know can get to the bottom of this.'

Anna saw how desperately the girl wanted to believe what she was saying, but she also saw the depth of her fear. 'I'd like to believe you, my lady, but—'

'Believe me, Eliza. I won't let Edward hurt you or your sister. Now, pack your things and let's be off.'

'You'll have to get past Betty first!' Eliza whispered. 'And that won't be easy. She knows Edward will make it the worse for her if she lets me go!'

'Then I'll find a place for Betty as well,' Anna said, aware that matters were getting more complicated by the minute—but she had no choice. She refused to see these women's lives made worse as a result of their association with her brother. She opened the wardrobe and took out the girl's tiny valise. 'What will you take?'

Eliza glanced at the array of dresses hanging in the closet and shook her head. 'Nothing. I don't want anything he bought me, because he never really wanted me, did he, my lady? Only what I could steal for him.'

Anna wasn't sure how to answer that. What could she say that wouldn't destroy the poor girl more than she already had been? 'You must forget what my brother has done, Eliza,' Anna said gently. 'When you leave here, you'll have no reason to see him again.'

'I'd like to believe that,' Eliza said again, 'but he won't take the blame for the theft of the necklace. He'll tell people I took it, and once that gets around, I'll be arrested.'

'That's why you're not going to stay in London,' Anna said firmly. 'I know people in the country. Good people who will be only too happy to give you and your sister positions. My brother will never find either of you.'

'But the necklace—'

'The necklace has been found and will be returned to the baroness without her ever knowing how it came to be stolen. Now, come along. We have much to do before this day is over.'

Removing Eliza Smith from her brother's house was one of the easier tasks Anna had to do that day. She hustled her down the narrow staircase and after checking to make sure that Betty was nowhere in sight, opened the front door and pointed her in the direction of the waiting carriage. Then, telling the driver to wait, Anna went back in search of the housekeeper, knowing the poor woman had to be made aware of the situation.

Betty didn't have to be told twice. Aware that her employment would be terminated as soon as Edward learned of Eliza's escape, she threw off her apron, grabbed what few personal belongings she had, and left the house at the same time as Anna and Eliza, with two more of Anna's guineas jingling in her pocket.

'Can we stop and pick up Justine?' Eliza asked when Anna gave the driver the direction of the Park Lane home of the Marquess of Bailley.

'There isn't room,' Anna said. 'I'll go back for her once you're safely out of sight.'

Arriving at the Marquess of Bailley's house, Anna walked up to the front door with Eliza at her side and knocked on the door. It was answered in moments by Hilton, the family's long-standing butler. 'Good afternoon, Lady Annabelle.'

'Good afternoon, Hilton. Is Lady Lydia in?'

'She is, my lady. In the rose salon.'

'Thank you. Would you be so kind as to take Miss Smith down to the kitchen? She would be most grateful for a cup of tea.'

The unflappable Hilton didn't bat an eye. 'Of course, my lady.' Signalling a maid, he told her to take the young lady downstairs. Once that was taken care of, Anna made her way to the rose salon and within minutes, she was giving her friend a terse though somewhat abbreviated version of all that had happened.

'You wish me to keep Miss Smith and her sister *here*?' Lydia asked at the conclusion.

'Only for a little while,' Anna said. 'For obvious reasons, I can't risk having either of them stay with me. And I promise it will only be for a few days. I'm going to see Sir Barrington right now and tell him everything that's happened.'

'He's not going to be happy when he hears that you've involved yourself in this,' Lydia warned.

'Why not? He should be delighted that I've solved his case for him,' Anna protested.

'Not when he learns that you put yourself in harm's way to do so!'

'I was hardly in harm's way,' Anna said drily.

'You think going to Edward's house and kidnapping his battered mistress isn't going to spark a reaction?' Lydia demanded incredulously. 'I shudder to think what he would have done had he arrived and caught you in the act.'

'He would have been angry and told me to mind my own business, but it's silly to suggest that I was in any kind of danger,' Anna said. 'He is my brother, after all.'

'That doesn't absolve him. Edward is a wicked man and wicked men are capable of anything. Have you forgotten what happened to Sarah Wentworth?'

Anna's jaw tightened. How could anyone forget what had happened to that poor woman? Her husband had mistakenly believed her guilty of having an affair and had had her committed to an institution, even though it was clear to anyone who saw her that there was absolutely nothing wrong with her mind. Nevertheless, she disappeared one night and it was months before someone happened to see her in the asylum and made a complaint to the lady's father. Even then, it had taken considerable effort on her family's part to have her released and the resulting scandal had been horrendous.

'Please help me, Lydia. Will you keep Eliza and her sister here? It won't be for long,' Anna said. 'I shall write to a very good friend of mine this very night and see about sending both of the girls to her. Edward would never even think of going there. She runs a small school near York and her sister married well and has a very large house. I'm sure one of them will be able to give the girls some sort of employment.'

'You don't have to convince me, of course they can stay,' Lydia said. 'I shall put them in the room next to mine. In fact, their arrival has solved something of a problem in that my own maid asked for time off to visit her ailing father. If anyone asks, I shall simply say I hired them on a friend's recommendation. And I shall be sure not to send them out of the house on any errands.'

Anna pressed a kiss to her friend's cheek. 'Thank you, dear friend. I'll just go back and fetch Justine—'

'Oh, no, you won't.' Quickly getting up, Lydia went to the writing desk and took out parchment and quill. 'I refuse to see you venture alone into that part of town. It's dangerous; besides, someone might see you and start asking awkward questions.' She wrote a few words on the paper, sanded and folded it, then rang for a servant. 'I'll have John take the carriage and retrieve Miss Smith. A male servant going into that kind of place won't arouse any suspicions. And he can drop you at Sir Barrington's on the way.'

Touched by her friend's willingness to help, Anna gave her a hug. 'You are too good, Lydia. I promise I shall make it up to you.'

'Just get this mess straightened out,' Lydia said grimly. 'That will be thanks enough!'

Barrington had forgotten what a restful sleep was. For five nights in a row, he'd ended up pacing the drawing room because, for five nights in a row, he'd been unable to think about anything but Anna. She'd kept him awake—and aroused—into the wee hours of the morning. He couldn't explain why. He had trained himself to ignore what he couldn't have, to resist temptation in all its wide and varied forms. He couldn't be bought, bribed, or browbeaten. God knew, enough men had tried and failed. Yet when it came to her, it was as though he had no will at all. He became as docile as a kitten. And like a kitten, he craved her touch. He wanted to wrap himself around her, to immerse himself in her warmth and to lose himself in her body.

Knowing he couldn't do any of those things was driving him mad. Even now, as he sat at his desk, staring out the window instead of reviewing papers concerning a complicated case, all he could think about was Anna. Remembering the expression on her face during their last meeting—

'Sir Barrington...'

Recalling how angry she'd been at his refusal to abandon his pursuit of her father, her misplaced belief that he assumed the earl guilty—

'Sir Barrington?'

Her—

'Sir Barrington!'

'Yes, what *is* it, Sam?' Exasperated, Barrington turned to see his secretary standing in the open doorway, and right behind him—'Anna!' He leaped to his feet, sending a flurry of papers to the floor. 'That is...Lady Annabelle!'

She stepped in front of the younger man, hesitation and uncertainty written on her face. 'I hope I haven't come at a bad time?'

'Of course not. Come in. Sit down.' He stared at her greedily, devouring the sight of her, wondering how it was possible for a woman to grow more beautiful by the day. 'Thank you, Sam, that will be all.'

The door closed with a quiet click. Anna came towards him. 'Are you sure this isn't a bad time. You seem...preoccupied.'

'I am.' *With you.* 'I was going over the details of a case.' He glanced briefly at the papers on the floor and then walked around to the front of his desk. Leaning back against the edge, he crossed his arms over his chest and tried not to notice how the sunlight danced on her hair, turning it a warm, honeyed gold. Her complexion was as smooth as alabaster, her mouth a bright red berry, ripe for the taking—

Desire exploded, hardening him where he stood. And with a degree of resolve he didn't know he had, he forced it down and away. 'You look like a woman on a mission.'

'I am. I came here to tell you that I know who took Julia's necklace. *And* how it came to be in my father's wardrobe.'

His eyebrows lifted. 'Indeed.'

'My brother's mistress took it.'

'Elizabeth Paisley?'

He said the name without thinking, and watched as a delicate line formed between her brows. 'No. Eliza Smith.'

'Your brother's mistress is a girl by the name of Elizabeth Paisley,' Barrington said. 'I know because I was asked to find her by a gentleman who was...concerned about her welfare.'

'A gentleman by the name of Colonel Tanner?'

Barrington raised an eyebrow. 'How did you know?'

'Eliza told me about him. And I remember you speaking to a gentleman you referred to as Colonel that night at the Billinghams' soirée. I suspected they might be one and the same.'

Hiding his surprise, Barrington inclined his head. 'Elizabeth Paisley was originally Colonel Tanner's mistress. When she disappeared from his house, he began to worry so he asked me to see if I could find her. Initially I was afraid that foul play might have been involved, but when I learned through my visit to Madame Delors that someone else was paying for her clothes, I realised she had simply transferred her affections.'

'Madame Delors?' Anna said, wide eyed. 'Is *that* why you went to see her?'

'Of course. A good modiste dresses a wide range of women and sends the bills to their husbands or protectors. It seemed the logical place to start. Why? Did you think I had some other reason for going?'

Anna coloured, but firmly shook her head. 'No, of course not. Go on.'

'Because I knew the Colonel had ordered clothes for Miss Paisley from Madame Delors, I hoped she might be able to tell me what had become of her. After some careful prompting, she kindly provided me with your brother's name.'

'So you *knew* about Eliza's involvement with Edward.' Anna abruptly sat down. 'Why didn't you tell me?'

'Two reasons. One, because I was investigating her in confidence for another client, and, two, because I was afraid you might ask Edward what his involvement with her was.'

'And so I should! Eliza was the one who took the necklace!'

'Not possible,' Barrington said. 'The baroness's maid said she saw your father take the necklace.'

'That's right. Eliza *was* Julia's maid.'

'Wrong,' Barrington said. 'I interviewed all of the household help. No one matching Miss Paisley's description worked there at the time of the robbery.'

'That's because Eliza wasn't there the day you questioned the staff. Her sister, Justine, was.'

'But I didn't interview a Justine Paisley,' Barrington said. 'The baroness's maid was a girl by the name of Eliza Smith.'

'Exactly. Eliza Smith *is* Elizabeth Paisley,' Anna said patiently. 'She changed her name when she went to work for Julia. And she asked her sister, Justine, to stand in for her on the day you went to interview the staff because she was afraid that if *she* spoke to you, her nerves would give her away. Justine knew nothing of what Eliza had done so Eliza knew she would be entirely convincing.'

'Are you telling me the baroness didn't know she had two different girls working for her?'

'Not when the only difference between them was the colour of their eyes,' Anna said triumphantly. 'Justine and Eliza are twins.'

There it was. The missing piece of the puzzle. Barrington hadn't been able to trace Elizabeth Paisley because she had changed her name to Smith and because she and her twin sister were pretending to be the same person.

He picked up the crystal paperweight and turned it over in his hand, the sunlight sending shards of silver dancing around the room. Elizabeth *and* Justine Paisley. Damn.

'So it all started,' he said slowly, 'when Edward saw Elizabeth Paisley...or Smith as she was then, at the baroness's dinner party.'

'Actually, it started a little before that, but I suspect they first became lovers that night. Eliza told me she spotted Edward the moment she walked into the dining room and he must have noticed her because I saw them together later that night.'

'Where?'

'In the study. After you and I...parted company on the balcony, I went back into the house through another door and came upon Edward and Miss Smith.'

He watched the colour spring to her cheeks and his eyebrows rose a fraction of an inch. *'In flagrante delicto?'* When her colour deepened, he couldn't help smiling. 'That must have been awkward.'

'Apparently more so for me than for Edward,' Anna said ruefully. 'A few days later, I overheard him telling two of his friends that he had installed a new mistress at his house. I put two and two together.'

'So she went to him willingly,' Barrington said.

'Oh yes. Eliza said that while Colonel Tanner had been good to her, she wasn't in love with him.'

In love with him. So, his hunch had proven true. 'Is that how Edward convinced her to steal the necklace?' Barrington asked. 'By telling her he loved her?'

'Of course. He told her she would be doing it for them, so they could be together.'

'And she was gullible enough to believe it,' he said wryly.

'A woman in love is all too ready to believe anything she's told,' Anna pointed out. 'Edward made her believe that selling part of the necklace would provide the money they needed to start a new life together. And Eliza was too much in love with him to see how impossible a reality that was.'

'Of course. We always think the best of those we love,' Barrington murmured. 'Only to discover that love blinds us to the truth. Eliza was no different.'

'Until she found out it was all lies. When she threatened to leave, Edward realised she had the power to expose him and his method of persuasion took on a more…physical form.' Anna looked at him and Barrington saw the anger in her eyes. 'That's why I had to take her away.'

He froze, hardly able to believe what she'd said. '*You* took her out of his house? Dear God, Anna, do you realise how dangerous that could have been?'

'The only danger would have been to Eliza if I'd left her there!'

'And what if Edward had arrived whilst you were helping her to escape?' he said.

'He likely would have been angry and put a stop to it.'

'He might have done a damn sight more than that.'

'Why does everyone insist on believing that Edward would hurt me?' Anna asked in exasperation. 'He's my brother, for heaven's sake!'

'He's also a man with a grudge and guilty of having plotted a serious crime,' Barrington retaliated. 'He attempted to destroy your father's reputation and apparently had no qualms about using violence against Miss Paisley or her sister. Speaking of which, we have to find the other sister as quickly as possible. Once your brother discovers what's happened, she won't be safe.'

'I know. That's why a carriage is on its way to pick Justine up now and take her to the Marquess of Bailley's house,' Anna said. 'I asked Lydia if the girls could stay with her until I've had a chance to contact some friends of mine in the country who might be able to provide positions for them.'

'Good girl,' Barrington said approvingly. 'While I don't like involving anyone else in this, Lady Lydia's house is probably the safest place in the short term. Your brother would never think to look for Miss Paisley or her sister there.' He turned away from her, dragging a hand through his dark hair. There was still much to be done, but when he thought of what Anna had already endured, and what could have happened… 'I'm sorry you had to get involved in this, Anna. I would have spared you, if I could.'

'I know,' Anna said softly. 'But none of this is your fault, Barrington. Edward's turned out to be the villain. I would never have believed him capable of such treachery, but it seems I didn't know him *or* Peregrine as well as I thought.'

'You can't know what people don't want you to. That's what makes this such a dangerous business,' Barrington said, walking towards her. 'Please don't do it again.'

His voice was soft, barely above a whisper, yet it reverberated through her with the force of a hurricane. 'You don't have the right to tell me what to do,' she whispered back.

'No, but I'm going to regardless. And do you know why?' He came to a halt in front of her, so close that he could see the pulse beating beneath her skin. 'Because if something were to happen to you, I would never know peace again.' He raised his hands and placed them on either side of her face. 'If I never had the chance to kiss you again, I would slowly go insane. Much as I'm doing now...'

He waited for her to pull away, but when she leaned into him and closed her eyes, Barrington knew there was no turning back. He took her face between his hands and angled her mouth to his, desperate to feel the softness of her mouth under his.

It was more than he expected. Her lips, sweet, soft, and maddeningly erotic, wiped every thought from his mind but how much he wanted her. He touched his tongue to her upper lip, heard her breath catch and felt his world shift when she opened her mouth to him.

The taste of her nearly drove reason from his brain. The warmth of her in his arms, the hunger he tasted in her kiss, were all that mattered. And when her arms came around him and her fingers pressed into his back, urging him closer, he knew he couldn't let her go. With a groan, he slipped one hand around to cup the nape of her neck, tilting her head back, exposing her throat. She smelled like heaven and, like a starving man, he feasted on her, savouring the scent and the taste of her skin. Her breasts were warm and heavy against his chest, rising and falling as the tempo of her breathing increased.

He reclaimed her mouth, his kiss no longer gentle, his tongue exploring the shadowy recesses of her mouth. He kissed the pulse beating at the base of her throat, and when she groaned and arched against him, he cupped one breast, feeling the nipple harden through the slight material of her gown.

Anna moaned, a whisper into his hair, and he went as hard as iron. God, he needed her. Needed to peel away the layers of clothing until they lay skin to skin, to caress her until they were both aching with desire, to hear her cry out his name as he claimed her for his own…

'Anna,' he whispered against her throat. 'Oh, my love…'

He spoke without thinking, the endearment slipping naturally from his lips. He no longer cared if she knew how he felt. All he wanted was to be close to her, as though, in this intimate embrace, all the reservations he'd felt had suddenly evaporated.

But something was different. Anna was pulling back. Her arms fell away, leaving him cold where he had been hot. Empty where he had been full. And when he looked at her, it was to see tears rolling down her cheeks. 'What's wrong, my love?'

'Don't *call* me that,' she protested, her voice tremulous. 'Don't talk to me of love when, by your own admission, you have none to give me.'

Her words stabbed at him like the point of a rapier. 'You know why I said that. I told you of the risks—'

'But you kissed me as though you cared—but you don't.'

'I do! Just—'

'Just not enough to marry me, yes, I know,' she threw at him. 'Then why torment me like this, Barrington? I won't be your mistress.'

'I would never ask that of you,' he said, aware that his own heart was thundering in his chest. 'But neither will I be the cause of you putting yourself in danger. You've already seen what I bring to your life: Rand's life in shambles; your father held up for ridicule; and you, forced to speak out against your brother and forcibly remove a woman from the prison he was holding her in. Do you not see the dangers of being involved with me?'

'What I see,' she said huskily, 'is a man trying to put right what others have put wrong. A man who chooses to expose the weaknesses that turn good people bad and which destroy families along the way. You did not *ruin* Peregrine's life, Barrington. He did that by involving himself with Lady Yew. And you certainly didn't hold my father up for ridicule. That was all Edward's doing.'

'And what of the dangers from Edward now? You've seen what he's capable of,' Barrington said. 'And while you might not want to believe it, *all* men are capable of violence. All it takes is one spark to ignite the fire.'

'Does that include you?' she asked.

He swallowed hard as an image of Hayle raising his hand to her appeared in his mind. 'If it came to the possibility of your being hurt by another, yes, I would most definitely be capable of violence.'

He had no idea if it was the answer she expected, or even the one she wanted. But it was the only one he could give and he knew that she was shaken by the intensity of his declaration.

'I have no wish to inspire such behaviour,' she said in a low voice. 'It has always been my desire to bring out the best in people, not the worst. And violence of any kind can only be the worst.'

'That's why I need you to be careful,' Barrington warned. 'Your brother is guilty of having tried to implicate your father in the theft of the necklace. If he suspects you of going public with that information, how do you think he's going to react? His standing in society means a great deal to him. He won't look kindly upon anyone who exposes him for what he really is.'

'Maybe not, but how *can* I expose him, Barrington? He's

a member of my family. Think of what it would do to my father. How disloyal it would be—'

'Did Edward consider loyalty when he asked the Marquess of Yew to persecute Rand over the affair?' Barrington said brutally. 'Knowing it would cause Rand public humiliation and disgrace?'

She blanched. 'Edward *asked* Lord Yew to bring charges against Peregrine?'

'Yes. The marquess is actually quite proud of his wife's ability to seduce younger men. He doesn't care that she slept with Rand, and neither did Edward. All your brother wanted to do was humiliate Rand in the eyes of society.'

'But why?'

'Because he's jealous.'

'Jealous! Why on earth would Edward be jealous of Peregrine? He's heir to an earldom, for heaven's sake! Peregrine is merely my father's godson—'

'No, Anna. Edward hates Peregrine Rand because he *is* your father's other son—'

'*What?*'

He'd gone too far. The moment he saw the look of disbelief on her face, Barrington knew he'd said too much, because contrary to what he'd believed, she hadn't worked it out. As astute as she was when it came to analysing and fixing relationships between other people's families, she was blind to the truth when it came to her own. 'You didn't know,' was all he said.

'Didn't *know*?' she demanded in a tortured whisper. 'How could I possibly have known? Papa introduced Peregrine as his *godson*. I had no reason to believe he was anything else.'

'What about the physical resemblance between them?'

'I thought it barely noticeable. Even Edward doesn't resemble my father all that much. Or are you going to tell me he's not really my brother either?'

Barrington heard the tension in Anna's voice and, though his first instinct was to apologise, he knew silence was the better choice. It was too late for apologies now. The damage was done. Anna hadn't moved an inch from where she stood, but she was as distant from him as the moon was from the earth. 'It was never my intention to hurt you, Anna.'

'Then why would you say such a thing to me?'

'Because I know it to be the truth. I did some digging into your family history,' Barrington said, not bothering to mention that it was Lord Richard Crew who had discovered the truth about Peregrine's background. 'It was all there, in the parish registers.'

Anna didn't move, but her eyes grew suspiciously bright. 'So that's why Edward hates Peregrine so much,' she whispered. 'He worked it out as soon as Peregrine arrived.'

'I suspect so, yes.'

She was silent for a long time, her expression one of mute despair. Barrington didn't say anything either, knowing it was better that she work matters out for herself. Anything else he said now might only make the situation worse.

Finally, she spoke. 'Why didn't Papa tell us? Surely we had a right to know.'

'Perhaps he thought to spare you the hurt you're suffering now. And while it pains me to say it, he wouldn't be the first nobleman to father a child outside marriage.'

'How *dare* you!' she cried. 'My father *loved* my mother. He was faithful to her until the day she died! How do I know *you're* not the one telling lies? You could be making this all up!'

'Why would I do that?'

'I don't know.' Anna wrapped her arms around her chest, as though to stop herself from shattering into a million pieces.

'You once told me that people lie to protect themselves or someone they care about, but we both know those aren't the only reasons. People lie to influence others, or to make them feel better about themselves. They lie to inflict hurt.'

'So you believe I'm deliberately trying to hurt you by lying to you about your father's relationship to Peregrine Rand?'

Anna shook her head. 'I don't know what you're trying to do. All I know is that my father is an honourable man. He would never have done something like that. It would have destroyed our mother. And he would *never* bring a child he'd had with another woman to live under the same roof as Edward and me. It would be too painful for all of us.' Her chin came up. 'If Peregrine *is* my father's child, he would have told us. I *know* he would.'

Barrington said nothing. What could he say? She was a daughter defending the father she loved. She trusted him, as she'd trusted her brother, believing that she knew the ways of the world. The ways of love.

Yet she didn't know how love could twist and warp until it was unrecognisable to anyone who saw it. She didn't know how it could wound with a single word, or destroy with a single glance. For what was jealousy but love without trust? What was obsession but love without reason?

Hayle was jealous of Rand because he was the product of his father's love with another woman. Elizabeth Paisley had stolen for the man she loved because she believed it would strengthen their bond and allow them to start a life together. And the earl had lied to his family in an effort to protect them from a devastating truth. He probably *had* been faithful to his wife while he was married to her, but Peregrine was his child by a woman he'd met *before* he married Isabel. Likely before their marriage had even been arranged or the two of them had met.

Sadly, none of that mattered now. Anna was looking at

him as though *he* was the serpent in the Garden of Eden. As though he was the source of all the rumours and lies. There was nothing he could do now but finish his investigation and walk away. Out of the case, out of her life.

'I will call upon your brother this evening, Lady Annabelle,' Barrington said quietly.

'Not at home!' she gasped.

He shook his head. 'Lord Hayle spends Thursday nights at his club. I shall speak to him there.'

'What will you say?' she asked, not looking at him.

'That is between your brother and myself. But when the interview is over, I shall send word to your father of the outcome.'

'And what about me, Barrington?' Anna said, finally raising her eyes to his face. 'What would you say to me?'

He stared down at the blotter, knowing there was only one thing he could say. 'I will say goodbye. Because after what's happened between us today, I can't imagine there possibly being anything else appropriate.'

Chapter Fourteen

Contrary to what he'd told her, Barrington did not find Hayle at his club that evening. He called in at White's on his way to another society event, only to be informed by the manager that the earl's son had not yet put in an appearance.

Thanking him, Barrington left and climbed back into his carriage. Where did he go next? There were any number of hells to which Hayle might have gone, but it would take the entire night to investigate them all. Had he gone to see his mistress? Possible, Barrington reflected. And if so, he would have found the house in darkness and Eliza gone. How would he react to such a development? With anger? Or with fear? Would he suspect Eliza of having revealed the part he'd played in the theft of the necklace and realise that information now existed that could connect him to the crime, thereby exonerating his father?

The likelihood of that was even more possible; afraid of what that might mean for Anna, Barrington gave his coach-man the direction of Regent's Park. He intended to keep a close eye on Hayle for the next few days. Anna might like to think her brother was guided by family loyalty, but having seen what loyalty meant to him, Barrington decided it was best to play it safe. Any man that twisted by jealousy and anger was a danger to anyone he came into contact with—and that *included* his only sister.

The carriage pulled into the darkened street a short while later. Barrington knew the number of the house, but even from this distance he could see that there were no lights on inside and that neither a private carriage nor a hackney stood outside. If Hayle had paid the house a call, he hadn't bothered to wait around.

So where was he now—and in what state of mind?

Abruptly, Barrington remembered something Crew had told him during his last visit. As well as providing him with the surprising but very useful information regarding Cambermere and his relationship to Peregrine Rand, Crew had informed him that Hayle had taken to spending time with Lord Andrews. Apparently they were often seen heading in the direction of Andrews's favourite hangout, a disreputable tavern close to the Thames, down a dark alley most decent men knew better than to travel. A place known to opium users needing a place to hide.

Barrington thumped the roof of his carriage and gave the driver the address. Whatever he was going to say to Hayle had to be said tonight. And if that meant following him into the mouth of hell, that's what he'd do. But he'd go in prepared. He reached under his seat and pulled out the ebony cane. If he was to take Hayle on in an unfriendly atmosphere, the cane might well save his life. In places like the Cock's Crown, he was only going to get one chance.

Anna walked listlessly into the drawing room as the clock on the mantel struck nine. She and Peregrine were expected at Lady Bessmel's for cards, but the thought of having to spend an entire evening making light-hearted conversation and acting as though nothing was wrong was far from welcome. She perched on the arm of a high-back chair, only to get restlessly to her feet a few minutes later. She felt cold though the room was warm and even an extra shawl couldn't banish the chill, nor was it likely to given the source of her distraction.

Was Peregrine truly her half-brother? Barrington certainly thought so. He would never have made the comment to her otherwise. But the only person who could give her a definitive answer to that question was her father and he had gone out earlier in the day. And even if she knew when he was coming home, would she have the courage to ask him such a question?

How did one go about enquiring if the young man now living with them, a man who had been introduced to them by their father as his godson, was, in fact, their half-brother?

Her father's bastard.

No. Definitely not the kind of question a daughter asked. Because if Barrington was wrong, her father would be devastated by her questioning of his honesty. Indeed, of his very honour. And if he wasn't wrong?

Anna closed her eyes, retreating from the thought.

Unfortunately, Barrington didn't make mistakes. Everything he'd said to her from the moment they'd met had been proven true. What reason had she to doubt him now? His approach to everything he undertook was logical, unemotional and based purely on fact. Sentiment didn't enter into it, whereas with her, *everything* revolved around emotion. People didn't make mistakes because they were logical. They made them because they allowed their emotions to get the upper hand. Emotions like anger and jealousy and hate.

Having to listen to such accusations made against the members of her own family was horrible—but having to agree with them was even more so. It called into question the degree of loyalty she owed her family. A responsibility she'd never questioned until now—and Barrington was the one who was making her question it. Was it any wonder she had no desire to see him again?

Yet she *did* want to see him. Desperately, because he had become the only constant in her life, the one person she could count on. He consumed her every waking thought. Not an hour went by that she didn't think of him. Not a minute passed that she didn't remember every exquisite detail of the moments they'd spent together: the heady sensation of his hand caressing her breast; the warmth of his mouth on hers; the incredible eroticism of his body pressed intimately against hers.

But what was all that worth if love and tenderness weren't present as well? Intimacy without love was the reason men went to prostitutes. Barrington might not be able to deny the strength of the attraction between them, but he was still reluctant to encourage anything more. He used the charges he had laid against the men in her family as proof of the destructive force he brought into her life.

How was she to tell him that she didn't care about that any more? That all she cared about was loving him and of finding some way of getting him to love her in return?

How on earth did she tell a logical man something so thoroughly illogical?

'Anna? Are you ready to go?'

She looked up to see Peregrine standing in the doorway—and the sight of him caused her heart to turn over all over again. Peregrine Rand. Country gentleman—or unknown half-brother? It was impossible not to wonder in light of Barrington's stunning revelations.

And yet though she stared hard at Peregrine, she still couldn't find the confirmation she was seeking. The knowledge that he truly was her father's son by another woman…

'Anna? Are you all right?'

'Hmm? Oh, yes, of course.' *Don't think about it. It won't help you get through the evening.* 'Are you sure you want to go to Lady Bessmel's tonight?'

Peregrine's mouth twisted and, suddenly, there was no mistaking the hesitation in his eye. 'I'm quite sure I *don't* wish to go, but I can't hide in the house for ever. I'll have to show my face in public at some time.' He walked into the room, hands thrust into his pockets. 'If it was only the affair, I could bear it. But knowing that people are whispering about what I reputedly did to your father is a thousand times worse.'

Anna looked at him and saw how deeply he was suffering. The colour had gone from his face and his eyes were shadowed with despair. Even his attire was subdued: his cravat simply tied, his waistcoat plain, his collar points of moderate height.

'I know you didn't start the rumour about having found the necklace in Papa's possession, Per,' Anna said softly. 'You wouldn't have done that to him.'

His laughter had a hard, bitter edge to it. 'Then you're one of the few who believes it.'

'How did you find out what people were saying?'

'Lord Richard Crew was good enough to inform me.'

Hearing the name of the well-known lady's man, Anna raised an eyebrow. 'I'm surprised *he* would be the one to tell you, given his own less-than-sterling reputation. Did he happen to mention whether or not he believed it?'

'He didn't say and I didn't ask,' Peregrine replied, his expression bleak. 'Frankly, I didn't want to know.'

'Oh, Peregrine,' Anna said, coming to stand beside him. 'This really hasn't been a very good visit for you.'

'No, it hasn't, but much of it's been my own fault,' Peregrine said ruefully. 'Making a fool of myself over Lady Yew wasn't the best way to start and this has certainly made matters worse. But I can't believe people would think I would betray your father like that. Yes, I saw the necklace in his wardrobe. We both did. But I would never say so in public. Your father's been good to me, Anna. He brought me to London and let me live here. He made it easy for me to enter society when my background lends nothing to my being there, and he even forgave me for the débâcle with Lady Yew.'

'He did?'

'He said it was the right of every young man to sow his wild oats.' Peregrine gave her a lopsided grin. 'I just picked the wrong field in which to sow them.'

In spite of the situation, Anna was actually able to laugh. 'Yes, well, I suppose everyone must be forgiven one mistake.'

'Would that it was only one.' Peregrine said. 'I wish I was more like you, Anna. I doubt you've ever done anything stupid or irresponsible in your life. You would never let yourself be compromised by your feelings.'

'Oh, Peregrine,' Anna breathed. 'I am no more sensible than you when it comes to matters of the heart.'

'Nonsense. You're never out of humour. You don't allow familiarity from gentlemen and you act with moderation at all times.'

Except when in the arms of the man I love, Anna wanted to tell him. *Waiting for him to say the things I so desperately want to hear...and probably never will.* But all she said was, 'The young ladies I counsel would think me a poor example if I didn't follow my own advice. Besides, we both know how destructive unbridled passion can be. Surely it is better to love moderately than to lose oneself completely.'

'Perhaps, but I would never wish that for you. Or for myself. When I fall in love, I want it to be without reason or logic. I want to feel light-headed over it,' Peregrine said. 'Giddy with the excitement of it all. I want the woman I love to be all I think about—my reason for getting up in the morning and the motivation for everything I do during the day. I want her to be my queen. My Guinevere.'

Anna smiled. 'You're a poet and a dreamer, Peregrine, but I have no doubt that you *will* find your Guinevere one day.'

'And what about you, Anna? Do you think you'll ever find your Lancelot?'

Anna stood up. She already had…and his name was Barrington Parker. But he was lost to her, the bitter words they'd thrown at one another severing the tenuous connection that existed between them. 'I doubt it. There just aren't that many knights in shining armour left.'

As expected, walking into the Cock's Crown was like descending into the dungeons of hell. The dimly lit room was thick with smoke, the cloying scent of opium burning the eyes and addling the brain. Pictures both dark and disturbing hung from the walls and there was a sense of desperation and despair about the place.

It took only a moment to locate the figure of Viscount Hayle. Sitting at a table in the corner, he appeared to be well into his cups, though in truth, he was in better shape than many of his companions. Lord Andrews was sprawled out on the table next to him and a younger man Barrington recognised as the heir to a dukedom lay face down on the floor. The humid air was rank with the smell of booze and fear.

Hayle looked up as Barrington approached. His eyes were bloodshot and, in the dim light, his skin had a decidedly greyish tinge. 'Well, well, if it isn't the admirable Parker,' he drawled. 'A little out of your area, aren't you?'

'It's not one of my favourite haunts,' Barrington said,

resting his hands on the knob of his ebony cane. 'But something told me I might find you here.'

'And why should you wish to *find* me?' Hayle said, enunciating each word.

'You and I have business to discuss.'

'Really? I can't imagine what manner of business would be so important that you would need seek me out here. As you can see, I am with friends, and friends would resent me speaking to you on matters that do not concern them.'

It was hard to tell if Hayle was foxed or drugged, but either way, Barrington knew it was going to be a difficult conversation. 'Your friends can listen if they wish, but we *will* have a conversation.'

'I think not.' Hayle closed his eyes and rocked back on the legs of his chair. 'You take yourself far too seriously, Parker. You should learn to relax and enjoy life, as I do.'

'What, by viewing it through a veil of opium? Thank you, but I prefer reality to hallucinations.'

'Obviously, you've never tried it.'

'No, but it would no more be my idea of fun than forcing a helpless young woman to do my dirty work, then hold her prisoner for fear of her exposing me,' Barrington said contemptuously.

Hayle's eyes opened, the chair slowly righting. 'What the hell are you talking about?'

'I think you know. I'm sure the name Elizabeth Paisley rings a bell.'

'Eliza?' To Barrington's surprise, Hayle actually laughed. 'I'm not holding her prisoner. She came to me willingly. She loves me, don't you know.'

'She may believe herself in love with you, but you and I both know it was fear that kept her from running away from you.'

Hayle's smile slowly disappeared. 'And I suppose I have

you to thank for her unexpected departure. And for that of my housekeeper?'

Not even the most unholy of tortures would have prompted Barrington to tell Hayle it was his sister who had orchestrated Eliza's escape. 'The young lady was too afraid to leave on her own, so it was necessary that I assist her in that regard,' he said quietly. 'Once I realised she was the one who'd stolen the baroness's necklace and given it to you, I had no choice but to speak with her.'

'Gave the necklace to me? What a bizarre notion. And entirely wrong, of course.' Hayle unsteadily picked up his glass. 'My *father* is the thief, Parker. Surely you've figured that out by now. The much revered Earl of Cambermere stole the baroness's necklace and it was none other than his *godson*, Mr Peregrine Rand, who made it known to society. Were you aware that it was Rand who found the necklace amongst my father's things?'

'I did hear something to that effect,' Barrington remarked, 'though it seems a bit strange that you would ask him to fetch something from your father's room…a watch, I believe… when you were the one who was supposed to take care of it.'

The man gave a non-committal shrug. 'My father asked me to attend to it, but I was busy, so I asked Rand to do it for me. I thought him competent enough to undertake a trifling matter like that.'

'So you had no idea he would find the necklace lying right next to the watch when he went in search of it,' Barrington said blandly.

Again, the shrug. 'Had I known, I would have gone myself. I have no desire to see my father humiliated in the eyes of society, Parker. Or to see our family name tarnished by such a dishonourable act.'

'No, I'm sure you do not,' Barrington murmured, impressed

by the man's ability to lie so convincingly when under the influence of the drug. 'And, of course, it makes no sense that your father would steal anything from the woman he has asked to marry him.'

It wasn't the truth, but it got the response Barrington was hoping for.

'He hasn't asked her to marry him,' Hayle snapped. 'Julia would have told me!'

'You wouldn't have heard it from your father first?' Barrington probed.

'My father doesn't confide his plans to me any more. He hasn't for some time.'

Barrington heard the note of resentment in Hayle's voice and knew the loss of his father's confidence, and perhaps his respect, rankled. 'Still, it can't come as a great surprise that he wishes to marry her,' Barrington went on. 'He's made no secret of his affection for the lady. Your father is, in all ways, an honourable man. If he was in love with the baroness, he would naturally offer her marriage.'

'Oh yes, just like he offered Rand's mother marriage,' Hayle said contemptuously. 'But he didn't, did he? He married my mother and ignored his bastard for the first twenty-seven years of his life. Hardly the behaviour of an *honourable man*.'

'It's possible your father didn't know of Rand's existence,' Barrington said. 'It may have been brought to his attention only a few months ago.'

'He knew he'd bedded Rand's mother,' Hayle said with contempt. 'And the consequences of *that* are all too easy to predict.'

'As I said, the relationship may have ended without his knowledge of there being a child,' Barrington said reasonably. 'Rand is older than you, so the association between your father and his mother was an early one.'

'I don't give a damn when he had the relationship or what they were to one another!' Hayle burst out hotly. 'What bothers me is that the moment my father learned of Rand's existence, he brought him to London without so much as a by your leave.'

'What did you expect him to do?'

'He could have asked me how *I* felt about it. I *am* his legitimate son and heir, after all!'

'Perhaps he didn't think it concerned you. Rand is his son by a woman you don't even know. It's hardly surprising that he would be suffering feelings of guilt—'

'If my father was stupid enough to rut with a woman of low birth and then have feelings of guilt, he should have gone to the country, made his apologies to the family and left it at that,' Hayle bit off. 'He should *never* have brought his bastard to London and tried to pass him off as his *godson* so I might be made a laughingstock in society!'

'And that's what really bothers you, isn't it, Hayle? That you have a brother you never knew anything about and whose existence is an embarrassment. A brother who shares your bloodline—'

'He is nothing to me! Less than nothing!'

'He is your half-brother. And because you sensed that the moment he set foot in your house, you set out to humiliate Rand *and* your father by showing them both in the worst possible light,' Barrington said mercilessly. 'You had your mistress steal a necklace from the woman your father loved and then you tried to pin the blame for the crime on him, knowing that by exposing him, you would be humiliating your father as deeply as you felt he had humiliated you.'

If Barrington was hoping for a confession, he was destined for disappointment. 'I don't know what you're talking about, Parker. All I know is that the baroness's necklace was found in my father's possession and that he must bear the consequences for his actions.'

'And Miss Paisley? Would you see her hang for a crime she didn't commit?' Barrington pressed.

'Why should I care? She's a whore. She made her interest in me plain enough the first time I saw her and I wasn't about to pass up the invitation. Unlike you, I have hot blood running through my veins,' Hayle sneered.

Ignoring the slight, Barrington said, 'So you expect me to believe that you didn't take her as your mistress simply because she worked for the baroness and you knew that, through her, you could get your hands on the necklace.'

'That's right.'

'You'd also like me to believe that you didn't feed Miss Paisley a parcel of lies about how much you loved her, telling her that if she could steal the baroness's necklace, the two of you would be able to start a new life together.'

'Most certainly not.'

'Nor did you tell her that you actually wanted the necklace so you could set up your father to look like a thief.'

'You really have got the wrong end of the stick, Parker.'

'Have I?' Barrington shook his head. 'I think you planned the entire affair as a way of getting back at your father. You seduced Miss Paisley and then persuaded her to steal the necklace for you. You planted the necklace in your father's things and made sure Rand would be the one to find it, then *you* started the rumour that he was the one who named your father as the thief. Everyone knew that relations between Rand and your father were strained as a result of the affair with Lady Yew, so you reasoned it wouldn't come as any great surprise if Rand took an opportunity to get back at your father. But the fact is that Rand would never do something like that because, unlike you, he has a conscience.'

'A conscience!' Hayle threw back his head and laughed.

'You have the gall to say that after he slept with another man's wife?'

'Ah, but you laid the groundwork for that affair, didn't you, my Lord?' Barrington said. '*You* told Rand about the state of the Yews' marriage and *you* made a point of introducing him to her, knowing full well that she had a passion for younger men. Then, you made sure her husband found out and you asked him to go after Rand in public, knowing how furious your father would be when he learned what Rand had done. And by doing that, you thought you were giving Rand a reason for revenge against your father. It really was very well thought out. By trying to implicate your father and Rand, you attempted to destroy *both* their reputations at the same time.'

'My God, Parker, you really should be writing lurid Gothic novels for love-struck young females. Either that, or the opium has already got to your brain,' Hayle said derisively.

Barrington smiled. 'Pleading innocence won't wash, Hayle. I *know* what you're guilty of. That's why both Miss Paisley and her sister are safely beyond your reach. And if *you* know what's good for you, you'll confess to the part you played in this whole ugly affair.'

Again, Hayle laughed, but there was a nastiness to it that warned Barrington to be careful. 'Why should I? It's all supposition on your part. You don't have a shred of evidence. And even if I was guilty, it's not something that's going to put me in jail.'

'No, but it would make living in London intolerable and I think to a man like you, that would be almost as bad. When society hears what you've done, they *will* turn against you. No one will receive you and your reputation will be in shreds.'

Hayle's eyes darkened with hate. 'Get out!' he snarled. 'Get out before I forget I'm a gentleman and thrash you to within an inch of your life.' As if to make good on his threat, he rose unsteadily to his feet and took a lurching step forwards.

But Barrington merely stepped back and raised his cane. 'I'd advise you to think again, Hayle. This isn't the typical gentleman's walking stick. It doesn't break when it's brought down with force on a man's head. I know because I've done it before. And my reactions haven't been slowed by the numbing effects of opium or alcohol. I guarantee that if you take me on now, you *will* lose.'

Eyeing the lethal-looking cane, Hayle hesitated, but his voice was rough with emotion when he said, 'You won't get away with this, Parker. By God, I'll make you pay.'

'No, my Lord,' Barrington said. '*You're* the one who's going to pay. Because if I have my way, you won't be getting away with anything.'

It was nearly two o'clock in the morning when Barrington left the Nottinghams' soirée. He'd had enough of glittering society for one night. He was tired of the games he was called upon to play, weary of the desperation he saw in the eyes of so many. When had it all begun to lose its lustre? When had moving in society become a chore rather than a pleasure?

He remembered how it had been when he'd first come home from France. How surprised he'd been at the extent of society's welcome. Within days of his arrival, invitations to select gatherings had begun to roll in, as had sponsorships to the right clubs from gentlemen who had seemed genuinely interested in his welfare. He had been told which families to befriend and which to avoid in the same breath as he'd been told which tailors to patronise and which to ignore.

Then, of course, had come the ladies. All of them beautiful, many of them titled, a fair number of them married. They had shamelessly flirted with him, some in the hopes of eliciting a proposal of marriage, others in the hopes of prompting a very different type of proposal. Had he chosen to partake, he could have had a dozen of them lining up to warm his bed.

But he hadn't accepted their come-hither looks and it wasn't long before the rest of the pleasures had begun to pall as well. A brief affair with the widow of one of his father's friends, though sexually fulfilling, had left him feeling curiously dissatisfied, much like a hungry man who, having sat down to a magnificent buffet, discovered that the wine was bad and the food tasteless.

But the final blow had come during the investigation of the two men his late father had trusted and done business with. Men with whom Barrington had socialised and for whom he'd felt admiration and respect. Men who had turned out to be nothing more than parasites on the flesh of society. Greed had fuelled their quest for power and money and once their masks of civility had been stripped away, Barrington had seen them for the monsters they were.

The discovery had come too late to be of help to his father, but from that night on, Barrington had done what he could to make sure that other decent men were not so foully put upon. He'd begun listening to conversations, and when he heard something he didn't like, he'd started asking questions. Quietly. Unobtrusively. Always careful not to raise suspicions in anyone's mind. But he'd asked the questions he'd needed to get the answers that mattered.

He'd also started cultivating different friends. Friends not as highly placed in society. Friends who put more stock in a man's worth than in his title. People he found himself able to trust. He also stopped putting faith in a person's appearance. A lovely face could hide a heart of stone, just as an ugly one could disguise a generous and giving nature. He'd stopped basing his decisions on emotion and gut feeling and turned to uncovering facts, doing whatever he'd had to in order to get at the truth.

It hadn't always made him popular, but he hadn't done it to win friends.

As the soirée wasn't far from his house, Barrington decided to dismiss the carriage and walk home. He needed time to think through his situation with Anna. They hadn't spoken since their last conversation and Barrington was beginning to think they never would again. Of all the disagreements they'd had, this was by far the worst…because he'd found her vulnerable spot and struck it hard. He had called her father's honour into question. He had accused him of having a child with another woman and of not telling his legitimate son and daughter the truth.

And she, loyal to a fault and believing wholeheartedly in her father's integrity, had retaliated by accusing Barrington of being a liar and completely insensitive to her father's feelings. When he had tried to make her see her brother for what he was, Anna had told him he'd had no right to criticise and had steadfastly refused to believe that she was in any danger from Edward at all.

Unfortunately, Barrington had absolutely *no* doubt that Hayle was capable of violence and it infuriated him that Anna still tried to see the good in him, believing that his role as her brother would prevent him from visiting upon her the cruelty he so freely visited on other people. So it was up to him, Barrington realised, to keep her safe. Until Hayle could be dealt with, his priority had to be in keeping him away from Anna.

But apart from that, there was the other far more emotional situation between them: the one concerning their feelings for one another. Growing slowly but steadily, his had changed from simple liking and admiration to a deep and abiding love. Thoughts of Anna filled his days with longing and his nights with hours of sleepless frustration. He wanted her in his bed. In his heart. In his life.

But the life he offered was not one most well-bred young ladies would wish for—and it certainly wasn't what Anna deserved. For one thing, she would be settling for far less than was her due. As the daughter of an earl, a marquis or a duke wasn't out of the question; given her incredible beauty, Barrington knew she would have no trouble attracting either. And yet she remained single, professing to want *him*. She'd told him as much in the way she'd kissed him, in the way her body had melted into his, in the way her arms had closed around him and drawn him close. She was a passionate woman with a heart that beat for those she loved and she would defend them to the bitter end, Peregrine Rand being a case in point.

So how did he go about resolving this mess? How did he change her opinion of him without hurting her—or convince himself to marry her despite all the reasons he should not?

More importantly, how was he to go on living, if he was unable to do either?

He was passing a small copse of trees when he heard it. The snap of a twig. The sound of laboured breathing. Someone hiding in the bushes, waiting to spring. But even as he jumped to the left and drew the sword from its ebony holder, Barrington knew it was too late. His enemy was upon him, the sudden, sharp pain in his right shoulder proof that the danger was much closer than he'd anticipated.

Clamping his teeth against the pain, Barrington whirled and saw the man standing behind him. Darkness hid the contours of his face, but he had no need of lamplight to know who his enemy was. The hatred emanating from Hayle was a tangible force. And when he lunged again, Barrington knew it was in the hopes of finishing him off.

Fortunately, this time, the lethal blade missed its mark.

'The opium must have muddled your brain,' Barrington said, switching the sword to his left hand, knowing his right was now useless. 'A skilled fencer wouldn't have missed an opportunity like that.'

'I didn't miss with my first strike,' Hayle growled. 'Shall I take pity on you and finish you off quickly, Parker? Or are you as good with your left hand as you are with your right?'

Barrington shifted his weight to compensate for the change in fencing arm. 'I am, by nature, a right-handed fencer, but I learned to use a sword in my left so I might be doubly prepared.'

'Then we shall see how well you were taught,' Hayle cried, lunging again.

The sharp clang of blades echoed in the night, but Barrington knew better than to look for help. No sensible person was abroad this time of night and the watchman was likely asleep in his box. Hayle had chosen the time and place of his attack well.

'I must have caused you considerable alarm,' Barrington said, the edge of his blade gleaming dangerously in the moonlight, 'to provoke you into coming after me.'

'You said enough.' The earl's son aimed a deadly blow at Barrington's right side, obviously hoping to worsen the damage he'd already inflicted. 'I don't intend to let you or anyone else humiliate me again and I certainly don't intend to let you expose me.'

Barrington skilfully deflected the attack, but Hayle was fighting like a man possessed. While his skills were inferior to Barrington's, his anger and fear combined to make him a dangerous adversary. Fortunately, with that much opium in his system he couldn't hope to last long in a sustained fight. 'Killing me won't change the situation with Rand,' Barrington threw out. 'He'll always be your father's son.'

'His bastard, you mean!' Hayle shouted. 'And I'm damned if I'll let him take what's rightfully mine.'

'Don't be stupid, Hayle. Your father won't leave his estate to Rand. You're his legitimate son and heir.'

'But he *likes* Rand,' Hayle spat contemptuously. 'He wishes I was more like him. But I'm not and I'm never going to be. Rand's a spineless interloper who's going back to the country as soon as I can make it happen.'

Barrington felt a sudden wave of light-headedness. He must be losing more blood than he thought. And the pain in his right shoulder was a constant reminder of his carelessness…

'Feeling the strain, Parker?' Hayle taunted. 'It's all well and good to put on a fancy show in front of others, but we both know *this* is what it's all about. The fight to the death.'

Barrington took a deep breath. He *was* getting weaker, which meant he had to change his strategy. If he hoped to survive, he had to convince Hayle that he was failing. Lull him into believing that he could close in for the kill at any time.

Fortunately, Barrington had a feeling his opponent wasn't looking to make this a quick kill. Hayle was the kind of man who enjoyed prolonging the agony. By doing so, he would unwittingly give his opponent the advantage he needed.

Barrington let his arm fall, as though weakening. 'What do you hope to gain by killing me, Hayle? Freedom from persecution?'

'You could say that.' Hayle withdrew a few paces, but kept his fighting arm extended, the point of the blade level with Barrington's chest. 'With you dead, there will be no one to challenge my father's guilt. He won't go to jail, but he will be ostracised. And Rand will go back to the country where he belongs and I'll see to it that Anna is married off to some harmless bumpkin who prefers life in the country. Maybe

I'll push her in Lord Andrews's direction. She'd do nicely for him once he has knocked the spunk out of her.'

Fighting down rage at the thought of Andrews getting anywhere near Anna, Barrington took a step, exaggerated a wince and made sure his opponent saw it. 'You've thought of everything.'

'I always do. It's taken a while, but it's all come together,' Hayle said. 'Rand's humiliation, Father's disgrace and, eventually, my marriage to the lovely baroness. And with it, an end to all my financial worries.'

'So that was the final part of your plan.'

Hayle inclined his head. 'I've already told her it was my father who stole the necklace. She didn't believe me, of course, but she won't have a choice once it all comes out. And I have been very careful in my addresses to her. I am, of course, in utter despair over my poor father's circumstances. But if a man cannot bring himself to act according to the law, he must suffer the consequences. Julia will see that and, in time, she will agree to be my wife. I have expensive habits and they need constant feeding. I intend to make damn sure no lawyer puts her money beyond my reach.'

It was shameless, Barrington reflected, but he couldn't fault Hayle's strategy. Through careful planning, he had removed each of the obstacles that stood in the way of his getting what he wanted. Barrington saw the anticipation of victory on the other man's face and knew he believed success lay within his grasp, confident it was only a matter of minutes before it was his.

But he'd reckoned without his opponent's equally fierce determination to prevent any of that happening. Barrington let his arm fall another inch and saw the smile break out on Hayle's face.

'Well, I think it's time to bring an end to this. Goodbye, Parker. I hope your skills with a foil serve you better in hell than they did here.'

Chapter Fifteen

⚜

Anna stared through the window of the carriage as it made its way home from the card party. Peregrine was dozing quietly beside her, but even though the hour was late, she was far too wide awake to sleep. She had hoped an evening with friends might help her forget her concerns about Barrington and her family, but not even the constant chatter about balls and betrothals had been enough to do so—because she couldn't stop thinking about Barrington. She couldn't stop remembering everything he'd said to her. Everything he had come to mean to her.

And in remembering all that, Anna knew she had no choice but to tell him she loved him and dare him to turn her away! She would suffer the embarrassment of being spurned, take whatever chances she had to, but she was *not* going to let him walk out of her life without having made one last effort to get him to stay. She had no intention of spending the rest of her life alone, knowing she had no one to blame but herself if that's how it ended up.

They were passing the end of the park when she saw a flurry of movement in the trees. Two dark figures—then a shimmer of silver in the moonlit darkness. Swords! She sat forwards and pressed her face to the glass. 'Peregrine! Wake up!' She thumped on the roof of the carriage. 'Stop!'

'What's the matter?' Peregrine said, groggily coming to.

'There's a fight,' she said, throwing open the carriage door. 'In the park.'

'Anna, wait, are you mad?'

She ran across the grass, deaf to his cries. Some sixth sense warned her that this was no ordinary fight. She hadn't seen her brother or Barrington the entire evening, but Lord Richard Crew, appearing late at the home of Lady Bessmel, said he had been at a hell earlier in the evening and that both Barrington and her brother had been there and that neither of them had looked happy. Had Barrington gone to confront Edward about his conduct with Eliza and been met with threats of violence?

Those words echoed in Anna's ears now as she ran towards the two men. One of them was tiring. He was staggering backwards, hunched over, his right arm hanging limp at his side. The other man raised his sword for the killing blow and she felt the scream build in her lungs. *'Barrington!'*

A split second before he heard Anna scream, Barrington straightened. With deadly intent, he lunged, moving at incredible speed and catching Hayle completely off guard. He stabbed him first in the left leg to disable him, then in his right shoulder to render his sword arm ineffectual.

The earl's son screamed in pain as the sword fell uselessly from his hand. As he sank to the ground, Barrington saw the look of disbelief on his face. He hadn't expected that final rally. Hayle had been preparing himself for victory, readying his blade for the killing blow, his wounded opponent all but vanquished.

Instead, he was the one now down on the ground, blood flowing freely from wounds in his leg and his shoulder. He would live, but he would never fight with that arm again. Only then did Barrington turn and see Anna flying across the grass towards him. Anna, her eyes wide, her face white with fear. 'Barrington! Oh, dear God!'

And then she was in his arms, heedless of his blood soaking into her gown. He gasped at the pain her embrace caused, but there was no way in hell he was going to push her away. Not now when he felt the wetness of tears on her face. He closed his eyes and held her close as his knees finally gave way and he sank wearily to the ground.

'Barrington!' she cried, falling with him.

'I'm fine, Anna,' he whispered. 'Fine. I just need to…sit down.'

Seconds later, Peregrine came running. 'What the hell's going on?' He looked in horror at Edward lying on the ground, and then at Barrington bleeding in Anna's arms. 'What in blazes—?'

'Lord Hayle and I had some…unfinished business,' Barrington murmured over Anna's head. He handed his sword to Peregrine with the instruction that he watch Hayle, then he tipped Anna's face up to his. 'It's over, love. Everything's going to be all right now.'

He stared down into her eyes and saw everything that mattered to him. Everything that ever would matter. She was his now and for always. And he was never going to do anything to risk losing her again.

That was his last thought as he slipped into darkness and the pain in his shoulder mercifully disappeared.

It was a tense party that gathered in the Earl of Cambermere's library just over an hour later. Barrington, his shoulder bandaged and wearing a clean shirt lent to him by Peregrine, held a large glass of brandy in his good hand and Anna sat next to him wearing a new gown, her previous one having been liberally stained with his blood. Peregrine sat in the chair in front of the fireplace, looking deeply upset by all that had gone on, and the earl sat behind his desk, looking equally troubled as he nursed an even larger glass of brandy.

Only Edward was absent, his injuries being tended to upstairs by the surgeon his father had called in immediately upon the party arriving home.

A few minutes later, the door opened and the surgeon came in. Instantly, the earl was on his feet. 'Well?'

'Your son will be fine,' Mr Hopkins said with a weary smile. 'I've stitched the wound and given him a sedative for the pain. I doubt he'll wake up for some time.'

'How serious are his injuries?' Anna asked.

'The injury to his thigh was superficial, but he won't have much use of his right arm.' The surgeon glanced at Barrington. 'I suspect the only reason he's still alive is because you knew exactly where to strike.'

'It was never my intention to kill him,' Barrington said quietly. 'Only to prevent one of us from being killed.'

'Then you have my congratulations on a job well done. I've left some laudanum on the table by the door for you, Sir Barrington. It will help ease the pain.'

Barrington nodded. 'Thank you, Mr Hopkins.'

'Yes, thank you, Hopkins,' the earl said gruffly. 'Good of you to come so quickly.'

The surgeon smiled. 'I'll add it to the bill. Goodnight, all.'

Cambermere waited for the surgeon to leave before saying,

'Now would someone please tell me what in God's name happened tonight?'

Barrington glanced at Anna, but realised she was still too shaken to talk about it. Given that Peregrine didn't look much better, Barrington said, 'I think it falls to me to explain, my Lord. And as much as I regret some of what I am about to say, I'm afraid you need to hear it all.'

The earl grimaced. 'Say what you must. I shall bear it as best I can.'

So Barrington told him, beginning with Hayle's taking up with Elizabeth Paisley, followed by the details of his plan to have her steal the baroness's necklace and finally his reasons for placing the necklace in his father's room. He purposely made no mention of the conversation he'd had with Hayle regarding his feelings towards Peregrine, knowing it would reveal more than he—and likely the earl—wished to, but what he did say was damning enough.

At the end of the lengthy telling, the earl abruptly stood up, his face devoid of colour, his brown eyes deeply troubled. 'Why?' was all he said. 'I've never been hard on Edward. Never forced him to do anything he had no wish to do. And I gave him everything he asked for.'

'I'm sure you did all that and more,' Barrington said. 'But when you invited Peregrine to come and stay with you, everything changed. It's time, my Lord,' he said softly. 'You can't keep this a secret any longer.'

He felt Anna stiffen on the sofa beside him, but knew the time for deceit was over. She had to hear the truth and she had to hear it from her father's lips.

Cambermere obviously knew it, too. 'You're right, of course,' he said finally. 'It was naïve of me to think I could keep the secret for ever. A man's past is never truly past.' He looked at Anna and sadly shook his head. 'I'm sorry, my dear. I should have told you the truth straight away. Before Peregrine even got here. But I was afraid you would think badly of me.'

'I could never do that, Papa.'

'You might over something like this.'

'Like what?'

The earl sighed. 'The fact that Peregrine *is* my son.'

Barrington heard Anna's muffled gasp, but it was to Peregrine's starkly white face that his gaze was drawn. 'I'm *what*?'

'It's true,' the earl said. 'I met your mother when I was nineteen. We fell madly in love and it was my dearest wish that we be married. But my father wouldn't allow it. Olivia wasn't well born and I was heir to an earldom. So while my parents didn't object to our friendship in the beginning, they did once they saw it getting serious. When I told my father I was in love with Olivia, he forbade me to see her ever again.'

'Oh, Papa,' Anna said softly.

'We were both heartbroken,' the earl said quietly. 'At that age, love is so keenly felt, as was the pain of our enforced separation. But I had no choice. I had duties and obligations. Responsibilities to my name. So I made the decision to break it off. I never saw Olivia again.'

'But what about Mama?' Anna asked. 'Did you not love her?'

'Yes, but not in the way I loved Olivia. I'm sorry, my dear, but you may as well know the truth. My marriage to your mother was arranged and the love we came to feel for one another developed over time. But what I felt for Olivia was entirely different. Something that only comes along once in a lifetime. Peregrine is the result of that love.'

'But how could you just leave her like that?' Peregrine

asked in a harsh whisper. 'You got her with child and then just…walked away?'

'I never knew she was increasing,' the earl said, the sadness in his voice reflected in the bleakness of his expression. 'I was sent away to Europe. When I got back, it was to find the preparations for my marriage to Isabel already underway.'

'How did Mama feel about the marriage?' Anna asked.

'We liked each other well enough. Your mother was high born and beautiful, everything a man could ask for, and we were married a few months later. The problem was, I was still in love with Olivia.'

'But you never saw her again,' Peregrine said grimly.

Cambermere shook his head. 'I went looking for her when I got back, of course, but she was gone. And I had no idea there was a child until two months ago when the man you believed to be your father wrote to tell me about you.'

'But how did he know?'

'Apparently, Olivia fell ill not long after I was sent away. When she found out she was…dying—' the earl's voice caught, but he forced himself to go on '—she gave you to her sister, Mary, to raise. But she made Mary promise not to tell *anyone* who your father really was. Mary kept that promise until the night before she died. Only then did she tell her husband who you really were and that it was only right I be contacted and made aware of your existence.'

It was a shocking story and Barrington wasn't at all surprised that no one in the room spoke for a few minutes. They all had much to come to terms with. The knowledge that Cambermere had been in love with another woman before he'd met his wife. The fact there had been a child from that ill-fated love, and the fact that only three people had known the truth about Peregrine's existence.

'So, Peregrine really *is* my half-brother,' Anna said, the first to find her voice.

'Yes, my dear, he is,' her father said. 'And I hope you will believe me when I say that I was as deeply shocked when the letter arrived telling me about him as you are now.'

Anna nodded, her eyes heavy with regret as she glanced at Barrington. 'I'm so sorry, Barrington. I should never have doubted you.'

'It doesn't matter.'

'Yes, it does.' Anna turned to glare at her father. 'You should have told us the truth, Papa. As soon as you found out.'

'I know. I thought you might have realised it the first day Peregrine arrived,' Cambermere said. 'Edward saw it straight away.'

Anna shook her head. 'I wasn't looking. You introduced him as your godson. I had no reason to suspect otherwise.'

'But if you knew who I was when you wrote to me,' Peregrine said slowly, 'why didn't you tell *me* when I first arrived in London?'

'Because I wanted the three of you to get to know one another without any kind of prejudice standing in the way,' the earl explained. 'Perhaps that was naïve of me, but I thought it would be easier for you to become friends if you didn't know about the connection. Wrong, I know now, but that was the decision I made.' He glanced at his daughter, his eyes pleading with her to understand. 'I knew it would be difficult to explain my having a child with another woman. You loved your mother deeply and I feared you would see it as a betrayal of her that I had been with another woman, even if happened before your mother and I were introduced. I didn't want you to hold that against Peregrine. It wasn't his fault.'

'But it mattered to Edward,' Anna said sadly. 'He knew who Peregrine was and he wanted nothing to do with him.'

'It was worse than that,' Barrington said. 'Your brother wanted to humiliate Rand, the way he felt he'd been humiliated by your father's bringing Peregrine to London. Edward was convinced that if *he* knew Peregrine was your father's son, so would the rest of society.'

'And did they?' Anna asked.

'I'd be lying if I said there hasn't been speculation about it. Nevertheless, it was Edward's intention right from the start that Peregrine should fail.' Barrington said. 'He introduced him to Lady Yew, knowing her penchant for younger men, and made sure that Peregrine knew the truth about the state of the Yews' marriage. He encouraged him to become Lady Yew's lover, and he used that to try to set your father against Peregrine, and perhaps against you as well.'

'That's why he tried to make it look as though I'd stolen the necklace,' the earl said sadly.

Barrington nodded. 'He knew you wouldn't go to jail, but that your standing in society would be hopelessly compromised. That's what he was counting on. He also planned on courting the baroness in the hopes of eventually marrying her. He felt that by showing you in such a bad light, and himself in such a good one, she would eventually transfer her affections to him.'

'Dear God,' the earl whispered. 'What did I do to deserve such hatred from my own son?'

'He didn't hate you, Papa,' Anna said sadly. 'He was just eaten up by jealousy.'

'And by his fears, irrational as they were,' Barrington said. 'Perhaps he was afraid you might have made Peregrine your heir.'

'No,' the earl said firmly. 'Whatever my feelings for

Peregrine, Edward is my legitimate heir. The title must devolve to him.'

'But what of his future now, Papa?' Anna said. 'He cannot stay here. Not after what he did to you and Peregrine. To say nothing of the fact that he tried to kill Barrington tonight.'

'My lord, if I may…?' Barrington interjected.

The earl nodded. 'Of course.'

'It might be in everyone's best interests if Edward were to…go away for a while.'

The earl frowned. 'Go away?'

'To the Americas, perhaps. Or Australia. A man can do well in such places if he applies himself and your son is far from stupid. He is simply a victim of his own insecurities. This could be a chance for him to make something of himself. More importantly, it would get him away from London and give the rest of you time to work matters through. And, hopefully, to put all of this behind you.'

Anna nodded. 'I think it's an excellent idea. I don't see how any of us would be able to carry on as normal, given what's happened.'

'No, I don't suppose we would. But what about you, Parker?' the earl asked, his voice laced with regret. 'There's no getting around the fact that my son would have killed you. You would be perfectly within your rights to have him brought up on charges.'

'Perhaps, but I have no intention of doing so. I would never wish that kind of grief on your family. Your son acted out of jealousy and fear. He is tortured enough by his demons. There is no need for me to add to his suffering,' Barrington said.

All eyes turned to the earl, who seemed to be considering the suggestion. 'Are you sure you would be amenable to seeing him walk away? You may never wield a sword with that arm again.'

Barrington shrugged. 'Since I am able to fence with either hand, it is of no real consequence. It is enough that Edward experience life elsewhere. Perhaps it will force him to take a closer look at his life and to rethink his priorities.'

'I sincerely hope so,' the earl said heavily. 'A man's son is said to be a reflection of himself. I hate to think that in some way I inspired that kind of belief system in him.' He glanced at Peregrine, who was sitting quietly in the corner, and said, 'And what about you, sir? What have you to say about all this?'

Peregrine looked up, still clearly in shock. 'What *can* one say upon learning that the man he has always believed to be his father is not, and that a man he never knew existed until a few weeks ago is.'

'A shocking revelation indeed,' the earl agreed.

'Also, that I have a half-brother and half-sister I never knew, and that one of them hated me enough to wish his own father grievous harm.' Peregrine shook his head, his eyes troubled. 'It is a great deal to come to terms with.'

'Indeed it is,' the earl said quietly. 'But it is my sincere hope that you will stay here and get to know us better while you are endeavouring to do so. However, if you feel you cannot stay under the present circumstances, you are free to leave. Perhaps you will wish to return to the family you left behind.'

'Actually, I would rather stay in London,' Peregrine said slowly. 'One of the reasons my father…that is, the man I thought was my father wrote asking you to take me, was so that I might have a chance to experience life beyond the farm. I think he knew I wasn't cut out to be a farmer. And while

they were good to me, I doubt going back there now would be in anyone's best interests.'

'Then you are welcome to stay,' the earl said. 'If Anna has no objections?'

'None whatsoever,' Anna said immediately. 'I don't like Peregrine any the less for having found out he's my half-brother. In fact,' she added with a smile, 'I like him a great deal more.'

'Good. Then the decision is yours, Peregrine. If you wish to stay in London, we will be happy to have you. And if you do not wish to live in this house, you may choose another,' the earl said. 'I shall see to it that you *are* taken care of and that you are acknowledged as my son.'

Peregrine stared. 'You would do that?'

'Why not? I'm not ashamed of you. Far from it,' the earl said softly. 'You are all I have left of Olivia and I loved her with all my heart. I see so much of her in you and I deeply regret that you did not have a chance to know her. She was… an exceptional woman.'

'Perhaps you could tell me about her,' Peregrine said slowly. 'I would like to know who she was.'

'I would be honoured,' the earl said. Then, roughly clearing his throat, he got to his feet. 'Well, it's late and I think enough's been said for now. Parker, my carriage is at your disposal. Or, you are welcome to stay here if your injuries are such that you would rather not travel.'

'Thank you, my Lord, but I would like to return home.' Barrington stood up, wincing slightly. It was one thing to pretend his injuries weren't serious; it was quite another to believe it. 'You have enough to contend with here, I think.'

'I'll see you out,' Anna said, quickly getting to her feet.

They walked to the front door in silence. Barrington was very aware of Anna beside him, but the situation was too fraught with emotion to speak of important matters now. The embrace they had shared in the park, the passionate words they had exchanged, would all have to be addressed, but not tonight. 'May I call upon you in a few days' time?' he asked as they stood together at the door. 'There are things that need to be said.'

'Of course,' she said, her expression faltering ever so slightly. 'Are you sure you're well enough to drive home, Barrington? You've been through so much tonight.'

He gave her a weak smile. 'We all have. Given that I won't be the one driving, I'll be fine. But I am in need of rest.'

'Yes, of course.' She looked at him then, and to his surprise she stood on her toes and kissed him full on the mouth in a long, intimate kiss that left his head spinning. 'Sleep well, my love,' she whispered against his lips. 'And thank you from the bottom of my heart for everything you did tonight.'

Incredible. As much as his body ached, the touch of her mouth instantly aroused him. 'I did nothing.'

'You let my brother live,' she said. 'But, more importantly, *you* lived. I wouldn't have liked having my brother's death on my hands, but I fear that's what would have happened had you died at his tonight.'

Barrington wanted to believe she was joking, but the look in her eyes told him otherwise. 'You would have destroyed your life.'

'It wouldn't have mattered,' she told him. 'If he had killed you, it would already have been destroyed beyond all hope of repair.'

As expected, over the next few days, Peregrine and the earl spent a great deal of time talking through their unusual situation. There were twenty-seven years to make up for and a lot of ground to cover. And though, at first, the words were slow in coming, it wasn't long before they were flowing freely, bringing the two back on an even keel. Peregrine was anxious to hear about his mother and Cambermere was delighted to talk about her. Given that he'd had to keep the truth about Olivia bottled up for so many years, it was a relief to finally be able to talk to someone about her—especially when that someone happened to be her son. And in learning of his true parentage, Peregrine seemed to mature into the man Anna knew he wanted to be. Lady Yew was never mentioned again.

As for Edward, he had been happy to go away. Aware that his future in London was in jeopardy, both because his family knew what he had tried to do and because it was quite likely society would find out at some point, he elected to go to California, where he'd heard stories that it was possible for a man with a good head on his shoulders to acquire vast tracts of land and make a fortune into the bargain. If there was one thing Edward wasn't lacking, Anna acknowledged wryly, it was confidence in his own ability to succeed.

As for Julia, she was thrilled at having her necklace safely returned to her. So much so that, when she learned the truth about what happened, she decided not to press charges against Miss Paisley and even offered the girl her position back.

'Why ever would she do such a thing?' Lydia asked as she and Anna walked their horses along Rotten Row a few days later. 'Miss Paisley has proven herself anything but trustworthy.'

'I know, but if you could have seen Eliza's face when Barrington told her she wasn't going to be charged and that the baroness was willing to take her back, you would understand. Eliza hasn't had an easy life,' Anna said. 'She told me the happiest she's ever been was during her brief time with the baroness and she apologised to Julia so sincerely that I actually saw tears in Julia's eyes. Eliza said she was willing to do whatever the baroness asked and that she could check her jewellery every night to make sure it was all there. She was just that happy to have a second chance.'

'Well, I'm glad it all worked out for Eliza, but what about Justine?'

Anna laughed. 'I was able to find a position for her and you will never guess with whom.'

Lydia looked blank. 'Who?'

'Miss Mercy Banks. Or, as she will shortly become, Mrs Giles Blokker. I think they will suit admirably.'

'How marvellous! And your father? This must have been a very trying time for him.'

'It has been dreadful,' Anna admitted. 'Learning about the existence of a son he never knew he had and finding out what kind of man Edward was were very hard on him. But some wonderful things have come out of it, too. He has acknowledged Peregrine as his son and Peregrine is delighted that he doesn't have to go back to the country. He's promised us all that he'll forget about sowing wild oats and stick to his papers and archaeological investigations.'

'And what of your father's hopes with regard to Julia?'

Anna slowly began to smile. 'In spite of my brother's best efforts, Julia never believed that my father was guilty of stealing her necklace. She didn't understand Edward's sudden interest in her and says she found it rather sad, since it was obvious he didn't love her the same way Papa did. I believe he will ask her to marry him once a suitable time has passed and the memory of all this has faded.'

'So,' Lydia said with a smile, 'your father and Peregrine are settled and Edward has been banished to the Americas. It would appear that matters have worked out splendidly for everyone…except you.'

'Nonsense, I am perfectly happy.'

'Has Sir Barrington spoken to you?'

Anna felt her cheeks grow warm. 'Not yet, but he did say we had things to talk about.'

'And do you wish to talk to him about these matters?'

'Yes, though there really is no hurry,' Anna said, knowing it for the lie it was.

But Lydia just smiled. 'Perhaps not on your part, but I believe the gentleman is quite anxious in that regard. No doubt that is why he is approaching us now with such a determined look on his face.'

Anna gasped and, lifting her head, saw that Barrington was indeed riding towards them. 'Oh, no, I'm not ready!'

'I don't think we ever are for moments like this,' Lydia said with a wink, 'but they come along regardless. And in case you're wondering, this isn't a chance meeting. Sir Barrington sent a note asking me if we would be riding in the park this morning. I told him we would.'

Anna felt her pulse begin to race. He had planned this? He'd wanted to see her that badly?

'Good morning, Lady Annabelle. Lady Lydia,' he greeted them, resting his hands on the pommel. 'Lovely morning for a ride.'

'It is indeed, Sir Barrington, and I think I shall take advantage of it,' Lydia said, gathering her reins and smiling at Anna. 'I shall return in a little while.'

In the silence that followed, Anna turned to study the face of the man watching her and realised her heart was beating so hard she could barely speak. 'I could say this is a surprise but I understand it was planned.'

Barrington gave her a wry, fleeting smile. 'It has been my experience that important matters are best not left to chance. I wished to speak to you in private, which meant not at your house or at a society gathering. So, I had to arrange for some other meeting place and I thought this the most suitable. I did ask Lady Lydia to stay close by so there could be no question of impropriety.'

Anna looked up and saw that Lydia was still within sight, having stopped under the shade of a large tree just beyond. 'You appear to have thought of everything.'

'I try,' he said quietly. 'Though when it comes to you, I find myself constantly falling short of the mark.'

Anna bit her lip so as not to smile. 'I can't imagine why you would say that. You always seem so completely in control of yourself, no matter what the situation.'

'Because I am used to dealing in logic and reason. Yet all of my dealings with you involve emotions, and rather strong ones at that,' he admitted.

'And emotion clouds judgement so as to totally obscure the truth,' she teased.

'I should have known you would use that against me,' he said wryly.

'It wasn't intended as a slight. I would never knowingly hurt you, Barrington.' Anna's smile faded, her fingers tightening convulsively on the reins. 'You look…much better than you did when last I saw you.'

Clearly intent on setting her mind at rest, Barrington grinned. 'I have fully regained my strength and the surgeon is very pleased with my shoulder, though my valet has been heard to complain that I have, at times, been a rather difficult patient.'

Anna laughed, a welcome relief from the tension she'd been carrying for too many days. 'I was so afraid, Barrington. That night, when I ran across the park and saw you and Edward fighting…when I saw all the blood…I was terrified I was going to lose you.'

'There was really never any danger of that,' he said quietly. 'Your brother was too far under the influence of the opium to be a real threat.'

'But he wounded you all the same.'

'Yes, because I was careless,' Barrington admitted. 'I lowered my guard. Preoccupied with thoughts of you, I wasn't expecting the attack. But he only managed to get in one thrust.'

'One good one,' she whispered, glancing at his arm, still in its sling. 'You may never use that arm again.'

'Not to fight to my previous standard, perhaps, but it is perfectly capable of doing other things. Like holding you close,' he murmured.

Anna closed her eyes, feeling the warmth of his words pierce her heart. 'Is this where you tell me again about the risks involved in loving you?'

She opened her eyes and caught his gaze. A minute passed, and then he slowly began to smile. 'No. It's probably what I *should* say, but I'm not going to. What I feel for you isn't rational, Anna, but I'm not willing to fight it any more.'

'Good, because love isn't rational,' Anna said. 'Elizabeth Paisley did what my brother asked because she loved him and thought he loved her in return. Just as Peregrine lied to me because he thought Lady Yew had deep feelings for him. Love excuses all things and forgives all things.'

'Do you honestly believe that?'

'No. It's a pretty sentiment, but it doesn't justify lies or deceit. Peregrine's belief that Lady Yew wasn't in love with her husband didn't make it right for him to enter into an affair with her. Just as being in love with my brother didn't justify Miss Paisley's stealing Julia's necklace.'

'So you're saying that truth and emotion will always clash,' Barrington said.

'Probably. I suspect men will always do bizarre things in the name of love.'

'Which brings me back to our ongoing conversation.' At her look of confusion, he said, 'The one we started the night we met at Lady Montby's and that we have been having ever since. The one concerning...us.'

Her pulse accelerated. 'I wasn't sure there *was* an us.'

'Oh, there most definitely is an us,' Barrington replied. 'I've spent the last few weeks trying to deny it, but finally realised I'm fighting a losing battle. And you know why.'

Anna stared down at her hands. 'You have taken pains to tell me and on more than one occasion. But you must feel there is hope for us or you wouldn't have sought me out.'

'You're right. Because the idea of *not* having you in my life is one I can no longer contemplate. You *are* all I think about, Anna,' he said quietly. 'And a man cannot be effective if his mind is constantly engaged upon something or someone he believes...unattainable.'

'I have always been attainable...for you,' Anna said, her voice husky. 'It was *you* who chose to believe otherwise. And I don't care if being with you involves risk. I would rather take the risks than live without you.'

'Even if it endangered your life?'

Anna suddenly felt wise beyond her years. 'You said yourself that life is never entirely without risk and you're right. But I like to think I demonstrated that I am not some witless female prone to running away at the first sign of danger.'

'No, you're not.' His mouth lifted at one corner. 'You have proven that most admirably. But would you allow yourself to become intimately involved with a man like me? Knowing that what I do might always put you in danger.'

Anna shook her head. 'The greatest danger to *both* of

us thus far has been from my own family. I couldn't be any closer to the source of the danger if I tried.'

'In that case...' Barrington dismounted and, crossing to her side, held out his hand. Anna placed hers within it and allowed him to help her down from the saddle. His hands lingered on her waist and they were so close she could feel the warmth of his breath on her face. 'I haven't spoken to your father, and if you say you have no desire to *be* my wife, I will not do so. But if you consent to marry me, Anna, I'll make you a promise here and now that there won't be any more risks to either of us, because I won't take on any more assignments.'

Her eyes widened in shock. 'You would do that for me?'

'I would do whatever it took to keep you safe,' Barrington said softly. 'I love you, Anna. There's never been a woman in my life for whom I've felt a deeper or more powerful passion. I love everything about you. Your enthusiasm for life, your unstinting concern for others, the genuine goodness that is so much a part of you. If you refuse to marry me, I will go on, but only because there won't be anything else for me to do. If you accept, you'll never have to worry about your happiness again.'

'Or yours,' Anna said. 'My brother almost killed you, Barrington, and I suspect there are others who would no doubt like to try. A man doesn't make friends by exposing other men's deepest, darkest secrets.'

'That's what I've been trying to tell you.'

'Nevertheless, someone has to try to stop them, and as I've been trying to tell *you*, I don't want you to give up what you do. I love you. There's no doubt in my mind about that. And, yes, I'll be afraid for you, but what you do is part of who you are. I couldn't ask you to give that up for me.'

'You don't have to ask. I've given a great deal of thought

to what I would be giving up and it doesn't compare to what I would be gaining. I want you as my wife, Anna,' he told her fervently. 'I want to hold you in my arms and tell you every day how much I love you. I want to cover your body with kisses and hear you cry out my name when we make love. And I want to see your beautiful eyes in the faces of our children. Marry me, sweetheart, and I'll spend the rest of my life not only telling you how much I love you, but showing you.'

His smile was slow and sensual, filling her with a giddy sense of pleasure. 'Good, because I *am* saying yes, Barrington, so you'd better be prepared to make good on your promise.' Uncaring as to who might be watching, Anna walked into his arms and tilted her head back, her eyes glowing. 'As far as I'm concerned, you can start telling me *and* showing me, just as soon as you like.'

* * * * *

IMPROPER MISS DARLING

To Donna Baspaly.

A gifted artist, a wonderful friend,
and a truly remarkable woman.

Chapter One

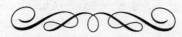

The three letters arrived on Lord Stewart's desk within a few days of one another. Each had been written in the author's own distinct style and each was intended to sway the reader to the writer's assessment of a situation never before encountered: the unexpected engagement of Alex's younger brother, Peter, to a young lady unknown to his family or to society at large.

The letter from his father, the earl, had been typically bombastic—a strongly worded missive condemning his youngest son's behaviour, throwing out words like duty and obligation and saying that such conduct was not at all in keeping with what he expected from a member of his own family.

The letter from his mother had been more gently phrased, blaming the error of Peter's ways on the impulsiveness of his nature and pleading with Alex to intervene before it caused irreparable rifts within the family.

But the third and most heartwrenching letter had been written by Peter himself; a desperate outpouring of emotion inspired by his love for the lady to whom he had blithely pledged his troth, along with a request for Alex's support in light of his father's blatant disapproval and his mother's resultant unhappiness.

All Alex could think of as he reread the three letters was how remarkable it was that a single engagement could have spawned such a wide and diverse range of reactions.

Still, he supposed it was only to be expected. Peter might not be first in line for the title, but he was still the Earl of Widdicombe's son, and their father always had been a stickler for propriety. No episodes of drunkenness, excessive gambling, or contracting of unsuitable marriages had ever been permitted to tarnish the family name. Alex's ancestors prided themselves on their ability to rise above such weaknesses, eschewing the vices that had crippled so many other noble families. They had been responsible family men and landowners for centuries, and, in time, Alex would follow in their footsteps and take up the role he had been groomed for from birth. Peter would likely settle into religion or law, either being an acceptable occupation for the younger son of a peer, and both would marry ladies of high birth and exceptional breeding suitable to producing children worthy of carrying on the line.

At least, that *had* been the expectation until Peter had done the unthinkable by betrothing himself to an unknown girl from the country, who, in his father's words, ...*while no doubt possessed of a pretty face, has absolutely nothing else to recommend her...*

Now it seemed the entire family was looking to Alex for a resolution, and time was of the essence since Peter was planning a family dinner for the coming week, followed by a grand ball and gathering two weeks after that at Ellingsworth Hall, his recently acquired country estate. And while Alex wasn't sure *anyone* was up to the task of smoothing an entire family's ruffled feathers in so short a time, he realised he was probably in the best position to try. If there was one thing at which he *did* excel, it was cutting through the layers of emotional chaos to get to the heart of the problem and resolve it before any lasting or serious damage could be done.

'Godfrey, have I anything of importance scheduled for the next few weeks?' he enquired of his steward.

That impeccably groomed gentleman turned the pages of a large leather-bound diary and scanned the entries. 'Nothing a few well-worded letters of regret won't take care of, my lord. Why?'

'It seems I am required in the country for a time.'

'In the *country*?' The steward looked at him askance. 'Now?'

'Unfortunately, my brother does not concern himself with the goings on in society. No doubt it slipped his mind that the Season would soon be underway.'

'No doubt,' Godfrey said, though his tone clearly indicated incredulity that anyone in the Earl of Widdicombe's family should be so negligent in their planning. 'I take it there is no chance he will change his mind?'

'None whatsoever.'

'Very well. I shall prepare the letters and have them ready for your signature by this evening.'

'Thank you.' Alex paused, frowning. 'When is Lady Glynnis due back?'

'The twenty-fourth, my lord. A week Friday.'

Friday. The day *after* his brother's dinner to introduce the members of his family to those of the young lady he intended to marry. Pity. Glynnis's presence would have gone a long way towards calming the troubled waters this first meeting was sure to stir up. His father *liked* Lady Glynnis Pettle. He heartily *approved* of Alex's plans to marry her. And he was far less likely to fly off the handle or to embarrass Peter in front of a houseful of guests if she was there lending her graceful manners and soothing influence to the proceedings.

Of course, there was always that *other* kind of soothing influence, Alex reflected. One his father was known to be particularly fond of…

'Godfrey, have we any of the earl's favourite whisky tucked away in the cellar?'

'I believe so, my lord.'

'Good. Have a case of that put in the carriage as well.'

'I shall see to it at once.'

Might as well go in prepared for all eventualities, Alex thought as he slid the letters into his desk and locked the drawer. If it didn't help sweeten his father's mood, it would certainly improve his. He could sit back and watch as the rest of his family battled around him, all the while thanking the gods of fortune and fate that love had not chosen *him* to be the unfortunate recipient of Cupid's annoying little arrows.

If there was one thing Emma Darling longed for, it was harmony—the blissful absence of the emotional strife that turned one's life upside down and made rational people do completely irrational things. Witness her Aunt Augusta. For the last three weeks, Emma had been staying with her aunt in Bath, listening to her go on about her daughter's unhappy marriage and her son's unsuitable bride, about the loneliness of her life and the scandalous affair her husband was supposedly having with the widow next door. When she became too emotionally overwrought to function, Emma had made the tea and run errands, baked Chelsea buns and read poetry, all in an attempt to console her aunt in what was obviously a very trying time.

Then, without a word of explanation or thanks, Aunt

Augusta had simply packed her bags and walked out, saying she was going to stay with a friend in Newport and that she wasn't coming back!

Not sure what else to do, Emma had hastily written letters to her cousins, explaining that their mother had gone to Newport and that it would be a good idea if one of them contacted her as soon as possible. Then she had written a note for her uncle with much the same message, adding that she would be leaving Bath the following day and returning home to Hampshire.

Emma doubted he would care. She had scarcely seen the man since her arrival in the spa town three weeks ago. And had she *known* the state of affairs in her aunt's house *before* boarding the coach, she would never have come in the first place. The only reason she had come to Bath was as a result of her father's other sister, Dorothy, suggesting upon her arrival at Dove's Hollow for her twice-annual visit, that Augusta 'wasn't well' and perhaps seeing Emma's smiling face would help lift her spirits.

Aware now that it would have taken a Belzonian pulley to lift her aunt's spirits from the abyss into which they had fallen, Emma closed her eyes and breathed a sigh of relief that she was almost home—back at Dove's Hollow, where life was, for the most part, tranquil and uncomplicated. When she went downstairs in the morning, it would not be to find a middle-aged woman weeping into her tea, but her father, quietly perusing yesterday's copy of *The Times* as though there were nothing of greater importance that needed to be done. Rory and Ranger, their two ageing spaniels, would be lying at his feet and there would be pleasant conversation, perhaps something of interest to be shared, until her younger sister, Linette, came downstairs to fill the room with chatter about hairstyles and dress patterns and whatever gossip happened to be circulating in the local shops the previous day.

At that point, Mr Darling would pick up his paper and escape to his study for the rest of the morning, leaving his daughters to discuss the latest goings on in London and to speculate upon who was marrying for love and who was marrying to better their position in life.

Emma, who tended to believe that everyone wed for material gain, would eventually finish her tea, bid her sister good morning and then go about her day. If the summer months were upon them, she would head into the garden to cut fresh flowers for the various table arrangements, or take a book into the shady recesses of the garden to read. In autumn, she would don her riding habit and enjoy a brisk canter along the leaf-covered roads, or collect apples from the trees in the nearby orchard. Once winter fell and the air grew chill, she might harness Bess and take the trap down to the village to shop for fabric, or, if too cold to go out, gather up her embroidery and settle in front of the fireplace to sew.

But now in the spring, her days were devoted to painting, to capturing the myriad shades of the new season on canvas, from the pastel greens of the freshly burst buds to the delicate pink-and-white blossoms of apple and cherry trees. With brush in hand, she would venture into the garden and try to replicate the glorious panoply of colour all around her.

Having to spend three weeks with Aunt Augusta at such a time had been agony!

However, that was all behind her now, and with her brother away at Oxford and Linette in a lull between passionate storms, Emma had every expectation of life being uneventful. As the carriage finally rumbled to a halt in front of the old stone house, she found herself counting the minutes until she could escape into the peace and quiet of the garden with her easel and brushes—

'Emma, dear, welcome home,' Aunt Dorothy cried, appearing in the courtyard as the carriage door swung open. 'Did you enjoy your stay in Bath?'

Emma frowned. Aunt Dorothy was still here? 'Not exactly, but I dare say you'll be hearing why from one of your nieces in the not-too-distant future. But what are *you* still doing here, Aunt?' she asked, climbing down from the carriage. 'I thought you were to have gone back to London weeks ago.'

'That was my intention, but there have been some interesting developments while you've been away and your father asked me if I would stay on a little longer.'

Developments? Emma wasn't sure she liked the sound of that. 'What kind of developments?'

'You'll see. Your father is waiting for you in his study.'

Emma paused, arrested by the expression on the older woman's face. 'Aunt Dorothy, you look like the cat that swallowed the canary. What *has* been going on?'

'I would love to tell you, my dear, but your father insists on giving you the news himself. But once he has, come to us in the drawing room and we will tell you all the things he has most likely forgotten.'

Emma didn't miss her aunt's use of the words *us* and *we*. 'Has this something to do with Linette?'

'It has, but more than that I dare not say.' She kissed Emma fondly on the cheek, smelling vaguely of sherry and peppermint, and then turned to lead the way into the house. Emma followed, wondering what could have happened to warrant such an inexplicable turn of events. Aunt Dorothy was not fond of country living. She only came to stay with them twice a year, saying it was the least she could do for her poor widowed brother and his three motherless children, but Emma knew she counted the days until she could return to London again.

What kind of 'development' could have prompted her to stay on, *and* to look as though there was nowhere else she would rather be?

'Linette is *engaged*?' Emma repeated after her father gave her the news. 'To whom?'

'Can you not guess?'

'In truth I cannot. The only gentleman of whom she has spoken with any affection is Mr Taylor, but I cannot imagine that he...' Emma stopped. 'Never tell me *he* has proposed.'

'Yes, and very sweetly, according to your sister.'

'But...the youngest son of the Earl of Widdicombe? Why on earth would he propose to Linette?'

'For all the usual reasons, I suppose. Apparently he is head over heels in love with the girl and cannot imagine life without her.'

'Good Lord.' Emma sat down in the nearest chair. 'Did he really say that?'

'He did, and naturally your sister is over the moon. There is to be a ball held in a few weeks' time to celebrate their betrothal.'

Emma's eyes widened. 'Not here!'

'Good Lord, no, we are not nearly grand enough. The festivities are to take place at Ellingsworth Hall. I believe Lady Widdicombe is coming down to oversee the arrangements. That's why I asked Dorothy to stay on. I thought it might be helpful for Linette to have an older woman to talk to. One who has...experience of marriage and would be able to offer advice in that regard. You understand.'

Oh, yes, Emma understood. Educating a young girl as to the 'expectations' of marriage was a job that usually fell to the mother or married older sister; but in the absence of both, her father had obviously decided that his widowed sister was the best person for the job.

Pity, Emma reflected drily. If her father had wanted his youngest daughter to learn about the expectations of marriage, he should have sent her to Bath. Linette would have learned a great deal more there than she had by staying here.

'When did all this happen?' Emma asked. 'I've only been gone three weeks.'

'The proposal was offered a few days after you left.'

'And no one wrote to tell me about it?'

Her father had the grace to look embarrassed. 'We thought it best not to. We knew you would wish to come home at once and Dorothy felt it better that you stayed with Gussie.' He tugged at his ear, a sure sign of his discomfort. 'I understand she is having some…family issues.'

'You could say that,' Emma muttered, not about to go into the details. 'Have you heard anything from Lord and Lady Widdicombe?'

'Not yet. They are in London and no doubt very busy with the Season. But I expect I will be hearing from his lordship quite soon.'

'I wonder what they think of this engagement,' Emma mused. 'Linette is the sweetest girl in the world, but the disparity between her social standing and Mr Taylor's cannot be denied. I would have thought it an insurmountable barrier to marriage.'

'As would I,' her father agreed. 'But young Mr Taylor doesn't seem to mind and there is nothing one can object to in Linette. She is as lovely as a spring day and as sweet as custard pie, although perhaps a trifle naïve.'

A great deal naïve, Emma was tempted to say. There was a world of difference between life at Dove's Hollow and the role she would be expected to fulfil as mistress of Ellingsworth Hall. Linette had never been exposed to society before. She had been to London once and had seemed happy enough to leave it. Her only social interactions since then had been at the local assemblies and dances that were held in the village of Little Moreton.

What a turnabout now to find her engaged to one of the most eligible bachelors in the county!

'I hope she knows what she is doing,' Emma murmured. 'I love Linette with all my heart, but she is a hopeless romantic and tends towards impulsive behaviour. What seems like a good idea one day is positively the worst the next, with scarcely a breath in between.'

'I know, and only time will tell how genuinely happy the two of them will be,' her father said. 'But you will have an opportunity to see for yourself tomorrow evening.'

'Tomorrow?'

'We have been invited to dine at Ellingsworth Hall. Just a small gathering of the immediate family. Your aunt will have all the details. In fact, you had best run along now, my dear, I'm sure she and your sister are at sixes and sevens waiting to tell you all about it.'

'Yes, I'm sure they are.' Emma managed a smile as she slowly got to her feet. 'Imagine, our little Linette engaged to the son of an earl. It is a tremendous match for her.'

'Yes, though considerably less so for him. But they are not wed yet.'

'Do you think one of them will cry off?'

'My dear, when it comes to matters of the heart, I have learned that nothing is impossible.' Her father retired to the comfort of his favourite chair beneath which Rory and Ranger slept and picked up one of his books. 'A burning passion can be doused with a few ill-chosen words and undying love can, in fact, die a quick and painful death. Nothing is as fickle as love. We would all do well to remember that.'

For the next hour, Emma was treated to a complete and extensive list of the Honourable Peter Taylor's qualities. According to Linette, he was the most handsome, the most charming, the most good-natured and the most patient of men. He was an accomplished rider, an excellent shot, spoke French like a native and even played the pianoforte.

By the time Emma reached her room, she was beginning to wonder whether her sister was marrying a saint rather than just a mere man. However, since Linette was also happier than Emma had ever seen her, establishing the difference seemed unimportant. She had found the man of her dreams and tomorrow evening they were to dine with Mr Taylor and his family at Ellingsworth Hall, a magnificent Elizabethan house nestled in over one hundred acres of rolling English countryside.

Not only that, two weeks later, friends and family would be arriving for an extended house party. It would commence with a grand ball on the Friday evening, followed by a series of outdoor events on the Saturday afternoon and a formal dinner that evening. Guests would likely begin leaving Sunday morning, and by the time it was over, Emma was sure she would know everything there was to know about the illustrious Peter Taylor and his family. Even her brother, Ridley, had been sent a note, strongly suggesting that he make himself available for the festivities.

Emma thought longingly of her easel and brushes. It was a beautiful afternoon and she would have loved to spend some time enjoying the sights and sounds of nature, especially after the long, dreary hours she had been forced to spend with Aunt Augusta.

However, it was clear that artistic endeavours would have to wait. Her sister was to be married to the youngest son of the Earl of Widdicombe. There would be a hundred-and-one details to sort out, and, knowing Aunt Dorothy's tendency to tipple during times of high emotional stress, Emma suspected most of the decisions would have to be made by her. She would try to be as patient as possible, and make herself available for Linette in whatever capacity her sister required. Other than that, all she could do was offer up silent prayers that it wouldn't be too long before the whole dizzying affair was behind them.

Prior to leaving for the country, Alex stopped off in Mayfair to pay a call on his parents. He hadn't heard from either of them since making them aware of his intention to travel down to Ellingsworth and he was curious to know if they planned on attending the dinner Peter was giving to introduce his fiancée to whichever members of his family were present. Considering his father's sentiments about the match, Alex knew better than to consider his parent's attendance a foregone conclusion.

He found his mother seated at her desk in the Wedgwood Salon, going through a large pile of correspondence. Garbed in a morning gown of deep-turquoise silk, she looked the picture of serenity; but, upon closer inspection, Alex noticed that her complexion was pale and that she looked to have lost weight, something she could ill afford to do. He quietly crossed the room and bent to drop a kiss on the top of her dark, shining head. 'Good morning, Mother.'

'Alex!' Lady Widdicombe jumped. 'I'm sorry, darling,

I was that caught up in my notes I didn't hear you come in. How are you?'

'Well. I'm on my way to Ellingsworth and thought I would stop by to find out if and when you and Father were driving down.'

His mother sighed. 'I shall be leaving tomorrow, but your father won't be joining me. He's worked himself into such a state over this engagement, I've had to call in Dr Harrow.'

'Harrow? That can't have made Father happy. What did the doctor say?'

'That Richard could do with losing a little weight and have one less whisky before retiring. And that he was to rest for a few days.'

'Sage advice for any man, I suppose,' Alex said. 'Is he in his study?'

'No. He wasn't feeling quite the thing this morning so he decided to remain in his room.'

'Then I shall go and see him—'

'Alex, there's something I have to tell you,' his mother said abruptly. 'Something you need to know before you go upstairs…'

It was bad news. Alex knew it from the way she suddenly refused to meet his eyes. 'What's wrong?'

'It isn't just Peter's engagement that has upset your father. Last week he…collapsed, in his study,' she said slowly. 'Dr Harrow said it…could be his heart.'

His *heart*? Alex was stunned. His father was only fifty-nine years old and as fit as most men half his age. When had he suddenly developed problems of this nature? 'Has this happened before?'

'I don't know. He says it hasn't, but you know he doesn't like worrying us and he hates having to see the doctor.' His mother sighed. 'Naturally, he didn't want me to say anything to you at all. He said there was no point in upsetting you because in a matter of days it would all be fine. And maybe it will be. But I felt you had a right to know before you went down to see your brother.'

Alex walked slowly across the room, stopping by the long window. 'What did Harrow suggest?'

'That we restrict your father to a light diet. Boiled fish and broths, no rich desserts or sauces. And he must be kept as calm as possible.'

Calm. With his youngest son about to marry a woman of whom he heartily disapproved. It was like telling a starving fox to ignore the rabbit jumping up and down in front of his nose.

'On second thought, perhaps it's best Father not come down to Ellingsworth just yet,' Alex said. 'At least not until I've had a chance to see how things stand. With luck, I'll be able to rectify matters without Father ever having to be involved.'

'Oh, that *would* be wonderful, Alex,' his mother said. 'I do want Peter to be happy, but I would be lying if I said I wasn't concerned. We know absolutely nothing about this young woman. Who her people are, where she comes from, what her background is. And naturally that worries your father very much. He is afraid Peter has engaged himself to some fortune-hunting social climber.'

'We can't deny that the possibility exists,' Alex acknowledged, 'but I'll find out what I can. And I understand if you would rather stay here with Father than travel all the way down to Hampshire.'

To his surprise, his mother shook her head. 'There's really nothing I can do here. Your father will be happier having Murdoch look after him. He thinks he's more likely to get that glass of whisky. But I've warned Murdoch not to indulge him and Dr Harrow did say he would look in while

I was gone. Besides, I promised Peter I would take care
of the arrangements for the ball. Being a man, he won't
have a clue where to start. That's what I've been doing
this morning,' she said, indicating the pile of papers on
her desk. 'And to be honest, I do want to meet this young
woman without your father being there to glower at her.
If Peter cannot be dissuaded from going ahead with the
marriage, I want to know what kind of person I am going
to be welcoming into the family.' She sighed. 'I would
like to feel there is at least *one* area of my life over which
I have some control.'

The earl was dozing when Alex walked into his room,
and though only a few weeks had passed since his last
visit, Alex could definitely see a change in his father's
appearance. His complexion was grey, his hands lay limp
at his sides and there was a definite rattle in his chest
when he breathed. Hard to equate the elderly-looking man
slumped in his chair with the vital, powerful figure Alex
had known all of his life. 'Father?' he ventured quietly.

'Hmm?' The earl's head moved, his eyes slowly opening. 'Oh, it's you, Alex. Didn't hear you come in.' He
tried to sit up. 'Must be all this medication Harrow's been
forcing down my throat. Told him I didn't want any of the
damn stuff.'

'If he's giving you medication, it's because you *need* it,'
Alex said, pulling up a chair next to his father's. 'And if
you don't take it, I shall force it down your throat myself.
We cannot have you messing about when it comes to your
health.'

'Damnation! She told you, didn't she!' the earl railed.
'I knew she wouldn't be able to keep it to herself.'

'Yes, Mother told me and she was right to do so.'

'She was *not* right to do so and I'll tell you now, it is

not my heart! It was indigestion. Brought on by a bit of bad pork.'

'A man does not collapse from indigestion,' Alex said calmly.

'Of course he does. I told Harrow as much too, the old quack! Said all I needed was a good glass of whisky!'

'I trust he didn't give you one.'

'He did not. Neither did Murdoch, damn his surly Scottish hide! I've a good mind to send him packing.'

Alex smiled. 'That would be a mistake, Father. Murdoch's been with you for nigh on forty years.'

'Yes, and he's getting far too uppity in his old age,' his father grumbled. He briefly closed his eyes, took a moment to catch his breath. 'So, what are you going to do about this situation with your brother?'

'Too early to say, but I'm on my way to Ellingsworth now.'

'Good, Alex, good, I have every confidence you'll be able to take care of it. And your timing couldn't be better. You know Peter's planned a dinner for the chit and her family on Thursday evening.'

'I heard.'

'Trumped-up little harpy,' the earl muttered. 'It was likely *her* idea that he hold a celebratory dinner in her honour so that she can get a taste of what her life is going to be like once she's lady of the manor. But we're not going to let that happen, are we, Alex? We're going to nip this in the bud long before it gets to that point.'

Unwilling to give his father false assurances, Alex merely said, 'I'll do what I can, sir. I take it you're not planning to be there.'

'Ha! I'd as soon spit in her eye as see her sit at my son's table. But Harrow has confined me to bed for a few days so I won't be able to go regardless. But *you* know what's what, Alex. You know we can't allow this marriage to take place.'

'It may be out of our hands. Have you spoken to Peter recently?'

'What's the point?' The earl's face twisted. 'He says he loves her and that's all there is to it. But we both know he's marrying beneath himself. And mark my words, he'll live to regret it.'

Alex decided not to address that for the moment. Marriages between mismatched social partners often did work out, but it wasn't easy and it usually required a considerable degree of sacrifice on one part or the other. 'Do you know anything about the girl?' he asked instead.

'Not yet, though I've engaged someone to make enquiries. And you needn't look at me like that,' he said when Alex raised an eyebrow in surprise. 'If there's bad blood in the family, I want to know about it *before* my son puts a ring on her finger!'

'It is possible you're exaggerating things, sir,' Alex said. 'She may be a perfectly charming young woman.'

'Really? Have you ever heard of the Darlings of Little Moreton? No, I thought not. Mark my words, she's after his money and an easy life. Peter won't believe that, of course. Reading his letter, you'd think she was an angel from heaven complete with fairy wings and a blasted halo! But I'll wager she's a common little chit with no breeding and bad manners. Pretty, but not at all suitable to being the wife of a Taylor.'

And that's really what it all came down to, Alex reflected drily. The appropriateness of the ladies his sons wished to marry. 'Well, I'll do what I can, but you should be prepared for the worst,' Alex said, getting to his feet. 'Peter's sensible enough to make up his own mind—'

'No man's sensible when it comes to women,' his father

interrupted. 'That's why I'm so proud of you, Alex. You take your obligations seriously. Always have. Lady Glynnis Pettle is precisely the sort of woman your brother *should* be marrying. A woman who knows her place in society. One you'll never have to worry about. She's an earl's daughter, after all.'

Alex smiled. 'Yes, she is, but she's also a good friend and has been for a long time. As to the other matter, I'll do what I can, but I'm not making any promises.'

'I have faith in you, my boy,' his father said. 'You've been a good and dutiful son all your life. You've never once given me any reason to doubt you. If *anyone* is going to be able to resolve this mess and make Peter listen to sense, it's you.'

Chapter Two

Ellingsworth Hall was an exquisite Elizabethan house perched prettily on the edge of a vast wood. Unlike many such grand houses, it had not been ruined by tasteless additions thrust upon it by succeeding generations; but had retained the dignity of its origins, the mellow gold stone reflecting warmth and welcome to all who came near.

'The formal gardens in the back are exceptionally lovely,' Linette said as the carriage drew to a halt under the portico. 'Mr Taylor took me for a walk through them last week. He was remarkably knowledgeable about the names of the flowers. I just said they were all very pretty and that my sister would create the most beautiful arrangements if she had such a garden to draw upon.'

Emma smiled, silently adding botanist to the growing list of her future brother-in-law's accomplishments. 'I am content with the selection I have in our own gardens, Linette, but I suspect you will be grateful for the variety. The need for flower arrangements will be that much greater in a house the size of Ellingsworth.'

'Without question,' Aunt Dorothy said. 'Mrs Connelly

told me the house has twenty-seven rooms, including twelve bedrooms.'

And Mrs Connelly would know, Emma thought drily. The wife of the local squire made it her business to know everything that went on in Little Moreton. In a bucolic village where the arrival of the post was the most exciting thing to happen in a day, the upcoming marriage of a peer's son to a local girl must have seemed like manna from heaven.

'Can this really be happening, Emma?' Linette asked in a voice of wonder. 'Or shall I wake up to find that it has all been a dream?'

'I certainly hope it is not a dream,' Emma said. 'Otherwise I shall have expended a great deal of time and effort getting dressed, and all for nothing.'

'It is never a waste of time to make oneself look pretty, Emma,' Aunt Dorothy chided. 'On such an auspicious occasion, we must all try to look our very best. Even your father has made more of an effort than usual.'

'I have made no more or less of an effort than I would have for any other occasion,' Mr Darling objected.

'Nonsense, Percy, you look quite the thing in your new mulberry jacket. And I do like the way Jenks has tied your cravat. Simple, yet elegant. The hallmark of a gentleman.'

Emma smiled, aware that how they looked would likely be of secondary importance to how they behaved. They were about to meet the Earl and Countess of Widdicombe, two of society's most illustrious and influential members. Lord Widdicombe sat in the House of Lords and Lady Widdicombe was a close confidant of the patronesses of Almack's. They owned an elegant town house in London, a sprawling estate in Kent, and likely several other establishments with which Emma was not familiar.

By contrast, Emma's father was a former tutor and her

late mother was the daughter of a well-to-do merchant. They had acquired Dove's Hollow upon the demise of Mr Darling's older brother, Cyril, who had apparently won the house and all its contents at the faro table. After Cyril's unfortunate death in a drunken brawl, the house had passed to Emma's father, who had been only too delighted to move his young family in and take up the life of a gentleman. They were not well travelled, did not go regularly to the theatre or museums, and though Emma had been to London once, she had not been formally presented at Court, having had no one to sponsor her or cover the costs of a Season.

Still, at least they made a presentable party as they climbed the steps to the front door of the house her sister would soon be calling home. Aunt Dorothy was wearing a stylish new gown of *terre d'Eygpt* sarsenet, Linette was radiant in white muslin trimmed with double bands of gold embroidery and Emma's own gown was a shade of pale green she knew to be flattering to her dark hair and fair complexion.

Nevertheless, she was thankful she was not the one who would have to bear the brunt of the scrutiny tonight. This evening, she was simply a bystander. She would support her sister in every way she could, but if the earl and countess took it into their heads to be disdainful, she suspected there would be little any of them could do but smile as bravely as they could and count the minutes until it was all over.

They were greeted at the door by a tall and rather impressive-looking butler and shown into the elaborate Chinese drawing room. Linette had already informed them that Mr Taylor intended on having all of the reception rooms redone and that he had decided to start with this, the largest of the saloons. Emma, whose eye was always drawn to line and colour, paused on the thresh-

old, impressed by the elegant proportions and by the deep
crimson and gold colour scheme. Fire-breathing dragons
and sword-wielding warriors were prominent throughout
the room and the furnishings were Oriental in design.
Two magnificent black-lacquer cabinets with ornate battle
scenes hand painted in gold and crimson stood on either
side of the long window.

The Countess of Widdicombe was seated on a red-velvet
chair by the fireplace, hands folded calmly in her lap. She
was a regal-looking woman, still relatively young, with a
smooth, unlined complexion and glossy black hair art-
fully arranged in an elegant coiffure. Wearing a gown of
rich crimson silk, she seemed almost an accessory to the
room, her elegance and grace very much in keeping with
her surroundings.

Emma thought she would have looked a great deal
friendlier had she troubled herself to smile, but apparently
smiles were not required of a countess when meeting a
prospective daughter-in-law and her family for the first
time.

Two other men occupied the room and stood on either
side of the fireplace like mismatched bookends. Emma
recognised Peter Taylor at once and, though he was not
the kind of man that appealed to her, she could well understand Linette's attraction to him. He was not overly tall,
but his slenderness conveyed the impression of height and
the combined skills of his tailor and valet did the rest.
His thick, nut-brown hair tapered neatly to his collar, and
with quite the most charming smile Emma had ever seen
and a demeanour that was totally without arrogance, he
reminded her of an anxious puppy, desperate to be loved
by one and all.

The other man, who was clearly too young to be the
earl, was obviously the eldest son, Viscount Stewart.

Lord Stewart towered over his younger brother by a good four inches and possessed the kind of looks that would invariably send young girls swooning. Thick black hair, luxurious as sable, was swept back from a broad forehead already tanned by the warm spring sun. His jaw was square, his mouth full lipped and sensual, his lashes dark under even darker brows.

Only his eyes were light, the clear, cornflower blue seemingly at odds with the rest of his appearance.

But where was Lord Widdicombe? Surely he should be here to greet his son's intended bride and her family?

'Mr Darling, I am so pleased you were able to come,' Peter Taylor said, quickly stepping forwards. 'Mother, may I present Mr Darling and his family.'

As Lady Widdicombe inclined her head, Emma studied her face for some indication as to what she was feeling. But apart from a slight stiffness of manner, there was nothing to indicate either pleasure or resentment. 'Good evening, Mr Darling. I do not believe you have met my eldest son, Lord Stewart?'

'I have not, Lady Widdicombe, but I am very pleased to do so.' Mr Darling bowed to both the countess and the heir, and then turned to introduce the members of his own family. 'May I present my sister, Mrs Grand, my eldest daughter, Emma, and, of course, my youngest daughter, Linette.'

'Mrs Grand, Miss Darling,' the countess said, her gaze resting on each of them for a moment. 'And Miss Linette Darling. Step forwards, child.'

Linette did, her cheeks taking on a deeper-pink hue as she moved closer to the countess's chair. Stopping a few feet in front of her, she executed a graceful curtsy.

The countess nodded her approval. 'How old are you, child?'

'Seventeen, your ladyship.'

'Seventeen. And you think you can make my son happy.'

'Of course she will make me happy, Mother,' Mr Taylor said, springing to Linette's defence. 'That is why—'

His mother's upraised hand silenced him. 'My question was addressed to Miss Linette, Peter. Kindly allow her to answer.'

All eyes swung back to Linette, who suddenly looked like the sacrificial lamb being led to the slaughter. 'I...I—'

'Speak up, child. I'm not going to eat you.'

'Of course not, Mother, but judging from the look of terror in Miss Linette's eyes, I'm not sure she believes you.'

It was Lord Stewart who spoke, the rich timbre of his voice drawing every eye in the room. He stepped away from the fireplace and offered Linette a surprisingly friendly smile. 'Good evening, Miss Linette. We are very pleased to welcome you and your family to Ellingsworth Hall.' His voice was low and deep, the tone undeniably reassuring.

Linette visibly relaxed. 'Th-thank you, Lord Stewart.'

'I regret that my father is not able to be with us this evening, but his health is not the best and it was necessary that he remain in London for a few days.'

'We are very sorry to hear that, my lord,' Mr Darling said in a tone of mingled relief and regret. Obviously, he too had been wondering at the reason behind the earl's absence. 'I hope he will be recovered in time for the coming festivities.'

'We certainly hope that will be the case,' Lord Stewart said. 'The doctor has advised a period of rest before resuming his social obligations. Especially one of this consequence.'

'Will there be...a lot of people in attendance?' Linette asked nervously.

'Indeed, most everyone has written to say they will be here,' Lady Widdicombe replied. 'I had my doubts about Lord and Lady Martindale, but their acceptance arrived yesterday, and even Lord and Lady Huffton said they would be willing to leave town for a weekend. Then there will be Sir George and Lady Monk, and of course, the Earl and Countess of Leyland and their daughter, Lady Glynnis Pettle, whom Alexander is soon to marry.'

'Marry?' Peter Taylor's eyebrows rose. 'I wasn't aware you'd proposed to Lady Glyn, Alex.'

'I haven't,' Lord Stewart said with a speaking glance at his mother.

'But we all know it is only a matter of time.' Lady Widdicombe turned to Emma's father with a complacent smile. 'There has been an understanding between the families for some time. Lady Glynnis's father is the Earl of Leyland and her mother the former Lady Georgiana Croft, daughter of the Marquis of Tunney. It is an excellent match.'

Mr Darling and Aunt Dorothy both offered dutiful murmurs of approval and Lady Widdicombe looked suitably appeased. Emma, who was not impressed by the countess's reluctance to appear as welcoming towards Linette as she was to this other unknown lady, rolled her eyes, only to flush when she caught Lord Stewart watching her.

'Miss Darling,' he said, his gaze moving over her so quickly she felt a draught. 'I would not have taken you for Miss Linette's sister. The resemblance between you is not immediately discernible.'

'Pray do not trouble yourself to be polite, Lord Stewart, the resemblance is not discernable after several hours of intense study. Linette has always been the beauty in the family,' Emma told him. 'I tend more towards the academic and the practical.'

'Oh, now, Emma, you are being far too critical of yourself,' Linette was quick to say. 'You play the piano, manage the household and paint the most wonderful landscapes.'

'All at the same time?' Lord Stewart favoured Emma with a brief smile. 'A remarkable talent indeed.'

Resisting the impulse to trade sarcasm for sarcasm, Emma said, 'It no doubt would be if I were able to do all three simultaneously, but I prefer to do them separately and I admit to painting with far more skill than I play.'

'How unfortunate,' Lady Widdicombe observed. 'A lady's talent on the pianoforte must always be deemed more valuable than her ability to paint. Painting is such a solitary occupation and one cannot socialise when one is alone.'

'True, but if a lady does not entertain well, surely it is kinder to her audience that she not make the attempt? I would far rather look at a well-executed painting than listen to a poorly played sonata.'

'Surely the answer is to practise more often, Miss Darling.'

'Only if there is something to be gained by the effort.' Emma smiled. 'Apart from Linette, my family is not particularly gifted in the musical arena.'

The remark was followed by a rather startled silence, leaving Emma to conclude that speaking truthfully about one's abilities or lack thereof was probably not recommended. She couldn't be sure, but she thought her father was not the only one who breathed a sigh of relief when dinner was announced a short time later.

Dinner in the baronial dining room was exceptional, though Emma thought eating in the smaller, more intimate family dining room would have been far less intimidating. The great table, which could easily have sat forty, was set with crisp white linens, sparking crystal and the family silver. A magnificent silver epergne graced the centre of the table, while smaller flower arrangements at either end provided a welcome splash of colour against the backdrop of white and silver.

As host, Peter Taylor took his place at the head of the table, with his mother on his right and Linette on his left. Lord Stewart sat to Emma's right, while her father was on Lady Widdicombe's right with Aunt Dorothy beside him. And, as expected, the meal was outstanding. A variety of courses, each more tempting than the last, was served by liveried footmen while the butler poured the wine and kept a sharp eye on every servant in the room.

Emma couldn't help but smile as she thought of Jenks, their man of all trades. A country fellow at best, poor Jenks would have felt decidedly out of place here at Ellingsworth Hall. No doubt the servants below stairs were every bit as intimidating as the lofty family above.

'Something amuses you, Miss Darling?'

Emma looked up to find Lord Stewart's blue eyes fixed upon her. 'Yes, though I doubt anyone but myself would find it so.'

'How can you know if you do not give us an opportunity to hear it?'

'Because I learned long ago that while some things are amusing to all, others are not.' Emma's gaze moved around the room, touching on the elegant, the beautiful and the priceless. Somehow she knew her musings would definitely fall into the latter category. 'I am sorry to hear of your father's illness, Lord Stewart. I hope it is nothing serious.'

'I'm sure it is not.' Lord Stewart's practised smile moved easily into place. 'The doctor simply advised rest for a few days.'

'Still, such things are worrisome. While I'm sure the

doctor is doing everything he can to speed Lord Widdicombe's recovery, it always weighs on one's mind.'

'As you say.' He raised his glass and glanced at her over
the rim. 'Will your brother be joining us in two weeks'
time? I understand he is presently studying law at Oxford.'

'Yes, but we sent word to let him know of the engagement and Ridley has assured us that he will be here in
time.'

'As, hopefully, will Father,' Peter Taylor said, glancing
at his mother. 'We must have *everyone* in attendance for
such an important occasion. Isn't that right, Mother?'

Lady Widdicombe looked up and shared a brief glance
with her eldest son. After a pause, Lord Stewart said, 'Of
course everyone will be here, Peter. It is, after all, the
celebration of your engagement. And, on that note, may I
ask you to rise, raise your glasses and join me in a toast,'
he said, getting to his feet. 'To my brother and his lady.
May they experience good health, prosperity, and may
they always be as happy as they are today.'

Emma dutifully raised her glass. It was not the most
romantic of toasts, but perhaps Lord Stewart was not a
romantic man. Just because he looked the part didn't mean
he had the temperament to go along with it. She spared
a quick glance for her sister, who was smiling blissfully
into her fiancé's eyes and knew Linette didn't care a whit
about flowery tributes or good wishes. She was in love
and the man she loved, loved her in return.

Not even the most pedantic of toasts was going to rob
her of the pleasure she found in that.

At the conclusion of meal, Lady Widdicombe led the
ladies into the elegant Green Saloon, leaving the gentlemen free to enjoy their after-dinner indulgences. Emma,
who was decidedly relieved to be away from the probing

eyes of Lord Stewart, found the Green Saloon far more to her liking. It was peaceful after the dramatic Chinese room, due no doubt to the absence of snarling dragons and sabre-waving warriors everywhere she turned.

'Mrs Grand,' Lady Widdicombe said as she settled into an emerald-green wing chair. 'You are, I understand, a widow?'

'Yes. My husband died three years ago.'

'So you now live with your brother and take care of his family?'

'Oh, no, your ladyship. I live in London with a companion. I'm not one for country life,' Aunt Dorothy admitted. 'I prefer the hustle and bustle of town. Always something going on and plenty of shops to spend your time and your money in. But I try to come down at least twice a year to be with my brother and his family.'

'I see. Then I take it *you*, Miss Darling, have the responsibility of running the house and looking after your siblings,' the countess said.

Emma smiled. 'I look after the housekeeping and the accounts, and I take care of Papa and Linette as best I can, but my brother, Ridley, is presently away at Oxford and quite able to look after himself.'

'And neither you nor your brother is married.'

'No.'

The countess turned to regard Aunt Dorothy again. 'Is it not unusual, Mrs Grand, for a younger daughter to be settled in marriage before the older son and daughter have made a suitable match?'

'I suppose it is, your ladyship.'

'Am I to assume, then, that Miss Darling has not been to London?'

The older woman's cheeks coloured. 'I believe she has.'

'But obviously met with no success.'

'On the contrary, I was most successful,' Emma said, having had enough of people talking about her as though she wasn't in the room. 'I spent a good deal of time at the British Museum and, by the time I left, I had sketched nearly the entire contents of the Egyptian wing *and* made a decent start on ancient Greece.'

The comment was clearly unexpected and the resultant look of surprise on Lady Widdicombe's face prompted Aunt Dorothy to say, 'Emma is quite gifted when it comes to drawing, Lady Widdicombe. Her sketches of the Elgin Marbles were really quite astonishing.'

'Indeed.' Lady Widdicombe turned her attention to Linette, obviously finding Emma's achievements less than noteworthy. 'Miss Linette, are you able to play the pianoforte?'

'I am, Lady Widdicombe.'

'Then pray be good enough to entertain us.'

'Yes, of course.' Linette quickly got up and moved to the instrument. 'Oh! A Broadwood grand piano.'

'Yes. Peter had it brought down from London.' Pride resonated in the countess's voice. 'He plays exquisitely.'

Linette ran her fingers lightly over the keys, picking out a simple tune. 'What a lovely sound. Emma, you must come and turn the pages for me.'

Dutifully, Emma got up and joined her sister.

'What shall I play?' Linette whispered. 'I am so nervous.'

'You have nothing to be nervous about.' Emma calmly flipped through the sheets of music on the platform and pulled one out. 'You play beautifully and your voice is that of an angel. And here is one of your favourite pieces.'

'"Greensleeves,"' Linette said, relieved. 'Yes, I shall be able to do justice to that.'

She began to play and though Emma dutifully watched

her progress so as not to miss turning the page at the appropriate time, she did risk an occasional glance at Lady Widdicombe to see if she was enjoying the performance. She hadn't missed the ambivalence in the countess's attitude towards Linette. While she wasn't precisely hostile, neither was she warmly welcoming. Fortunately, she seemed to appreciate Linette's skill on the pianoforte. She actually closed her eyes once or twice during the performance and was gracious in showing her appreciation at the end.

'Very nice, Miss Linette. You play tolerably well and have a very pleasant singing voice.'

'Thank you, Lady Widdicombe.'

'Of course, both would be improved by regular practice. I would advise you to take the required time during each day to do so.'

'Yes, Lady Widdicombe.'

'And now, it is Miss Darling's turn to entertain us,' the countess said. 'Unless she feels it will be too embarrassing for her.'

Emma smiled. Had Lady Widdicombe not tossed in that last line, she might have gracefully demurred. But never one to back away from a challenge, she sat down on the bench recently vacated by her sister and said, 'I do have one or two tolerable pieces in my repertoire. I simply shall not sing for that would be most humbling after Linette's performance. And I doubt *that* would be improved if I were to practise every hour of every day from now until I died.'

Lady Widdicombe said nothing, allowing Emma a brief moment of victory. The countess might be able to tell Linette what she should and should not do, but she certainly wasn't going to exert the same influence over her. One had to draw the line somewhere.

It would have been a great deal better, Emma reflected later, had *she* been the first to perform and Linette the second. Because by the time Linette had taken Emma's vacant seat next to Aunt Dorothy and Emma was ready to play, the door opened again and the gentlemen walked in. And it became immediately evident that no one had been expecting to see *her* seated at the pianoforte. Emma saw a look of startled pleasure on her father's face and a slightly more cautious one on Mr Taylor's.

Lord Stewart's expression was unreadable. Nor could she glean anything from the tone of his voice, when, moving to stand beside the fireplace, he said, 'I did not expect you to honour us with a performance, Miss Darling.'

'I did not say I was unable to play, my lord,' Emma said evenly. 'Only that I do not play as well as I paint. Nor do I sing as well as my sister, whose performance you just missed.'

'Then I hope we may prevail upon Miss Linette to sing for us again. But we should regret not hearing you play first.'

Equally sure he wouldn't have cared had she left immediately after dinner, Emma turned her attention back to the piano. Normally, she would have quailed at having to perform in front of such dignified company, but having recently discovered a piece by Bach that she liked very much, and having spent more time than usual practising it while at Aunt Augusta's house, Emma had managed to imprint the score firmly in her mind. Now, after giving herself a few minutes to recall the intricate opening, she placed her fingers upon the keys and began to play.

Music rolled forth. Not sweet and sentimental like Linette's 'Greensleeves,' but strong and powerful, the melody filling the room. It was one of passion and unrequited love, and on the exquisite instrument the notes rang true and clear. For once, Emma forgot about her audience and lost herself in the music. She had never performed on such a marvellous instrument before and she was astonished at how well the piece sounded. As she brought her hands down on the final chords, her heart was beating hard, her exhilaration at having executed the complicated piece without a mistake bringing an unexpected glow of triumph to her cheeks.

There was a moment's stunned silence. Then, enthusiastic applause broke out as Emma rose to take her bows. She saw a variety of expressions on the faces turned towards her. On her father's, pride, pure and simple. On her aunt's, pride mingled with relief, and on Linette's, astonished admiration. Peter Taylor's mouth was open and Lady Widdicombe was staring at her in disbelief.

Only Lord Stewart's expression bore no indication of surprise. 'You did not tell us the truth of your ability, Miss Darling. Seldom have I heard that piece played better or with more emotion.'

'Indeed, I believe you were having sport with us, Miss Darling,' Peter said. 'I vow she would give Lady Glynnis a run for her money. What say you, Alex?'

'I'd say Miss Darling could hold her own with anyone,' he answered evenly. 'Well done, Miss Darling.'

'Indeed, Emma, well done!' Linette said with unconcealed joy.

Emma politely inclined her head, grateful for the praise, but more relieved that she hadn't made a fool of herself in front of everyone in the room. She'd told herself when she'd sat down at the piano that she had wanted to make a good showing for Linette's sake and that she hadn't played the piece to impress anyone, but that wasn't entirely true.

She *had* wanted to make a good impression. She had wanted to impress *him*.

'Thank you, but it is one of the few pieces I play well,' she said. 'As indicated earlier, my repertoire is extremely limited.'

'If you were only to play that one piece, you would find yourself welcome in any drawing room,' Lord Stewart said.

The subtle words of praise had Emma raising her eyes to his; something she immediately came to regret. She didn't want him thinking she cared, any more than she was willing to admit she did.

'Play something else, Miss Darling,' Peter implored. 'You must have at least one other song with which to entertain us.'

'What about "The Merry Piper"?' Aunt Dorothy suggested.

Emma nodded. 'Only if Linette will sing.'

Not surprisingly, Linette was delighted to sing and because they had performed the duet so many times, Emma knew they acquitted themselves well. The music was lovely and Linette's sweet soprano voice made easy work of the lyrics. At the conclusion, they were again met with enthusiastic applause.

'I say, the two of you must perform for our guests at the ball,' Peter said. 'I don't believe I have ever heard a lovelier duet.'

'Nonsense, Peter, musicians have already been engaged,' his mother said. 'It is hardly the thing for your… fiancée and her sister to entertain.'

'In that case, I am delighted we were treated to the performance tonight.' He moved to stand beside Linette and taking her hand, raised it to his lips. 'Did I not tell you she was the most beautiful, the most gifted, the most remarkable young lady of my acquaintance?'

Emma hastily averted her eyes from the lovestruck look on her future brother-in-law's face and promptly locked gazes with Lord Stewart—whose expression was anything *but* lovestruck. What was he thinking as he watched the pretty scene unfold? That it was hopelessly romantic? An emotional embarrassment? Was he counting the minutes until he could politely slip away? The half-smile on his lips might be one of amusement, but it could just as easily signify boredom or contempt. He didn't strike Emma as the type of man who would find pleasure in such simple drawing-room entertainments.

'Well done, dearest,' Aunt Dorothy whispered as Emma sat back down beside her. 'Your father and I could not be more proud.'

Emma managed a fleeting smile, aware of being able to breathe a little easier now that the performance was over. But she was far from happy with her silly need to impress Peter's brother. Of what concern was it to her what he thought of her? The man was attractive, wealthy and heir to an earldom. He was no doubt used to women falling at his feet and to singing his praises in the hopes of attracting his attention.

Emma had no intention of becoming one of those women. She was not some simple-minded female easily swayed by good looks and an impressive title. She judged a man on the strength of his convictions, on the fairness of his mind and on the kindness of his words. What she had seen of Lord Stewart tonight was a man assessing a situation. One who had likely been asked to pass judgement on Linette and possibly on the rest of her family as well. Because when a man married, his bride's family became *his* family. Her assets became *his* assets. And her liabilities became *his* liabilities.

Was that what Lord Stewart had been sent here to find out? Emma wondered. The extent of the liability his brother was really taking on?

Chapter Three

Not surprisingly, a great deal of speculation followed the dinner at Ellingsworth Hall. Linette suffered alternating bouts of exhilaration and despair over what Lady Widdicombe's and Lord Stewart's feelings about her might have been, for while she was encouraged by her performance on the piano, she was equally convinced that her conversation at dinner had fallen far short of what was expected and that their impressions of her had been tainted as a result.

Naturally, Aunt Dorothy was of the opinion that Linette had done splendidly and that, in her estimation, the evening had been an unmitigated success. She declared the countess to be far more gracious than expected, that Lord Stewart was an elegant and handsome gentleman, and that Mr Taylor was exactly the type of man one might wish to have as a son-in-law.

Mr Darling was more reserved in his comments. Though he didn't say as much, Emma knew he believed that the real test of Linette's suitability would come during the weekend house party when many of Mr Taylor's friends and family would be in attendance and far more judgmental eyes would be focused on Linette than had been thus far.

In that, Emma tended to agree. Though Lady Widdicombe had been intimidating at the onset, by the end of the evening she had mellowed enough to give Linette a nod of approval and to tell her that she had played the pianoforte very nicely. Society, however, would take a far more critical view of the engagement and Emma felt sure there would be people at the ball who would be of the opinion that Mr Taylor could have done better. She feared a combination of ill will and jealousy would come together in the form of spiteful remarks that were neither fair nor warranted being directed towards Linette.

All of that she kept to herself, of course. Linette was anxious enough about the upcoming ball; there was no point in making matters worse by pointing out things that *might* happen. Besides, Emma had concerns enough of her own—not the least of which was the fact that the upcoming house party would again place her in the company of Lord Stewart.

She wished she could have said the thought didn't bother her, but she knew it for the half-truth that it was. The man unsettled her, arousing emotions and feelings she was not at all comfortable with. Several times throughout the dinner, she had felt his eyes on her and had looked up to find him watching her, as though hoping to find something lacking in her make-up.

It must have been that because she refused to believe it had anything to do with his interest in her as a woman. Not when he was all but engaged to a lady whose blood was as blue as his. But was he wondering, perhaps, if she thought to gain notoriety from her sister's success? To use Linette's connection to Peter as a way to move into better society herself?

The unpleasant speculation no doubt accounted for the terseness of her reply when Linette chanced to ask her about the gentleman as they strolled through the garden a few days later. 'What did *I* think of Lord Stewart?' Emma said. 'Why would you ask?'

'No particular reason.' Linette bent down to lift a slow-moving caterpillar off the path and settled him gently in the grass. 'I simply noticed him watching you throughout the evening and wondered what your opinions of him were.'

Emma took a deep breath. So Linette had noticed it too. 'I thought him…pleasant.'

'Nothing more?'

'What else would you have me say?'

'That he was exactly what he seemed. Handsome, charming and highly intimidating.'

'You found him intimidating?'

'Never tell me you did not?'

'I thought him serious, but hardly intimidating.' Emma drew her shawl more closely about her shoulders. 'But he is very different from his brother. Your Mr Taylor is certainly the more light-hearted of the two.'

'Yes, thank goodness. And now that you have spent an evening with him, do you not agree that he is wonderful, Emma?' Linette said, her face alight with love and happiness. 'I am convinced I am marrying the perfect man.'

Equally convinced there was no such thing, Emma said, 'I think the two of you will be very happy together.'

After a pause, Linette said, 'I wonder what Lady Glynnis will be like.'

'Lady Glynnis?'

'The young woman Lord Stewart is going to marry. Don't you remember? The countess seemed very pleased about the match.'

'I expect she would, given Lady Glynnis's position in society,' Emma said. 'As Lord Widdicombe's heir, it is Lord Stewart's duty to marry well.'

'It sounds as though she is very accomplished on the pianoforte.'

'I suspect the lady is accomplished in all areas of feminine endeavour. He would not have chosen her otherwise.'

'Do you think he loves her?' Linette asked.

Emma laughed. 'Good Lord, Linette, how am I to know that?'

'Well, did he strike you as the type of man who would marry for love?'

'I've no idea. I spoke to him briefly and in no great depth. You were there the entire time.'

'I know, but you are so much more perceptive about people than I. You see things I do not.'

'That is not always a good thing.'

'Well, perhaps we will know when we see the two of them together.' Linette fell into step beside her. 'You can always tell when two people are in love.'

'Oh yes?' Emma said, chuckling. 'And how do you do that?'

'The lady blushes and the man looks as though his heart is lost to all but her. They stand close together, even when there is no reason to do so, and they frequently exchange glances. Especially when they think no one is watching.'

'Gudgeon. You are making all of this up.'

'No, it's true!' Linette said with feeling. 'I saw Penelope Faith and Sir Wensley Cottonwood acting like that at the Parthingers' ball and they were betrothed the following week!'

'I cannot imagine Lord Stewart looking at *any* lady with stars in his eyes,' Emma said. 'He doesn't strike me as the type. Mr Taylor looks at you that way, but his temperament is vastly different from his brother's.'

'Yes, thank goodness. I think I am a little frightened of Lord Stewart, for all his being so handsome and charming,' Linette admitted. 'Nevertheless, it will be interesting to see him with Lady Glynnis on Friday evening. After all, if she is to be my sister-in-law, I do want her to like me.'

Impulsively, Emma stopped and hugged her sister close. 'No one can help but like you, dearest. You are the sweetest, gentlest, most kind-hearted person I know. If Lady Glynnis does *not* like you, we shall simply not like *her*.'

'That will not make for very pleasant family gatherings,' Linette said unhappily.

'I shouldn't worry about it.' Emma slipped her arm through her sister's. 'I doubt Lord Stewart is all that fond of country living. Once he and Lady Glynnis are married, we likely won't see either of them around Little Moreton for quite some time.'

Emma was seated at the far end of the garden when she noticed the horse and rider approaching from the direction of Ellingsworth Hall later that same day. The horse did not look to be of local stock. Big boned and with long, delicate legs and a proud arch to its neck, it was clearly a thoroughbred and therefore well beyond the reach of most of the young men who resided in Little Moreton.

As to the rider, Emma suspected it was Peter Taylor come to pay a call on her sister. Linette had informed her that he often stopped by for afternoon visits now they were officially betrothed, and, unconcerned, Emma went back to her painting. The sun was creating a fascinating interplay of light and shadow on the lily pond, and the ever-shifting patterns of blue and green were far more interesting to her than the gentleman coming to call. And when a dragonfly landed on the edge of a lily pad, the insect's huge silver wings shimmering in the sunlight, Emma caught her breath.

How did one capture something so magical? What colours did one use to replicate the translucence of its wings and the iridescent shading of its body? She thought about that for a while, mixing colours in her mind, and reached down for her palette—only to see a pair of dark-brown boots standing in the grass a few feet away.

'Good afternoon, Miss Darling.'

Emma knew the voice. Having heard it at dinner, she would have recognised it anywhere. But it was the last one she had been expecting to hear in her garden today. 'Good afternoon, Lord Stewart.' She raised her head and peered at him from beneath the brim of her bonnet. 'If you are looking for my father, you will find him in the house, most likely in his study.'

'Thank you, but it was you I came to see.'

'Oh?'

'I wondered if we might have a chat. If you do not mind me singling you out.'

'That would depend on what you were singling me out for.'

'I wish to talk to you about a matter of considerable importance.'

'Oh dear, that does sound alarming.' Emma put down her brush. 'Pray, forgive my attire. I was not expecting visitors.'

'No apologies are necessary. You look charming.'

Emma was too much of a lady to roll her eyes, but she was sorely tempted to do so given how easily the lies fell from his tongue. She was wearing a wide-brimmed sunhat with ribbons tied loosely beneath her chin, a painter's smock liberally smudged with paint, and though her hair was pinned up, she could feel the breeze tugging at loose wisps. Charming was decidedly not how she would have described her appearance. Still, he hadn't come with a view to courting her.

'Very well, Lord Stewart, you have my undivided attention. What is this important matter you wish to talk to me about?'

'Your sister, my brother and the unfortunate inequity of the match.'

Emma's eyes widened in shock. Mercy! The man certainly didn't beat around the bush. 'You will forgive me if I say I am somewhat taken aback by the remark, my lord.'

'I would have been more surprised had you said you were expecting it,' Lord Stewart acknowledged. 'But it is a subject I believe warrants further discussion.'

'I fail to see why. The inequity of the match obviously wasn't of concern to your brother when he asked Linette to marry him.'

'Of course not. My brother is romantic by nature and more impulsive than is wise.'

'Attributes shared by my sister, I'm afraid.' Emma looked up, shading her eyes with her hand. 'But what's done is done, wouldn't you agree?'

'Forgive me,' he said, belatedly aware that his position was causing her to stare directly into the sun. 'Perhaps we could take a walk?'

'As you like.' Emma put her brushes into a pot of water, then stood up and removed her smock. 'You do not tether your horse?' she asked, looking past him to the elegant thoroughbred grazing freely beyond.

'There is no need. He never wanders.' Lord Stewart stared at the easel for a moment. 'Impressive. You have a knack for blending colours so that they seem to melt into one another.'

'It is an attribute of watercolours. If a line is drawn too harshly, you simply brush a wash over it and the line softens. It is a very forgiving medium.'

'Only to those who know how to use it.' Lord Stewart smiled. 'You obviously do.'

It was a new and unusual experience to be complimented by a gentleman. Emma was used to most of the flattery going to Linette, but she had to admit to a warm glow of pleasure at hearing Lord Stewart praise her work. 'Thank you, but I am an amateur at best. My brother is the true artist in the family.' She fell into step beside him. 'So, you wish to talk about the unsuitability of the match between Linette and your brother.'

'Please don't misunderstand, Miss Darling,' he said quickly. 'Your sister is a lovely young woman with pleasing manners and a charming personality. But you cannot deny the disparity in their social situations.'

'Of course not, but your brother obviously doesn't care and given that your parents have not forbidden the match, I don't see what business it is of ours.'

He stopped, frowning. 'May I speak honestly, Miss Darling?'

'I wish you would.'

'Then I will tell you that my parents are *not* pleased with the engagement and that they would very much like to see it come to an end,' he said bluntly. 'Particularly my father.'

Emma turned to look at him. 'Is that why he was not at dinner the other night?'

'No. His doctor *has* restricted him to bed, but I am not entirely sure he would have come had he been feeling well enough to do so. He has very strong opinions about the obligations owed to one's family.'

Emma wished she could have said she was surprised, but how could she when Lord Stewart was echoing her own concerns about the inequality of the match? 'Why did your father not voice his concerns when your brother first made him aware of his intentions to approach my sister?'

'Because Peter didn't tell him of his intentions until it was too late,' Lord Stewart admitted. 'Now, relations between them are strained to the point where it is difficult for either of them to speak about the situation with any degree of rationality.'

'I am sorry to hear that,' Emma said slowly. 'Does the countess also object to the marriage?'

A pained expression flashed across Lord Stewart's face. 'That is not as simple a question to answer. My brother holds...a very special place in my mother's heart. Above all, she wants him to be happy.'

Emma supposed it was not an uncommon failing of mothers, to wish their children well, but it was obviously a feeling not shared by her husband. And their antipathy towards the marriage at so early a stage did not bode well for Linette's future relationship with her in-laws. 'What did you hope to achieve by mentioning this to me, Lord Stewart?'

'Before I answer that, I would ask you a question.' He stopped by the base of a large tree and crossed his arms over his chest. 'Is your sister marrying my brother for love or for what she stands to gain by becoming his wife?'

It was only because the nature of the question caught her so completely off guard that Emma did not immediately take offence to what was a highly impertinent enquiry. 'Of course she loves him. Linette is not in the least mercenary. She would never marry if her heart was not fully engaged. You cannot be expected to know this, of course, but she has spoken of nothing but your brother since the day the two of them met.'

'I feared as much,' he said. 'Love is always harder to discourage than gain.'

'But surely it is not your place to discourage the relationship,' Emma said. 'If they are truly in love—'

'Oh, I believe they both *think* themselves in love, Miss Darling, but will it last? You strike me as being a sensible young woman, one who knows what the world is all about. And it is not about kindness and love. It is about establishing one's place through the acquisition of power and wealth. Love plays very little part in that.'

Emma said nothing, not at all sure she liked being coupled with this man when it came to their feelings about matters of the heart. She might not dream about finding romantic love for herself, but that did not mean she belittled it when it came to others.

'Does that also apply to your forthcoming engagement to Lady Glynnis?' she asked boldly. 'Is that union also based on the premise of what each of you stands to gain, with no consideration for love or other feelings?'

He raised one dark eyebrow. 'I did not come here to discuss *my* relationship, Miss Darling.'

'No, but in being so cavalier about my sister's, it seems only fair that I should ask you about the basis for yours. I may be sensible, my lord, but if I were ever to marry, I would hope to do so for love rather than gain.'

'Very well. My betrothal to Lady Glynnis was arranged by our parents and accepted by the lady and myself as being eminently sensible. Our interests are similar, our natures compatible and our desires and goals identical. And we happen to like and respect one another.'

'So, all in all, a very convenient partnership,' Emma said.

'You could say that.'

'Do you love her?'

He clearly wasn't expecting the question and Emma knew from the look on his face that he wasn't pleased about being asked. 'You don't believe in mincing words.'

'Not when the issue concerns me as deeply as this one. Do you love the lady you are planning to marry, Lord Stewart?'

He took his time, suddenly more interested in the antics of a robin pulling a worm from the grass than he was in giving her an answer. Finally, 'If being comfortable with a lady and enjoying time spent in her company is an indication of love, then, yes, I suppose I do.'

'My, how passionately you speak.'

'Would you have me quote sonnets?' he retorted sarcastically. 'Proclaim my undying love in the manner of poets and kings?'

'I would have you speak of nothing you did not feel,' Emma said. 'But neither will I listen to you condemn two people who so obviously *are* in love simply because you put no stock in the emotion. Your brother has proposed to my sister and been accepted. Were he to break it off now, he would suffer the consequences of his actions and she would be left heartbroken.'

'Perhaps, but if your sister were to cry off, she would be thought flighty, but not socially irresponsible,' he countered. 'Indeed, proceeding with this marriage would be the more socially irresponsible of the two options.'

To a degree, he was correct, but Emma had no intention of letting him think she agreed with him on this or any other front. Or of letting the remark go unchallenged. 'Why do you dislike Linette so much, my lord? Apart from having spent a few hours in her company, you know absolutely nothing about her.'

'Whether I like her or not has nothing to do with it. My brother's birth is such that he should have done better.'

'Then your parents should have stopped him from proposing to her!'

'And I've already told you they had no idea he intended to do so. And even if they had, it would not have made any difference.' He turned away so she might not see his face. 'My mother can deny him nothing. Even when she should.'

They were past the point of polite discussion now. They were arguing—and as someone who disliked conflict intensely, Emma knew they would achieve nothing by it. 'Lord Stewart, you are the heir to your father's title and estates. As long as you marry well, what does it matter how your brother settles his affairs?'

'It matters a great deal. I do not wish to see Peter take stock of his life in ten years' time and come to regret what he did in a youthful burst of passion. I would rather see him suffer now than in the future.'

'*Suffer?* You think your brother will *suffer* from being married to Linette?'

'That's not what I said—'

'But it is what you meant.' Dear Lord, the arrogance of the man! Did he really expect her to ask Linette to reconsider her acceptance of Mr Taylor's offer? To throw over the man she loved for the sake of…what? Lord Stewart's misplaced notion that his brother might be happier for it in the long run? 'Lord Stewart, I…appreciate the concern you must feel for your brother, but you must also understand that the concern I feel for my sister is equally great,' Emma said, forcing herself to speak in a calm and rational manner. 'I believe her to be deeply in love with Mr Taylor and I could not counsel her against marrying him when I *know* how unhappy it would make her.'

'Then you will not encourage her to think on it again.'

'I will not.'

'You could be sparing them both a great deal of heart-ache and embarrassment.'

'Apart from the fact of Linette's birth not being as lofty as you might like, she will not embarrass you or your family. She is good and loving and I know she will make your brother an excellent wife. I cannot do what you ask, my lord, nor am I sure your brother would thank me for doing so,' Emma said quietly. 'You saw how they looked at one another the other night. You heard how he spoke to her.'

'Lies can be convincingly enacted, Miss Darling. So much so that, sometimes, we only see and hear what we wish to.'

Emma's mouth hardened. 'I like to think I see what's there, my lord.' How dare he suggest that Linette would *lie* about her feelings! Linette, who was no more capable of deceit than a child. 'Now if you don't mind—'

'Excuse me, Miss Darling?'

A man's voice interrupted, one Emma did not recognise. Until she looked up and saw the newly appointed vicar of the church in Little Moreton approaching. 'Mr Tufton?'

John Tufton was a handsome young man with a shock of light brown hair and warm brown eyes. He had come from a parish in Sussex to take over St David's and was at least thirty years younger than his predecessor—a fact that had not gone unnoticed by the single ladies in Little Moreton. 'Good afternoon.' His smile was somewhat hesitant as he glanced from Emma to her companion. 'I hope I haven't come at a bad time?'

Aware that he couldn't have come at a better one, Emma said, 'Not at all, Mr Tufton. Lord Stewart was just leaving.'

'Lord Stewart?' The vicar's eyes widened. 'I was not aware you resided in the parish, my lord.'

'I do not.' Lord Stewart's voice was less than conciliatory. 'I am here visiting my brother.'

'Ah, yes, Mr Taylor. A most excellent gentleman. I made his acquaintance last week. I, myself, am newly arrived in Little Moreton and so am calling upon all of my parishioners in an attempt to get to know them better,' Mr Tufton said. 'There is generally so little time after Sunday service.'

'Of course.' Lord Stewart's mouth lifted in a sardonic smile. 'Everyone rushing home to enjoy their dinners.' He turned to Emma, his expression growing even more cynical. 'Well, I shall take up no more of your time, Miss Darling. But I hope we may continue our conversation in the near future.'

'Only if the subject differs from what we spoke of today, Lord Stewart. Mr Tufton,' Emma said, turning to smile at the parson. 'Perhaps you would be good enough to make your way to the house. I know my father and my aunt will be pleased to see you. I shall collect my things and join you there.'

'Excellent. And I do hope we will see you and your family at church on Sunday, Lord Stewart?'

'I really couldn't say.' Lord Stewart's eyes briefly connected with Emma's. 'There are so many other things of importance to concern oneself with when in the country.'

With a brief nod, he whistled for his horse. Emma didn't say a word as the elegant creature trotted obediently to his side. It made no sense that she should be annoyed that even the horse seemed to fall under his spell. Instead, she turned her back on him and walked purposefully towards her easel, heavy in heart and low in spirit.

Poor Linette. What would she say if she knew what her future brother-in-law was saying about her? Linette had gone to Ellingsworth Hall in fear of Mr Taylor's parents, yet now it seemed it was his brother who offered the biggest threat to her happiness. *He* did not want the marriage to take place. And where his father did not have the courage to show his displeasure and his mother hadn't the heart to, it seemed Lord Stewart had more than enough of both. He intended to march in and destroy his brother's and her sister's chances at happiness by spouting duty and obligation and all the other things that obviously mattered to him far more than love.

It was just as well the vicar's arrival had put an end to her artistic endeavours, Emma thought moodily. Her creative urges had vanished, leaving her no more able to see the beauty in the lily pond than she could in a warty frog. She was angry and upset, yet she knew that directing her anger at Lord Stewart really made very little sense. Had *she* not questioned the inequity of the match herself? Was *she* not the one who had expressed concern over Linette's ability to take responsibility for her decisions? The one who had told her father that Linette was changeable by nature?

Why, then, was she angry at Lord Stewart for having said *exactly* the same things?

Mr Tufton did not stay long. A quiet gentleman with agreeable manners, he was careful not to wear out his welcome. After enjoying a cup of tea and a slice of seed cake, he spoke to Emma's father and Aunt Dorothy, saying how pleased he was to meet them and how much he looked forward to seeing them on Sunday. Then, after exchanging a few words with Linette and offering congratulations on her betrothal, he left.

Emma was not sorry to see him go. Not because she disliked the man. There really wasn't anything about Mr Tufton one *could* dislike. But the entire time he had been seated in their parlour, Emma had lived in fear of his bringing up Lord Stewart's visit and *that* would have been awkward since she had no intention of telling Linette Lord Stewart had called.

'Had he come to talk about the dinner?' Linette would surely have asked. Or *'Had he come to speak to her father about the upcoming wedding?'* And the thought of having to tell her sister the truth made Emma shudder. Such an admission would only have brought on grief and uncertainty, and tears were most effective at destroying harmony in a house.

Then her brother Ridley came home—and that fragile harmony vanished for good.

He arrived at eight o'clock in the evening. Dinner was over and they were all sitting quietly in the drawing room when the door burst open, causing the dogs to start barking as though the four horsemen of the Apocalypse had appeared, and then Ridley blew in like a westerly.

'Well, here I am,' he announced dramatically. 'The prodigal son returned. Have you all missed me dreadfully?'

'We can scarce speak for emotion,' Mr Darling said in a dry voice.

But Aunt Dorothy was already on her feet, anxious to greet her favourite nephew. 'Ridley, dear boy, of course they've missed you. And I haven't seen you in an age,' she said, kissing him soundly on both cheeks. 'But what *have* you done to your hair?'

'It's all the rage in London,' Ridley said, grinning. 'What do you think, Em?'

Emma looked up. 'That you look like Caesar and you know what happened to him.'

'Darling Emma,' Ridley said fondly. 'I can always count on you to say the nicest things. And here is little Linette,' he said, turning to his sister and pulling her to her feet. 'Who I vow is even more beautiful than when I left.'

'Don't be silly, Ridley, you've only been gone a few months,' Linette said, blushing.

'Nevertheless, there does seem to be an additional bloom on the rose and I suspect that has much to do with the fact you are soon to marry the venerable Mr Peter Taylor,' Ridley said. 'Well done, Linny. If all goes well, you might just end up a countess.'

'Highly unlikely,' Emma drawled, 'given that there is an older brother in line for the title.'

'Ah, yes. Alexander the Great.'

Emma blinked. 'I beg your pardon?'

'Alexander Taylor. Lord Stewart,' Ridley explained, flopping down in his favourite chair. 'The lads call him Alexander the Great because he's a cracking good rider and a dashed hand with a whip. I won't mind having him as a brother-in-law, I can tell you.'

'You must be hungry, Ridley,' Aunt Dorothy said. 'Shall I ask Cook to prepare something?'

'You may indeed. I did stop for a bit of overdone beef on the way, but I wouldn't mind a slice of Mrs Dunstan's excellent apple pie if there is any to be had.'

'I'm sure that can be arranged. Ring for Jenks, would you, Emma?'

'So, when are the nuptials to take place?' Ridley enquired, fondling Rory's silky head.

Linette blushed. 'We haven't set a date yet.'

'What? I thought you would have been anxious to reel him in.'

'Really, Ridley!' Aunt Dorothy exclaimed. 'The man is hardly a fish to be landed.'

'Of course not. He's already been hooked and I am very proud of my little sister for having done so. Imagine Linette snapping up the youngest son of an earl. It certainly trumps anything you or I have been able to pull off, Em. Unless there's something you haven't told me?' He grinned. 'Turned any gentleman up sweet yet?'

'If I had, I'd know better than to tell *you*,' Emma said, returning to her chair. 'You would likely tease the poor man to death.'

'Naturally. What are brothers for?'

'To tell you the truth, I haven't quite worked that out.'

'All right, stop bickering, you two,' Mr Darling said. 'Ridley, how are you going on with your studies? Finding the intricacies of the law to your liking?'

For the first time, Ridley looked a little uncomfortable. 'Actually, I've been meaning to write to you about that, Father.'

'Oh?'

'There's something I have to tell you. And I don't want you getting upset because I have given this a great deal of thought.'

Her father's eyes narrowed. 'Given *what* a great deal of thought?'

'My decision to become a solicitor. Or rather, my decision…not to become one.'

His father dropped his book. 'Not become a solicitor. Why the devil not?'

'Because I'm really not cut out for it.'

'Indeed! Then what, pray tell, *are* you cut out for?'

'Painting,' Ridley announced decisively.

Aunt Dorothy frowned. 'Painting?'

'Yes. As in portraits.'

'Of what?' his father demanded.

'Of society's most beautiful and aristocratic families.' Ridley stood up and affected an elegant bow. 'Of grand lords and titled ladies, of cherubic daughters and stalwart sons. And of their noble dogs and horses, of course,' he said, leaning down to scratch Ranger behind the ear.

There was a moment of stunned silence before Linette said, 'Goodness, Ridley, whatever possessed you to do such a thing?'

'Indeed! Giving up law to dabble in paints and brushes?' his father said stiffly. 'I thought you had more sense.'

'Sense I have in limited supply, but talent I possess in abundance,' Ridley quipped. 'I've already completed five commissions and have five more waiting. And they pay me very well.'

'Then he must be good, Percy,' Aunt Dorothy commented. 'The aristocracy are very particular about who they engage to paint their portraits.'

'Exactly!' Ridley agreed. 'They are *very* particular and I *am* very good. More to the point, those for whom I've done work have passed my name along to others and I actually have more work than I can handle.'

'And I suppose you expect me to clap you on the back and say, well done, sir, well done!' his father demanded.

'That would be nice.'

'Well, I shall not! Being a barrister is a respectable occupation. One that would stand you in good stead for the rest of your days. The same cannot be said for artists.'

'Of course not, because we are all licentious reprobates who drink too much and have naked women lying around our studios,' Ridley muttered. 'God knows, I'll probably be dead by the time I'm thirty.'

'Really, Ridley, such language in front of your sisters!' Aunt Dorothy chastised.

'Indeed, *and* in front of your aunt,' his father added. 'I am not pleased, Ridley. Not at all pleased.'

'But why should you be upset? It's not as though I'm drinking myself into oblivion, or trying to cadge money from you. I make a very good living.'

'But it is not the occupation of a gentleman!'

'And I have never aspired to *be* a gentleman,' Ridley said in exasperation. 'I want to paint. I've *always* wanted to paint. It is the only thing I'm good at and likely the only thing I ever will be.'

The conversation was mercifully interrupted by the arrival of Jenks.

'Ah, Jenks,' Emma said quickly. 'Would you be so good as to bring some fresh tea and either a slice of cake or a piece of pie for my brother?'

'Don't bother.' Ridley abruptly got up and headed for the door. 'I've lost my appetite. I'm going up to my room.'

'We'll talk about this in the morning, Ridley,' Mr Darling called after him. 'Don't think we won't!'

Emma exchanged an anxious glance with her sister, then nodded at the servant who was still standing patiently in the doorway. 'Thank you, Jenks, it seems we won't be needing anything after all.'

'Very good, miss.'

After he left, the room settled into an uneasy silence. Linette picked up a book, Emma reached for a magazine and Aunt Dorothy went back to her tambour, muttering something about mismatched threads and too-tight knots.

'Oh well, that's just splendid!' Mr Darling finally burst out. 'My youngest daughter about to marry into an earl's family and my only son announces he's given up law to paint pictures.'

'Portraits, Father,' Emma corrected tactfully. 'And it is not such a disreputable occupation. Mr Gainsborough and Sir Joshua Reynolds were both highly respected for their work.'

'Ridley is *not* Gainsborough,' Mr Darling drawled.

'You don't know that. You haven't seen any samples of his work.'

'And I have no desire to. Knowing Ridley, I can just imagine what kind of pictures—'

The door opened and Ridley walked back in. Ignoring his father, he handed a framed picture to Emma. 'Lord Mortimer paid me six guineas for that and his recommendation brought in two more commissions for which I shall charge double. You may not like what I've turned my hand to, Father, but you cannot deny I'm good at it.'

With that, he left again, this time closing the door firmly behind him.

Emma glanced at the painting and slowly began to smile. The subject was a little girl no more than three years old. She was sitting on a stool with a spaniel at her feet and a small grey kitten clutched in her arms. Her hair was the colour of ripe corn and she was wearing a pale pink dress dotted with silver stars. She was a pretty little girl, to be sure, but it was the wistfulness of her expression and the innocence of her smile that Ridley had captured so perfectly on the canvas.

'It is excellent,' Emma said, handing the painting to Linette.

Linette didn't say a word, but her eyes opened wide and when she looked up, Emma saw the admiration on her face. Clearly, she'd had no idea that Ridley was so talented. None of them had. The portrait was not the work of a rank amateur. It was the work of a man who deserved to be recognised for his skill and ability.

Unfortunately, thinking about paintings took Emma back to that morning and to the unpleasant confrontation she'd had with Lord Stewart. Pity she couldn't so easily relegate *him* to the back of her mind. But, there he was, front and centre once again, and she had a sinking feeling he was going to stay there until she had decided what she was going to do about this situation with Linette and Peter.

Lord Stewart didn't want his brother to marry Linette and Emma didn't want to see Peter and Linette break up. And now Ridley had given up law to become an artist. Was it any wonder she had a feeling it was going to be a long time before harmony found its way back inside the peaceful walls of Dove's Hollow again?

Chapter Four

Alex had been fortunate enough to enjoy a close relationship with his younger brother ever since they were boys. Always a happy-go-lucky lad, Peter was easy to be around and was never moody or quick to anger. Loyal to a fault, he could be counted on to tell the truth, and though that honesty that had cost him the friendship of several boys who tended towards mischief, it had stood him in good stead in all other areas of his life.

His one failing, if it could be called that, was his tendency to fall too easily in love. Peter often mistook friendship for affection and when a young lady smiled at him, he was prone to reading more into it than was intended. Thankfully, since most of the girls they had grown up with had tended to look upon Peter as a brother rather than a potential suitor, his youthful escapades had not landed him in any serious trouble. But Alex feared his brother's engagement to Linette Darling now *was* trouble. Trouble of the most ominous kind.

'So how did you and Linette meet?' he asked as the two

of them stood reviewing renovation plans the following morning.

'We were introduced at the Christmas fête.' Peter picked up the architect's drawing of the new parlour and held it towards the light. 'Linette was looking after the children. The vicar introduced us and we spent a few minutes in conversation. I thought her delightful.'

'So you went to see her after the fête?'

'No.'

Alex frowned. 'No?'

'I didn't think it would be a good idea.'

'I don't follow.'

Peter put down the drawing. 'Father's always had very high expectations of us and while Linette's birth is acceptable, I knew it wouldn't be good enough for him, so I purposely did not seek her out.'

'Then how did you come to be engaged?'

'A week before Christmas, I was invited to a small dinner party. An informal gathering, the hostess said, with three or four other families to whom they were close. Given that I had nothing else to do that evening, I agreed. Linette was there, along with her father and sister.'

'I see. And did she seek you out?'

'No.' Peter drew forwards another sketch, this one of changes to the formal dining room. 'In fact, she went out of her way to avoid me. She admitted afterwards that she had never associated with anyone of high rank before and that she was terrified of embarrassing herself. But she never put a foot wrong. And, as the evening wore on, I found myself making excuses to be near her. I enjoyed talking to her and I loved hearing her laugh.' He stared down at the plans, but Alex knew he was seeing something quite different. 'I believe I fell in love with her that very night.'

'You didn't think it simply a case of infatuation?'

'Briefly, yes,' Peter admitted. 'But as the months passed and I couldn't stop thinking about her, I realised it was more. And the idea she might be seeing someone else nearly drove me insane. So, I started planning ways in which we might meet. Accidentally, of course. I went to a few of the local assemblies. Started accepting invitations to events I knew she would be attending, and, eventually, I got up the courage to call at her house. And the more I saw her, the more I realised how much I loved her. Finally, I had no choice but to speak to Mr Darling. When I had his approval, I asked Linette to marry me.'

Alex stared at the drawings, aware that the answers weren't at all what he had been hoping to hear. He had expected to find fault with his brother's reasoning, sure there would be something upon which he could hang his hopes of breaking them up. But there was nothing. Peter had used logic and family obligation to try to resist the young lady's charms—and had fallen in love regardless. They were not off to a promising start.

'By the way, I talked to Mother last night,' Peter said.

'Oh?'

'I wanted to know how upset Father really was over my engagement.'

'What did she say?'

'That he doesn't approve and that he expects me break it off as soon as possible.'

'Is there any chance you would?'

'No. It would break Linette's heart, not to mention mine.'

So, he would stand by his decision. Alex sighed. Their father would *not* be pleased. 'Did Mother say anything else?'

'No. Why?'

Surprised, Alex turned and walked towards the window.

Why hadn't their mother made mention of their father's illness? Surely she felt it important enough. Why else would she have told *him*? 'No reason,' he said, deciding to leave it for the moment. 'Tell me, what does Mother think of Miss Linette Darling now that she's met her?'

'That she is lovely and sweet and seems to come from a nice enough family.'

'But…?'

'But do I really think I am doing the right thing by marrying her.'

Alex hadn't expected his mother to agree with the betrothal, but neither had he expected her to condemn it as harshly as his father had. Her relationship with Peter wouldn't allow it.

'You haven't told me what *you* think about all this yet,' Peter said.

Alex shrugged. 'Does it matter?'

'Of course it matters. You're my brother. I've always looked up to you. I care about what you think.'

'So if I were to tell you that I agree with Father in thinking you should have done better…?'

'I'd say it's not what I wanted to hear, but that I can understand your reasons for saying it.'

'Unfortunately, understanding what I'm saying doesn't solve the problem, Peter,' Alex said. 'If something were to happen to me, you would become the next earl. Do you really think Linette Darling is suitable to being the next Countess of Widdicombe?'

Peter smiled unhappily."I'm sorry, Alex. But in my eyes, she already is.'

Ridley's startling admission that he had given up law to paint portraits for a living was an endless source of fascination to Emma. It seemed a thoroughly illogical, but totally understandable, thing for her brother to do; curious to find out more about that part of his life, she waited until their father had gone for his daily walk and then went to seek him out.

She found him, not unexpectedly, in the stables, devoid of jacket and with his shirt sleeves rolled up to his elbows. He had a soft brush in his hand and was running it over the sides and back of his chestnut, both he and the horse seeming to enjoy the peaceful occupation. Ridley was different from most gentlemen in that regard. He liked looking after his horses almost as much as he enjoyed riding them.

'Hello, Emma,' he said as she appeared at the stall door. 'What brings you down here?'

'I wanted to talk to you about your painting. Away from the house.'

'Away from Father, you mean.' Ridley resumed brushing. 'At least I know you don't think I'm dicked in the nob for going ahead with it.'

'Not at all. I admire you for having had the courage to follow your heart. But weren't you nervous, giving up your legal studies for something as unpredictable as art?'

'In truth, I was terrified,' Ridley admitted with a smile. 'But only for a day or two. In my heart, I *knew* I was doing the right thing. I wasn't cut out for the law, Em. All those boring precedents and tedious pleadings. I never would have been any good at it. But painting is like breathing to me. It's natural. It's what I need to do to be happy.'

Emma understood that. Though her own enjoyment of painting wasn't the passion it so clearly was for Ridley, she knew the joy of sitting down in front of an easel and getting ready to create, the freedom of allowing her imagination to soar. 'But you said you had commissions. With so many successful portraitists in London, how did you get anyone to hire you?'

'I was lucky enough to be friends with Lord Bickerson's son at Oxford,' Ridley said, moving the brush over
the chestnut's hindquarters. 'Tom knew of my interest
because I had shown him a few of my sketches. So when
he came in one evening and told me his father was looking
for someone to do a family portrait, I jokingly suggested
that he put my name forward. He told me he already had
and that I was to meet with his father the next day to go
over the details.'

'How wonderful!' Emma said.

'Yes, it was, rather. So I met Lord Bickerson and told
him I'd do the painting, and that if he didn't like it he didn't
have to pay me.'

'Very noble of you.'

'Not really. Bickerson knew I'd never done a commission before. He had already engaged an established artist
before Tom even mentioned my name. So giving me a
chance wasn't much of a risk on his part. It was something
he did as a favour to his son. And if it turned out I wasn't
any good, he'd still have a painting from someone else
and all I would have been out was the cost of a canvas
and some paints. But, as luck had it; he was delighted with
the painting and paid me what I considered to be a very
fair sum. More importantly, he recommended me to Lord
Huston—'

'*Viscount* Huston?' Emma asked on a gasp of surprise.

'That's right. And when Huston saw what I'd done for
Lord Bickerson, he hired me to paint a portrait of his
wife and another one of his two young sons. After that, I
received a commission from a titled gentleman, followed
by one from a lady who wished me to paint her portrait
as a gift for someone.'

Emma smiled. How wonderful to hear that Ridley was
enjoying success in his new career. Why, then, the faint

echo of regret in his voice? 'So you are now an established artist with enviable credentials and a growing list of clients,' she said.

'Indeed. But Linette tells me *you* have improved immeasurably since I left,' he said in an overly hearty voice. 'When are you going to show me some of your work?'

'Are you mad? After showing me that delightful painting of the little girl with the kitten in her arms? Not a chance. I paint for my own pleasure. Not for your eyes or anyone else's!'

But someone else *had* seen her work. Lord Stewart, the morning he had come upon her painting down by the pond. He had complimented on her ability and told her that her work was *impressive.* High praise indeed from a man like that.

Good thing she'd known better than to believe him.

On Wednesday morning, Emma donned a plum-coloured riding habit with a matching bonnet and had Jenks saddle her mare. It was a glorious morning for a ride. The sky was a bright sapphire-blue with a few white clouds drifting by like tufts of cotton. Dark-green hedges criss-crossed lighter green fields dotted here and there with clumps of golden buttercups and white-and-yellow daisies. A painter's palette of colours! Unfortunately, caught up as she was in her study of the world around her, Emma failed to notice the approaching rider until he was close enough to speak. 'I suspect your artistic eye is seeing all this in a vastly different light than those of us who cannot tell blue from turquoise.'

The voice was teasing, lighter in tone than it had been the last time they'd spoken. Nevertheless, Emma couldn't suppress a *frisson* of awareness at hearing it. 'You surprise me, Lord Stewart. The fact you know there is a difference leads me to believe you already know more about colour than you are willing to let on.'

His smile widened. 'I always try to exceed a lady's expectations.'

'But since I have none, there is nothing to exceed.'

'Come now, Miss Darling, surely you have *some* expectations of the man who will soon be your brother-in-law.'

'Really? I thought you were doing everything you could to prevent that from happening.'

He shrugged. 'If neither party is willing to cry off...'

'Then you have not succeeded in changing your brother's mind?'

'No more than I suspect you have succeeded in changing your sister's.'

'Ah, but I have not tried,' Emma informed him. 'There have been so many other things to occupy my time. Fittings for new gowns. Paying calls on all the people who are desperate to hear details of my sister's upcoming nuptials. Meetings with Mr Tufton to talk about the ceremony.'

'Ah, yes, the dedicated vicar.' Lord Stewart did not smile. 'I wonder if he is taking as much of an interest in *all* of his parishioners as he seems to be taking in you and your family.'

Emma cursed the warmth that flooded her cheeks. She did not blush prettily. Patches of red stood out on her cheeks like droplets of blood on snow, resulting in her chin and forehead appearing all the more pale. 'It is part of his job to get to know the people of this parish, my lord. And since Linette is to be married in his church, he is spending time with her to familiarise her with the ceremony. As well, he and my father discuss matters of philosophy and religion. The time he spends with Ridley and myself is minimal.'

'If you say so.' He didn't meet her eyes, but Emma could sense his annoyance and for the life of her she couldn't imagine why.

'You haven't answered my question as to what you expect of me as your brother-in-law,' he said, reverting to their earlier topic of discussion.

Wondering why it mattered, Emma lifted her shoulders in a shrug. 'Only that you are good to my sister and mindful of your obligations to her. Although,' she said, hoping to lighten the mood, 'I suppose if you were to occasionally take your mother and two sisters-in-law to lunch at some hideously expensive but exceptionally good restaurant in London, it would not go amiss.'

'Hideously expensive but exceptionally good,' he mused. 'That would have to be the Clarendon. A pricey ticket, but worth it under the circumstances. Have you ever eaten there?'

'No, though Ridley may have. He has a taste for the finer things. What would you suggest?'

'Many believe their Coquilles St Jacques to be without equal and their crêpes Suzette better than those served at the Hôtel Le Meurice in Paris. Personally, I prefer the *langoustine d'anglais*, followed by a tender fillet of beef, and to finish, either a chocolate soufflé or *crème brûlée*,' Lord Stewart said. 'And I would start with a chilled bottle of champagne. I find it stimulates the appetite and lends a rosy glow to the surroundings.'

'Not to mention the diners,' Emma said.

He actually smiled. 'Only if one imbibes too freely. Then a piquant white for the fish course and a robust Burgundy for the beef.'

'Goodness, after all that, I shouldn't think you would be able to taste the food!'

'Ah, but a good wine enhances the flavours,' he

informed her. 'As well as lending a certain *joie de vivre* to the proceedings.'

'Yes, I've heard my brother talk about *joie de vivre*,' Emma said drily. 'As I recall, they had to carry him to his room afterwards.'

'That is the result of *too* much *joie de vivre*. A man must know where to draw the line.'

'And I suspect you always know when and where to do that.'

He shot her a sardonic gaze. 'I would have thought the ability to avoid falling into a drunken stupor something to recommend a man. You make it sound like a failing.'

'Did I? It wasn't my intention,' Emma said with a smile. 'I can think of nothing more demeaning than to see a man tumble into his host's rhododendrons.'

His mouth lifted in a smile. 'So, apart from entertaining you with good food and wine and not falling headlong into the bushes, what other expectations have you of me?'

'None I can think of at the moment. As long as you and Linette contrive to be happy in one another's company, I shall be content.'

'I wonder if the rest of your family's expectations will be as straightforward.'

'Well, my brother expects nothing of himself and even less of others, and my father will only be concerned with Linette's happiness.'

'Then it would seem I have only your opinion to worry about.' Lord Stewart narrowed his eyes against the brilliance of the morning sun. 'Is that your brother I see coming over the brow of the next hill?'

Emma turned to follow his gaze. 'Yes. Ridley arrived the night before last and will be staying for the duration of the spectacle.'

He shot her an amused glance. 'Did I detect a note of sarcasm in your voice?'

'Unintentional, but yes. I find all the pomp and ceremony excessive.'

'Your sister is marrying the son of an earl,' Lord Stewart pointed out. 'Some would say that worthy of ceremony.'

'I suppose, though I would enjoy it far more if it were all a little less grand.' Emma risked a quick glance in his direction. 'Do you like weddings, Lord Stewart?'

'I'm not sure one can like or dislike them. They are a necessity of life. But I enjoy seeing a well-matched pair come together.'

Emma laughed. Had he any idea, she wondered, how much like an old pair of boots he made the bride and groom sound? 'I take it by that you mean a lady and a gentleman of similar circumstances.'

'Of course.'

'Unlike my sister and your brother.'

He shot her a penetrating glance. 'We've already had this discussion, Miss Darling. Why bring it up again now?'

'Forgive me. Perhaps I should look to *your* marriage as the model for all others.'

'Now you are being cruel.'

'Not at all. I am quite sure your upcoming engagement to Lady Glynnis will be, in the eyes of the *ton*, an ideal match. She has all that you require in a wife, and you, all a woman could ask for in a husband. Why would you say I am being cruel?'

'Because on the basis of our brief association, *you* know that I have chosen to put practicality first and *I* know you decry the idea of marrying for anything *but* love.'

Emma tilted her head to one side. 'I said I would rather marry for love, my lord. I did not say it was the only reason for marrying.'

'Yet you mock me for saying that Lady Glynnis and I are well suited, rather than being madly in love.'

'If I mock anything, it is the way in which you say it. And, in truth, I should not mock you at all—while I do not like to think of two people marrying without love, it is, perhaps, the more intelligent reason for them to do so.'

'Have you ever been in love, Miss Darling?' he asked. 'Or know how it feels to have your heart broken?'

'Oh, I have most definitely had my heart broken. When I was seven years old, Johnny Beaton stole my beloved stuffed elephant and threw him into the pond,' Emma said. 'I could not speak of it for days. And I did not speak to Johnny Beaton for several months.'

The smile transformed him, lighting up his face and making him look years younger and far more approachable. 'Now you are teasing me and for that I demand a forfeit.'

Emma snorted, even though her stomach did the silliest flip flop. 'Don't be ridiculous, my lord. Teasing does not warrant a forfeit. I am constantly being teased by my brother and as you are soon to be my brother-in-law, that falls under the heading of family privileges.'

'Nevertheless, until I *am* related by marriage, you owe me for being impolite.'

'I was not impolite!'

'Sarcasm is a gentleman's prerogative. It is not a quality to be admired in a lady.'

'Oh, very well. What is my penalty to be?'

He turned his eyes to the rolling countryside around them. 'A painting. The subject of which will be of my own choosing.'

Emma stared at him. 'Are you mad? I'm not talented enough to do the kind of work someone like you would wish to hang on his wall.'

'On the contrary, what you are *not* is a good judge of your own talent. I like what I've seen of your work and, since I am the one naming the forfeit, I shall be the one who says what it is to be. And if I say I want a painting, you have no choice but to agree.'

'And what would you have me paint, my lord?' Emma asked mockingly. 'A tranquil landscape? A bowl of fruit? A picture of your horse?'

His gaze moved over her face in a way that caused her breath to catch. 'I shall tell you at the ball what I wish the subject to be. But do not think I will forget. I've a far better memory than that. Good day, Miss Darling.' He touched the brim of his hat and turned the bay around, galloping back in the direction of Ellingsworth Hall.

Emma watched him go, trying to make sense of what had just happened. He wanted her to do a painting for him? Ridiculous! A man like that could afford to buy the works of the finest artists in the world. Why on earth would he ask for a painting from an amateur like herself?

Given that Aunt Dorothy and Linette could talk about nothing but the upcoming ball, Emma decided it was a good time to run a few errands. She needed to replenish some of her painting supplies and Mrs Wilbers, who ran the village shop, made a point of keeping most of what Emma required in stock. As well, Aunt Dorothy had asked her to pick up two lengths of lace and the latest fashion magazines from London. Her aunt might not be living in London, but her heart never left the bustling metropolis for any length of time.

Emma enjoyed her trips into the quaint little village. Thatched roofed cottages lined the main street, each with gardens bright with colourful flowers. And while there were only a few shops, they seemed to provide all the residents required. There was a bakery and a linen draper, a bookstore and a greengrocer, and whatever those establishments weren't able to provide, visitors to London could often be called upon to bring back. Consequently, two hours later, with all of her errands done, Emma returned to the trap, her arms piled high with purchases.

'Miss Darling, how nice to see you again. Here, let me help you with your purchases.'

Turning, Emma was surprised to see Mr Tufton walking towards her. 'Thank you, Mr Tufton, but it really isn't necessary—'

'Nonsense, I wouldn't be able to sleep knowing I had allowed a lady to struggle unaided beneath the weight of her purchases.' He relieved her of several of the boxes and placed them carefully in the trap. 'I suspect a good deal of this has to do with Miss Linette's wedding.'

'Some of it,' Emma agreed, 'though just as much is for me. Painting supplies and the like.'

'Ah, yes, your sister told me you were a talented artist. It must run in your family.'

Emma smiled, assuming from his comment that word of Ridley's new profession had also made the rounds.

'Still, there must be a great deal of excitement in your house,' Mr Tufton went on, 'with your sister about to be married to the Earl of Widdicombe's son.'

A little too much, Emma was tempted to say, but feeling it might sound disloyal, said, 'There is indeed. And with Ridley home, we are quite a houseful.'

'I'm sure you are an admirable hostess and well able to keep everyone under control,' the vicar complimented her. 'You strike me as being a supremely organised young woman, entirely capable of managing a household.'

Emma inclined her head, wondering if he thought

'organised' the type of compliment a woman liked to hear. 'How are you getting on with your visits to parishioners?'

'Very well indeed. I have eaten more cake and drunk more tea in the last two weeks than in the previous six months,' he said with a rueful smile. 'But I have been made to feel welcome and for that I am exceedingly grateful. It is not easy to fill the shoes of a man like Mr Humbolt. He was a gifted orator, loved by one and all.'

Emma was touched by the note of humility in his voice. 'He was vicar here for a long time, Mr Tufton. It is only to be expected that he would garner a loyal following. You will too, given time.'

'You are kind to say so, but there are those who think I am too young to do the Lord's work.'

And likely too handsome. Emma already knew of several young ladies who had taken to attending Sunday service with a great deal more enthusiasm than they had in the past. 'Never mind, they'll come round. Country folk do not like change and resist it for as long as they can. But you have a very pleasant manner and I feel sure you will be as well loved as Mr Humbolt in no time at all.'

'Thank you, Miss Darling. Your support and your friendship mean a great deal to me. I hope you know that.'

He smiled down at her and Emma saw a glimmer of earnest affection in his eyes.

'Well, I had best be getting home,' she said quickly. 'Thank you for your help, Mr Tufton. It was most appreciated.'

'My pleasure. I look forward to seeing you again in the near future.'

Emma felt her cheeks grow warm as she climbed into the seat. Was it possible Mr Tufton was interested in her? She didn't have a great deal of experience in that area, but it was hard to ignore the warmth in his voice when he spoke to her. The last time they had met, she had assumed his attentions were merely those of a man of the cloth towards one of his flock, but after today's encounter, she wasn't so sure.

Emma flicked the reins and set the mare to a brisk walk. How did she feel about the idea of Mr Tufton courting her? On a practical level, she knew she could do worse. He held a position of respect within the community, had a nice home and garden, and if he was at all ambitious, his chances for advancement were as good was any man's and better than most. And he was certainly handsome enough.

Not, perhaps, as handsome as Lord Stewart, but then she had met very few men who were. But his manner was pleasing and she did not feel as unsettled with him as she did with Lord Stewart. Nor did she feel the need to be on guard with everything she said.

No, Mr Tufton's was definitely the more tranquil presence. Lord Stewart was about as tranquil as a tiger. She couldn't believe she was even *thinking* about the two men in the same light. Lord Stewart was heir to the Earl of Widdicombe, practically engaged to Lady Glynnis Pettle. He clearly had no interest in her, and she certainly had no interest in—

Craaccccckkk!

It happened without warning. The trap suddenly lurched to the left. As the mare whinnied, Emma toppled backwards off the seat, the reins wrenched from her hands as she landed on her back, her head hitting the floor of the trap hard.

For a few minutes, she just lay there, staring up at the sky. Though she'd heard that people often saw stars when they hit their heads, she had never experienced that particular sensation until now. And it was not in the least pleasant. Nor was the rest of her predicament. She was lying on an angle, with her feet higher than her head and her dress up around her knees. She was also over a mile from Dove's Hollow. How on earth was she going to get everything home?

She tried to sit up, only to sink back with a moan. Never mind getting home, how was she to sit up when every time she tried, the world started to spin madly around her?

'Miss Darling. Are you injured?'

Oh, wonderful! And now Lord Stewart had happened upon her. Of all the people who *could* have ridden by, why did it have to be him? 'I'm fine, though I'm not so sure about the trap,' she said in a depressingly weakened voice. 'Is Bess all right?'

'If you're referring to the mare, she's fine.' She heard him dismount and, seconds later, saw his face looming over hers. 'The trap's thrown a wheel. Are you sure *you're* all right?'

Strangely enough, she was—now that he was here. But when she went to sit up, not only did her head swim, but the angle of the trap made it virtually impossible.

'Here, let me help you,' he offered.

'That won't be necessary—'

He brushed her objections aside. Leaning down, he slid his left arm behind her shoulders, and his right arm under her knees. Thank goodness she had pulled her dress down, but the cool air on her ankles told her it wasn't far enough. 'Lord Stewart, I hardly think this is necessary—'

'Put your arms around my neck,' he ordered.

Her cheeks flamed. 'That wouldn't be proper!'

'It might not be proper, but it will make getting you out of the trap a good deal easier.'

'But—'

'Miss Darling. Either do as I ask or I shall leave you here until dark. Which would you prefer?'

Too weak to argue, Emma put both of her arms around his neck and, seconds later, felt herself lifted out of the trap as though she weighed nothing at all. She had never been carried by a man before and she found the sensation startlingly intimate. The scent of fine linen and starch clung to his clothes, the scent of bay rum and lemon to his skin. Unfortunately, when her head suddenly came up higher than her legs, the world began to spin in a most alarming fashion. Perspiration dotted her forehead and stars danced in front of her eyes again. The sound of him calling her name was the last thing she heard before the white light exploded and silence blanketed her world.

Chapter Five

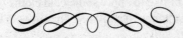

Emma came to slowly, rising from the depths of sleep to an awareness of soft grass beneath her back and a canopy of green leaves over her head. She blinked a few times, waiting for memory to return. When it did, she groaned and went to sit up, only to feel a hand at her shoulder gently pressing her back down.

'You might like to think twice before doing that,' Lord Stewart advised. 'Judging by the size of the lump on the back of your head, you would only pass out again.'

Emma reluctantly subsided, aware that he was probably right. Obviously she'd hit her head harder than she'd thought. She closed her eyes and drew a long deep breath. When she opened them again, it was to see him sitting beside her. 'Lord Stewart, where is your jacket?'

'Folded up beneath your head. I thought the lump needed cushioning.'

That explained the fragrance of lemon. 'It will not be fit to wear.'

'A small price to pay for your comfort. How do you feel?'

'I don't know,' she admitted. 'I should probably try sitting up.'

'Only if you go slowly.'

When she nodded, he slipped his arm beneath her shoulders and carefully brought her to an upright position. Emma kept her eyes closed and took a few deep breaths, trying to ignore the pleasurable feeling of his arm behind her back. Oh, yes, her head was definitely spinning, though whether that was from bumping her head or being in such close proximity to him, she really couldn't say.

'You might like to apply some cold cloths to that lump when you get home,' he advised. 'It will help bring down the swelling.'

'Thank you, I will.' She finally opened her eyes—and found herself staring into his: two clear blue mirrors that reflected her own face back at her. And try as she might, she couldn't look away.

'I've…taken the liberty of disengaging the mare from her harness,' he said abruptly. 'The trap is of no use now. I'll put you up on Thunder and walk alongside with the mare. We can take a few of the packages you'd rather not leave behind, but I'm afraid the rest will have to stay. I'll send someone back for them later.'

Emma nodded. He was being very sensible. Very gallant. Both of which were making her feel very guilty. 'I don't want to be a bother, Lord—'

'Alex.'

She glanced at him. 'Lord Alex?'

'Just Alex. I think we can drop the formality given what's happened. Besides, if I'm to be your brother-in-law, it is perfectly acceptable for you to call me Alex and for me to call you Emma.'

It did make sense. Unfortunately, it also made things a great deal more intimate, at least as far as she was concerned. 'I'm sure it would raise eyebrows if we were to be heard addressing one another in such a manner.'

'You worry too much. I already call your sister Linette. Why should I not call you Emma?'

Because it is my sister who is marrying into your family, Emma wanted to tell him, but she doubted he would understand. She wasn't sure she understood herself.

'I think I am well enough to stand. I need to get home. They will be wondering where I am.'

'Very well. But I shall get up first and help you to your feet.'

Emma nodded her agreement. It would be too embarrassing to try to regain her feet, only to collapse in a heap at his feet. She watched him rise, admiring his ease of motion. For such a tall man, he moved with surprising grace. Once standing, he bent down and placed his hands under her arms, then slowly raised her up.

It seemed right that she should put her hands on his forearms as he drew her to her feet. Even right to leave them there as they straightened together. But it was not right to think about letting them slip around his waist as she leaned into his strength…or to close her eyes and press her face against the warmth of his chest…

Unfortunately, that was exactly what happened. The moment she tried to stand on her own, Emma's knees buckled and the world began to waver… 'Oh!'

His arms went around her in an instant. 'You're not strong enough to ride alone,' he murmured against her hair. 'I'll ride with you.' Changing his position so that his arm encircled her waist, he led her back towards his horse. 'Lean against him while I fetch the mare,' Alex advised. 'And don't worry. He won't move and he doesn't bite.'

Emma did as she was told, thankful the big bay stood as motionless as he did. Alex walked across to where Bess stood flicking her ears back and forth and picked up the reins. He led her back across the grass, then swung up into his own saddle and looped the mare's reins through the leather strap of his saddle bag. 'All right, Emma, up you come.'

He lifted her with no more effort than had she been a child, gently placing her on the saddle in front of him and settling her so that her left side was resting against his chest, his arms on either side of her, holding her steady. Emma couldn't believe she was so weak. Just the act of being lifted on to Thunder's back had made her head spin. 'I'm sorry to be so silly,' she muttered. 'This has never happened to me before.'

'No need to apologise.' Alex pressed his heels gently into the bay's sides. 'It's not always easy to predict the effect a head injury will have.'

In spite of herself, Emma snorted. 'I don't have a head injury. I merely bumped my head. There is a difference.'

'Only if one has an effect and the other does not,' Alex said. 'In this case, you're dizzy and disoriented. Those are signs of a head injury as far as I'm concerned.'

Fearing that arguing might only make her feel worse, Emma subsided into silence. There was nothing she could do. The big horse's gait was surprisingly smooth; as she nestled against Alex's chest, it was all she could do to stay awake. Every time she closed her eyes, her head lolled back against his shoulder.

'Stop fighting, Emma,' he whispered. 'If you want to close your eyes, do so. I won't let you fall. You have my word as a gentleman.'

She didn't doubt him. Not for a moment. She would never fall as long as she was in his arms—but it was just unconscionable that she should enjoy it so much.

Finally, however, she did stop fighting. She lay back

against him, aware of the rhythmic beating of his heart; with his arms enclosing her and the mare trotting peacefully behind them, they made their way home.

Alex knew the moment Emma settled into sleep. He felt her body go limp and heard her breathing settle into a deep, even pattern. How small she seemed in his arms. The first time they'd met, he'd thought her more substantial, but today, the top of her head barely reached his chin.

Strange the protective instincts she aroused within him. Alex thought he had experienced the full range of emotions when it came to women—fascination, admiration, lust—but he had never experienced this overwhelming need to protect. Perhaps because he had never been called upon to do so. The women with whom he associated were either the society ladies he flirted with or the demi-reps he bedded. And, given that the latter had no interest in holding anything back, Alex had never felt anything but the need to indulge himself.

Why, then, was this feeling for Emma Darling so different?

Whatever it was, he'd have to get it in hand. His unwelcome awareness of Emma Darling as a woman was something he hadn't anticipated and it definitely wasn't part of his plans. His plans were to propose to Glynnis after the house party and get on with his life. That was what everyone expected.

Certainly it was what Glynnis expected. They had been friends for a long time. When she had first made her debut in society, it was Alex to whom she had turned for guidance and Alex with whom she had danced her first dance. And when, over the course of those first few weeks, she had spent time in the company of other men, she had never taken any of them seriously. She was typically cool and reserved, almost analytical in her assessment of them, and she had always come back to Alex.

Perhaps that's why their relationship had become the eminently suitable partnership it was. Neither of them was ruled by passion. They liked each other and made decisions calmly and intelligently, the way decisions were supposed to be made. Matters were always far less complicated when emotions weren't involved.

Why, then, was he having so much troubling separating the two when it came to Emma?

She awoke within sight of Dove's Hollow. Alex felt her stir, heard the softness of an unguarded sigh, then felt her body stiffen as she realised where she was.

'Relax, Emma, we're almost home,' he murmured against her hair. 'You have nothing to worry about.'

'I'm not worried,' she said huskily. 'But my family will be if they see me slumped against you like this.'

He smiled, aware they would worry far more about the fact the two of them were riding the same horse than they would about how erect her posture was. Nevertheless, he was sorry to see their enforced closeness come to an end. He had enjoyed, more than he cared to admit, the softness of Emma's body against his. Perhaps because it had been such a long time since he'd held a woman in his arms. Once he had made up his mind to marry Glynnis, he had parted company with his mistress, feeling it was unfair to his future wife to carry on with the affair. And naturally, there hadn't been anything of a physical nature between himself and Glynnis. Their time together was usually spent in conversation or in the company of others. They had held hands on more than one occasion, and twice they had kissed, but at Glynnis's request they had gone no further than that.

There would be plenty of time for passion after they were married, Alex assured himself.

Still, holding Emma Darling now was a pleasurable experience beyond any he had ever known. Her hair felt like strands of silk against his chin and he was aware of the most delightful fragrance emanating from her. Something sweet, yet sensual. And not for the first time that day, he was grateful for whatever whim of fate had sent him down that particular path, resulting in his finding a wrecked trap in the road and its winsome owner in desperate need of his help.

As expected, their arrival at Dove's Hollow created quite a stir. Linette ran out first, followed closely by her aunt and then by her father, his face lined with concern as he ran up to greet them. 'Lord Stewart, what's happened?'

'Your daughter is fine, Mr Darling,' Alex was quick to reassure them. 'The trap broke a wheel and Miss Darling hit her head when she fell backwards into the cart.'

'Gracious, it was very good of you to stop and help,' Mrs Grand said.

'Indeed it was.' Mr Darling reached up his arms and, carefully, Emma slid down into them. 'Emma, my dear, are you all right?'

'I'm fine, Papa,' Emma said, even though Alex suspected the motion set her head to pounding again. 'It's really not at all serious.'

'We'll let the doctor be the judge of that. Linette, send Jenks for the doctor. Ask him to come as quickly as he can.'

'Yes, Papa,' the girl said and promptly disappeared.

'Lord Stewart, we are indebted to you,' Mr Darling said. 'Will you stay and take some refreshment with us?'

'Another time.' Alex had dismounted and was already unfastening the mare's reins. 'I think Miss Darling needs to rest.' He glanced at Emma's white face and knew she didn't need a stranger around right now, especially one of whom she had no reason to be overly fond. 'But I would ask that you send me word of her condition so that I may be assured no complications have set in.'

'We will certainly keep you apprised,' Mr Darling said. 'And again, we are in your debt for having brought her safely home.'

Alex inclined his head as the three of them walked back into the house. He watched until the door closed behind them, but as he swung up into the saddle, he refused to ask himself why it mattered that Emma had not turned to look back at him.

He waited impatiently for word of her condition. He assured himself there was nothing to worry about. That it had been only a light bump to the back of her head. If it had been more, he would have seen signs of it straight away. Nevertheless, Alex was relieved when he finally received Mr Darling's letter, saying that the doctor had called and that the bump Emma had sustained was not serious. The application of cold cloths had brought the swelling down and she had managed to sleep for most of the afternoon.

He refolded the letter, pleased by the news that Emma was all right, but alarmed at how much better he felt upon receiving it. He had been on tenterhooks all afternoon. A natural reaction, he tried to tell himself, for the young lady whose sister would soon be his brother's wife.

'Ah, there you are, Alex,' Peter said, walking into the billiards room. 'I thought you'd gone up. Is that a letter from Lady Glynnis?'

Alex glanced at the parchment in his hand. It seemed a waste of time to tell Peter about the events of the afternoon now that everything had been satisfactorily resolved. 'No.' He folded it up and slipped it into his jacket. 'Care for a game?'

'Yes, though you'll probably just beat me again.'

'Only if you don't concentrate.' Alex racked the balls as Peter took down his cue. 'You may break.'

Peter did, then stood back to survey the table. 'So, Mother tells me you're planning to ask Glynnis to marry you in the very near future. That must have made Father happy.'

'It did.' Alex also surveyed the table. Bending down, he sighted his cue, then smoothly drew it back. 'He's always thought highly of Glyn.'

'The two of you have been friends for a long time. I remember the day you told Father you were thinking about her as a wife. He didn't stop smiling for a week.'

'I know. He used to tease Glyn unmercifully,' Alex said, watching the ball drop into the pocket. 'Said she was too tall and skinny and that she squeaked when she got excited. But she was never afraid of him. Not like the other girls. ' He bent down to take another shot. 'Glyn always gave as good as she got. That's why he liked her so much. And why I did.'

'No doubt,' Peter said, leaning against the edge of the table. 'So, when were you going to tell me about Father's being ill?'

Alex glanced up. 'If you recall, I mentioned it while we were at dinner with the Darlings.'

'Telling our guests that Father had to stay in London because he wasn't feeling well isn't quite the same as telling me he collapsed as the result of a bad heart. How serious is it?'

'I honestly don't know.' Alex took his shot and then watched the ball roll the length of the table, stopping just short of the pocket. 'Serious enough that Mother had to call in Harrow.'

'Good Lord.'

'I know. Came as a shock to me as well.'

'Do you think it's his heart?'

'That's what Harrow said.'

'But he can't know for sure?'

'Your guess is as good as mine. All I know is that Harrow said Father has to start taking better care of himself.'

'And to avoid stressful situations,' Peter murmured drily. 'God knows I'm not helping in that regard, am I?'

'Well, I'd be lying if I said the circumstances of your engagement haven't caused him some additional aggravation,' Alex said, straightening. 'But I doubt you're the only source of frustration in his life.'

'So what am I supposed to do?' Peter asked, his forehead furrowing. 'End my engagement to Linette just to make Father happy?'

'Is that so unreasonable?'

'It is to me.'

'Maybe you should look at your reasons for wishing to marry her,' Alex said. 'Analyse what you stand to gain from the alliance.'

'My reasons for marrying her are simple,' Peter said. 'I love her. And what I expect to gain from the marriage is the opportunity to spend the rest of my life with the woman I want to be with more than any other. What more *could* a man ask?'

'The respect of his friends and society,' Alex said quietly. 'The knowledge that he has lived up to his obligations with regards to his family and his name. There are those who share Father's concern about the wisdom of this marriage, Peter. People who expected you to do better.'

'I couldn't have done any better. Linette makes me happy.'

'But a man cannot always concern himself solely with his own happiness. Marriages are made for the good of both parties and for the benefit of the family.'

'Your marriage, Alex, not mine,' Peter said quietly. 'I don't need to worry about producing an heir.'

'That's a rather narrow point of view.'

'Is it? I prefer to think of it as being realistic, the same as my acceptance of your superiority at billiards. See? You've won again.'

Alex didn't give a damn about the billiards game. He cared about his brother. And the more time he spent in conversation with him, the more he feared he wasn't going to be able to change Peter's mind about Linette Darling.

'Alex, would you be willing to do something for me?' Peter said, putting his cue back on the rack.

'If I can.'

'Come out with us this week. Spend some time with Linette and see what kind of woman she is. I guarantee you won't be disappointed. And if you speak up on her behalf, I know Father will feel better about the marriage. He won't listen to me, but he respects your opinion. He always has.'

It was a lot to ask. Alex knew it wasn't so much Linette Darling his father resented, but what she represented. The earl expected both of his sons to marry well-born ladies. Linette didn't fit into that mould. She had been raised and educated in the country. She was not well read, had very little fashion sense and likely hadn't been taught any but the most rudimentary of country dances. She was not a lady born to the role.

And no matter how lovely or pleasant she was, nothing was ever going to change that.

* * *

Emma was in the garden sketching when Alex arrived to pay a visit the next morning. Given that her neck and shoulders were still tender as a result of her tumble into the trap, she had decided not to venture out as far out as the pond, but to sit in the shade of the towering oak tree, beneath which stood an old stone angel.

The angel had long been a source of artistic frustration to Emma. Not only was the colour of the stone difficult to replicate, but the details of the angel's features had all but worn away. Only her wings seem to have maintained any semblance of their original texture and Emma was fully engaged in trying to replicate their feathery look when she heard the crunch of gravel and turned to see the gentleman walking towards her.

The quiver of anticipation was automatic—and instantly quelled. She had no right to feel anything beyond the mildest friendship for Alex, but facts were facts and she knew there was no use in pretending otherwise. She liked Alexander Taylor. Worse, she was attracted to him. Not only because he was a remarkably handsome man, but because he was turning out to be a surprisingly compassionate one. She had been startled by the degree of concern he had shown towards her yesterday, and though it was pointless to complain about the way he had brought her home, she certainly couldn't pretend she hadn't enjoyed being held in his arms. He was a man who commanded respect and affection simply as a result of who he was.

And with every day that passed, Emma grew more and more aware of how deeply she was coming to like and admire him.

'Good morning, Emma,' he greeted her. 'I hope I'm not disturbing your concentration.'

'I was already disturbed by my inability to capture the

wispy quality of the angel's wings.' Emma kept her sketch pad poised, glad to have something other than him upon which to focus. 'As you can see, it is an ongoing battle.'

He stopped and glanced over her shoulder at the sketch-pad. 'But you have captured it.' He leaned forwards to indicate a line. 'See here, how you've made this piece look so wispy and this one so bold. It is exactly how the statue looks.'

Emma tried to ignore the warmth of his arm as it pressed against her shoulder. 'Thank you, my lord, but if you look more closely, you will see that the edge of this wing is too heavy, and up here, there isn't enough shading where the top of the wing curves over. And I've done a terrible job of capturing her expression.'

'On the contrary, it is the angel's expression that is lacking,' Alex said, straightening. 'You have given her a very nice smile. The statue's is somewhat…evil.'

Emma chuckled. 'Only because a piece of her mouth was knocked off during a windstorm. Poor thing. She originally had a very pretty mouth.'

'Not unlike the lady attempting to sketch her.'

Emma's head snapped up. He was smiling at her—and, stupidly, it went straight to her heart. How in the world was she to keep him at a distance if he continued to be charming like this?

She set the sketchbook aside and slowly stood up. 'Thank you for collecting the rest of my packages and having them sent home, Alex. *And* for having the trap fixed. It was very good of you to go to all that trouble. You really shouldn't have bothered.'

'It was no bother. You couldn't have driven the trap the way it was and I didn't like the idea of your packages sitting at the side of the road where anyone could have taken them.'

'I doubt a thief would have been interested in painting supplies,' Emma said drily. 'But I was glad to have them returned. If you have a moment, Papa would like to thank you as well. He was most grateful for everything you did.'

'Never mind that, how are you feeling?'

'Did you not receive Papa's note?'

'Yes, but I wished to know for myself that you are feeling better. You took a nasty spill.'

His concern was flattering, but Emma knew better than to let herself read too much into it. 'I am much better, thank you. Even the swelling has gone down.'

To her dismay, he brought his hand to the back of her head and gently felt for the lump. 'So it has. There is only a slight swelling there now.'

Emma took a short, hard breath. His hand was warm, his fingers gentle against her scalp. The urge to close her eyes and lean into his hand was overwhelming—and indefensible. 'The result of…frequent applications of cold clothes,' she said in a halting voice. She took a step back and watched his hand fall away. 'Shall we return to the house?'

Not surprisingly, it took only a few minutes to gather everyone in the drawing room. Aunt Dorothy and Linette were already there, the latter refurbishing a bonnet, the former embroidering handkerchiefs. Her father arrived shortly thereafter, and upon seeing Alex, stretched out his hand in welcome. 'Lord Stewart, how very good of you to call.'

'I thought to enquire after Miss Darling's health, but she has informed me she is fully recovered.'

'Mercifully, she is, but it is extraordinarily kind of you to be so concerned. And I must ask you to let me know the cost of repairing the trap. I was grateful you repaired one wheel. There was certainly no need to replace all four.'

'We will not talk about cost where the safety of your family is at issue,' Alex said. 'I was told it was only a matter of time before the other wheels went the way of the first and I would not have been able to live with myself had an accident occurred that I had had the knowledge to prevent.'

'Nevertheless, it was an exceedingly generous thing to do,' Aunt Dorothy said. 'Without the trap, we are quite housebound. And though there is little enough to be had in the village, it is nice to be able to get there when one is in need.'

There was a clatter of boots in the hall, followed by the appearance of Ridley at the door. 'Have I missed all the excitement?'

'Not a bit. Your timing is, as always, excellent,' Mr Darling drawled. 'Lord Stewart, my son, Ridley.'

Alex bowed. 'Your servant, sir.'

'Lord Stewart,' Ridley said. 'A pleasure.'

Emma glanced at her brother in surprise. Was it her imagination or did he actually sound a little in awe?

'Lord Stewart stopped by to see how Emma was feeling,' Linette explained.

'Really? Ah, well, you've no worries there,' Ridley said. 'Emma's head is as hard as mine. Takes more than a little bump to keep either of us down. Isn't that right, Em?'

Emma could have cheerfully murdered him. 'I dare say it does.'

Alex just smiled. 'I understand you're an artist, Mr Darling.'

'I am. Gave up chasing the bar to paint portraits of aristocratic gentlemen like yourself,' Ridley quipped. 'I find it far more entertaining.'

'But not nearly as respectable,' his father muttered.

'Now, Percy, let's not start in on that again,' Aunt Dorothy said. 'Ridley has assured us that he is making a good living, and as long as he is in demand, he will no doubt continue to do so.'

'Speaking of which, I've decided what I am going to give you as a wedding present, Linny,' Ridley said. 'How would you like a formal portrait of you and your fiancé in a setting of your choice?'

'Oh, Ridley, that would be wonderful!' Linette said, clapping her hands together. Then, with an anxious glance at her father, added, 'It would be all right, wouldn't it, Papa?'

'I don't see why not,' Ridley said before his father had a chance to object. 'The aristocracy all have portraits painted of themselves and as you are going to be the daughter-in-law of a peer, why shouldn't you have one done too?'

'I think it is a very generous offer,' Aunt Dorothy said. 'And we all know Ridley will do an excellent job.'

'Although you may wish to wait until they *are* actually married before starting on the work,' Alex said.

Emma sent a suspicious glance in his direction. 'Why would you say that?'

'Because it takes a good deal of time to paint a portrait and getting two people together at a time convenient to both during the preparations for a wedding can be challenging. However, once they are married and living in the same house, it will be much easier to arrange sittings.'

'Very sensible, Lord Stewart,' Aunt Dorothy commented. 'And I think a portrait of the newly married couple will make a fine wedding gift. Who knows, Ridley, perhaps Lord Stewart will commission you to do one of himself and his lady once they are married.'

'I should be delighted.' Ridley glanced at the other man

with interest. 'But forgive me, my lord, I was not aware you were to be married.'

'My mother was a bit hasty in announcing the engagement,' Alex acknowledged. 'I have not yet actually asked the lady for her hand.'

'But what woman in her right mind would turn down the opportunity to become a countess?'

'I doubt that is of concern to Lady Glynnis,' Linette said. 'She is already the daughter of an earl and has no need to marry in order to acquire a title or status.'

'Lady Glynnis?' There was a brief pause before Ridley said, 'Lady Glynnis Pettle?'

'Yes, that's right.'

'Do you know her, Ridley?' Linette asked, blue eyes bright with excitement. 'I thought you might given that you are moving in such high society now.'

'I do not move in high society, Imp,' Ridley replied. 'I merely bump into them every now and then. But I have heard the lady's name mentioned in conversation. I believe it came up in regard to a charity auction she and Lady Trilby's daughter were arranging.'

'Oh.' Linette's disappointment was plain. 'Then you are not acquainted with her.'

'I am not.' Ridley put his hands on his knees and got to his feet. 'Well, if you will all excuse me—'

'Where are you off to now?' his father asked. 'You've been out more than you've been in since you arrived home.'

'Oh, leave the boy be, Percy,' Aunt Dorothy said. 'You can't expect him to keep you apprised of what he's doing every minute of the day. Think how you would have felt had your father treated you that way when you were Ridley's age.'

'My father *did* treat me that way and it certainly didn't

do me any harm,' Mr Darling said. 'You've seen what happens when young men are left to their own devices. Ridley gave up a perfectly respectable occupation to become a painter.'

'I did not *give up* an occupation,' Ridley said in frustration. 'I simply decided not to become something I didn't want to be. If you can't understand that, we have nothing more to talk about.'

He left, slamming the door behind him.

'Oh dear,' Aunt Dorothy said. 'I didn't mean to upset him.'

'I shouldn't worry about it, Aunt,' Emma said, aware of Alex standing quietly off to one side. 'I suspect Ridley didn't want to tell us where he was going because he is off to visit a young lady in the village.'

'I beg your pardon? Which young lady?' Mr Darling demanded.

'Miss Harkness, most likely. Or Miss Stone. I know they were both very excited about the prospect of Ridley coming home for Linette's wedding.'

'And why would they not be excited?' Aunt Dorothy said, relief colouring her voice as she picked up her embroidery. 'Ridley is such a handsome lad. Always has been. Reminds me of a young man I knew once. Albert, his name was. Did I ever tell you about him, Linette?'

Linette smiled. 'No, Aunt Dorothy.'

'Almost married the dear boy, I was that smitten with him. And he wasn't near as handsome as your brother. Still, it wasn't meant to be and I suppose it's just as well. Your uncle came along soon after and he was far better off than poor Albert.'

Emma only just managed not to smile. Aunt Dorothy must have been at the sherry again. She tended to reminisce when she'd had a drink or two and she obviously didn't care that Lord Stewart was still in the room.

Still, at least her anecdote had served to take the attention away from Ridley and Emma was definitely grateful for that. Her suggestion that he had gone to see a young lady in the village had been pure fabrication because she was quite sure his reasons for leaving had nothing to do with having to be anywhere. His expression had changed the moment Lady Glynnis Pettle's name had been mentioned. And the tightening of his jaw indicated something far more troubling than a mild case of surprise.

Ridley had been *distressed* by the mention of Lady Glynnis's upcoming marriage to Lord Stewart. And the reasons behind *that* were neither pleasant to contemplate, nor possible to ignore.

Chapter Six

Emma felt nothing but relief when Alex took his leave shortly thereafter. Not because she wished to see him gone, but because the effort of having to pretend that everything was all right was definitely wearing on her nerves. She had no idea if Alex had noticed the change in her brother at the mention of Lady Glynnis's name, but he was not a stupid man and she knew better than to underestimate his powers of observation. Until she knew why Ridley had left so abruptly, she was happier keeping Alex at a distance than she was at having him close.

They walked outside together and found the bay waiting patiently, his reins having been tied to the hitching post. 'Strange,' Alex said. 'I don't recall leaving him tethered.'

'That's likely Jenks's doing,' Emma said with a smile. 'He isn't used to horses being left to their own devices. Certainly none of our horses are so well behaved.'

'Thunder is unusual in that regard, but it does come in handy when one takes a spill in the hunting field,' Alex said, patting the big bay's neck. 'Nothing worse than having to trek miles back to the house on foot, especially in the rain.'

'That cannot be good for one's boots.'

'Most definitely not.' Alex untied the horse's reins. 'Emma, my brother tells me there is to be an assembly held tomorrow evening at a house on the outskirts of the village.'

'Yes, at Mr and Mrs Jacobs's. Linette mentioned it to me the other day.'

'Were you planning to attend?'

'I thought I might. The Jacobs are good friends,' Emma said. 'They have a large house and they enjoy holding dances in it. We always have a good time.'

'Then perhaps I shall see you there.'

Emma gasped. 'You're *going*?'

'Yes. Do you find that strange?'

'Well, yes, I suppose I do,' Emma said, at a loss for a tactful reply. 'It will surely pale in comparison to the elegance of the soirées you normally attend in London.'

'Perhaps, but I thought it might make for an interesting diversion. There is not a great deal to do here in Little Moreton.'

Emma sighed. No, there really wasn't, especially for a man like Alex. To him, Little Moreton must seem almost paralytically boring because it wasn't his world. *His* world was in London, with the beautiful Lady Glynnis Pettle at his side. An assembly at the Jacobs's would be, at best, a pale imitation of what he was used to. 'Well, I dare say you'll find something with which to amuse yourself,' Emma said. 'There will be cards for those who don't like to dance.'

'But I do like to dance,' he told her. 'In fact, I hope you will reserve a dance for me. A waltz, if I may be so bold.'

Stupidly, her pulse quickened. He wanted to dance with

her…and not just any dance: a waltz, that most intimate of ballroom dances. He would be required to take her in his arms and to twirl her around the room, with one hand at her waist and the other holding her hand. And throughout it all, she would be expected to remain calmly indifferent and commendably aloof.

She *had* to remain that way. There would be far too many eyes watching them to permit any other kind of expression.

'I shall make a note of it on my card,' Emma said lightly. 'Until tomorrow, Lord Stewart.'

He stared at her for a long time. Then, with a brief but unusually genuine smile, he swung up into the saddle and touched the brim of his hat. 'Until tomorrow, Miss Darling.'

No sooner had Alex disappeared than Emma went in search of her brother. It was better she face *him* down than let her thoughts dwell on Alex. In that direction dwelt heartache and disappointment. The less time she spent longing for the unattainable, the better.

Ridley was another matter entirely. Emma was convinced there was more going on between her brother and Lady Glynnis than he was letting on, and for everyone's sake, she had to find out what it was, though Lord knew if he'd tell her. Her brother could clam up tighter than an oyster when it suited him.

She found him in the conservatory, sitting on a stone wall, his sketchpad open in his hands. 'Ridley?'

He flushed and quickly turned the page over. 'What do you want?'

'Only to talk. I was concerned when you left the drawing room so abruptly.' She sat down on the wall beside him. 'I wondered if someone had said something to offend you.'

'You mean other than Father *demanding* to know where I was going?'

Emma laughed. 'He did not demand that you tell him.'

'He would have,' Ridley muttered, 'had Aunt Dorothy not stepped in to intervene. Thank God she'd been at the sherry again. I doubt she would have said anything if she'd been sober.'

'Probably not. But you and Papa have never seen eye to eye about the proffering of information.'

'And I doubt we ever will. He doesn't seem to understand that I'm not a child any more,' Ridley grumbled. 'I'm old enough to do as I please and I don't appreciate having to account for my whereabouts every time I set foot outside the door.'

'But you didn't have anywhere to go, did you, Ridley? You just wanted to leave the room. Why?'

'No particular reason.'

Emma shrugged. 'As you wish.' She glanced at the sketchpad. 'What are you drawing?'

'Nothing. As you can see, the page is blank.'

'I mean on the one you just flipped over.'

'Oh, that. A poor rendition of a folly I came across on Lord Garrickson's estate,' he said in an offhand manner.

'Lord Garrickson,' Emma repeated, impressed. 'You *are* moving in illustrious circles these days, Ridley. Hobnobbing with Lord Bickerson. Accepting commissions from Viscount Huston. And now whiling away the hours on Lord Garrickson's estate. No wonder you're acquainted with people like Lady Glynnis Pettle.'

Nothing altered in Ridley's face. Not so much as an eyebrow flickered. But Emma saw his fingers tighten on the piece of charcoal. 'I have no idea what you're talking about. I've already said I don't know the lady.'

'But I believe you *do* and better than you would have any of us believe,' Emma said softly. 'And not just as a result of hearing her name mentioned in conversation.'

'It would be impossible for me to give you an accounting of *all* of the people I hear spoken of in a day, Emma.' Ridley began to sketch the wicker chair opposite, making quick, bold strikes with the piece of charcoal. 'We would be here until doomsday.'

'But we weren't talking about a lot of people. We were talking about Lady Glynnis Pettle. Now stop prevaricating and tell me the truth, Ridley. Have you met the lady or not?'

He hesitated briefly. 'What if I have?'

'Why didn't you want to admit it in front of Lord Stewart?'

'Because it's none of his business.'

'None of his business? Ridley, Lady Glynnis is going to *marry* Lord Stewart. I would say that *makes* it his business, wouldn't you? And since there is no getting around the fact that you and the lady are going to *be* in the same house together, I suggest you stop playing games. Now, what's the real reason you didn't want Lord Stewart to know that you were acquainted with Lady Glynnis?'

Ridley sighed in exasperation. 'Damn it, Emma, you are no less a badger at four-and-twenty than you were at six. Even then you refused to let anything go.'

'Then you should know better than to try to keep things from me now.'

'I wasn't trying to keep anything from you. I simply didn't want to tell Lord Stewart that I knew Lady Glynnis, because…I didn't want him to know that I had painted her.'

Emma blinked her surprise. 'She *sat* for you?'

'Remember I told you a lady had hired me to paint a portrait of her as a gift for someone else? Well, that was Lady Glynnis.'

Emma stared at her brother in bewilderment. He had run out of the room as though the hounds of hell were after him…because the woman Alex was going to marry had hired him to paint her portrait? 'You're not making any sense, Ridley. You are an artist and Lady Glynnis wanted her portrait painted. Where is the harm in admitting that *you* were the one she hired to do it?'

'Because I was afraid such an admission would have spoiled the surprise.'

'What surprise?'

'Did I not just tell you the portrait was to be a gift?'

'Yes.'

'Did it not occur to you that the person Lady Glynnis had in mind for the gift might just be Lord Stewart?'

'Oh!'

'Exactly.' Ridley resumed his sketching. 'It wouldn't have been very sporting of me to spoil her surprise. Now, may we please move on to another topic?'

'What did the two of you talk about?'

'Emma!'

'I'm just curious to know more about her. After all, she is going to be related to us through Linette's marriage to Peter.'

Ridley's face darkened. 'Then you'll have to ask her yourself. I don't remember what we talked about.'

'Did she mention Lord Stewart at all?' Emma persisted.

'No.'

'Strange. You'd think she would have if the painting was to be a gift for him.'

'Sometimes there's just no accounting for the ways of the aristocracy.'

'Was she pleased with her portrait?'

'I believe so.' He glanced from the wicker chair to his sketchpad, his hands constantly moving. 'I painted her in the rose garden at Devonwood. She said she preferred that to a more traditional setting.'

'How long did it take?'

'A few weeks.' Ridley deftly drew a few more lines so that, as Emma watched, not only the chair but the entire corner began to take shape. 'She asked me to come at different times of the day so it was difficult to finish the painting without having to keep retouching the background. Mid-morning light is entirely different from afternoon light. It took me several days to get the warmth of her complexion and the variations of her hair colour just right.'

'Yes, I'm sure it was,' Emma murmured, watching his face. 'You know she's going to be at the ball.'

'I suspected as much.'

'Will you be all right with that?'

'Of course. The lady engaged me to paint her portrait. I did. Nothing more to it.'

'So when you see her again, there won't be any feelings of awkwardness between you?'

'Why should there be? I completed the commission and we parted. Most likely, she won't even remember my name.' Ridley closed the sketchpad and stood up. 'People like that never do.'

He walked away, hands in his pockets, the sketchpad tucked under his arm, as though he hadn't a care in the world—but Emma didn't believe it for a moment. Ridley had always been good at making others believe what he wanted them to, but she had always been able to see through him because she knew where to look. The truth was there in his eyes. They were open and honest—sometimes in direct contrast to what came out of his mouth.

And the truth had been there just now, when he had talked about his feelings for Lady Glynnis. His mouth had said one thing, but his eyes had said something entirely different.

For once, Emma desperately wished that she could have believed the former.

The next afternoon, Emma sat with paintbrush in hand, staring at her own blank canvas. She wanted to believe that her inability to paint was the result of a lack of creative thought, but that was like trying to convince herself that the sky was purple and the clouds red.

How *could* she paint with everything that was going on around her? Her sister was about to enter into a marriage the groom's parents didn't approve of. She was unable to shake the feeling that Ridley hadn't been honest with her about his previous encounters with Lady Glynnis Pettle. And, worst of all, *she* had to deal with the inappropriateness of her feelings for Alex.

If all that wasn't enough to stifle creativity, she didn't know what was!

Still, while there was nothing she could do about Linette's or Ridley's situations, there was definitely something she could do about hers—and that was to stop thinking about Alex. The man was all but engaged to another woman. A woman his family approved of and who was eminently more suited to being his wife than she ever would be.

She didn't even know why she *couldn't* stop thinking about him. It wasn't as though she was lonely, or in need of male companionship. Emma was proud of her ability to find contentment without the presence of a man. Why, then, was *his* face the first thing she saw upon waking and the last thing she thought of at night?

It made absolutely no sense. Apart from that one afternoon when he had come to her rescue, Alex's treatment of her had been utterly cordial and predictably correct. He had given her no encouragement, nor had she looked for any. And yet, the thought of seeing him at the Jacobs's assembly tonight, and the knowledge that they would be dancing together, made her pulse race in a most alarming fashion. How silly that the thought of being held in his arms, that the anticipation of his hand closing around hers, should make it so difficult to breathe. Unfortunately as the carriage drew to a halt in front of the Jacobs's sprawling house later that evening, Emma realised it was all she was able to think about.

'Oh, look, Emma,' Linette whispered as they made their way into the ballroom after greeting their host and hostess. 'There's Mr Taylor. And Lord Stewart is with him.'

As her sister raised her hand to wave at her fiancé, Emma smiled and glanced in the other direction. Linette could wear her heart on her sleeve if she wished, but she didn't have that luxury when it came to Alex. She had to clamp down on these ridiculous urges and get them under control. She couldn't risk making a fool of herself in front of everyone she knew.

Worse, she couldn't make a fool of herself in front of him.

For that reason, she was exceedingly grateful when relief presented itself in the form of Mr John Tufton.

'Good evening, Miss Darling,' he said, coming up to them. 'Miss Linette. How lovely you both look this evening.'

'Thank you, Mr Tufton,' Emma said. 'I didn't expect to see you here.'

'I enjoy gatherings of this sort,' the vicar said. 'And though I don't usually dance, it is very pleasant to watch others do so.'

'Mr Tufton,' Linette said, 'I hope you won't think me rude, but I would like to go and speak to Mr Taylor.' She glanced at her sister. 'Emma, do you mind?'

'Of course not. I shall catch up with you later.'

Linette smiled and left them, all but skipping across the room in her eagerness to join her fiancé.

'Your sister seems very happy,' Mr Tufton remarked.

'I have never seen her happier,' Emma said softly. 'I suppose that is a true indication of love.' She watched them and was suddenly reminded of what Linette had said about the way people in love act. She saw Peter smile down at her, saw them briefly lean towards one another and touch hands, and then both blush and pull away again. Oh, yes, there was a very strong connection there. And to think Alex had asked her to try to break them up—

'…excited about the wedding.'

Emma turned her head, aware that Mr Tufton must think her abominably rude. 'I'm so sorry, Mr Tufton. What were you saying about the wedding?'

'Only that your sister must be very excited about it.'

'You would think so, but in fact, she is dreading it.'

The vicar looked shocked. 'She is?'

'The ceremony,' Emma said quickly. 'Linette wants nothing more than to be Mr Taylor's wife, but she is terribly shy and would much rather it be done without a great deal of fuss. However, she is marrying into the Earl of Widdicombe's family and that calls for a certain amount of formality.'

'Yes, I see what you mean,' Mr Tufton said. 'I should think it would be daunting for anyone, let alone someone as shy as Linette, to face the challenges that lie ahead.

Especially given the dissension that I hear exists within the family over the marriage.'

Emma turned to look at him. 'Dissension?'

'There are those who say the earl is not pleased with his son's choice of bride and that he is not going to attend the wedding. There has even been speculation that he isn't here because of his refusal to meet her.'

'The reason my father is not here,' said a cold voice behind them, 'is as a result of his ill health. It has *nothing* to do with his reluctance to see my brother and Miss Linette celebrate their engagement.'

Emma blushed hotly. It was impossible to miss the note of irritation in Alex's voice and Mr Tufton clearly had not. 'Forgive me for speaking out of turn, Lord Stewart,' he said quickly. 'I was only repeating what I had heard.'

'Then I suggest you verify your facts before passing along gossip. It does no one any good for lies to be taken as fact, Mr Tufton. You of all people should know that.'

Chastised, the vicar inclined his head. 'Indeed I do, my lord. And I shall be more mindful of what I say in the future.' With that, he bowed and walked away.

Emma, feeling decidedly sorry for the man, said, 'You could have been more tactful.'

'And he could have been more circumspect,' Alex snapped. 'I don't care for a clergyman who gossips. Why my father isn't here is no one's business but his own.'

'On the contrary, your brother is about to marry a woman your father hasn't even met and on the two occasions where he might have done so, he was noticeably absent,' Emma said boldly. 'Questions are bound to be raised in other people's minds.'

'I repeat, my father is not well.'

'But he has not even sent her a letter saying how sorry he is that he has had to miss both occasions. So naturally,

Linette is imagining all manner of reasons as to why he hasn't come. She believes he has taken her in dislike.'

'Does that surprise you?' Alex replied. 'Have I not already told you that neither he nor my mother are happy about the marriage?'

'But if your mother can set aside her feelings, why can your father not do the same? You said yourself the marriage *is* going to take place.'

'Only because Peter will consider nothing else.'

'Then does it not behove *both* of your parents to come to terms with the arrangement as quickly as possible? For the benefit of all concerned?'

Emma hated arguing with him, but she simply could not let his father's continued absence at these gatherings go unchallenged. Surely he could see that other people must find it questionable in the extreme.

'Good Lord, Emma, what are you and my future brother-in-law talking about?' Ridley said, suddenly appearing on the scene. 'If looks could kill, I swear you'd both be lying dead on the floor.'

Emma felt her cheeks burn, but Alex rose to the occasion masterfully. 'It is nothing to be concerned about, Mr Darling. Your sister and I were simply discussing the painting she has agreed to do for me.'

Emma glanced at Alex in horror, but Ridley was even more shocked. 'Emma is doing a *painting* for you? Good Lord, and here I thought I was the only artist in the family.'

'You *are* the only artist!' Emma said, blushing furiously. 'Lord Stewart happened upon me one day as I was painting a dragonfly and said he wanted one of my paintings—'

'Of a dragonfly?'

'No, silly! Of something of his own choosing.'

'And you *agreed*?'

'Not exactly.'

'But he just said you were discussing the painting you agreed to do for him. How is it you were going to sell him a painting when you're not even willing to *show* me anything you've done?'

'Lord Stewart isn't buying the painting, Ridley!' Emma said, cursing Alex for having brought it up. 'He mistakenly believed I insulted him and that I owe him a painting as a forfeit.'

Ridley's surprise quickly turned to incredulity. 'You insulted our future brother-in-law?'

'Of course not! I said he *thought* I'd insulted him, when in fact I did nothing of the kind—'

'I think,' Alex cut in smoothly, 'it would be best if we were to continue this discussion at a later date, Miss Darling. I do believe this is our waltz.'

Sure enough, the orchestra had begun to play and the opening strains of the waltz could be heard drifting throughout the room. With Ridley looking on, Alex extended his hand.

Emma stared at it, furious at having been backed into a corner. She hated having to explain herself and she didn't like having to defend her actions to Ridley. He was already watching them with far more interest than was called for and the last thing she needed was to give him more ammunition with which to tease her. But neither could she refuse to dance with Alex. She had given him her promise and if she reneged on that now, he would likely only end up demanding another forfeit. And God only knew what *that* might be!

And so, keeping her smile firmly in place—while wishing them both a long and lingering malady—she placed her hand in his, raised her chin and in chilly silence let him lead her on to the floor.

* * *

Alex did not regret his decision to attend the Jacobs's assembly. While lacking in the number of titled guests, it could not be said to be lacking in any other way. The refreshments were far superior to those served in many of the best London houses and the warmth of his host and hostess was undeniable. Now he was on the dance floor with Emma Darling, a woman who aroused more conflicting emotions in him than any woman he'd ever met. She was a baffling mixture of innocence and independence—a woman who could freeze with a glance or charm with a word. He couldn't remember the last time he had been so fascinated by a woman. Or so aware of one. 'You dance very well, Emma,' he said, hoping to break the tense silence between them. Since they had stepped on to the floor, she had scarcely spoken a word.

'Did you think I would not know how?' she shot back.

For some reason, her anger amused him. 'Not at all. I had no reason to believe you would not be as accomplished in feminine undertakings as any other lady of my acquaintance. But while the waltz is accepted in London, I thought it might not have received widespread approval in places like Little Moreton. A fact borne out by the expression on *that* lady's face.'

Emma turned her head to glance at the woman in question, and struggled not to smile. 'Mrs Proctor is not as forward thinking as some, my lord. She doesn't approve of single ladies and gentlemen…touching.'

'Then I dare say she would be shocked by some of the dances I saw during my travels in Spain.'

'Why? How do they dance in Spain?' Emma asked.

'Provocatively,' he whispered against her ear. 'They dance as though they were lovers.'

He wasn't surprised when she gasped, but when she

tried to pull away he merely tightened his grip. 'You asked me a question, I answered it.'

'But surely there was no need to be so descriptive,' she threw back at him.

He laughed, a fact which only angered Emma more. 'Stop it, Alex! Mrs Proctor is staring at us.'

'Let her stare. I don't care about Mrs Proctor, Emma,' he murmured. 'We're not doing anything wrong. Our bodies aren't touching, only our hands.' But as if to make matters worse, he curled his fingers around hers, pressing his thumb into the centre of her palm, gently caressing the creamy-smooth skin. And when he saw her swallow, he knew she wasn't immune to his touch.

'Did you…dance any of those dances?' she asked. 'The ones you saw in Spain.'

'No, but I enjoyed watching them. The Spanish are a passionate people. They are not afraid to demonstrate that passion when they dance.' He glanced at the stiffly erect bodies moving around them. 'We English have a long way to go.'

Emma said nothing more for the rest of the dance, but Alex knew she was aware of him, and in a way she hadn't been before. Her breath was coming faster, her colour was high, and when they were bumped by an overly-enthusiastic pair, he heard her gasp as she was pushed up against him, the softness of her breasts crushing into his chest. It made him think of those sultry nights in Spain and the whispers in the darkness of the night.

It would have been worth it, he thought, to take her there. If for no other reason than to watch the expression on her face when the Spaniards danced.

At the conclusion of the waltz he escorted her back to the sidelines, aware that a number of people were still watching them. Emma must have noticed it too. 'Thank you, Lord Stewart.'

'My pleasure, Miss Darling. I can't tell you how much I enjoyed it.' He would have said more had the vicar not suddenly appeared and extended his hand to Emma.

'I believe this is our dance, Miss Darling.'

Uncharacteristically annoyed, Alex said, 'I thought clergymen didn't dance.'

Mr Tufton's handsome face creased in a smile. 'I don't as a rule, but Mrs Jacobs has been most persistent, given the number of single ladies in attendance. I thought it would not hurt to make an exception this one time.'

Alex watched the blush rise in Emma's cheeks and silently cursed the vicar's charming manners. He watched them take their positions on the floor and while he knew he should have asked one of the other single ladies to dance, he suddenly wasn't feeling that charitable. Instead, he signalled the waiter for a drink and then stormed out into the garden.

His brother found him there some time later. 'Ah, so this is where you ran off to,' Peter said. 'Are you not having a good time?'

Alex took a mouthful of wine. 'No. Are you?'

'I am enjoying myself immensely.'

Of course he was, Alex thought darkly. His brother had danced as many dances as was polite with Linette, and had then turned his attention to the other ladies. He had even danced with Emma, allowing Alex the opportunity of observing her as she moved gracefully through the steps, her beautiful smile frequently appearing, without the restrictions she so often placed on those she offered him.

'Emma seems to be having a good time,' Peter said innocently. 'I saw her dancing with Mr Tufton.'

'Yes. The vicar is a man who enjoys getting to know his parishioners. Especially the pretty ones.'

'What's this?' Peter said in amusement. 'Is that jealousy I hear in my brother's voice?'

'Don't be ridiculous,' Alex snapped. 'She can dance with whomever she likes.'

'Yes, she can. And Tufton's a good man. She could do worse than to marry him.'

'Marry a village clergyman?' Alex said derisively. 'Surely she could set her sights a bit higher than that? Her sister set her cap at an earl's son and got him.'

Peter laughed. 'Linette did not set her cap at an earl's son. The earl's son fell in love with *her.*'

'Foolish young man,' Alex murmured. 'You know there will be those in attendance next weekend who will take you to task over it.'

'Yes, I know.' Peter sighed, his easy smile fading. 'And Father's not coming, is he? Even if he's well enough.'

It wasn't really a question and they both knew it. 'I think it would be best if you didn't get your hopes up,' Alex agreed.

'It isn't fair,' Peter said quietly. 'His absence will send a message.'

Yes, it would. Soon, everyone in London would know that the Earl of Widdicombe did not approve of his son's marriage to Linette Darling and, sadly, she would be treated accordingly. Not by the people of Little Moreton with whom she had grown up, but by those in society who knew of the earl's antipathy towards her and who would naturally take his side. They would eat shy little Linette for breakfast and spit out her bones.

'Peter, have you given any thought to what it's going to

be like for Linette if you do get married without Father's approval?' Alex asked, feeling sorry for the girl in spite of himself. 'If he doesn't acknowledge her, society never will, and doors that have always been open to you will suddenly be closed in your face. Linette will not be welcomed by those it is necessary she be welcomed by and you will be forced to live on the fringes of society.'

'I don't care. I'll never set foot in London again if that's the way we're treated. We can live here, where Linette is loved and admired for the woman she is. I don't need society's approval.'

'And what of your children? Would you have them shunned because of their mother?'

Peter blanched. 'That's not fair.'

'Life isn't fair, but we have to deal with it on its own terms,' Alex said. 'I'm not saying Father will do any of this, but the possibility exists. Think carefully about this, Peter. Because it's not only *your* life that is going to be affected by your decision.'

Emma did not dance with Alex again, though she was painfully aware of his presence in the room. She felt his eyes on her several times throughout the evening, watching with whom she danced and with whom she spoke. Once or twice, she even looked up in time to catch his thoughtful gaze resting upon her, but he was always the first to turn away and eventually she stopped looking. But her nerves were on edge regardless.

There was also no question that Alex's presence at the assembly was a tremendous coup for the host and hostess. Mrs Jacobs had been delighted at the prospect of having the youngest son of the Earl of Widdicombe in attendance, but to also have the eldest son there was an unexpected boon. The fact he was charming and handsome and single only added to his cachet.

The young ladies, of course, flocked to him like bees to honey. Since no one knew of his plans with regard to Lady Glynnis Pettle, he was seen as an eligible bachelor and both the young ladies and their mothers were anxious that good impressions be made. After all, Mrs Jacobs whispered to Emma later that night, if dear Linette could capture the heart of one of the earl's sons, why should Mrs White's daughter or Mrs Feeny's niece not secure the other?

By midnight, Emma was more than ready to leave. Her head was pounding and there was a queer, unsettled feeling in the pit of her stomach. Needing a moment's quiet, she slipped out on to the terrace, welcoming the freshness of the cool evening air against her cheeks. Perhaps she shouldn't have eaten the lobster...

'Emma, are you all right?'

She turned, and her heart plummeted. *Dash it all!* Why did the man have to keep on finding her? 'I'm all right.'

'Are you sure?' Alex said. 'You're as white as a sheet.'

'Perhaps I'm just a little tired.' Despite her best intentions, his concern touched her and she mustered a shaky smile. 'I must be out of practice. I haven't danced this much in years.'

'Yes, I noticed the vicar claimed two dances,' Alex muttered.

'Then you probably noticed he also claimed two dances with all of the other ladies present,' Emma told him. 'And his attentions were very well received. I thought Miss Brown seemed particularly taken with him.'

'And here I thought clergymen didn't dance,' Alex mumbled.

Emma laughed and leaned in closer. 'It would appear this one does.'

It was a mistake. When Alex abruptly turned, Emma found herself only inches away from his face. And when he glanced down at her lips, her heart gave a most unsettling lurch. 'Oh!'

'You're not well.' He grasped her arm, his long fingers curving gently around her elbow. 'Let me get you a chair.'

'No, I'm all right. Really,' she assured him, aware that her skin was burning where he touched her. 'I just need to go home.'

'Are you sure?'

She closed her eyes, nodding. 'My head is hurting. Perhaps a leftover from the bump I received.'

His eyes darkened with concern. 'Is the rest of your family ready to leave?'

'I don't think so. Papa and Aunt Dorothy are playing cards and I hate to take Linette away when she is having such a good time.'

'Then I shall send you home in my own carriage.'

'Oh, no, I couldn't—'

'Yes, you could. I shall go and let your father know you are leaving.'

Wearily, she nodded. 'Thank you.'

A few minutes later, Emma found herself standing outside the Jacobs's front door. She could see the line of carriages winding out into the driveway, but even at this distance, Alex's was easy to pick out. Not only because it was the only one drawn by four perfectly matched blacks, but because it was the only one bearing a coat of arms. A coat of arms that signified how truly different they were—and how ridiculous were the direction of Emma's daydreams.

'Thank you, Hobbs,' Alex said when the coachman

finally brought the elegant equipage to the door. He carefully helped Emma inside, then surprised her by climbing in after her.

'My lord, this really isn't necessary—'

'I wish you wouldn't call me that when we're alone,' he said. 'And you can let me be the judge of what is and isn't necessary.' He settled the fur rug over her lap. 'I'm sorry the bricks aren't warm. Your feet must be cold, standing on the front step all that time.'

And before Emma could object, Alex had slipped off her left slipper and was cradling her foot in his hands.

Shock waves ran up her leg. Dear Lord, was the man part-god of fire? His hands were blissfully warm, his touch unbelievably gentle. She could feel the cold recede as welcome heat seeped back into her skin. He massaged her toes through her stockings, the gentle caress bringing them slowly back to life.

'Does that feel better?' he enquired.

Emma gazed at the dark head bent over her foot, about to tell him she had never felt anything better in her entire life when he suddenly reached for her other foot and slipped that shoe off as well. Oh, no, this was definitely *not* a good idea. While rubbing someone's foot wasn't exactly a prelude to making love, Emma was finding it incredibly intimate and it was made even more so by the privacy of the carriage.

She bit her lip as she listened to the sound of his breathing, aware that she was alone in the carriage, that both of her feet were bare, and that Alex was caressing them in a way that was making her head spin. If someone were to see them now…

'Alex, I really think you should…stop,' she whispered.

'Yes, I know.'

But he didn't stop. He went on touching her, his long fingers curving around the base of her ankles, caressing the sensitive spot just beneath the bone before running his thumbs along her insteps and then back.

Emma closed her eyes, lulled by the sensual massage. She heard the tempo of his breathing quicken as his fingers climbed higher, gently kneading the flesh of her calves. She wanted to groan out loud at how blissful it felt, but she knew such a sound would send the wrong message entirely. Thank goodness the carriage was dark. His touch was making her warm all over, her body strangely heavy and lethargic. But she had neither the will nor the desire to stop him.

She gazed down at his head, fighting the urge to put her hands in his hair, to run her fingers through the ebony strands. She wanted to touch him. To hold him. To—

No, no, *no!* She was mad even to think it. He wasn't hers. He *never* would be hers. And every step she took down that treacherous path only made the return journey that much more painful. 'Stop it, Alex,' she whispered harshly. 'For pity's sake, *stop.*'

It was the anguish in her voice that finally stilled his hands. She held her breath as he looked up, the space between them crackling with tension. She was sure he must be able to hear her heart. It was pounding so hard it deafened her to everything else.

Slowly, he drew back his hand and even more slowly he sat back, and slowly he backed out of the carriage. But he did not stop looking at her. Not as he folded in the stairs. Not as he closed the carriage door. Not as he stood and gazed in at her through the window. Only when he stepped away and the carriage moved off did she finally lose sight of his face, and only then did Emma close her eyes and lay her head back against the cushions.

In the space of five minutes, her entire life had changed. From this moment, there was no going back. But sadly, there was no going forwards either.

Chapter Seven

Emma heard the carriage with the rest of her family arrive home later that night, though she couldn't have said at what time it did. She heard, shortly thereafter, a light knock at her door, followed by the flickering brightness of a candle as someone pushed the door open a crack. But she kept her eyes closed and said nothing, too afraid of the words that might have tumbled out had someone given her the chance.

She was falling in love with Alexander Taylor. Of all the idiotic, imbecilic things to do, that had to be at the top of the list. All of her life, Emma had prided herself on being the sensible sister. The one who scoffed at the idea of love at first sight and who said passion was the purview of poets and dreamers. Then Alex had come along and she'd discovered that she was no more impervious to Cupid's arrows than anyone else.

But she had to be! She had to be strong for everyone else's sake. Linette was marrying a man whose family didn't want her. Ridley had feelings for a woman who could never be his. And somewhere along the way, *she* had been stupid enough to fall in love with a man who was promised to another. Surely one of them had to save themselves from the arrows of that scheming little monster!

Morning came, and with it the memory of everything that had happened the night before. Emma gazed at her reflection in the glass and saw all too clearly the ravages of a sleepless night. Faint purple shadows lingered in the hollows beneath her eyes and there was a noticeable pallor to her complexion.

She prayed her family would be too caught up in their discussions of the dance to notice that her appearance was considerably less than vibrant.

'Ah, there you are, Emma,' her father said as she walked into the breakfast parlour. 'Feeling better this morning?'

'Yes, thank you.' She managed a faint smile and quickly went to the sideboard where breakfast had been laid out.

'Dashed good of Lord Stewart to send you home in his carriage,' Ridley said between mouthfuls of ham.

'Yes, it was,' Emma said, keeping her answers as non-committal as possible.

'Well, I think he's quite the gentleman,' Aunt Dorothy observed. 'Welcoming Linette into the family the way he did. Taking care of Emma not once, but twice now. I can tell you he made a very big impression on everyone who was there last night. Mrs Jacobs was positively over the moon at having *both* the Earl of Widdicombe's sons at her assembly. Definitely a feather in her cap!'

'Poor Lord Stewart,' Linette said. 'He was positively besieged by the ladies. Mrs Connelly cornered him every time he was alone and Mrs Hewitt followed him around the entire night, trying to introduce him to any one of her three daughters.'

'As if he'd be interested in any of them,' Ridley said with a snort. 'Not a pretty face amongst them.'

'Now, Ridley,' Aunt Dorothy chided. 'A pretty face isn't always a guarantee of a sweet disposition.'

'Perhaps, but if she hasn't a pretty face, why bother to look? I know I wouldn't.'

'No, because *you* put entirely *too* much stock in a lady's appearance,' Mr Darling criticised. 'And given your chosen field, you'll be lucky to have *any* woman look at you, let alone one worthy of attracting.' He went back to his paper. 'You should have stuck to the law.'

'Jupiter, Father, are you never going to let that go?' Ridley asked. 'At least I can paint pictures of my future wife. What can a barrister do but bore her to death with legal pleadings?'

Emma was thankful the conversation did not require her to take part. She sat down at the table next to her sister and applied herself to her eggs.

'Did you have a good time before you went home?' Linette leaned over to whisper.

'Yes, of course,' Emma said. 'But you were the belle of the ball!'

Her sister blushed. 'I wasn't that at all. Cynthia Brown was. Everyone was talking about how lovely her gown was and how very pretty she looked. Even Mr Tufton seemed to notice. But I did have a nice time and I'm so sorry you weren't feeling well. Was it the bump on your head?'

That, and Alex tenderly massaging her feet in the darkness. Oh Lord, there went her stomach again. 'I think it must have been.'

'Lord Stewart seemed very concerned about you,' Linette said, reaching for the salt cellar. 'He said you were in a bad way and that sending you home was the kindest thing he could have done.'

Emma tried very hard not to remember the other kindness he had shown her. Some things just didn't bear thinking about. 'It *was* good of him and I was very grateful for his assistance, but I'm all right now and I think we need say no more about it.'

'He really is a very nice man though, Emma. He spoke to me last night, you know.'

'He did?'

'Yes. After you left and when Peter was dancing with Loretta Jacobs. He came over to me and asked me about myself and what it was like living at Dove's Hollow. I told him I couldn't have imagined a nicer place to grow up and when he asked me about London, I said I really had no desire to go there at all. He said he could understand that, and then I told him about Ridley, and we actually laughed about it together. He didn't seem in the least intimidating. In fact—'

'Linette, please!' Emma said in desperation. 'I really have heard quite enough about Lord Stewart for one day, thank you.'

Unfortunately, her comment fell into a lull in the conversation.

'What's this?' her father asked as all eyes turned in her direction. 'Have you taken Lord Stewart in dislike, Emma?'

'That doesn't seem very charitable after he was good enough to send you home in his carriage,' Aunt Dorothy added.

'I have not taken Lord Stewart in dislike!'

'Then why don't you want to talk about him any more?'

'Very well. Talk about him all you like. I really don't care.'

A strained silence followed her words. Her father looked

at Aunt Dorothy, Ridley and Linette exchanged a glance, and then everyone returned their attention to their plates.

Not surprisingly, Emma felt the onset of another headache.

The eleven o'clock service on Sunday morning was very well attended. Not only because it was a lovely morning or because Mr Tufton was presiding, but because it was a wonderful opportunity for people to gather and discuss what had taken place at Mrs Jacobs's assembly.

It was generally agreed that the assembly had been one of the most successful ever held, mainly because no one could remember an event where not one, but two members of a peer's family had been present. It was also agreed that Lord Stewart's presence at the event made it that much more memorable, especially to the young ladies who'd had the good fortune to speak with him, or to those who had been even more fortunate in being asked to dance with him. And though it did not go without notice that Lord Stewart had waltzed with Miss Emma Darling, or that he had demonstrated a marked partiality for her company, it was also agreed that because the gentleman's brother was engaged to Emma's sister, the family connection warranted a closer association than might otherwise have been allowed.

Emma, who refused to offer any comment with regard to the gentleman's attentions towards her, her sentiments about him, or what he was like to waltz with, sat quietly in the pew, leafing through the pages of her hymn book as she waited for the service to begin. A few minutes before it did, however, the church doors opened and Lady Widdicombe, Lord Stewart and Mr Taylor walked in.

Emma heard the muffled gasps, predominantly female, and saw heads turn to watch the late arrivals make their way up the aisle. The front pew was always reserved for the aristocracy and as the three settled into their places, she heard the whispers begin. Mr Tufton merely smiled down at them from his pulpit. 'Good morning. I am delighted to see all of you here on this fine day. And I bid special welcome to those visiting us for the first time.' He nodded at Lady Widdicombe and her sons. 'Please open your hymn books and let us begin with "Hail the day that sees Him rise."'

It was a moving service about sin and forgiveness and Mr Tufton spoke passionately about man's need to forgive his fellow man for wrongs committed. Several young ladies surreptitiously wiped tears from their eyes, but Emma simply allowed the comforting words to wash over her, enjoying the sense of peace she so often found in the old stone church.

John Tufton was an eloquent speaker. He did not drone on about God's unending mercy, or speak in that boring monotone that threatened to put people to sleep. His voice was musical, almost lilting, as it touched on man's vices and virtues. Sometimes, he drew on humour to illustrate his point; other times he called on pathos to drive his message home. But no one fell asleep during his sermon and, at the conclusion, Emma stepped out into the sunshine feeling much better than she had going in, because listening to Mr Tufton's words had allowed her to examine her feelings for Lord Stewart and to put them in perspective.

She wasn't in love with Alexander Taylor. She admired and respected him, yes, but she certainly wasn't in love with him. True love took months to develop, sometimes even years. She had known Alex less than two weeks! Obviously, she had been caught up in a girlish infatuation and swept away by his dashing good looks. She wasn't proud of that, but at least she could explain it. And she could forgive herself for it, as Mr Tufton advised.

'Excellent sermon, Mr Tufton,' Mr Darling said as he greeted the vicar on the steps of the church. 'Always a thought-provoking topic, forgiveness.'

Mr Tufton smiled, his eyes sparkling with amusement. 'Thank you, Mr Darling. I have always thought so.' He turned to Emma and smiled. 'I hope you enjoyed the sermon, Miss Darling?'

'I did, Mr Tufton, very much. It came at a most appropriate time.'

She gave him a warmer smile than she had in the past and was surprised to see his cheeks redden. 'Yes, well, I like to think my words help many people through difficult or challenging times,' he said. 'Ah, good morning, Lady Widdicombe. Lord Stewart. Mr Taylor.'

'Good morning, Vicar,' Lady Widdicombe said. 'Excellent sermon.'

'Thank you, your ladyship.'

'Mr Darling,' the countess said, turning to regard Emma's father. 'I am pleased to see that you and your family honour the Sabbath.'

'We always have, Lady Widdicombe,' Mr Darling replied. 'Sunday is a day for quiet reflection and contemplation. To thank the Lord for all He has given us. Speaking of which, how does the earl go on?'

'I believe he is feeling better,' Lady Widdicombe said. 'I had a letter from his physician yesterday and he seems quite pleased with my husband's progress.'

'Then it is possible he may be here for the ball?' Linette asked impulsively.

Emma spared a glance for her sister's hopeful face, before looking at Alex. She was surprised to see compassion rather than annoyance reflected there. 'I'm sure if he is feeling well enough to attend, he will be here, Miss Linette.'

'Of course he will,' Peter said, reaching for her hand. 'Nothing would please him more. Mr Darling, may I have the pleasure of walking your daughter home?'

'I have no objection if Linette does not,' Mr Darling said.

Linette beamed. 'I would like it very much. Good day, Lady Widdicombe, Lord Stewart.'

On the heels of their departure, Lady Widdicombe set off in the carriage and Mr Darling resumed his conversation with Mr Tufton, Aunt Dorothy went to speak to Mrs Brown and her daughter, Cynthia, and Emma found herself alone with Alex.

'Are you feeling better, Miss Darling?' he asked in a casual tone.

'Much better, thank you.' Buoyed by the strength of Mr Tufton's words and by her new awareness of how silly her brief infatuation was, Emma offered him a genuinely warm and engaging smile. 'I am most grateful for your kindness last night, Lord Stewart. I hope it did not delay your departure from the assembly for too long.'

He looked down at her and shook his head. 'The moment I returned I was set upon by Mrs Jacobs and Mrs Connelly, both enquiring after your health. Word of your accident seems to have spread throughout the village, and when they noticed you looking so pale, they were concerned that you might have suffered a relapse. I was called upon to give my medical assessment of the situation.'

Emma frowned. 'But you're not a doctor.'

'As you and I know, however, they questioned me as though I was and I assured them that you had revived somewhat upon venturing into the cooler night air and that I was sure you would be feeling much better by the morning. So, as you can see, my time was fully occupied until my carriage returned.'

Emma smiled. 'I heard you were also kept very busy on the dance floor. The residents of Little Moreton cannot stop talking about the assembly. Indeed, I suspect it will be the topic of conversation for months to come.'

His mouth lifted at one side, making him look somewhat rakish. 'I'm sure it will grow tedious long before then. But I shall remember the evening too, Emma...' he looked at her and his smile changed '...though I venture to say for reasons far different than anyone else's.'

And just like that, Emma's newfound conviction vanished. He couldn't have been more clear had he said the words aloud, and her heart ached within her breast. 'Well, I had best be returning home. Good day, Lord Stewart.'

'Emma.' He put his hand out, stopping her. 'There's no one around. No one to overhear us.'

'I know.' Emma knew exactly what he was referring to. She glanced in the direction of her father and the vicar, relieved to see that they were still enjoying their conversation. 'But I think it better that we maintain a more formal distance between us.'

'Better for whom?'

'For everyone.' She gently disengaged her arm. 'Life is complicated enough, my lord. It will not benefit either of us to complicate it any further.'

She didn't wait for his answer, but turned and started in the direction of Dove's Hollow. It was over a mile and her father would no doubt question her decision to walk home, but at the moment, she needed to be alone. She needed time to sort through her feelings.

In a little less than a week, she would be seeing Alex again, but this time, it would be in the company of Lady

Glynnis Pettle. The woman he was going to marry. If she did not ready herself for that, if she was not mentally prepared for the sight of Alex with another woman, she didn't know how she would be able to bear it. She was already so confused, so out of her depth.

'…I shall remember the evening too, Emma, though… for reasons far different than anyone else's…'

What was he saying? That he, too, had enjoyed the time they had spent alone in the carriage? That he remembered with fondness the intimacy of caressing her feet and calves? Surely that was wrong. Surely a man in his position knew what he invited by dwelling on such memories. He certainly knew better than anyone the impossibility of their relationship. Was he not the one who had counselled her to have Linette end her engagement to his brother on the grounds of her unsuitability? And Peter wasn't even the heir. The future of the line didn't depend on him. It depended on Alex. What possible chance could there ever be of the two of them having a life together?

More to the point, why was she suddenly beginning to think that she was not the only one asking that question?

After a bruising ride across the hills, Alex returned to the stables at Ellingsworth no happier than when he'd left. He had striven to banish all thought from his mind by flinging himself and his mount at hedges and turnstiles with a careless abandon not at all in keeping with his usual sense of responsibility. But even then he'd found no peace. He didn't even know why his mood was so foul. Only that it was and that it hadn't been improved by the sight of Emma smile so engagingly at Mr Tufton this morning. Surely it was not her intention to encourage the man. Surely she knew she could do a thousand times better than a simple country parson.

And yet, why the hell should he care? If she wanted to marry the local butcher, that was entirely up to her. He hadn't any more say in who she married than did a fly. Because *his* future was settled...or would be as soon as he asked Glynnis to marry him.

'Give him a good rub down,' he said to the stable lad who came running out. 'And an extra ration of oats. He deserves it.'

The young lad tugged the edge of his cap, then turned to lead the steaming bay into the stable. Alex headed in the direction of the house, his thoughts on Glynnis as an image of her face appeared in his mind. He'd always thought her beautiful, with those aristocratic features, lithe, slender body, and bright, golden hair. It was longer than Emma's and fell in a shimmering ribbon almost to her waist.

By contrast, Emma's hair was shorter and far less disciplined. Wispy tendrils all too often escaped to dance around her face, blowing across her eyes and cheeks so that she constantly had to push them back. The colour was darker, too. Richer.

He tried to remember the colour of Glynnis's eyes, but all he kept seeing were Emma's: that soft, melting brown, reminiscent of molten chocolate. And when she smiled, dimples popped out in both cheeks. He didn't think Glynnis had dimples, though he couldn't be sure.

He couldn't be sure of anything any more...

'Alex, dear, did you have a good ride?'

Alex turned to see his mother approaching and quickly marshalled his thoughts. 'I did, thank you. I'd forgotten how beautiful the countryside around here is.'

'I've always thought it the most picturesque in England,' Lady Widdicombe said. 'But then I grew up not far from here so my roots are in Hampshire.' She tilted her head to one side and looked at him. 'What's wrong? You seem unsettled.'

'Do I?' He gave her a rueful smile. 'Maybe it's just everything that's going on between Peter and Father. I don't like to think of them at odds with one another.'

'I know. It makes me unhappy too.' His mother sighed. 'As a child, Peter adored your father. And Richard couldn't spend enough time with him. He loved carrying Peter on his shoulders. You never liked being carried. You preferred to walk beside him.'

'I did?'

'Mmm. Said you were too big to be carried. That you might hurt him.'

Alex tried to remember those days, but they were lost in the annals of time. 'Is it truly such a bad thing, Peter marrying Linette Darling?' Alex asked. 'She is a lovely girl and the family seems respectable enough.'

His mother sighed. 'I know. I've tried to find something to object to in Linette's conduct, but I really cannot. The older girl is a touch bold and a little odd, but Linette is quite sweet and I've come to like her very much. And when I see her and Peter together...' The countess pressed her lips together, tears forming in her eyes. 'I love him so much, Alex,' she whispered. 'I just want him to be happy. That's all I've ever wanted. Especially after...what happened.'

Alex nodded and drew his mother into his arms. Few people knew the story of Peter's childhood accident. It was one the family had taken pains to conceal, but it burned in his mother's heart like acid. Because on the one day she had left Peter alone in the nursery, the unthinkable had happened. She had only been gone a moment, but it was long enough for the little boy to have climbed out of his crib and fallen down.

He hadn't cried. He had knocked himself unconscious.

And when his mother had come back in and seen him lying motionless on the stone floor, she had believed him dead and started screaming.

Naturally, the servants had come running. They had stood in the doorway, horrified by the sight of the countess clutching her youngest son in her arms, his body limp, his eyes closed, blood pouring from a gash on his face.

Thankfully, the diagnosis had been good. Peter had suffered a mild concussion, but he had regained consciousness soon after and had gone on to lead a normal healthy life. But the memory of that scare and the knowledge that, because of her inattention, her youngest son could have died stayed with Lady Widdicombe all through the years. It was the reason she could deny him nothing. Whatever Peter needed to make him happy, she was more than willing to give.

'This can't be helping matters between you and Father,' Alex said, knowing it wasn't the first time his parents had experienced differing opinions when it came to Peter.

'It isn't, but we are dealing with it as best we can.' She straightened, and pulled away. 'Your father doesn't understand why I cannot see his side in this. Why I won't stand with him in refusing to allow Peter to marry Linette. But I cannot.' She turned bright eyes towards Alex. 'I simply cannot.'

'I understand. But if Father chooses to make matters difficult for them, there won't be much any of us can do. He could revoke Peter's allowance and leave him without anything upon which to live. And given that Peter hasn't shown any inclination towards the law or the church, he will have no occupation.'

'I know,' his mother whispered. 'I would give him some of my own money, but your father would be furious and that would only make matters worse.' She hung her head.

'I really don't know what the answer is, Alex. I don't know what to do.'

'Well, why don't we see how matters go over the weekend?' Alex suggested. 'Everyone is coming to celebrate the engagement so the mood should be festive. Besides, Glynnis will be here; if she speaks favourably about Linette to Father, perhaps it will be enough to change his mind.'

'That would be a blessing,' his mother agreed. 'Your father has always been so fond of Lady Glynnis. She's like a daughter to him.' She shook her head. 'If only Peter had been able to find someone like that, everything would have been so much easier.' She laughed softly. 'I've often thought it a pity Glynnis didn't have a sister.'

'Yes, I suppose it is,' Alex murmured. 'Though there's no saying she would have turned out as well as Glynnis.'

'No, that's true. And there is no point wishing for the impossible,' the countess said. 'At least we know you are going to make a marriage of which your father approves. He keeps asking if I know when you plan to propose. Naturally I've said that's up to you. But I know he's looking forward to it.'

Alex nodded, trying not to allow an image of Emma's face to intrude. As his mother said, there was nothing to be gained by wishing for the impossible. 'I thought to ask her after the house party,' he said. 'Perhaps when we all return to London.'

'That would be wonderful, darling. I know it will make your father so happy. Both of us, really. I've always liked Glynnis. Such a sensible, down-to-earth girl. Well, I suppose I'd best get back to work. There are still many things to do before the weekend. Thank you, Alex,' she said, kissing him on the cheek. 'I don't know what I would do without you. You've always been so strong. You stand firm while the rest of us crumble. No wonder your father's so proud of you.' She raised her hand and brushed it across his cheek. 'And in case I haven't said it lately, so am I.'

All too soon, the weekend arrived and with it the ball to celebrate Peter and Linette's betrothal. Guests began arriving early on the Friday afternoon, or so Emma was informed by Mrs Connelly when she went into the village to purchase a length of lace. Of course, Mrs Connelly was in the perfect position to see the carriages as they rumbled through town, given that her shop fronted on to the main street. Some had borne elaborate coats of arms, while others were just very stylish as they clipped along behind teams of matched black, grey, or brown horses.

And of course, the occupants had been very fashionably turned out, Mrs Connelly had assured Emma. She had caught glimpses of stylish bonnets and elegant travelling gowns in many of the carriages, and such handsome gentlemen riding such very fine horses! It was clearly going to be a very exciting weekend. And to think it was all in honour of little Linette and that Emma's entire family were going to be there. Wasn't she just beside herself with excitement?

Emma had smiled, agreed that she could scarcely think straight and had then taken her leave. Mrs Connelly would have given her right arm to be a guest at the betrothal ball, but that honour had been reserved for invited guests only. While a general invitation had gone out to the residents of Little Moreton to attend the outdoor festivities planned for tomorrow, only family and friends would be in attendance at the grand ball tonight.

Mrs Connelly would have to be satisfied with that.

As expected, by the time Emma got home, Linette was in a rare state of nerves. Several times throughout the

afternoon, Emma had to repeat herself as a result of her
sister staring off into space, oblivious to what was going
on around her. She was terrified of the evening ahead and
there seemed to be nothing Emma or Aunt Dorothy could
say that could change how she felt.

Emma had to admit she wasn't looking forward to the
evening either. Thanks to the summer she had spent in
London, she was more at ease with strangers than her
sister, but she knew that many of the guests would be titled
and that all of them would be well to do. At such a gathering, her family would naturally be out of their league. If
they managed to acquit themselves with only a few *faux
pas*, Emma would think them lucky.

As a result, she took more care with her appearance
than usual and at the last minute had decided not to wear
her favourite gown of white India muslin, but to bring
out a new dress she hadn't worn before. The gown of pale
ivory shot through with gold thread had been a present
from Aunt Dorothy, brought with her from London for
Emma to wear during her stay in Bath. But because it was
far more daring than the gowns Emma usually wore, she
hadn't taken it with her.

Now she put it on and gasped at the amount of smooth
white skin visible above the neckline. It was bordered
in two inches of the finest lace but it was also far more
revealing than anything she'd ever worn before and the
sight of her breasts all but popping out over the top took
some getting used to.

'Oh, Miss Emma, what a beautiful gown!' her maid
said. 'You'll surely be turning heads, looking like that.'

Emma glanced at the girl, wishing she felt a little more
confident and a little less exposed. 'Are you sure, Jane? It
does seem a trifle…immodest.'

'Of course it does, miss, but that's what all the fine ladies are wearing in London.'

Yes, judging by the latest magazines Aunt Dorothy had been reading, it was—which meant it was also what most of the ladies at Ellingsworth would be wearing tonight.

With that in mind, Emma decided to grin and bear it—literally. She even allowed Jane to arrange her hair in a more elaborate style than usual. Fortunately, the girl was as much an artist with a brush and comb as Ridley was with his paints, and the upswept hairstyle, fastened with a pearl-studded comb that had belonged to Emma's great-grandmother, could not have been more flattering. With excitement lending a natural blush to her cheeks, Emma knew she looked her best. But would it be enough for the discerning eyes of Lord and Lady Widdicombe and their guests?

For Alex?

Ridley was already in the drawing room when Emma went down. He was standing by the window gazing out and, even to her eyes, he looked remarkably handsome. Somewhere along the way, the boy had disappeared and the man had taken his place. His body had filled out and his clothes looked to have been cut by one of London's better tailors.

It seemed they had all grown up, almost overnight.

Ridley turned as she walked into the room, a thoughtful frown quickly replaced by a smile of approval. 'I say, Emma, you're looking quite the thing. You might just outshine our little sister.'

Emma's mouth twisted. 'Thank you, Ridley, but we both know there's as much chance of that as there was of you being named first in your class.'

'You wound me,' he said, pretending to be hurt. 'I never thought you could be so cruel.'

'Do you disagree with what I said?'

'Not a bit, but that doesn't make it sting any the less.'

Moments later, the door opened and Linette and Aunt Dorothy walked in. 'Oh good, you're both here,' Aunt Dorothy said, looking rather more flushed than usual. 'Jenks is bringing the carriage around. Pour me a sherry, there's a good boy. I take it we do have time for a drink?'

'Not really, but if you're quite quick...' Ridley walked over to the decanter and poured his aunt the requested glass.

'Thank you, Ridley. Never hurts to have a little liquid courage, I always say.'

As long as it was only a little, Emma thought. Aunt Dorothy enjoyed a drop of sherry. More than a drop, though no one in the family had been tactless enough to mention it. But tonight was an occasion—something out of the ordinary. It definitely wasn't the time for Aunt Dorothy to end up lying face down in the trifle.

'Good Lord, Linny, are you going out like that?' Ridley asked.

Linette gasped, her lovely face turning white. 'Like what?'

'What *are* you talking about, Ridley,' Aunt Dorothy asked. 'Linette looks beautiful.'

'I didn't say otherwise.'

'But you said—'

'I simply asked her if she was going out like that,' Ridley said, his mischievous grin flashing. 'I didn't say she wasn't beautiful.'

'That's horrid, Ridley!' Linette complained, suddenly looking close to tears. 'I thought you were criticising me.'

'Then take that as a lesson, my dear,' he said. 'Never

jump to conclusions until you've heard everything a gentleman has to say and don't try to read something into his meaning that isn't there.'

'Most important of all,' Emma said drily, 'never try to read *anything* of intelligence into anything Ridley says. That would most definitely be a mistake.'

The good-natured bickering carried on until Mr Darling appeared, but for once Emma was glad of it. They were all a little on edge, and why would they not be? It wasn't every day one's sister was guest of honour at a ball hosted by an earl and a countess. A ball where lords and ladies would be in attendance and where all eyes would be focused on her from the moment she stepped into the room.

How would Linette handle such intense scrutiny? Her exposure to the upper crust had been virtually non-existent and Emma knew how deeply a careless word or a thoughtless gesture could wound. Would there be awkward silences as common ground was sought and found lacking, or would the conversations flow easily, as they did at home? More to the point, what would Linette do if she began to suspect she was falling short of everyone's expectations? Or that her future brother-in-law, a man she had come to like and admire, even to trust, might well be leading the pack?

Chapter Eight

Ellingsworth was ablaze with lights when the Darlings' carriage arrived in the courtyard. Liveried servants were on hand to help the ladies and gentlemen alight, to take capes, hats, canes and gloves, and to generally make sure the guests' arrivals went as smoothly as possible.

Having been in the house before, Emma thought she knew what to expect, but even she was unprepared for the splendour that greeted her eyes upon arrival. It was evident the servants had been up since before dawn preparing the house. There were flowers everywhere, their sweet fragrance perfuming the air and serving as a bright dash of colour against the pale walls. Brass-and-silver candle-holders glowed warmly in the candlelight, the floors had been polished so that one could see one's reflection in the black-and-white tiles and there wasn't a speck of dust or dirt anywhere.

Peter and his mother were waiting to greet them in the hall. Lady Widdicombe looked magnificent in a gown of rose-coloured silk, a glittering diamond necklace encircling her throat and long white gloves covering her arms.

Peter was equally dashing in formal black and white, his embroidered waistcoat a tribute to the tailor's art. But Lord Widdicombe was still noticeably absent and Emma's heart plummeted when she realised that Alex was missing too.

'Mr Darling, Mrs Grand, how nice to see you again,' Lady Widdicombe said. 'And Miss Linette, you look charming. Miss Darling, you look very well too.'

Emma dipped one knee in a curtsy. 'Thank you, your ladyship.'

Mr Darling stepped forwards. 'Lady Widdicombe, allow me to present my son, Ridley.'

The countess inclined her head. 'Mr Darling. I understand you've come down from Oxford just for the occasion.'

'Yes, your ladyship,' Ridley said. 'To see my little sister marry into such a grand family I would have sailed all the way from America.'

The countess raised an eyebrow, but said nothing as Ridley was likewise introduced to Linette's fiancé. Emma stood back and watched the exchange of greetings with interest, surprised by how easily Ridley seemed to fit in. In fact, with his dashing good looks and elegant clothes, he appeared right at home with the lords and ladies drifting through the beautiful rooms. But then, he moved in this sort of crowd now, Emma reminded herself. His clients were drawn from the ranks of the wealthy and titled and he was used to moving amongst them.

Linette, on the other hand, was like an anxious little bird, constantly looking around for the reassuring presence of her fiancé. Thankfully, he never went far from her side, preferring to stay with her as his mother moved off and the rest of them made their way into the Chinese drawing room. And finally, Emma saw Alex. He was standing alone by the fireplace, with a glass in his hand. He was watching her over the rim and Emma saw his eyes darken as they swept over her gown.

For the space of a heartbeat, she allowed herself the simple pleasure of looking back at him. What would it have been like, she wondered, had *she* been the one anticipating his proposal of marriage? She had been the object of his affections? Would she still feel this breathless every time he came near? Would her heart still hammer in her chest every time he stepped into a room? Or would she look at him the way so many other women regarded their husbands or lovers? Complacently. Smugly. Unemotionally.

The way Lady Glynnis Pettle might one day regard Alex.

Emma didn't want to believe it would be that way. In fact, it was hard to imagine *any* woman not falling in love with Alex given half the chance. He was easily the most handsome man in the room and certainly the one with the most presence. But it was also Alex who had told her there was very little romance in his relationship with Lady Glynnis. Was she wishing for something that didn't exist? Something he couldn't give?

Unconsciously, Emma found herself looking around for Lady Glynnis Pettle. Having no idea of the lady's appearance, it was impossible to make a positive identification, but Emma had a feeling she would know the lady when she saw her.

Her observations came to an abrupt end when Alex came over to join them.

'Miss Darling, you and your sister would make lovely subjects for a painting of spring,' he said after greetings had been exchanged. 'Or perhaps you have already done such a study.'

'Actually, I seldom paint people,' Emma said. 'I find facial expressions very difficult to capture.'

'But she is good at birds and insects,' Ridley said helpfully. 'Be thankful you haven't wings or you might find yourself sitting for her.'

Alex laughed, but Emma's father was less than amused. 'I hardly think your sister is about to become the second artist in the family, Ridley. Not as long as I have anything to say about it.'

And then, laughter, as melodious as silver bells, rang out, the sound drawing all eyes to the lady who had just entered the room in the company of Lady Widdicombe. She was tall and slender and impossibly beautiful, wearing a stunning gown of shimmering lilac silk. Her golden hair was arranged in an elegant chignon caught up with pearls and roses and she moved with the unconscious grace of a lady born and bred.

This, surely, must be Lady Glynnis Pettle, daughter of the Earl and Countess of Leyland.

'Behold, the lady cometh,' Ridley whispered in Emma's ear.

Emma turned to look at him. His complexion was pale, but otherwise, he seemed composed. 'Are you all right?' she whispered.

'Of course. Why wouldn't I be?'

Emma had a few ideas of her own on that score, but knowing this wasn't the time or the place, she turned back to watch Alex's future bride approach. Lady Glynnis was clearly very comfortable at Lady Widdicombe's side, and judging by the expression on the countess's face, the feelings were mutual. But then, Lady Glynnis had grown up with these people. She was the daughter of an earl. Just as Alex was the son of one.

'Ah, there you are, Alex,' his mother said, catching sight

of him. 'I was just telling Lady Glynnis about our evening at the Parkinsons'.'

'I am so sorry to have missed your performance, my lord,' Lady Glynnis said with a beautiful smile.

Alex sighed. 'I should have known you would be in a hurry to volunteer that information, Mother.'

'Now, you mustn't blame your mother,' Lady Glynnis said. 'I did hear rumours to the effect that you had reluctantly agreed to play and that you gave an outstanding performance. But since I could not find anyone to confirm which *étude* you played, I was forced to ask your mother.'

Emma just stared at him. Alex played the piano? He had never made any mention of that to her. But then, why would he?

'Lady Glynnis,' he was saying now, 'may I present Mr Darling and his sister, Mrs Grand, as well as Mr Ridley Darling, Miss Emma Darling, and of course, my brother's fiancée, Miss Linette Darling.'

'Goodness, so many Darlings,' Lady Glynnis said, her voice sounding just a little breathless. 'I am very pleased to meet all of you. And congratulations, Miss Linette. I hope you and Mr Taylor will be very happy.'

Linette blushed, but Emma could see that she was pleased, and why would she not be? Lady Glynnis was beautiful, and charming and kind, with just a hint of the reserve that would be expected from the daughter of an earl. She smiled at each of them in turn, though when she came to Ridley, Emma noticed she didn't meet his eyes. Instead, she turned her head to ask a question of Emma. 'Lord Stewart tells me you are an accomplished artist, Miss Darling. Is that true?'

'Not at all, Lady Glynnis. I merely dabble with colour and brush and my efforts are those of an amateur. My brother is the true artist in the family—'

Too late Emma realised the inappropriateness of the remark. A scarlet bloom appeared on Lady Glynnis's cheeks, but it was Lady Widdicombe who stared at Emma in surprise. 'Your brother is an artist?'

'Yes, your ladyship.'

'Mr Darling, I thought you told me your son was studying law.'

'He was, Lady Widdicombe,' Mr Darling acknowledged reluctantly. 'But upon arriving home, he informed us that he had given up his studies to become…a portraitist.'

'Really? That is not the usual occupation for a gentleman's son.'

'No, my lady,' Mr Darling agreed with a decided lack of enthusiasm. 'It is not.'

'But he *is* very good at it,' Aunt Dorothy piped up, clearly not wanting anyone to think less of her nephew's abilities. 'He has already received a number of commissions from members of society and apparently he has several more lined up. And he would not be so gainfully employed if he was not—good heavens, what is all that noise?'

The commotion was coming from the direction of the hall. Emma turned, as everyone else did, to see what the cause might be.

'Oh, dear Lord!' Lady Widdicombe whispered. 'He's *here*?' She glanced at Alex with something akin to panic in her eyes. 'I had no idea he was coming.'

'Perhaps he thought you would try to discourage him,' Alex said softly. 'I wonder if the doctor knows.'

'Chances are good he does not. Pray excuse me,' Lady Widdicombe said with an apologetic glance at her guests before heading quickly towards the door.

Alex glanced at his brother. 'I think we had best go too.'

'Peter, what's wrong?' Linette asked quickly.

'Nothing.' Peter raised her hands to his lips and fervently kissed them. 'I shall return as quickly as I can.' Then, he turned and followed his mother and brother out of the room.

'How strange,' Aunt Dorothy said. 'I wonder what that was all about?'

Lady Glynnis was still gazing in the direction of the door; it looked to Emma as though she was trying not to smile. 'I cannot be sure, but judging from the look of surprise on Lady Widdicombe's face, I would say that the unexpected has happened and that, contrary to opinion, the Earl of Widdicombe has most definitely arrived.'

Alex was two steps behind his mother as they walked quickly into the hall. Just in time to see his brother's butler and valet helping his father get up off the floor.

'Richard!' his wife cried. 'Is it your heart?'

'Don't be silly, woman, it's these damned slippery floors,' the earl grumbled. 'I simply lost my footing and fell.'

'Perhaps you should lie down for a moment, Father,' Alex suggested.

'I didn't come here to lie down.' The earl rose to his full height, shaking off the butler and valet. 'I came to see what kind of a mess my son is making of his life!'

Alex felt Peter stiffen at his side. 'Then I'm afraid you've wasted your time, sir. I am very happy with my life. In fact, I am having a grand ball tonight to celebrate it.'

Aware that his mother was about to say something, Alex said, 'Why don't we retire to the drawing room? I don't think our guests need witness any of this.'

Recognizing the wisdom in the suggestion, the four of them repaired to the nearest saloon. Alex shut the door and then turned to face his parents, aware that his father had already poured himself a glass of whisky and that his mother was looking none too pleased about it.

'Is that a good idea, Richard?' she said.

'Harrow wouldn't think so, but since he's not here I don't give a damn.' The earl raised the glass and tipped back the contents. 'Damn fine whisky, that.' When he'd emptied the glass, he smacked his lips in satisfaction. 'Damn fine. Now, about this engagement—'

'I won't hear anything said against Linette,' Peter said, quietly defiant. 'I love her. And I am going to marry her!'

'Not without my permission.'

'I don't need your permission. I am old enough to make my own decisions.'

'So you would defy me in this!'

'If you pushed me to it, yes,' Peter said. 'It is not what I would like to do, Father, but I will if you force my hand.'

'Force your hand? Of all the—!'

'Father, if I may,' Alex interrupted. 'I understand your taking exception to Linette Darling based on what little you know of her, but she is here tonight and anxious to meet you. Why not spend some time with her? I venture to say you will be surprised.'

His father's eyes narrowed. 'What's this? Has the chit charmed you as well?'

'I like her, yes,' Alex said simply. 'But, more importantly, Peter has already said he intends to marry her with or without your permission, and if the latter happens, the rift between you will never be healed. All I'm saying is that surely it is worth a few minutes of your time to speak to Linette and find out what kind of person she is.'

'And if I spend a few minutes with her and don't like what I see, what then?' The earl turned his gaze on his youngest son. 'Would you respect my wishes and walk away?'

Peter swallowed hard. 'No, sir, I would not. I have given my promise to Linette. I will not go back on my word. Not even for you.'

Alex felt the atmosphere in the room grow explosive. He watched his father's mouth begin to work and saw him stiffen as he turned away. 'Then it would seem we have nothing more to say to one another.'

'But you will meet her?' Peter said.

'No, sir, I will not. Nor will I acknowledge her family.'

'Richard!'

'Don't bother, my dear.' The earl's voice was coldly pre-emptive. 'I am still the head of this family and I say how matters are to go on. For your sake, I will not malign her, but neither will I speak of her in the terms you might wish me to.'

'You can't do that, Father,' Alex said quietly.

'Can't I? I'm not the one who's chosen to turn his back on the morals by which we live,' the earl snapped. 'The morals that have guided this family for generations. Your brother knows what kind of woman I expected him to marry. The kind of life I expected him to lead.'

'There's nothing to say he can't still lead that life,' Alex said, catching a glimpse of the despair on his brother's face. 'Miss Linette Darling is a lovely young woman. The least you can do is take a moment to meet her.'

'Why? Your brother's already told me he doesn't give a damn about my feelings.'

'That's not what I said!' Peter was stung into replying.

'Wasn't it? Did you not say you would marry her regardless of my opinion? That you would pay no mind to my concerns about her lack of position or breeding?'

'She may not have a title, Richard, but that doesn't mean

she has no social graces,' Lady Widdicombe objected. 'Her appearance and manners are most pleasing and she plays the pianoforte very well.'

'That's right,' Peter spoke up. 'Because Linette is the daughter of a gentleman.'

'She is the daughter of a former tutor who lives in a house obtained as a result of gambling,' the earl threw back. 'That does not make her a suitable bride for any son of mine.'

Lady Widdicombe gasped. 'Gambling?'

'Yes. Apparently, Mr Darling's older brother was something of a Captain Sharp. He won the house and everything in it at the faro table. When he died in a drunken brawl, it passed to his only brother, along with a tidy sum of cash that enabled him to give up teaching and settle down to the life of a gentleman. Not the most honourable way for a man to acquire the roof over his head.'

'You can hardly condemn the daughter for something the uncle did,' Peter said.

'Ah, but there's more. Mr Darling has two sisters, a younger sister living in Bath and an older one who lives in London. Both have a known propensity for drink, especially the widowed sister in London, while the husband of the sister in Bath is reputedly engaged in a scandalous affair with the woman next door.'

'Never!' Lady Widdicombe said. 'How do you know all this?'

The earl flushed. 'Never mind how I know. It is enough that I do. I should also tell you that the son, Mr Ridley Darling, has given up his studies of law to take up painting and that he has set himself up in a studio in London. And you know what they say about the morals of an artist.'

'In this instance, I can guarantee that whatever you've heard are exaggerations,' Alex felt disposed to say. 'I have made the acquaintance of Ridley Darling and he is good mannered and extremely affable.'

'I'm sure he is. No doubt he uses that affability to persuade impressionable young women to come and sit for him in his private studio.'

'Richard, really!'

'All I'm saying, my dear, is that the Darlings are not the genteel family they would try to make you believe they are. And if you'll take my advice, you will stay well away from them. All of them!' He glanced at his younger son, adding, 'And you, sir, would do well to take a page out of your brother's book. *He* is marrying a lady worthy of him. A woman who can hold her own with dukes and duchesses. Can your little country chit do that?'

Peter raised his chin. 'I would present her at Court if I could and be proud to do so.'

'Then you would embarrass yourself and the rest of your family by your efforts,' the earl said in disgust. 'Alex, for God's sake, try to talk some sense into him. Obviously nothing I say is having the slightest effect.'

'Only because you are being narrow minded and cruel,' Peter said.

'You would call me cruel, sir!'

'I would, because Linette has done nothing to deserve your condemnation!' Peter flung at him. 'You'd know that if you took even a moment to speak with her.'

'*Enough,*' Alex said sharply. 'This evening is not about debating the wisdom of the relationship. It is about celebrating Peter and Linette's betrothal. And since people know you are here, Father, you have no choice but to make an appearance and to put a good face on it. Unless you wish to bring down upon all our heads the type of embarrassment you fear Peter's association with Miss Darling will.'

'Alex is right, Richard,' Lady Widdicombe said. 'Whatever your feelings, you must put them aside for this evening. To cut the Darlings in your own son's home would be the height of ill manners and it would not be forgotten by those who are here to witness it.'

The earl muttered something about that not being his fault, but finally seeing the wisdom in Alex's words, reluctantly agreed to meet the family and to try to be civil whilst doing so. Alex could see that his mother, while relieved, was also anxious as to exactly how civil her husband was likely to be. He had got it into his head that Linette Darling was unsuitable and Alex knew he wouldn't give that up easily.

He was quite sure he wasn't the only one holding his breath as the four of them headed back to the ballroom.

Emma was also doing battle with family issues. Shortly after Alex and the rest of the family had left the ballroom, Ridley had excused himself on the pretext of securing refreshments for her and Lady Glynnis. An excuse that would have been believable had he actually returned with any.

'I cannot think what has happened to my brother,' Emma said some ten minutes later. 'He is usually most attentive.'

'Perhaps he stopped to speak to someone,' Lady Glynnis said, avoiding Emma's eyes. 'It really doesn't matter.'

Emma couldn't help thinking that the lady seemed relieved by his absence and she wasn't at all surprised when the earl's daughter bid her a clipped good evening immediately after.

As soon as she did, Linette appeared. 'Emma, do you mind if I slip upstairs for a moment? I've a mind to press a cool cloth to my face.'

'Are you all right, dearest?' Emma asked in concern.

'I'm not sure.' Linette bit her lip, looking far from happy. 'I don't know whether to be relieved or alarmed that Lord Widdicombe is here. Peter didn't look at all pleased upon hearing of his arrival.'

'Now don't start creating problems where none exists,' Emma cautioned. 'By all means, go upstairs and do whatever you need to settle your nerves. A cooling cloth will help. Your colour is a touch high. I shall find Ridley and, together, we will deal with whatever happens.'

She found her brother in one of the smaller saloons a short while later. He was standing by the window, staring out into the night. 'Ridley? What are you doing in here? You were supposed to be bringing back refreshments for Lady Glynnis and myself.'

'Yes, I know.'

'Then why didn't you?'

'Because I thought it would be better if I did not.' He pulled his gaze from the night and turned, his brow furrowed. 'Easier.'

'Easier for whom?'

'For me.' He sighed, and raised his head. 'And for her.'

Emma's heart did a flip. 'Lady Glynnis?'

She watched him nod, the candlelight accentuating the blue-black highlights in his hair. 'I haven't been entirely honest with you about my dealings with her, Emma. I led you to believe our relationship was strictly a business arrangement. That I didn't have any…personal feelings for her.'

Emma felt her breath freeze in her throat. 'So what are you telling me now? That you do have feelings for her?'

He glanced at her, then away. 'I'm afraid so.'

'Oh, Ridley. How could you? If you knew she was promised to someone else—'

'I didn't. Not in the beginning,' he said quickly. 'When she first came to sit for me, that's all she was. A client who wished me to do a painting of her. We didn't even talk about anything of a personal nature for the first few days. But as the hours passed and we came to know each another better, I found myself growing more and more fond of her.'

'Did you ever tell her how you felt?'

'Of course not! She is the Earl of Leyland's daughter. Who am I? A man who'd dropped out of Oxford to paint society portraits. Not exactly an equitable match.'

'So how did you part when the painting was done?'

Again, Ridley shook his head. 'I wish I could say we parted as friends, but the truth is, the last time I saw her, she was furious with me.'

Emma felt herself go pale. 'Why? What did you do?'

Ridley breathed a deep sigh. 'I let someone else see the finished portrait.'

'Someone else?'

'A friend. He often comes by the studio to see what I'm working on. Then we usually go out for a bite of supper and on to his club.'

'And he saw the painting when he came to collect you.'

'Yes. It wasn't even that I made a point of showing it to him.' Ridley's eyes were dark with misery. 'It was simply still on the easel when he walked in. I wanted to make sure it was completely dry before I framed it.'

'What did he say?'

'That it was stunning. The best piece of portraiture I'd ever done. Frankly, I didn't think anything of it. Tom's seen most of my work; as he was personally acquainted with Lady Glynnis's family, I didn't think it would be an issue. But when I delivered the painting to her two days later and happened to mention that a mutual friend had seen it, she tore a strip off me,' Ridley said unhappily. 'Told me I'd had no right to show it to anyone and that I had completely betrayed her trust.'

Something was missing, Emma thought. It made no sense that the lady would be so angry just because Ridley had allowed someone to see what was obviously a very beautiful portrait of her. 'You said this fellow was a mutual friend?'

'Yes. Lady Glynnis knows his sister quite well. That was another reason it never occurred to me that it would be a problem.'

'Ridley,' she said slowly. 'You didn't harm Lady Glynnis's reputation in any way by showing this fellow her portrait, did you?'

'Of course not. She was fully clothed and seated on a garden bench. It couldn't have been more proper.'

'Then why did she object so strenuously to his seeing it? Surely it would be no different than someone coming to her house and seeing it hanging on a wall. Portraits *are* for public viewing.'

Ridley sighed and turned back towards the window. 'That's what I tried to tell her, but it didn't make any difference. She took the painting, told me my professional ethics were lacking and made it clear she never wanted to see me again. That's why I thought it would be easier if I didn't linger in her company tonight. She was polite in her greeting of me, but it can't have been easy. I know it wasn't for me.'

'Unfortunately, you *will* have to see her again, dearest,' Emma said softly. 'Even if you manage to avoid her for the rest of this weekend, there's still Linette's wedding to get through, and any future family events and engagements we may be called upon to attend.'

Including Lady Glynnis's marriage to Alex, Emma thought sadly. An occasion that was going to be exceedingly difficult for both her and Ridley.

'Do you think I haven't thought of that?' Ridley ground out. 'I didn't want this to happen. In fact, it's the last thing I'd wish on anybody. It's just that…sometimes you meet someone at the wrong time in your life. And when you suddenly find yourself developing feelings for them, you can't just turn them off.'

A chill rippled through her body. 'Ridley. You're not… in love with Lady Glynnis, are you?'

He laughed, a harsh sound that was an unconvincing as the words that followed. 'Of course not. And it wouldn't matter if I was. She's going to marry Alexander the Great. And I am going home.'

'Home!'

'Yes. I have no intention of staying here and ruining Linette's special evening.'

'Now you listen to me, Ridley Octavius Darling,' Emma said firmly. 'I don't care what's happened between you and Lady Glynnis, you are *not* going home. Linette needs you right now. She needs all of us.'

Ridley frowned. 'Why?'

'Because Lord Widdicombe has just arrived and Linette is absolutely beside herself with worry. She's upstairs trying to calm herself down, which means you and I have to go back out there and lend her whatever moral support we can.'

'Shouldn't Mr Taylor be doing that?'

'Probably,' Emma admitted with a sigh. 'But to be honest, right now, I think supporting Linette is more than even he is capable of doing.'

* * *

Thankfully, Linette had not returned to the ballroom by the time Emma and Ridley arrived back, but a quick sweep of the room showed her that Alex and Peter had. The former was speaking quietly to Lady Glynnis, their heads close together. The latter hurried across the room to join them. 'Where's Linette?' Peter asked straight off.

'Upstairs,' Emma told him. 'She should be down soon.'

'Is she all right?'

'Nervous, but fine other than that.'

'I'm not surprised.' Peter looked decidedly unhappy. 'My father wishes to meet her. All of you. In the Chinese Salon.'

Oh, wonderful, Emma thought with a sense of fatalism. A meeting in a room filled with fire-breathing dragons and those sword-wielding warriors. She couldn't help wondering if the earl had chosen it for that very reason. 'Very well. As soon as Linette returns, we will make our way there.'

Peter smiled at her and Emma saw the look of gratitude in his eyes. He knew what this was costing Linette—probably what it was costing all of them—but there was nothing he could do. His father was the head of the family. All he could do was stick it out and hope that everything turned out for the best. He bowed and withdrew, likely to make his way to the Chinese Salon.

No sooner had he done so than Alex approached with Lady Glynnis.

'Oh, hell!' Ridley whispered.

'Courage, dearest. Remember, you're not the only one suffering over this,' Emma said, knowing her brother would think she was referring to Lady Glynnis—but she wasn't. She was talking about herself—about having to face the painful truth that the beautiful woman on Alex's

arm would soon be his wife. A realisation that was causing Emma more pain than she would ever have believed
possible. Her feelings for Alex were such that she could
not bear thinking about him being with any one else. The
thought of the tender moments they would share and the
loving words they would exchange was tearing her apart
because, in her heart, *she* wanted to be the one Alex turned
to for intimacy and warmth. The one he turned to for love.

But that wasn't going to happen. She'd had the misfortune to fall in love with the wrong man at the wrong
time. And sadly, there was never going to be a right time
for her.

'Mr Ridley, Miss Darling,' Alex said now. 'My father
has arrived and wishes to meet you and the rest of your
family in the Chinese Salon.'

'Yes, so your brother just informed us. Ridley,' Emma
said, 'why don't you go and find Papa and Aunt Dorothy
and tell them what is happening?'

Clearly relieved to have a reason for making himself
scarce, Ridley nodded. 'Yes, of course.'

After he left, Lady Glynnis said, 'Where is your sister,
Miss Darling? She should be here, mingling with her
guests.'

'I know, but she is not used to being the centre of attention.'

'If she is to marry into this family, she will have to get
used to it,' Lady Glynnis said, though not harshly. 'She
will be expected to take her place in society.'

Emma looked up and saw the expression of sympathy
on Alex's face. Did he know how she was feeling? She
had to believe that Lady Glynnis knew of his opinion
with regard to the relationship between Peter and Linette,
indeed how the entire family did. So was her question now
an indication that she agreed with his assessment of the

situation, even to wondering why the engagement was proceeding?

Emma managed a smile. 'I'm sure she will be fine once she gets used to it. This is all so new to her.'

'Emma?'

And then, thankfully, Linette was there. Her cheeks were still pale, but she held her head high and wore a valiant smile. No one looking at her would ever guess that her knees were knocking beneath her gown. 'We are to meet Lord Widdicombe,' Emma said. 'In the Chinese Salon.'

Linette's eyes went wide. 'All of us?'

'Yes. Ridley has gone to find Papa and Aunt Dorothy.'

'We may as well head that way now,' Alex said.

With an encouraging smile at Linette, Lady Glynnis put her hand on Alex's arm and the two of them turned to lead the way. Stifling the pain the sight of the proprietary gesture caused, Emma linked arms with her sister. 'Are you ready, Linny?'

'I don't have a choice,' Linette whispered. 'This is the meeting I've both longed for and dreaded. What will I do if he doesn't like me?'

'Of course he's going to like you. And Peter will be there to support you and you know he loves you madly. And really, in the end, that's all that matters.'

'I know it's all that *should* matter,' Linette said, her face softening. 'But will it be enough?'

Lord and Lady Widdicombe were standing by the taller of the two lacquered cabinets when Emma and her sister walked into the salon. Alex and Lady Glynnis had entered ahead of them and, glancing to the left, Emma saw that Ridley, her father and Aunt Dorothy had also arrived and were standing by one of the ornate Chinese pagodas.

Peter, who had been standing beside his mother, came towards them as soon as they entered. Lady Widdicombe touched her husband's shoulder and, slowly, the earl turned to face the assembled group.

The Earl of Widdicombe was an impressive-looking man. Tall and somewhat gaunt as a result of his illness, he was still a commanding and authoritative figure. He was faultlessly dressed, a tribute to the finest tailors in London, and his colouring was as dark as Alex's. Emma saw his gaze touch briefly on his eldest son before moving over to her, and then finally to Linette. Peter took Linette's hand in his and gave her a reassuring smile.

But it was not Linette or any other member of the Darling family to whom Lord Widdicombe spoke first. It was the lady at Alex's side.

'Lady Glynnis,' the earl said warmly. 'I am very pleased to see you again.'

'Lord Widdicombe.' Lady Glynnis executed a perfect curtsy. 'I'm glad you were feeling well enough to join us.'

'Thank you. Are your parents here?'

'They are, but I don't believe they have come down yet.'

'I look forward to seeing them again,' the earl said. 'It has been far too long since Leyland and I enjoyed some shooting together. We will have them out to Widdicombe Hill once the Season is over.'

'I know my father would enjoy that,' Lady Glynnis said with the ease of one talking to a long-established friend. 'Mama has always said Widdicombe is one of the last truly gracious country houses in Kent.'

'Father?' Peter said during a lull in the conversation. 'Pray allow me to introduce our guests. This is Mr Darling and his sister, Mrs Grand.'

Emma watched her father and aunt step up to make their greetings. Aunt Dorothy was visibly shaking, but Emma was pleased to see that her father acquitted himself well. The earl nodded, but the smile that had warmed his face during his conversation with Lady Glynnis was noticeably absent. 'Mr Darling,' he said. 'Mrs Grand.'

'And this is Mr Ridley Darling and his sister, Miss Emma Darling,' Peter continued.

'Ah, yes, the artist,' Lord Widdicombe said, his eyes narrowing.

Emma felt Ridley stiffen at her side and prayed he wouldn't do anything stupid. But obviously aware of the repercussions such a response would generate, he let the remark pass. The earl's glance rested briefly on her, but his interest was already on Linette.

'And this,' Peter said, drawing her forwards, 'is my fiancée, Miss Linette Darling.'

Emma hadn't realised she was holding her breath until Ridley nudged her gently in the ribs, forcing her to let it go. Linette walked the few steps towards Lord and Lady Widdicombe, and then, smiling up at the earl, made an elegant curtsy. 'Good evening, Lord Widdicombe.'

Her lovely face was so innocent, so devoid of artifice, that Emma wondered how anyone could ever believe ill of her. And the intense rush of fierce, protective love she felt in that moment was so strong that she knew if the earl made one single derogatory remark, she would confront him immediately.

'So, you're the one,' Lord Widdicombe said, raking Linette with his gaze. 'Very pretty, as expected. Well, what have you to say for yourself?'

'That I am very pleased to meet you at last,' Linette said quietly.

'At last? What's that supposed to mean?'

Linette flushed. 'I simply meant that…I had the plea-sure of meeting Lady Widdicombe and Lord Stewart at dinner the week before last, but not you. And I was so sorry to hear that it was due to illness. I hope you're feeling better.'

The earl snorted. 'I'm here, aren't I?'

It was a deliberate put-down and Emma felt her blood begin to boil. How *dare* he speak to her like that! Linette was doing everything right and still that wretched man was trying to make things difficult for her. And nobody was saying anything.

And then, to her astonishment, two people did.

'I think you are being overly harsh, Father,' Alex said. 'Linette meant no offence.'

'Indeed,' Lady Glynnis added quickly. 'She was being introduced to her future in-laws for the first time. Naturally, she would regret not meeting you at the same time and be concerned that it was your health that caused you to miss the dinner.'

It was the perfect response, Emma thought dispiritedly, and it couldn't have come from a better person. Lady Glynnis Pettle was clearly adored by both Lord and Lady Widdicombe. Even Alex was gazing at her with approval.

'Think that, do you, missy?' the earl said gruffly.

Lady Glynnis actually smiled at him. 'Yes, I do.'

'Then perhaps I shall give it some consideration. For your sake.' The earl turned to stare at Linette, his expression not quite as intimidating as it had been before. 'It seems you have a champion, young lady. Two, in fact, and a better pair I could not imagine. Perhaps we will speak again, you and I. But not tonight.' He glanced at his wife before briefly closing his eyes. 'I think I would like to retire. The journey must have been...more tiring than I thought.'

Lady Widdicombe immediately stepped forwards to take his arm. 'I shall accompany you upstairs and then

Murdoch can look after you. Peter, you have a houseful of guests. Please extend our apologies. If anyone asks, tell them your father is not fully recovered from his illness.'

'Of course.'

The earl did not look at Linette again, but somehow Emma knew the worst was over and that the atmosphere had lightened. As soon as the earl and countess left, she gave her sister a fierce hug. 'Linette, dearest, you were wonderful.'

'I was?'

'Yes, and I am so very proud of you.'

'Indeed,' Lady Glynnis said, coming over to join them. 'I doubt there are many young women who could have withstood the earl's intimidation as well as you did.'

Linette bit her lip. 'But I have *you* to thank for that, Lady Glynnis. You spoke up for me. You and Lord Stewart both,' she added with a grateful glance at Alex. 'I was so nervous when Lord Widdicombe first spoke to me. But I desperately wanted him to like me. For Peter's sake. So I kept on trying. But what you said changed his mind. I know it did.'

'Lord Widdicombe can be as prickly as a hedgehog at times,' Lady Glynnis said with a fond glance at Alex. 'But I've always believed his bark to be worse than his bite. Wouldn't you agree, my lord?'

'Yes, though I'm not sure a bark like that can't do as much harm as a bite. What say you, Mr Darling?' Alex asked Ridley as the door opened and a butler walked in with a tray of drinks. 'I thought for a moment he was going to start in on you.'

'I would have preferred that to watching him take a bite out of my sister,' Ridley murmured, reaching for two glasses of champagne and handing one to his aunt. 'We appreciate you stepping in. For a moment I wasn't sure who was going to go for him first, Emma or myself.'

'Ridley, really!' Aunt Dorothy said. 'I'm quite sure neither of you would have done anything so outlandish.'

Ridley laughed. 'Then you don't know either of us very well, Aunt.' His gaze rested briefly on Lady Glynnis's averted face. 'We are none of us exactly what we seem.'

For a split second, Lady Glynnis turned to look at him—and Emma sucked in her breath.

Dear Lord, had anyone else in the room been witness to that naked gaze? Was she the only one to have seen the expression of anguish in the young woman's face? The desperate longing in her eyes?

Apparently so. Mr Darling was already talking to Aunt Dorothy, who was happily tipping back her glass of champagne. Alex and Peter were speaking quietly between themselves and Linette was gazing in Peter's direction. She was the only one to have witnessed it and she could only thank her lucky stars that such had been the case. Whereas before she had only suspected this might be a weekend fraught with difficulties, now she knew it was going to be.

Her brother was in love with the woman Lord Stewart was planning to marry. And if Emma didn't miss her guess, Lady Glynnis was not entirely without feelings of her own!

Chapter Nine

Word of Lord Widdicombe's illness was accepted without question by the guests gathered for Linette and Peter's engagement ball, and when at midnight, the toast was offered by Alex rather than his father, not a single well-groomed eyebrow was raised. Most of the guests knew the earl had not been well, so it came as no shock that the rigours of the journey had forced him back to bed. They simply expressed their concern at hearing of his discomfort and sent wishes for his speedy recovery.

As for Linette, her future father-in-law's absence provided some much-needed breathing space; contrary to what Alex had feared, she was not shunned by the guests who were introduced to her, but was now welcomed by them, most probably because no outright rift between her and the earl had been declared. Everyone seemed to know that a meeting had taken place between the two families earlier in the evening, but, given that no obvious signs of condemnation had followed, the guests accepted as fact the earl's approval of the match.

And in light of that acceptance, Linette blossomed.

The pride on her face at being introduced as Peter's fiancée lent her a new and even more beautiful glow. Emma could hardly believe that the confident young lady moving around the room was the same nervous girl who had quaked at the thought of being the centre of attention only a few hours ago.

An opinion shared by more than one person in the room.

'Your sister is utterly charming,' Alex said quietly at Emma's side later in the evening. 'I am beginning to understand why my brother has fallen so deeply in love with her.'

They were the words Emma had been longing to hear—the words she had never expected to hear. But hearing them from Alex now made her pleasure in the evening complete. 'I admit, she has exceeded even my expectations,' Emma said. 'Linette has always been so quiet and unassuming. Completely unpretentious. She wears her heart on her sleeve; while she can fly as high as a kite, she can also be cut down by an unkind word. But I have never seen her rise to an occasion the way she did tonight, or shine the way she is shining now.'

'Obviously, love *does* work miracles for some people,' Alex commented drily.

Emma sent him a curious look. 'You sound as though you still doubt the power it wields.'

'Oh, I know full well its power. Wars have been waged over it. Kingdoms lost and reputations forfeited because of it. All as a result of man being a constant victim to his stronger desires.'

'But why do you see only the harm that it does?' Emma asked, turning to face him. 'Men have done miraculous things in the name of love. They have created masterpieces of art and music. Built magnificent castles and crossed vast expanses of land and ocean, all because they were inspired by something bigger than themselves.'

His gaze softened as he looked at her. 'You truly are a romantic, aren't you, Emma?'

'No!' His caustic tone made her flush. 'But neither am I deaf or blind to what has been accomplished in the name of love.'

She watched the play of emotions across his face. 'I wonder,' he said softly.

'What?'

'I wonder what you could achieve if you were ever to fall as deeply in love with a man as your sister has. I'd like to be there to see that.'

Her heart thudded once, painfully, the echo of it reverberating throughout her entire body. *I'd like to be there to see that.* It hurt, more than she could ever have expected, the knowledge that he didn't see himself as that man. And while she dearly wished she could have responded to his statement in as casual a manner as he'd made it, even that simple act was beyond her.

'I like to think I would be able to accomplish such things with or without the presence of a man in my life.' Emma gazed up into his face, saw everything she had come to love and admire about him, and said, 'We are all capable of great achievement, my lord, limited only by our own imaginations and by the resources we have at our disposal.'

'But you do not believe that love is necessary for the achievement of all things.'

'Not all things, no. But consider what a mother will do for her child,' Emma said. 'Most would move mountains if they thought it would make the lives of their children easier.'

'You speak of selfless love,' Alex said.

'But is not all true love selfless? Do you not think that what Linette and Peter feel for one another is selfless?

Your brother has gone against your father's wishes in order to be with the woman he loves, and such rebellion does not come without cost. But he has chosen his path and will not be diverted from it.'

'He says he can do nothing else,' Alex said.

'Exactly. That is what true love does. It inspires one to be better.'

His smile was infinitely gentle. 'Then I do not think I could bear to see you when you do find that man, Emma. Because try as I might, I cannot imagine you being any better than you already are.'

After another sleepless night due in large part to Alex's enigmatic remark, Emma arrived in the breakfast parlour the next morning to find her father, brother and aunt happily discussing the events of the previous evening.

'I always thought Linette had more spunk than we gave her credit for,' Aunt Dorothy said, spreading a liberal helping of lemon curd on her toast. 'She's just never had an opportunity to shine. But last night, she was given that opportunity and I think I can safely say that she made all of us proud. Wouldn't you agree, Percy?'

'She did indeed,' Mr Darling said, turning the page of his newspaper. 'She is much like her mother in that regard.'

'And I thought Lady Glynnis Pettle was very impressive too,' Aunt Dorothy went on. 'I know old Widdicombe's fond of her and that she is going to be Lord Stewart's wife, but it takes courage to stand up to a man like that. I vow he had me trembling in my boots when we first walked into that room.' She looked up and frowned. 'You're very quiet this morning, Ridley. Feeling a bit poorly after all the excitement last night?'

Emma glanced up from her toast, not particularly surprised when her brother didn't answer. Aunt Dorothy just frowned. 'Ridley?'

He finally looked up, his expression blank. 'Pardon?'

'Dear me, and here I thought only old ladies and love-lorn young women were prone to wool gathering. I asked you if you were feeling poorly.'

'No. I feel all right,' he said, glancing around the table. 'I was merely thinking about a new painting I've been engaged to do.'

'Oh, yes, I'm sure that takes a great deal of thought,' Mr Darling muttered into his paper.

'As a matter of fact, it does,' Ridley said stiffly. 'I have a family grouping to do and they have asked me to come up with a list of possible settings or locations other than those usually employed for such portraits.'

'You could put them in a boat,' Aunt Dorothy suggested. 'Floating on a tranquil pond.'

'And I would stand where?' Ridley asked. 'On the gun-nels? Tricky keeping the easel upright.'

'What about a folly?' Emma asked. 'You could use your sketch of the one on Lord Garrickson's estate.'

He stared at her without comprehension. 'A folly?'

'Yes, the one in your sketchbook. The one—'

Emma stopped. Ridley was looking at her as though she was spouting Greek—and suddenly, she knew the reason why. Her brother didn't *have* a sketch of Lord Garrickson's folly in his sketchbook. He had a sketch of something he hadn't wanted her to see.

Unfortunately, given what Emma had seen of his behaviour with Lady Glynnis Pettle last night, it wasn't all that difficult to puzzle out what—or who—that might be.

A wide range of outdoor events had been planned for the entertainment of the guests at Ellingsworth on Saturday, and by the time Emma and her family arrived around one o'clock, many of them were already underway. Emma saw targets for archery contests, buckets of water for apple bobbing, even a jousting course for anyone bold enough to try their hand at the medieval sport. There were also a lot more people milling around the grounds. Peter had kindly extended a general invitation to anyone in the village who wished to participate in the afternoon celebrations, and, always glad for a reason to hobnob with the well to do, many of them had come out.

Standing on the balcony looking out over the proceedings, Emma recognised Mr and Mrs Jacobs, as well as many of the guests who had been at their last assembly, strolling about the manicured lawns. Mrs Connolly was good-naturedly taking part in a three-legged race with Aunt Dorothy, while Mr Darling and Mr Connolly laughed and looked on.

Ridley had chosen to stay at home, saying he preferred to work on his new commission to running around fields playing silly games. Emma hadn't tried to change his mind. She suspected his reasons for not wanting to come had more to do with avoiding a certain lady than they did with shunning any of the festivities to be found. Ridley was usually a great lover of games.

There were also the well-dressed ladies and gentlemen who had been present at the ball the previous evening and who were staying at Ellingsworth for the weekend. Friends of Peter's and Alex's, all of whom were laughing and having a very good time, aided, no doubt, by the glasses of punch and beer the servants were busy handing around.

Peter played the part of the genial host to perfection, welcoming all of the guests as they arrived. Lord and Lady Widdicombe did not participate in any of the events, but sat comfortably on chairs on a private terrace at the back of the house, talking to Lord and Lady Leyland and the Marquess and Marchioness of Huffton.

Alex moved freely amongst all the guests, often with the beautiful Lady Glynnis at his side. At the moment, she was looking particularly fetching in a dark-green riding habit with a stylish, high-top bonnet that trailed long green ribbons down her back. Clearly she had been riding and hadn't gone up to change. But neither did she need to. She was breathtaking just as she was...

'She *is* lovely, isn't she? And she will make him a beautiful bride,' Linette said at Emma's elbow. 'Pity she doesn't love him.'

Emma's head spun around. 'What on earth are you talking about?'

'I watched them last night,' Linette said. 'They didn't exhibit any of the required signs. Not once did they stare longingly into one another's eyes, or make excuses to stand close to one another. They didn't even hold hands.'

'It *was* a rather harrowing evening,' Emma pointed out. 'As I recall, Lady Glynnis was more interested in defending *you* than she was in clinging to Lord Stewart.'

'I know, but in times of stress, two people in love will always look to one another for support and comfort.'

Linette's unexpected intuition might not have made such an impression had Emma not remembered the conversation she'd had with Alex about his relationship with Lady Glynnis shortly after meeting him. The one in which he had admitted that the basis for their marriage was not love.

'You were meeting Lord Widdicombe for the first time and Lady Glynnis was meeting our family for the first time,' Emma reminded her sister, trying to put the memory of that conversation aside. 'Surely such an evening would tend to make people act differently. I suspect Lady Glynnis was nervous.'

'She wasn't nervous at all,' Linette said. 'Lady Glynnis is the daughter of an earl. She is used to moving in society and to meeting all manner of people. She might have been a little on edge when she first met us, but she certainly wasn't nervous.'

No, she wasn't, Emma acknowledged bleakly. She'd had no reason to be. She was beautiful and well born and she was going to be Alex's wife. Not only that, her future father-in-law adored her. What on earth had a woman like that to be nervous about?

Emma turned to watch Alex approach the archery range. He was dressed for the outdoors and when he turned to smile at something Lady Glynnis said, Emma felt her heart turn over. Had she ever known a more handsome man? Or did he only seem so handsome because she loved him so much?

She glanced at Lady Glynnis's laughing face and decided she must have misread the situation with Ridley last night. Lady Glynnis would have to be mad to think of giving up a life with Alex to be with Ridley. As much as Emma loved her brother, he simply wasn't in the same league.

'Emma, can I ask you a personal question?' Linette said.

'Of course.'

'Do you have feelings for Lord Stewart?'

Emma coloured fiercely. How on earth was she to answer that? If she spoke too quickly, she risked sounding defensive, but if she took her time, Linette might think she was trying to concoct an answer. She decided on a half-truth. 'Of course I have feelings for him, Linette, just as I have feelings for Peter. They are both going to be related to me.'

'That's not what I meant. I meant do you have *feelings* for him. Of a romantic nature.'

Not even a half-truth would suffice here, Emma thought dimly. This called for an out-and-out lie. 'Of course not. Why?'

'Because remember what I said about how you can tell when two people are in love?'

'Yes.'

'Well, that's how you and Lord Stewart were behaving last night.'

Emma felt her face burn. 'We were not!'

'Yes, you were,' Linette said calmly. 'You were standing quite close together, looking as though there was no one else in the room. He spoke to you and you blushed, and when you spoke to him, you leaned in towards him ever so slightly.'

'I did?'

'Yes. Then at the end, *he* leaned in close to you and said something that made you look at him as though—'

'Stop it!' Emma said quickly. 'Immediately. Before you embarrass us both. I do *not* have feelings of a romantic nature for Lord Stewart. I like him as a person, but that's all. He is as good as engaged to Lady Glynnis and I am not so foolish as to risk my heart on someone who is not free to return my affection.'

'But they are not engaged yet,' Linette said softly. 'And if he has feelings for you—'

'He does *not* have feelings for me, Linette. He has feelings for Lady Glynnis. And he is going to marry her as everyone expects he should.'

And *she* would go to the wedding and throw rice at the newlyweds, and act as though she couldn't be happier.

And with any luck, the more times she told herself that, the sooner she would come to believe it.

For that reason, Emma contented herself with watching Alex from a distance, admiring the fine figure of a man he presented. It was a lovely afternoon and, like most of the other gentlemen, he had shed his jacket and now stood in shirt sleeves, breeches and boots, aiming a very impressive-looking bow at a straw target set up some fifty feet distant. She saw him take his stance, spreading his legs to balance his weight, then watched him nock the arrow and raise the bow. Slowly he drew it back, his extended hand and his draw hand parallel to the ground. When his lips lightly touched the strings, he released the arrow. Emma watched it fly, straight as a die, landing just above centre in the red-and-white target.

A cheer went up from several of the ladies, including Lady Glynnis, who clapped her hands in approval.

'Well, at least she seems to like and admire him,' Linette observed. 'I suppose that will have to be enough.'

'People do marry for reasons other than love, you know,' Emma murmured, keeping her eyes on the archers.

'Yes, but love is still the only reason that matters.' Linette watched Peter step up to the mark and take up his bow. 'I suppose I'd hoped that given how much love matters to Peter, it might be of importance to his brother as well.'

'Need I remind you that *you* were the one who pointed out how different Lord Stewart and his brother were,' Emma said. 'And time has proven you right.'

'Actually, it hasn't,' Linette said. 'The more I come to know Lord Stewart, the more I think he is like his brother in many ways. He simply doesn't show it. Likely because the role he has always been called upon to play demands that he keeps his deepest feelings hidden. But I believe love matters to him every bit as much as it does to Peter. Oh, well done, Mr Taylor!' Linette cried, clapping her hands as her fiancé's arrow struck the target about two inches from the centre. 'I had no idea he was so good. I must go down and compliment him.'

Emma and Linette waited until the bows were safely set aside before making their way on to the archery course. Lady Glynnis, Emma noticed, had already turned and started in the direction of the refreshment tent with two other ladies, leaving Alex alone.

'Ah, Miss Darling,' Alex said, slipping his coat back on. 'I thought I saw you watching me from the balcony.'

Flustered that he should have noticed, Emma attempted a quelling smile. 'I was not watching *you*, Lord Stewart. I was observing all of the archers. Including your brother, who I must say shot very well.'

'Peter's a keen sportsman,' Alex said without rancour. 'Where my talents at school ran more to the academic, his always tended towards the physical.'

Strange, Emma thought, given that Alex's build was the more muscular. 'You have nothing to be ashamed of. You acquitted yourself quite well.'

'Quite well.' His smile was slow and deliberate. 'Thank you, Miss Darling. I am at a loss for words in the face of such blatant flattery.'

Emma felt colour scald her cheeks. 'It was not intended as a slight, my lord. I was simply making a comment.'

'Of course you were. Just as if I were to say that you look *quite* charming in that dress, or that I've always thought your hair *quite* a lovely colour, there would be no danger of it going to your head because I would simply have been…making a comment.'

He thought she looked charming? And that her hair was pretty? 'It is not the same at all. I am making a judgement as to your ability. A comment about my dress or my hair addresses something over which I have no control.'

'On the contrary, does a lady not specifically choose clothing to flatter her figure and complexion?' Alex retorted. 'Does she not style her hair in a manner most becoming to her face? Of course she does. Because the whole point of the exercise is to attract the attention of a male.'

Emma frowned. 'You make us sound rather predatory.'

'We *all* are. What do you think the purpose of these gatherings is, Emma, if not to allow us to be seen at our best by members of the opposite sex? The goal of married couples is to provide venues like this so that those of us who *are* single are quickly absorbed into the wedded state. There is nothing a married man likes better than to see a happily single man trapped in the parson's noose.'

'And what about a happily single woman?'

'I doubt such a thing exists.'

'Odious man, of course it does! A woman loses everything when she marries. Her property. Her money. Her identity.'

'Ah, but look at what she gains,' Alex pointed out. 'A man willing to protect her virtue and honour her name. A banker who will pay her debts and keep her in the style she might not otherwise have known. And, if she is lucky, a man who will love her and make her happy in every way a man should.'

She wanted to mock him, but the words died on her lips. He hadn't been smiling when he had spoken those last words. He had been looking right at her. Daring her to disagree. Or waiting for her to tell him he was right… which, of course, he *was*. What did any woman want but a man who truly loved her? A man to whom she meant everything. She might not have believed that a month ago, but she believed it now. Linette had found that connection with Peter Taylor. Emma had not found it with anyone. Nor had Alex, who was marrying Lady Glynnis Pettle because she was suitable. Dear Lord, was there ever a colder, more emotionless reason for doing something so important? So life altering…

'My lord,' Lady Glynnis said, rejoining them, 'what has been keeping you? I was waiting for you at the tent.'

Alex looked round and quickly apologised. 'Forgive me, Glyn, Miss Darling and I were engaged in a verbal battle.'

'Oh?' Beautiful violet eyes turned to gaze at Emma. 'Dare I ask who the winner was?'

'I'm not sure there was one,' Emma said, afraid to look at Alex with Lady Glynnis watching her so closely.

But Alex only laughed. 'I think Miss Darling is right. It was more an exchange of opinions than an argument and it is difficult to establish a winner when there is no point to be won or lost. But now, shall we join the others in the tent for refreshments? This shooting of innocent bales of straw has made me devilishly hungry.'

On the way to the tent, Linette and Peter joined them, and somehow Emma found herself walking with Lady Glynnis behind the other three. She enjoyed watched the antics going on all around her: young men making fools of themselves in three-legged races, young girls skipping rope and tossing bowls, Aunt Dorothy imbibing champagne…

'I am surprised your brother did not come with you this afternoon, Miss Darling,' Lady Glynnis said casually. 'I would have thought this type of gathering the sort of thing he would have enjoyed.'

Surprised to hear her speak of Ridley, Emma said, 'He

told me he had to do some preparatory work for a…project he has in London.'

'A new painting, perhaps?'

When Emma turned to look at her, Lady Glynnis smiled. 'It's all right, Miss Darling. You don't have to pretend you don't know. You and your brother are very close. I'm sure he told you he did a portrait of me.'

Glad for the opening, but nevertheless aware of a need for caution, Emma said, 'He did mention it in passing, Lady Glynnis.'

'You must have been shocked to learn he had taken up painting as a living.'

'We all were, given that he started out with the intention of becoming a lawyer.'

'But he is very good. Has he shown you any of his work?'

'He brought home a painting of a little girl with a kitten. I thought it excellent.'

Lady Glynnis smiled. 'Lord Forrester's daughter. He was just finishing that one when I came to talk to him about my portrait.'

They proceeded on in silence for a few minutes. Lady Glynnis walked slowly, as if to let the other three get ahead of them. 'Miss Darling, did your brother tell you anything about the painting he did of me?'

'Only that it took him a long time to get it exactly right.'

'So you don't know anything about the nature of the painting?'

'No.'

'I commissioned it as a gift for Lord Stewart. You must have heard that we are promised to one another.'

Emma swallowed, but kept her eyes straight ahead. 'Yes.'

'The arrangements were made by our parents some

time ago, of course, but I had no complaint. I've known
Alex for years. Ever since we were children, in fact, and
I've always been fond of him. I don't suppose there was
ever any question that we would marry other people. And,
this last year, we have talked about it several times. That
is how I know he will be proposing very soon and why I
decided to have a painting done of myself. As a wedding
present. And I wanted it to be…beautiful.'

'How could it be anything else?' Emma asked.

To her surprise, the lady blushed. 'You are too kind,
Miss Darling. I have never thought of myself as beautiful. My cousin is the acknowledged beauty in the family.
But Alex has a keen eye for such things and I wanted him
to have a portrait that he would be pleased to look upon.
After seeing a sample of your brother's work, I knew he
was the one to do it.'

There was a wistfulness to her voice, a sadness, that
prompted Emma to say, 'Ridley told me you were happy
with the finished portrait, Lady Glynnis. Is that not the
case?'

This time, it was Lady Glynnis who kept her eyes forwards. 'The painting was…exquisite. It captured a side
of me I didn't even know existed. Yes, I was pleased with
it. And had I taken it with me the day he showed it to me,
everything would have been well. But he said he needed
a few extra days to frame it and that he would deliver it
in person to my home.' Lady Glynnis slowed to a stop,
forcing Emma to do the same. 'Unfortunately, before I
finally did receive the painting, he did the unforgivable.'

The sadness was back, along with the wistfulness.
Emma knew it would be wrong to pretend she didn't know.
'He let someone else see the portrait,' she said quietly.
'That's why you were so angry with him.'

'The painting was to have been a gift for my fiancé,

Miss Darling. As such, I felt Alex should be the first man to see it. I thought I could trust your brother in that regard. When he told me he had shown the painting to someone else, I felt betrayed. As though the level of trust I had placed in him had been misplaced.' Lady Glynnis started to walk again. 'I'm sure you can understand that.'

'I can understand your disappointment at your fiancé not being the first to see the painting,' Emma said slowly, 'but not your anger towards my brother for having let someone else see it. Ridley told me the gentleman, who is known to you both, simply dropped by the studio one evening and happened to see it sitting upon the easel where it was waiting to be finished. And I understand that his remarks about the portrait were highly complimentary.'

'All of that is true, Miss Darling. But the painting revealed…a state of mind,' Lady Glynnis said, a delicate rush of pink staining her cheeks. 'A very private state of mind. Had it been just a painting of a woman in a garden, I would not have cared, but your brother's painting gave away more of my feelings than I was comfortable sharing with other people.'

'But surely there is no embarrassment in seeing the face of a woman in love,' Emma said. 'Is that not how you wish Lord Stewart to see you when he looks upon the painting? Or anyone else who sees it.'

When Lady Glynnis made no reply, Emma sighed. She did not understand why the lady was reacting the way she was. All she could be sure of was that whatever she thought she had seen on Lady Glynnis's face in response to Ridley's comment last night must have been a mistake. Clearly, the lady was very much in love with Alex.

'I am sorry, Lady Glynnis,' Emma said finally. 'I know Ridley had no intention of hurting you and that it has upset

him greatly to know that he has. He is not a cruel or mean
spirited man.'

'I never believed he was,' Lady Glynnis said quietly.
'That's why I was so surprised when I found out he had
shown the painting to Mr Towbridge.'

'And I must repeat that it was not intentionally done,'
Emma said. 'My brother did not invite Mr…'

'Towbridge.'

'Mr Towbridge to come and see the painting—'

'I understand that, Miss Darling. And I am well aware
that Mr Towbridge is a good friend of your brother's and
that he was responsible for your brother receiving his first
commission. But Alex…Lord Stewart, should have been
the first man to see it,' Lady Glynnis repeated. 'The only
man.'

Emma sighed. Obviously nothing she said was going
to have any effect on the lady's opinion. 'Then I can only
say again how sorry I am, Lady Glynnis.'

'I realise this has…nothing to do with you,' Lady Glynnis said as they drew closer to the tent. 'But I wanted you
to know so that you would understand the tension between
your brother and myself. To understand why it is so…dif-
ficult for me to be in the same room with him.'

'I do understand. And I shall not speak of this to anyone
else.'

'You're very kind. And despite the difficulties, I do
hope your sister and Mr Taylor are able to find happiness
together. They are both dear people and I honestly believe
they should be allowed to marry.'

'I think what you said last night helped in that regard,'
Emma said.

By now they had caught up with the others and were
soon absorbed into the crowd of people moving along the
tables weighted down with refreshments of all kinds. But

Lady Glynnis's words stayed with Emma long after they had parted, as had the tone in which they had been spoken. There had been anger, but there had also been regret, as though the lady was sorry matters had turned out the way they had. But why should she feel that way? Emma kept asking herself. Why would a lady who was as good as engaged to the heir to an earldom feel regret that a relationship between herself and the man hired to paint her portrait had ended so badly?

At the conclusion of the afternoon's festivities, the villagers returned to their homes to talk about all the things they had seen and done, and the invited guests returned to Ellingsworth to prepare for the formal evening events. Alex had seen Emma and her family leave, though he had not gone over to say goodbye. He knew it was best he maintain a distance from her now. She was a lovely young woman and he knew himself well enough to know that he was attracted to her and that the attraction was only going to get stronger. She had such a refreshing and uncomplicated way about her. The afternoon he had arrived at Dove's Hollow to find her painting in the garden, she hadn't made any apologies for her appearance. She had smiled when he had offered the expected compliment, but he had seen in her eyes her awareness of its intention. He knew she hadn't believed him, which was a pity since he really *had* meant it.

He'd found her appearance that day utterly charming. The white painter's smock spattered here and there with splotches of both green and yellow paint had fit loosely, but had done nothing to disguise the sweetness of her figure. The straw bonnet had been casually undone, allowing tendrils of hair to escape, and her lips had been slightly parted as she had gazed intently at the canvas, her arm extended, bent a little at the elbow, as she moved the brush lightly over the canvas.

She'd had absolutely no idea that to him, *she* had been the work of art.

And when he had spoken and she had looked up at him, for an unguarded moment, he had seen surprised pleasure in the depths of those soft brown eyes. It had vanished the moment he had begun to explain his reasons for coming to see her, of course, but just for an instant, it had been there and he wanted very much to see it again. To see her smile at him like that again.

That was the reason he knew he had to back away now. The attraction was there, tangible and strong, but an attraction was all it could ever be. He had a duty to his name and he had made a promise to a lady. A lady who, even now, was waiting for his offer of marriage.

'Thank you, Barker,' Alex said as his valet finished brushing his jacket. He turned to face the glass and saw a composed face staring back at him. No trace of indecision was reflected there. No indication of the age-old battle being waged within. The battle against desire.

The battle to do what was right.

Chapter Ten

Dinner started out as a surprisingly enjoyable affair. Alex had come to dislike large formal gatherings, but tonight everyone seemed to be in good spirits. The guests expressed their pleasure over the events of the afternoon and many a laugh was shared over misfortunes encountered and games won or lost.

Seated three chairs down from him and on the other side of the table, Emma was too far away to converse, a fact that was both a source of relief and disappointment to Alex. He had been rendered almost speechless by the sight of her this evening, her voluptuous curves magnificently displayed in a gown that could only have been made by one of London's most fashionable modistes. Emma could have taken her place in any of the grandest of London houses, had such been her wish.

Instead, she was here, looking supremely composed and radiantly beautiful as she conversed with Lord Mallard on her left and Anthony Slayter on her right. Mallard was in his late fifties, recently widowed and looking for a wife. Slayter, younger and far more handsome, was looking for a mistress. Alex knew those facts to be well known in society, but he doubted word of them had spread to Little Moreton. A fact that made him less than pleased at seeing both gentlemen paying Emma far more attention that the length of their acquaintance warranted.

'So, what about you, my lord?' Tom Towbridge asked in a genial tone. 'Why aren't we celebrating two engagements this weekend, rather than just one?'

Alex mustered a smile. He liked Tom Towbridge. Though younger than him by a good few years, Tom was a sensible fellow who took his responsibilities seriously. 'Because, Mr Towbridge, this *is* my brother's celebration and the last thing I would wish to do is steal his thunder.'

'But you are still planning to marry Lady Glynnis?' Lady Gregory demanded from across the table.

Alex raised an eyebrow. He might have taken exception to the remark except for the fact that Lady Gregory was a close friend of Glynnis's Aunt Mary and knew how matters stood between the families. But he found he was not as comfortable talking about his marriage now that the direction of his feelings had changed. 'Our arrangement hasn't changed, Lady Gregory. I simply haven't found the right moment to ask her.'

'Good, because everyone knows how anxious your father is to see Lady Glynnis become the next countess.'

'Well, all I can say,' Tom said, 'is that I hope when it comes time for me to choose a wife, I am fortunate enough to find a woman who loves me as deeply as Lady Glynnis loves you.'

Surprised by the remark, Alex said, 'How do you know she does?'

'Good God, man, you only have to look at the painting to know how she feels about you. If that's not a portrait of a woman in love, I don't know what is.'

'The portrait?'

'Yes, the one she had—' Suddenly, Towbridge went white. 'Oh, God. Don't tell me…she hasn't given it to you yet.'

'Given me what?'

'Oh, *hell*!'

'Tom?'

'Forgive me. It was meant to be a surprise. Pretend we never had this conversation,' Towbridge said desperately. 'If anyone asks, say you know nothing about it.'

Alex sat back, frowning. 'That won't be hard since I have absolutely no idea what—'

The whoop of feminine laughter cut across Alex's words and brought the quiet murmur of conversation up and down the table to an abrupt halt. Alex glanced to his left, saw that Emma's face had gone deathly pale, then looked past her to find the source of the laughter.

At the lower end of the table, Mrs Grand was talking with great animation to Sir Stanford Buckle, an affable gentleman and recent widower who was clearly enjoying the lady's attentions. Both were looking a little flushed, and when Mrs Grand picked up her glass and tipped back the contents Alex understood why. It seemed his father had not been mistaken in suggesting that certain members of Emma's family were fond of a tipple.

He glanced quickly at his mother and father sitting at either end of the table, saw the horror-stricken expressions on both their faces, and then, seeing Peter's face, realised he wasn't any happier. Linette's face was crimson, as was her father's, who was seated across the table from his sister.

Thankfully, the last cover had been removed and without waiting for the butler to sweep the table, Lady Widdicombe abruptly got to her feet. 'Ladies, please join me in the Green Drawing room.' Without another word, she turned and led the way out of the room.

Emma and Linette quickly got to their feet and went immediately to their aunt's side.

'Come along, Aunt Dorothy,' Emma said, helping the lady to her feet. 'It is time for us to leave the gentlemen to their after-dinner pleasures.'

'Really? What a pity.' She giggled. 'Sir Stanford and I were having a most interesting conversation about—'

'Aunt, *please,* we really must go,' Linette whispered in mortification.

It was only then, as Mrs Grand looked around the table and saw how many of the guests were staring at her with disapproval, that her laughter abruptly died. She glanced at her nieces, the expressions on their faces giving her an awareness of what she had done, and her joy evaporated. 'Oh, yes. Yes, of course.'

Alex watched the girls help their aunt to her feet, noticed her teeter a little as she backed away from the table, then saw them quickly escort her from the room. The moment the door closed behind them, the buzz of conversation resumed. Alex watched his father get up from the table and abruptly draw Lord Leyland aside. Several other gentlemen also stood up to stretch their legs, but Mr Darling stayed where he was, his body rigid, his eyes downcast.

Alex went over and sat down next to him. 'Mr Darling, would you care to join me for a—?'

'I am so sorry, Lord Stewart,' Mr Darling said in a choked voice, his eyes never leaving the table. 'I cannot imagine what came over her.'

'A little too much champagne, I expect,' Alex said, trying to downplay the seriousness of the event. 'It happens to the best of us.'

'But not to a lady. *Never* to a lady. And certainly not at such an important occasion as this.' Mr Darling's face was a study in regret. 'One meant to celebrate her niece's engagement to the son of a peer.'

'Perhaps it was the nature of the event that compelled her to imbibe a little more freely than she normally would,' Alex said. 'Drink does tend to help settle one's nerves.'

'Yes, but all too often it also results in the loss of one's inhibitions and this is the *last* place such a thing should have happened.' The older man sighed deeply. 'Do you know what the sad part of this is, my lord? My sister has been more concerned with making a good impression on your family and friends than any of us. She knows how important this is to Linette and she was most insistent that we present ourselves in the best light possible on each and every occasion our families came together.'

'And you have.'

'Until tonight,' Mr Darling said ruefully. 'Your mother and father were not pleased by Dorothy's conduct and who can blame them? She behaved in a manner totally unbecoming to a lady. I dearly wish Emma and Linette had not been here to witness it.'

'But they are, I think, aware of your sister's tendency to drink,' Alex said as tactfully as he could. 'If it is an ongoing condition, they must have seen evidence of it in the past.'

'Yes. I dearly wish I could say that was not the case, but I would only be lying to both of us.' Mr Darling finally raised his head, but he did not meet Alex's eyes. 'My sister changed after her husband passed away, Lord Stewart. I think it shocked her, his dying so young, and she was totally unprepared for life on her own. She had servants, of course, but she was suddenly the one in charge and I know she missed him dreadfully. So she started taking a glass or two of sherry in the afternoon, just to settle her nerves. I didn't say anything in the beginning. After all, where was the harm? I thought. Why shouldn't she dull her loneliness a little in whatever manner she had at her disposal?'

Alex smiled. 'I suspect we've all done that at one time or another.'

'I know I have,' Mr Darling admitted. 'After the children's mother died, I often found myself heading for my study for a few hours spent in a whisky-induced haze. It was an easy way to escape the less pleasant aspects of one's life. But, eventually, I realised I had a family to look after and that I had to set an example. I saw what happened to my brother when the drink took over and I was damned if I was going to let that happen to me. So I stopped drinking then and there. Unfortunately, Dorothy didn't have anyone to look after, or to turn to for solace.'

'She has no family of her own?'

Mr Darling shook his head. 'She was never blessed with children.'

'But you have, I believe, another sister living in Bath. Could Mrs Grand not have gone and stayed with her?'

'It would never have worked,' Mr Darling said with a sad smile. 'Even as children, they fought. Always jealous of what the other had. Both wanting more than what life had given them. I doubt being together would have helped either of them.'

Alex managed a smile. 'They say misery loves company.'

'And never a truer word spoken,' Mr Darling agreed. 'But sometimes it is wiser to stay clear of someone else's unhappiness when you are so low in spirit yourself. Rather than buoy each other up, I fear they would have dragged the other down.' Then, as if realising who he was talking to and how he had been going on, Mr Darling abruptly stood up. 'Forgive me, my lord. This cannot be of the slightest interest to you and I am the last person in the world who should be monopolising your time.'

'On the contrary, I'm glad you felt you could talk to me about it.' Alex likewise got to his feet. 'I can assure you, I understand completely.'

'Thank you for saying that,' Mr Darling said. 'I only hope Dorothy's behaviour tonight did not reflect too badly on Linette and the rest of our family.'

Alex clapped the man on the shoulder, offered him as reassuring a smile as he could and then walked towards the French doors. The room had grown uncomfortably warm; needing a breath of fresh air, he stepped out in the night, only to overhear another conversation taking place between three gentlemen standing on the balcony.

'…haven't heard a laugh like that since my father took me to the fair and I went to see the Fat Lady,' Anthony Slayter was saying. 'Anyone know who she is?'

'A Mrs Grand, I believe,' said Lord Baird. 'Widowed aunt of young Taylor's fiancée.'

'An aunt? By Jove, they'd best hide the sherry when *she* comes to call lest she drink them out of house and home.'

'Old Buckle seemed quite taken with her,' Lord Whitby said.

'And why wouldn't he?' Slayter said. 'He's well known for bending the elbow himself and he *is* looking for a wife. They'd make a fine pair, as long as Buckle's income don't run out.'

'Speaking of a fine pair,' Baird commented, 'you seemed rather taken with the young lady sitting next to you, Slayter. Isn't she the older sister?'

'She is.'

'Tasty little piece,' Whitby said. 'Got more meat on her

bones than most society chits. I wager she'd keep a man warm in his bed.'

Alex had heard more than enough. 'I would advise you to keep a civil tongue in your heads, gentlemen,' he said, stepping out on to the balcony. 'The ladies you refer to will soon be members of my family.'

Lord Baird and Lord Whitby looked decidedly uncomfortable, but Slayter just laughed. 'Oh, come on, Stewart, we were simply having a little fun.'

'At someone else's expense.'

'Of course, we certainly wouldn't want it at our own. But you can't deny that the Darlings are an interesting family. Getting foxed in front of your father wasn't the smartest thing the aunt could have done.'

'I agree it was not the most prudent course of action, but Mrs Grand is not accustomed to moving in society,' Alex said. 'I expect she sought a way to calm her nerves.'

Slayter's smile was more of a sneer. 'She did that very nicely. Unfortunately, just a touch too vocally.'

'So what do you know of the family, Stewart?' Whitby asked. 'I'd never heard of them before receiving the invitation for this weekend.'

'I understand the father used to tutor Lord Gaylord's son,' Baird volunteered. 'But that he gave it up when he acquired a house and moved down here. And his own son recently became an artist. He painted that portrait of Forrester's youngest daughter.'

'*That's* where I heard the name!' Whitby said. 'Has the makings of a damn fine artist from all I hear.'

'And then there's the youngest daughter, presently engaged to your brother,' Slayter said, his smile as cold as his pale blue eyes. 'Tell me, Stewart, are your mother and father pleased about the engagement?'

'They are pleased my brother has found someone about whom he cares deeply, yes.'

'But it's not quite the same thing, is it?' Slayter said. 'I hear the earl has refused to give his permission for them to wed.'

'Then you heard incorrectly. And I suggest you stop listening to gossip and innuendo.' Alex's voice was cold, the warning implicit. 'It is most unbecoming in a gentleman.'

Slayter's expression clouded in anger, but Alex didn't give a damn. The man was an arrogant dandy who cared more about other people's business than he did his own and who was constantly running up gambling losses at the tables and the racecourse that frequently had to be covered by his family. Alex was surprised he had even been invited to the gathering, until he remembered that Sir Roger and Lady Slayter were good friends of his parents.

'Alex,' his father said, coming up behind him now. 'A word, if you don't mind. Excuse us, gentlemen?'

The other three bowed and drifted back into the dining room. Alex ignored the smug look on Slayter's face as he closed the doors and waited for his father to launch into his tirade.

It wasn't long in coming. 'Well? What have you to say about *that*?' the earl demanded.

'I take it you mean Mrs Grand?'

'Of course I mean Mrs Grand! Did you see any other lady at the table drinking and flirting outrageously with one of the guests?'

'I realise it was not becoming behaviour—'

'Not becoming? It was humiliating for everyone who had the misfortune to witness it!' his father snapped. 'And this is the family Peter has chosen to marry into. How do you think that reflects on us?'

Alex sighed. 'I agree it should not have happened, but

there is nothing we can do now but try to look at it in the best light possible!'

'There is no light in the *world* that could make this look good!' the earl said. 'Now, I think I have been patient, Alex, but your brother must be made to see that marrying into such a family is simply not acceptable.'

'Peter is marrying Linette Darling, Father. Not her aunt.'

'He is still tying himself to a family of drunkards and gamblers.'

'You exaggerate.'

'Do I? I told you how they came to be in possession of Dove's Hollow, and now you've seen proof that they have no social conscience whatsoever! How much more proof of their unsuitability do you need?'

The French doors opened and Peter appeared. He looked from one to the other and Alex saw the despair in his eyes. 'I think you should come back in. Your absence is being commented upon.'

The earl simply grunted and marched past his younger son without a word.

Alex sighed and glanced at his brother. 'Are you sure you know what you're doing, Peter? There are other young women out there. Women who would be more suitable to being your wife.'

'You mean women who would make Father happier than he is right now.'

'That too.'

Peter shook his head. 'There could never be anyone for me but Linette. I'm more sure of that every day. She is good and kind and she loves me. Not what I own or who my family is. *Me*. And I won't give her up, Alex. Not for Father. Not for you. Not for anyone. The only way I would give her up is if she asked me to.'

'Be sensible, Peter. You know Father's health is failing and this tension between the two of you isn't helping.'

'I know and I'm sorry. But if he cared more about patching things up between us, he wouldn't have suggested that I set Linette up as my mistress and look for a more suitable woman to be my wife.'

Alex swore softly. 'He said that?'

'Just now, before he came out to see you. Thank God I was the only one who heard it, but how do you think that made me feel, Alex? What does it say when your father suggests that the woman you've asked to be your wife is only suitable to being your mistress?'

'It just confirms what he's been saying all along. That he doesn't believe Linette Darling is good enough for you,' Alex said. 'That he never *will* believe she's good enough for you. And that if you proceed with this marriage, the two of you will remain at odds until one or the other of you dies.'

It was a sobering reality, Alex reflected as he watched his brother walk away. Because it also meant that Emma Darling would never be good enough for him. No matter how he'd come to feel about her, any type of relationship, other than the one his father had just suggested, was impossible. He was next in line to the earldom, which meant he had even less leeway than his brother when it came to giving away his heart. He owed his family his loyalty; an obligation that had been instilled in him since he was a boy. Honour. Duty. Responsibility. The pride one took in one's name and one's position in society. He was doing the right thing by marrying Glynnis because it was what everyone expected.

Why, then, did it suddenly feel as though it couldn't have been more wrong?

There was not a great deal of happiness to be found at Dove's Hollow the next morning. Aunt Dorothy, painfully aware of the grievous *faux pas* she had committed the night before, refused to come out of her room. She would not be swayed by her brother's pleas that she come downstairs and talk this out, and, when Emma tried to take her a breakfast tray, she steadfastly refused to open the door.

'Aunt Dorothy, please come downstairs,' Emma said. 'We are not angry with you.'

'You should be!' came the unusually frail voice. 'I am furious with myself.'

'But—'

'Go away, Emma dear. I would rather be alone.'

Emma pressed her ear to the door and heard the sound of muffled crying. 'Very well, but I shall leave the tray.'

'Take it away. I don't want anything.'

'I shall leave it regardless.' And Emma did, hoping her aunt would change her mind. Dorothy had always had a good appetite for food.

'How is she?' Linette asked when Emma arrived back downstairs.

'Not good. I left the tray outside her door, but she wouldn't let me in.'

'Oh, Emma, I feel dreadful about all this,' Linette said. 'I never meant to make everyone so unhappy. I had no idea matters would turn out like this.'

Emma drew her sister into her arms and held her tight. 'You have nothing to apologise for. You have no more control over Aunt Dorothy than I did over Aunt Augusta. They lead their own lives and, if they make mistakes, they have no one to blame but themselves. But you have a man who loves you desperately and who wants to marry you. That is what you have to concentrate on right now.'

'But will the earl still *allow* Peter to marry me?' Linette sadly pulled free of her sister's embrace. 'Lord Widdicombe did not look at me once after the gentlemen rejoined the ladies last night. He made a point of staying as far away from me as possible. And when Peter tried to come over to talk to me, his father called him away on some pretence or other. It couldn't have been more obvious that he did not want us to be together.'

That, unfortunately, was true. Keenly aware of the dynamics in the room, Emma had watched the earl effectively ignore Linette for the rest of the evening. Only when she was leaving had he nodded in her direction, but while it was enough to prevent people from thinking he had cut her entirely, it wasn't much more.

And neither had her own situation improved. She hadn't had a chance to talk to Alex at all. It was as though he had decided to ignore her the same way Lord Widdicombe had chosen to ignore Linette. When he had come back into the drawing room with the rest of the gentlemen, he had gone immediately to Lady Glynnis's side and Emma had watched them laughing and talking as though he had been trying to make her aware of the differences between them.

It had all but torn Emma apart. Even when Alex hadn't been with Lady Glynnis, he had stayed in the company of his other friends, part of the gilded circle in which he moved. If ever the differences between their families had been apparent, it was last night. The elegant society people on one side of the room and her family on the other. The gap could not have been wider.

'Well, as far as I'm concerned, you have absolutely nothing to be ashamed of,' Emma said fiercely. 'You were a perfect lady the entire weekend and everyone who was there saw that. If the earl wishes to wash his hands of us because of something Aunt Dorothy did, there is really nothing we can do. But I will not have you think any the

less of yourself because *he* cannot distinguish the goodness in you from the weakness in our aunt.'

Emma had no idea if she managed to convince Linette
of anything. She wasn't even sure she had convinced herself. But she refused to believe that the earl would force
his son to end the relationship simply as a result of Aunt
Dorothy's behaviour. Surely anyone looking at the two of
them could see how deeply in love they were.

And what did they see when they looked at you? the
nagging little voice asked. *Did they see how desperately
you wanted to be with Alex?*

Emma closed her eyes and prayed they did not. It would
be too humiliating to be seen as being in love with Alex
when he was so clearly dedicated to Lady Glynnis. She
could just imagine the whispers. *Who does she think she
is? Surely she isn't so naïve as to think Lord Stewart would
fancy* her? *It's bad enough his brother is consorting with
her sister.*

Oh, yes, she knew what the gossips would say. Her
brief exposure to society two years ago had given her a
very good insight into the ways of the *ton*. Most of them
were shallow and conceited and out for their own gain.
She had listened to them gossiping in their elegant salons,
heard them whispering in music rooms about this person
or that, and had seen them laugh at young unsophisticated
girls who came to London with stars in their eyes in the
hopes of finding the man of their dreams. A man who was
oft-times as shallow and conceited as all the rest.

No, it was imperative that she maintain an emotional
distance from Alex. She would not embarrass him by
asking for something he could not give. And she would
not embarrass herself by being seen to want it.

Aunt Dorothy eventually did come downstairs. It was
just past one o'clock and lunch was already over, but it

soon became evident that food was the last thing on her mind. She headed straight for the library where she knew her brother would be reading, and informed him—as he informed his children shortly thereafter—that she would be returning to London as soon as it could be arranged. She had disgraced the family beyond all hope of redemption and could not bear to show her face to any of them again. Especially to dear Linette, whose future with Mr Taylor she was quite sure she had put in jeopardy.

Mr Darling, not the most effusive or sympathetic man at the best of times, had asked if there was anything he could do, whereupon Aunt Dorothy had assured him there was not and had then returned to her room to pack. The carriage had called for her an hour later and after bidding them all a teary and embarrassed farewell, she left.

An hour later, Peter arrived.

Emma was not surprised to see him. He must have known how dreadful Linette would be feeling and he had obviously come to Dove's Hollow in the hopes of consoling her, as any loving and dutiful fiancé would do. Mr Darling received him most civilly and after again apologising for his sister's behaviour, he agreed to Peter's request that he be allowed to take Linette out for a drive.

Naturally, Linette was delighted to see him. She took his appearance to mean that Lord Widdicombe had not ordered him to break off his association with her and that all was forgiven. She hurried upstairs to change into something more appropriate and left Emma and Peter to walk out to his carriage together.

'I would ask you to join us, Miss Darling,' Peter said, 'but I have only the phaeton, as my brother is using the carriage to show Lady Glynnis and her parents the countryside.'

'Pray do not concern yourself, Mr Taylor,' Emma said, far more pained by the knowledge that Alex was occupied with Lady Glynnis than she was at having to miss her sister's outing. 'There are things I must attend to here.'

'Of course.'

Emma smiled and blessed the man for not looking as relieved as he probably felt. She was quite sure the last thing he wanted was an older sister tagging along as he tried to reassure the woman he loved that all would be well. And since the last thing Emma *wanted* was to have to sit there and listen to such reassurances, she was equally relieved not to be included. When Linette came downstairs, looking perfectly charming in a gown of lavender-sprigged muslin, Emma was perfectly content to see Peter help her into the high seat and then climb up after her.

'We shan't be long,' he said.

Emma waved them off, then drew her shawl more closely around her shoulders as she turned to regard the old stone house. How must Dove's Hollow look to someone like Peter Taylor, a man who had been raised in such a grand house and who now lived in one equally fine? Or to Lord Stewart, whose London home was said to be splendid, and who would one day inherit Widdicombe Hill, one of the finest houses in Kent? It must appear quite humble, Emma thought.

But then, their family had never pretended to be anything else. Her father was a good man, but far from sophisticated. He was educated and well read, as any man who tutors others must be, but he liked his home and his books far better than anything London had to offer. Emma's mother was the one who had sampled the delights of town. Growing up as the eldest daughter of a well-to-do merchant, she was the one who had taken in the theatre and the museums and the art galleries. She had met Percy Darling at one such place and had fallen quite madly in love with him.

Still, they had been happy. There had always been food on the table and a roof over their heads. The girls had enjoyed lessons with a governess while Ridley had been sent to a school in the village. It was only after they had moved into Dove's Hollow that their father had given up teaching and settled to the life of a gentleman. And all would have been perfect had it not been for their mother's declining health and subsequent passing.

That had been the hardest thing Emma had ever had to endure. She still missed her mother dreadfully. There were so many things she would have liked to talk to her about. Things only a mother and daughter could share, because a mother had special insights into a daughter's heart. While her father did his best, he was just a man. And dear Aunt Dorothy, well, she'd always had her own best interests at heart. She hadn't adapted well to life on her own and had taken to finding solace in drink.

However, everyone had their problems, Emma reflected, and everyone had their own ways of dealing with them. It was just unfortunate that Dorothy's manner of dealing with *her* problems had unwittingly created a problem for everyone else. But, as her father said, there was nothing any of them could do about it. The damage was done. The fact of Peter's coming here today was surely proof that the wedding was going to proceed. If he had come to break it off, Emma doubted he would have looked so happy at setting off alone with Linette in the phaeton.

Not ready to head back into the house, Emma ambled towards the stable. She thought Ridley might be back soon, having left just after Aunt Dorothy made her announcement, but Chesapeake's stall was still empty and the stable was quiet, the only sound being the contented sound of Bess munching hay.

Emma went to close the door of Chessy's stall when she noticed, of all things, Ridley's sketchbook lying on one of the bales of hay. Why on earth would he have left it down here?

She had her answer when she glanced at the page lying open. Ridley had started a sketch of the chestnut. Perhaps he thought to use it in his portrait for the family in London. He'd certainly done a masterful job. The musculature of the horse's hindquarters was beautifully depicted, as was the length and shape of its legs. More accustomed to seeing her brother's rendition of the human animal, Emma was astonished at how accurately he had captured the details of the horse's form, even to the coarse texture of the mane and tail.

Curious to see more of his work, Emma sat down and pulled the pad on to her lap. There were a variety of sketches within, some of animals, a few of buildings, but most often of people. There were even casual drawings of the three of them going about their daily routine. She saw one of her father absently rubbing Rory's head as he read the newspaper, and one of her working on her embroidery while Linette played the piano in the background. Ridley had a gift for capturing the tiny details other artists would surely miss. The dusting of freckles across the bridge of Linette's nose. The tranquillity of her father's expression, the smile that always hovered so close to the surface. There was even a second one of her, sitting at her easel with her brush poised against the canvas, her brow furrowed in concentration.

Then she turned the page again—and saw Lady Glynnis staring up at her.

Emma gasped. The portrait was uncannily lifelike.

Ridley had captured Lady Glynnis during an unguarded moment, her expression soft, her features relaxed as she smiled back at him. She was wearing a simple round gown and her head was bare, her hair casually arranged in soft waves around her face.

Hardly daring to breathe, Emma turned the page and found another sketch of Lady Glynnis, this time a more formal portrait of the lady seated in a wingback chair, elegantly garbed in a sumptuous silver gown with strands of pearls and flowers woven through her hair.

Then another of her in a riding habit, with a crop in one hand and her other resting on the head of a very large black-and-white dog.

And finally, the last sketch, almost medieval in nature. Lady Glynnis was standing in a doorway looking back at the artist. Her hair hung down her back, her eyes were soft, her lips full and inviting. It was a beautiful portrait. Seductive, without being erotic. But it was the expression on her face that Emma found the most disturbing. Because in every sketch, Lady Glynnis was gazing back at the man who had captured her so deliberately on paper and smiling at him in that special way. The way of a woman in love—

'What the hell do you think you're doing?'

Emma's head shot up. 'Ridley!'

He was standing in the doorway, and he was furious. 'You had no right—!'

'You left the sketchbook open on a bale of hay.' Emma got to her feet. 'Anyone could have found it.'

'But no one would have had the nerve to pick it up and look through it.' Ridley walked in and flipped it closed. 'No one else would have been interested.'

'You don't know that! And if you don't want people looking at your secrets, you shouldn't leave them lying around.'

This time, it was her brother who flushed. 'I have no secrets.'

'Oh, Ridley, do you think I'm blind?' Emma opened the book to the last sketch of Lady Glynnis. 'Do you think I don't recognise that look?'

Her brother's dark brows drew together. 'What look?'

'The look of a woman in love. The same look Linette's worn for the last six months!'

'All right, so it's a picture of Lady Glynnis in love. That's nothing to be remarked upon. She *is* in love—with Lord Stewart.'

'But she's looking at *you*.'

'Of course she is. I'm the artist,' Ridley said. 'But she was thinking of *him*. Now if you don't mind—'

'But Lord Stewart is going to *propose* to Lady Glynnis. But if she's in love with you—'

'She is not in love with me!'

'Look at this drawing, Ridley!' Emma said in exasperation. 'Look at the expression on her face. She isn't looking at Lord Stewart now.'

'Leave it alone, Emma.'

'I can't.' Emma knew she was badgering him, but she had to get at the truth. 'This is too important. Especially if there's a chance she's in love with you!'

'Damn it, Emma, she is *not* in love with me. She made that very clear the day she learned I'd shown the painting to Tom. She said she never wanted to see me again!'

'But *why* do you think she was so upset? Aside from the fact that she wanted Lord Stewart to be the first one to see the portrait.'

'I don't know.'

'You told me she was happy with the portrait?'

'Yes. She asked me to make her look beautiful and I did. But I just painted her as I saw her. I didn't have to *try* to make her look beautiful. She *was* beautiful. And the more I came to care for her, the more of my feelings I poured into the painting. Eventually, it became…a portrait for me.'

'Precisely!' Emma said, quietly triumphant. 'And I think Lady Glynnis was afraid Tom Towbridge saw exactly that. The fact that she was in love…but with you!'

'That's ridiculous!'

'Is it? A guilty conscience is a powerful thing, Ridley,' Emma said softly. 'It makes people go through all kinds of wild imaginings. Make them see shadows where none exist. Lady Glynnis was afraid Tom saw how much she loved you, rather than the man she was having the painting done for!'

Ridley shook his head. 'You're wrong. She was angry because I betrayed her trust. If she loved me, she would have *told* me.'

'Oh, yes, just like you told her!' Emma threw back at him.

'It wasn't my place to tell her! She was promised to another man. It wasn't the honourable thing to do.'

'And letting her marry a man who doesn't love her is?'

'Enough!' he shouted. 'I will not discuss this. Whatever her reasons for being angry with me don't matter any more. She obviously doesn't have any feelings for me or she would have made some kind of effort to speak to me alone. But she hasn't done that, has she? She's stayed at Ellingsworth even though she knew I was here. If that's how a woman in love behaves, I'm better off without her.'

'Ridley, please think about this—'

'No! I've done all the thinking I'm going to,' Ridley snapped. 'In a few days, I will be returning to London and carrying on with my life. Linette will marry Peter Taylor,

Lady Glynnis will marry Lord Stewart and everyone will be happy.'

'Everyone except you,' Emma whispered as her brother marched out of the stall with the sketchbook under his arm.

She didn't have the courage to add, *and everyone except me.*

Chapter Eleven

Alex knew it made no sense to want to see Emma again. He had enjoyed a good deal of time in her company over the last three days, but after spending a few pleasurable hours showing Glynnis and her parents the delights of the countryside, thoughts of another woman should have been the furthest thing from his mind. But they were not. Even as he sat next to Glynnis in the carriage, it was Emma he found himself thinking about, Emma's smiles he pictured and Emma's laughter he heard. And the more he thought about her, the more he realised how desperately he wanted to see her. But what possible excuse did he have for going to Dove's Hollow now?

Unexpectedly, his mother provided him with it. 'Oh, there you are, darling,' she said when he walked into the drawing room. 'I wonder if I could trouble you to pick up a few things from the village. I'd go myself, but I don't want to leave the Leylands alone.'

'I understand,' he said, taking the list she held out to him.

'Oh, and if you wouldn't mind, perhaps you could stop

by Dove's Hollow on your way back and give this earring to Miss Darling,' she said, handing him a small package. 'One of the maids found it when they were cleaning.'

'Yes, of course. I'm sure Emma will be pleased to have it returned,' he said without thinking.

'Emma?' His mother glanced at him quizzically. 'I wasn't aware you and Miss Darling had established such a close friendship, Alex. Surely such informality should wait until after the wedding? Besides, the earring belongs to Miss Linette Darling.'

Mentally cursing himself for the slip, Alex inclined his head. 'Of course. I simply had other things on my mind. We are all a little preoccupied these days. Speaking of which, have you decided when you and Father are returning to London?'

'No. I thought it might be a good idea for your father to rest here for a bit. His colour was not good at breakfast and Murdoch said he didn't get much sleep last night.' She sighed. 'I expect I shall have to call for Dr Harrow as soon as we get back.'

'Don't worry. Father's too tough to die.' Alex bent down and kissed his mother on the cheek. 'He'll probably outlast us all!'

Given that there were a few things his mother needed him to pick up, Alex decided to take the carriage into the village rather than to ride. Upon arriving, he was pleasantly surprised to be greeted by a number of people, some of whom he remembered from the Jacobs's assembly, others who had been at Ellingsworth for the festivities on the Saturday afternoon. But they were all very pleasant and Alex was surprised at how much he enjoyed the feeling of being part of the small community.

He thought back to the assembly and slowly began to

smile. Was it only last week he had held Emma in his arms and waltzed her around the room? Only last week that he had felt the softness of her hand in his, and caressed her bare feet in the darkness of a carriage? It seemed like an eternity. He needed to be near her again. To bask in the warmth of her smile and to hear the softness of her voice.

He hurried through his errands in the village and then set out for Dove's Hollow.

She was in the garden when he arrived. Not painting. Just standing still, gazing out over the pond, her arms folded across her chest, her brow furrowed in concentration.

'Emma?'

She turned, and to his surprise he saw not pleasure, but pain flash across her face. It was gone in an instant, but the knowledge that he had put it there caused him more grief than he cared to acknowledge. 'I've come at a bad time,' he said, ready to leave.

'No, no, you haven't,' she hastened to say. 'I was just… thinking. Trying to come up with answers.'

'For what?'

She looked up at him and didn't even bother to hide her unease. 'For a situation over which I have no control and that is going to cause untold problems for everyone involved.'

He knew better than to accuse her of exaggerating. Emma was not given to melodrama. 'Can you tell me who the people are and what the nature of the problem is?'

'I wish I could. But it is…a private matter.' She looked up at him. 'I'm sure you understand.'

He nodded, all too familiar with private matters of a painful nature. 'Then, perhaps we might take a stroll together? I often find I do my best thinking when I am walking. Perhaps the answers will come to you more readily.'

'Perhaps.' She sighed. 'If nothing else, it will be good to stretch my legs.' She looked at him with curiosity. 'Is there a reason you came to see me?'

'Hmm? Oh, yes. Mother asked me to return this,' Alex said, handing her the package. 'Linette's earring. One of the servants found it when they were cleaning. Perhaps you could give it to her?'

She stared at the small tissue-wrapped package he held out to her. 'Yes, of course.' When she took it from him, he noticed she was careful not to touch him. 'Linette will be relieved to have it back.'

After slipping the earring into her pocket, they headed out of the garden and along the path towards the gate. Pushing it open, they passed into the next field and started up the hill behind the house. The climb was not steep, but it was steady; at the top, Emma paused to catch her breath. 'Oh, my, I haven't been up here in ages.'

'What a spectacular view,' Alex breathed. 'You can see all the way to Little Moreton.'

'I used to run up here a lot when I was a child,' Emma said. 'I loved watching the clouds flying by overhead. I felt like I was standing on top of the world.'

The image of her as a little girl with her hair streaming out behind her, running up the hill with her arms spread wide, made him chuckle. 'It's hard to picture you as a little girl running up a hill.'

'Papa said I ran everywhere. I've never thought of myself as being impatient, but I must have been when I was younger. Always in a hurry to get wherever I was going,' Emma mused. 'I've slowed down in the intervening years.'

'I'd rather say you've acquired patience,' Alex said. 'I'm sure you still do hurry, if the need is really there.'

She flicked him an amused glance. 'Do you always know exactly the right thing to say, Lord Stewart?'

'Obviously not, because I've become Lord Stewart again.' He had hoped to make her smile. He was dismayed when he saw her frown. 'What's really going on, Emma? What's troubling you?'

'Nothing. And everything,' she whispered. 'After what happened with my aunt—'

'There is no need for us to speak of that again,' Alex began, only to see her shake her head.

'There is every need. I know my father apologised to you and that he spoke to your brother when he came to take Linette driving, but I feel I must also offer my apologies for the way my aunt behaved. It was…unforgivable.'

'It was an error in judgement,' Alex said. 'She didn't do it on purpose.'

'Of course not! But the damage is done and the tragic part is that no one regrets it more than my aunt. She went back to London because she could not bear to stay with us a moment longer. She felt her conduct reflected poorly on the rest of us. Most particularly, on Linette.'

Alex argued with himself as to what he should say, but in the end, he decided on the truth. 'I cannot deny that my mother and father were displeased, Emma, but Peter loves your sister very much and he intends to marry her.' He paused, trying to gauge her mood. 'Is there…anything else that's making you unhappy?'

Her sudden flush gave him his answer, but all she said was, 'No. Why should there be?'

He took a step closer, knowing the moment for honesty was at hand. He couldn't go on pretending that he didn't care. 'Perhaps because you are not the only one forced to keep painful secrets.'

Her eyes widened. 'I don't know what you're talking about.'

'Don't you? You must know I'm drawn to you, Emma. That I think about you…far too much.'

He watched her eyes darken in pain. 'Lord Stewart, this is not a good idea.'

'Perhaps not,' he said quietly. 'My father asked me to counsel my brother as to the unsuitability of his relationship with your sister. I shudder to think what he would say if he knew I was also having to counsel myself against my feelings…for you.'

It had to happen. Perhaps it had been building to this right from the start, but the inevitability of the kiss still left Emma breathless. She watched Alex slowly take a step towards her, felt the warmth of his hands as they closed around her upper arms and watched his head bend towards her with unmistakable intent. But when his mouth finally came down on hers, it was not with trepidation that Emma returned his kiss, but with desire, her heart pounding wildly against his chest, her entire body trembling with need.

He kissed her slowly, languidly, his lips moving over hers without urgency or haste. There was only need and longing. And when at length they drew apart, Emma slowly opened her eyes to find him gazing down at her without regret or recrimination. His hands still held her close, the heat of his body still warming her through the thin fabric of her gown. 'Forgive me,' he whispered.

She shook her head, wishing he had said anything but that. 'I can't. Any more than I can forgive myself for wanting it.'

He gazed down at her, his expression so gentle that

Emma feared she would cry. They could not undo what they had done or pretend it hadn't happened, but even before he said the words, Emma knew what they would be. 'I'm sorry, Emma. The expectations of me are such that…I cannot go any further with this.'

'I know. But that doesn't mean the feelings don't exist,' she said. 'Or that the longings are any the less painful to bear.'

He raised his hand, trailed his fingers over her temple and cheek to curl around the point of her chin. 'There are so many things I would say to you,' he said. 'So many things I would have you know. But I can say none of them. It would be unfair to everyone involved, but, most particularly, to you.'

Emma nodded. He was speaking to her, but he was referring to Lady Glynnis. 'I know. This was never meant to happen, but it did. And believe me when I say that *no one* is more surprised than I am.'

'I have been fighting it,' Alex admitted. 'Because I didn't want to hurt you. But the strength of my feelings for you is such that…I had to say something. I wanted you to know how I felt. And I needed to know if you felt the same way about me. Perhaps that was wrong—'

'It was,' Emma said, her voice unexpectedly husky. 'It would have been easier not knowing that you cared for me. Because then I could have pretended it was just me being foolish. That no matter what my feelings for you, you could never have felt the same way. But now I can't hide behind that any more because I know you do care for me. And that just makes it that much harder to bear.'

Alex's hand fell away. He took a reluctant step backwards and glanced at the clouds overhead. 'I've never felt this way about anyone before. You know what my feelings about marriage were. How I thought it should be approached. But with you, everything is so…different.' He finally looked back at her. 'Now I *know* how it is supposed to be between two people. And how cruel being forced to settle for anything less is going to be.'

Emma squeezed her eyes shut, hardly daring to breathe. How was it possible that the words that should have made her so happy were making her anything but? 'I think it would be best if we did not see each other alone again, Alex. It will be hard enough at the wedding, but other than that…'

He nodded. 'I understand. I have no desire to make this any more difficult for you than it is for me.'

He left her then, and Emma felt a pain so intense it stole the breath from her lungs. It was as though a hand was closing around her heart, tearing it out of her chest. She wanted to cry, but the tears wouldn't come, only this horrible, unending pain. This hollowness, as though someone had cut a hole in her soul.

She was in love with Alexander Taylor. And he was going to marry a woman who didn't love him while she was forced to sit by and watch. It was more than she could bear.

It was more than anyone should have to bear.

The pressure on Alex started early the next morning, over breakfast, when his father informed him that the Leylands would be leaving the following day.

'So if there's anything you want to say to Lady Glynnis, now would be the time,' Lord Widdicombe advised. 'They're all expecting it. And it would be a shining way to end an otherwise dismal affair.'

Alex said nothing. He was well aware that Lord and Lady Leyland were expecting him to propose to Glynnis, but it hadn't occurred to him that it had to be done here before they left. After all, the arrangements over settlements had been made, and he had already talked to Glynnis about where they would live. He owned a town house in London and a hunting box near Melton Mowbray, but until now the latter had been a bachelor's home that was sorely in need of renovation. Alex had shown Glynnis through the house months ago and told her she could do whatever was needed to turn it into a welcoming home. They had even talked about curtains, for heaven's sake. Why wouldn't they be expecting him to propose?

Glynnis must surely have been expecting it. As the days went by, Alex noticed her growing noticeably more quiet and withdrawn. She seemed to laugh less when she was around him and the sparkle he had always associated with her was gone. Was her disappointment in him so great that it was affecting her to this degree?

The question pained him deeply. Glynnis didn't deserve this kind of treatment from him. They had always been good friends and, until now, they had been able to talk about almost anything. But now their association seemed strained, the easy laughter and gentle banter gone. Everything was different…because he knew it was Emma he wished to marry, but that it was Glynnis he *must*.

He brought the subject up when they were out riding together after lunch. 'Glyn, is everything all right?'

They were walking their horses through a shady glen. Glynnis looked at him, and roused herself to smile. 'Yes, of course. Why do you ask?'

'Because you don't seem as happy as you did when you first arrived.'

'It has been…an interesting few days.' She turned her attention to the path ahead. 'A great deal has happened that I did not expect.'

'And perhaps something has *not* happened that you did expect?'

He saw the blush race across her cheeks. 'I'm not sure I know what you mean.'

'Don't you?' Alex reached for her mare's reins and drew both animals to a halt. 'You've never been shy when it came to talking about our marriage before, Glyn.'

Her head slowly came round, but she did not smile. 'To be honest, I wasn't sure if you still wished to marry me.'

The note of anxiety in her voice pierced his heart. 'Why would I not? We have been promised to one another these last two years, and we have been friends a good deal longer. It is what everyone expects.'

'Yes, I know. But things have…happened that I thought might have changed your mind.'

Her face gave nothing away, but her words were a clear indication that something was amiss. Was she talking about his feelings for Emma? Had he somehow given himself away? Alex thought hard about everything that had happened over the last few days, but he couldn't isolate one single incident or conversation that might have exposed him.

'Is there something I should know, Glyn? Something I haven't been told?' When she didn't answer, Alex put his hand on her arm. 'Glyn, please. What's this really all about? I have the feeling there's something you want to tell me.'

He waited, aware that even as she kept silent, hope flared within his heart. Had she met someone else? Was she trying to find a gentle way of breaking it off? At one time such a revelation would have caused him considerable concern, but now he found himself welcoming it.

Still, what good would it do him if she *did* wish to end it? He couldn't go running to Emma. His father would *never* approve of him having a relationship with her and would never forgive Alex for disappointing him. He would be furious at his heir's blatant disregard for everything that mattered.

'No, there's nothing I want to tell you,' Glynnis said finally. 'Forgive me, it must be everything's that happened this weekend. There has been so much conflict and unhappiness over your brother's engagement. Your father is clearly displeased by it, yet for the life of me I can't imagine why.'

Alex glanced at her in surprise. 'He doesn't feel that Linette Darling is well born enough to be Peter's bride. She doesn't have the kind of background he was looking for.'

'But she is a beautiful, genteel girl,' Glynnis said. 'More importantly, she loves him and he loves her. Desperately. You have only to see them together to know that.' She turned away, biting her lip. 'Surely that has to count for something.'

Alex stared at her in amazement. He had never heard her talk this way before. Like him, she had always adopted a practical approach to marriage, espousing the benefits of a well-thought-out liaison over sentimentality. He had never heard her speak about love or desire and, like him, had assumed she didn't care about such things, that they weren't part of what she was looking for in a marriage. Could it be he had completely misread her?

'So if my father were to ask you your opinion of Peter and Linette's betrothal,' Alex said slowly, 'you would tell him he should give his approval to the marriage?'

'Of course. Oh, I know it isn't what the earl wishes to hear, but surely when two people are so obviously in love, it would be wrong to stop them from being together. What kind of life would that be condemning them to? I know your father only wants the best for his sons and he is afraid that Peter is making a terrible mistake. But your brother is very much in love with Linette Darling. Everything he's done is proof of that. He's stood by her through every uncomfortable moment. He's faced up to your father and to anyone else who said she wasn't good enough. And even after what happened with Mrs Grand, he refused to abandon her.' Glynnis turned to look at him and he saw an unexpected shimmer of tears in her eyes. 'You see the way they look at each other, Alex,' she said huskily. 'How could I advise your father not to allow them to marry when it is clear they would only spend the rest of their lives pining for each other if they did not? What kind of life would that be?'

'I never knew you felt this way,' he said quietly. 'You've never spoken to me like this before.'

'I know. And I know it isn't the same for you,' Glynnis said. 'You are the heir. You don't have the freedom of choice your brother has. You have always been forced to weigh duty and obligation, as I have. That's why a marriage between the two of us seemed the ideal solution to our parents. I am the type of woman your father expects you to marry and you are the type of man my father wishes me to.'

Alex didn't know what to say. This was a side of Glynnis he'd never seen before. He had never heard her speak so passionately about something she obviously felt so strongly about. And clearly his failure to ask her to marry him was the cause of the sadness he saw in her now.

He suddenly remembered what Towbridge had let slip at dinner—the fact that Glynnis had hired an artist to paint a portrait of her as a gift for him. A portrait that had revealed the depth of her love so clearly that even another man had been able to see it.

And that must be the problem. Glynnis *was* in love
with him. She was waiting for him to ask her to marry
him, to do what they both knew he should. What everyone
expected. And in that moment, Alex knew there was only
one thing he could do. 'Lady Glynnis Pettle,' he said softly.
'Glyn. Will you do me the honour of becoming my wife?'

She didn't look at him, but he saw the tears that formed
in her eyes and ran silently down her cheek. 'Yes.' Her
mouth trembled, but she managed a smile. 'I will marry
you.'

He leaned over and kissed her, tasting the saltiness of
tears on her lips. But on an emotional level, he felt nothing. The kiss didn't inspire him the way Emma's had. It
didn't leave him longing to make love to her, or to hold
her as she cried out his name in that moment of passionate
awakening. Beyond the fondness he felt for her as a friend,
there was nothing.

Drawing back, he raised his hand to gently wipe away
her tears. 'Don't cry, Glyn. This is supposed to be a happy
moment.'

She laughed, more a gulping sound than anything else.
'Yes, of course. It's just that I'm more…emotional than I
expected to be. It isn't every day a lady receives a proposal
of marriage.'

He nodded, waiting for her to compose herself. And
while he did, he waited for it to come: the feeling of relief
that he had done the right thing. The certainty that she was
the only woman he was destined to be with. But it did not.
The knowledge that she would soon be his wife brought
with it no sense of deep and abiding satisfaction. He wasn't
looking forward to a future filled with the kind of love
he had discovered with Emma because Glynnis *wasn't*
Emma. And it was the most tragic thought imaginable
that no matter how long he and Glynnis were together, no

matter how many children they brought into the world, he would never feel for her after a lifetime of marriage what he did for Emma Darling right now.

The reaction to his announcement that Glynnis had agreed to be his wife was everything Alex expected. Lord and Lady Leyland expressed their heartfelt delight and his own parents left him in no doubt as to their pleasure at hearing that he had finally made up his mind.

'Oh Alex, my dear, I'm so happy for you!' his mother said, crushing him in an unusually affectionate embrace.

'Well done, my boy, well done!' his father said, pumping his hand. 'Damned if I don't feel better already.'

'I'm glad to hear it, Father,' Alex said, relieved that no one seemed to notice his own lack of enthusiasm.

'This calls for a celebration,' the earl said. 'Sarah, you'll start planning something as soon as we get home. An engagement party, followed by a grand ball, and then the wedding itself.'

'I suspect the Leylands will want to take care of that, my dear.'

'Ah, well, you know what's best. But it will be the social event of the Season,' his father went on proudly. 'Only the finest families in attendance. The *crème de la crème* of society.'

'I must go and speak to Glynnis's mother,' Lady Widdicombe said. 'We have so much to talk about and to arrange.'

After she left, Lord Widdicombe walked up to his son and, in an unexpected display of affection, hugged him close. 'Thank you, Alex. You've made me very proud. Lady Glynnis will make you an excellent wife. If you're as happy with her as I've been with your mother, you'll be a lucky man.'

'Thank you, Father, I'm sure I will be.'

'And don't wait too long before starting a family, eh? I'm longing to see grandsons.'

Alex smiled, thinking it typical of his father that he would only consider boys. 'There may be girls.'

'A token one or two,' the earl said with a laugh. 'But only after the boys. Because we all know it's boys that really matter. Especially the first one. The heir!' The earl choked up. 'Like you.'

Uncomfortable with emotion, he turned and left the room.

Alex stood where he was, listening to the ticking of the clock. He had done the right thing. The pride and satisfaction on his father's face was proof of that. He'd never seen him so jubilant. And his mother was delighted. Glyn's parents too. He had made everyone happy by doing what he was supposed to. Everyone but the two people who would suffer for it the most.

'So, you finally did it. Congratulations, brother.'

Alex turned as Peter walked in. 'You heard.'

'I just passed Father on the way out. I don't remember the last time I saw him so elated. Well done.' Peter put out his hand and grasped his brother's. 'At least he's pleased with one of us.'

Alex sighed. 'Give him time, Peter. The more he comes to know Linette, the more he'll grow to love her.'

'I'd like to think that,' Peter said. 'But who knows? Maybe now that you've finally done the right thing by Lady Glyn, he'll find it in his heart to look more kindly on *my* marriage.'

The pain came out of nowhere, a swift, sharp jab that tore at Alex's insides. Because his brother was marrying the woman he loved—and he was marrying the one he had to. 'Only time will tell,' Alex said, releasing Peter's hand. 'Care to join me for a drink?'

'Why not? It is an auspicious occasion.'

Alex shot him a keen glance as he walked to the credenza. 'So why the note of reserve?'

Peter sighed. 'Perhaps not so much reserve as regret.'

'Regret? What for? Everyone else is ecstatic.'

'Of course, because you are doing what's expected of you. What everyone else considers to be the right thing. I just hope it's the right thing…for you.'

Alex frowned as he poured brandy into two glasses. 'What's that supposed to mean?'

'Oh, come on, Alex. We both know you're not marrying Glynnis for love. Oh, I'm sure you like her well enough, but it's not the same as loving someone, is it? It's not like wanting to be with that woman because you can't imagine being with anyone else.'

Alex replaced the crystal stopper. 'It's all very well for you, Peter. You have the luxury of being able to follow your heart. I don't. You said it yourself. I have my duty to consider. My obligation to the family name.' He handed his brother a glass, his smile tight. 'You didn't have to take that into account when you asked Linette to marry you.'

The words were harsher than he'd intended, the tone considerably more bitter. But even when he saw the look of hurt surprise on his brother's face, he couldn't bring himself to apologise.

'I meant no offence, Alex. I'm just saying—'

'I know what you're saying, but that's the difference between you and me. Being the first-born means you have responsibilities. I live with them every day of my life. And whether I like it or not, they *do* rule my life.'

'I'm sorry.' Peter's expression grew troubled. 'It was never my intention—'

'I know. It's simply the way it is.'

And just like that, Alex's anger evaporated, leaving him feeling drained and not particularly pleased with himself. His brother hadn't been deserving of the set-down he'd just received, but Alex hadn't been able to stop once he'd started. He finished his drink and set his glass on the desk. 'You should be glad you're not next in line to the title, Peter. There are definitely times when being the heir isn't all it's cracked up to be.'

Alex waited until both the Leylands and his parents had gone out for a stroll before calling for his horse and heading in the direction of Dove's Hollow. He had to tell Emma straight away. He didn't want her learning of his engagement to Glynnis through the village grapevine. She had to hear it from him. He owed her that much at least.

His thoughts were scattered as he cantered along the road. How would he break the news? Should he do it quickly, hoping it would be less painful, or should he tell her slowly, setting out all his reasons for why he had done what he'd done? Or should he just tell her he was getting married and leave her to work out the rest on her own?

No, that would surely be the most hurtful. God knew it was going to be agony seeing the look on her face when he told her. To live with the knowledge that they would never be together and that their encounters from here on would have to be of the most polite and innocuous kind.

All he wanted to do was hold her in his arms and make love to her.

He closed his eyes, shutting out the images. It was too much to bear. As long as he lived, he would never forget the sweetness of holding Emma in his arms, the incredible softness of her skin beneath his fingers, the blatant sensuality of her body pressed against his. She was everything he had ever wanted: the woman he hadn't known he was looking for. And now she was lost to him.

Damn.

At Dove's Hollow, he was shown into the parlour where Ridley and Linette were enjoying a quiet game of cards. They looked up in surprise at his entrance. 'Lord Stewart!' Linette said, her eyes darting past him in hopes of seeing his brother.

'Sorry, Linette, Peter's not with me,' he said gently. 'I've come on my own. I need…that is, I'd like to speak to your sister.'

'She's in the garden,' Ridley said. 'Doing battle with the angel.'

Alex smiled, even as Linette frowned, and said, 'What are you talking about, Ridley? How can anyone do battle with an angel?'

Alex shared a knowing glance with Ridley. 'I doubt anyone but your sister could.'

He found her in the garden, her easel positioned about three feet away from the statue. It looked as though she had started a new sketch and that she was drawing the troublesome angel with charcoal first.

He stood for a moment, just allowing himself the pleasure of watching her. How had he ever thought her anything less than magnificent? The roundness of her cheek, the delicate curve of her neck and throat, the smoothness of her complexion. She wasn't wearing her painter's smock today, protecting her dress with a cloth, and had cast aside her shawl. It was a warm afternoon and she was sitting in the shade of a tree so as not to be browned by the sun. He saw the tempting swell of her breasts rising above the lace edging on her gown and the slender whiteness of an ankle where her gown had pulled up.

She was glorious. And she would never be his. 'Emma.'

She turned, her hand poised above the sketch pad. 'Alex!' He saw the pleasure in her eyes, the fleeting moment of joy at seeing him, then watched her smile fade as awareness of their situation came to the fore. 'Lord Stewart.' She put down the piece of charcoal, slowly, as though to give herself time to pull a protective cocoon around her. 'The festivities are over and you've come to say goodbye. When do you leave?'

'I'm not sure. Later this week, I suppose.'

'And Lady Glynnis?'

'Tomorrow, with her parents.'

'I see.' Emma nodded and looked as though she wanted to say more, but in the end she glanced back at the stone angel and said, 'I've started a new sketch. And I'm having more luck with her wing this afternoon.'

'Yes, I see.' Alex cleared his throat, feeling a lump the size of Gibraltar stuck there. 'Emma, I have to tell you—'

'No, you don't,' she said quietly. 'I already know.' She turned to look at him and her face was as white as the statue's. 'You and Lady Glynnis are engaged.'

Alex wished he knew what to say. When had she found out? The servants couldn't have spread the news that quickly. 'How did you know?'

She tried for a smile, but failed. 'It was a foregone conclusion. When you said she was leaving with her parents in the morning, I knew. It only made sense that you proposed to her before she left.' Slowly, she stood up, her hands pressed against her sides. 'Your father must be very pleased.'

'He is.' The words burned like hot coals against his throat. 'They all are.'

'Of course. Because it is…as it should be. You did what was expected.'

'Emma—'

'No, please, I beg you!' She closed her eyes, her voice thick with emotion. 'It will only make this harder. I wish you…much happiness, Lord Stewart. And Lady Glynnis too.' She slowly opened her eyes. 'I wish I could say I don't like her, but I do. She stood up for Linette at a time when my sister needed it most and I will always think kindly of her for that.' She paused, as if to draw more air into her lungs. 'She is a lady in every sense of the word.'

'Yes, she is.' His own voice was husky, his heart pounding fit to burst. 'But she is not you.'

With that, he turned and walked away. He couldn't bear to spend another moment in her company. If he had, he would have taken her in his arms and made love to her right there, with the damn stone angel looking on. Instead, he clenched his fists at his sides and walked back to where he had left his horse, willing himself to put one foot in front of the other. He knew Emma wouldn't call him back. That wasn't her way. Even if she was hurting as badly as he was, she knew what the realities of their lives were and she would abide by them.

Their worlds were too far apart. And at this moment, they had never been more so.

Chapter Twelve

Because she had no choice, Emma went back to the house and, taking Ridley aside, told him about Lady Glynnis and Lord Stewart. She planned on telling the rest of the family over dinner that evening, but she knew it would be kinder to Ridley if she gave him the information in private. He would need time to come to grips with the information and to compose himself, as she had.

She was not mistaken. He turned pale upon learning of the engagement; Emma saw on his face a reflection of the bleakness she felt within her own heart. 'So, that's it then,' he said in a flat, emotionless voice. 'They are to be married.'

'I'm afraid so.'

'When?'

'He didn't say. I expect they will discuss a date once they are all back in London.'

Ridley nodded woodenly. 'And Glynnis is leaving with her parents tomorrow?'

'That's what Lord Stewart told me.'

'And then life will revert to normal,' Ridley said, his

expression bleak. 'All the pieces having fallen into place. All very neat and tidy.'

'Are you going to see her when you return to London?'

'What's the point?' Ridley got up and began to walk around. 'She is now an officially engaged lady. There is no reason for me to call.'

'I'm truly sorry, Ridley,' Emma said softly. 'I know this isn't easy.'

He stopped in front of the window and gazed out. 'No, it isn't. But no one said life was going to be easy. Thank you, Emma. I'd rather have found out like this than at the dinner table, when no doubt everyone will be deliriously happy. You are the only one who understands.'

Yes, she was. But not for the reasons he thought, and it wasn't until her brother left the room that Emma finally allowed herself to cry, sobbing as though her heart would break, aware that nothing anyone could have said would have made the news any the less devastating to hear.

Emma told Linette and her father the news at dinner that evening, and, as expected, they were delighted. Ridley paid diligent attention to his soup and Emma was content to let Linette carry the bulk of the conversation after that. Having discovered a new friend in Alex and a new ally in Lady Glynnis, she was thrilled that the lady was soon to become her sister-in-law.

On a positive note, it did have the effect of easing Linette's despair over Lord Widdicombe's reaction towards her. She had already met with Peter, who had taken pains to assure her their marriage would take place at St David's as planned, and perhaps seeing in Alex's engagement the possibility of the earl's mellowing towards his other son, she was optimistic that everything was going to turn out well.

Having more of an insight into the situation, Emma did not venture an opinion. How it would play out now was completely out of her hands. She was a pawn in Fate's game—and she soon found out that the game could change in an instant, and not for the better.

It was a little after ten o'clock the next morning when she made the unwelcome discovery. She set out on a ride, desperate to get out of the house and be alone with her thoughts. She hadn't wanted to paint or to talk to Linette about the wedding. In fact, if she never heard the word wedding again, she would be just as happy!

Emma wasn't surprised to see that Ridley's chestnut was also gone from the stable. He, too, must have felt a need to get away and be alone with his thoughts. Thank God he didn't know what was going on between her and Alex. There would have been a small degree of comfort in being able to commiserate with one another over the similarity of their situations, but it would have served little purpose beyond that. They had each lost the person they loved to the person the *other* one loved.

Deciding not to follow her usual path up the hill, Emma turned the mare left and headed south. This route was more heavily forested than the one she usually took and unless she wished to incur a lengthy detour by going around the woods, she had no choice but to ride through them. At the best of times, they tended to be dark and gloomy, but this morning they were an exact match for Emma's feelings.

She had ridden in about a mile when she saw Ridley's horse standing in a small copse of trees. The chestnut's reins were tethered to the lowest branch of a tree, but Ridley was nowhere to be seen.

Concerned, Emma drew Bess to a halt and slipped out

of the saddle. After securing the mare's reins to the same
tree as Chesapeake's, Emma went in search of her brother.
Given the state of mind he was in, she worried about him
being alone in the woods. She doubted he would intentionally injure himself. Ridley loved life too much for that.
But there were definitely times when one's thoughts could
turn dark and Ridley was enough of a romantic to fall into
an emotional depression.

She moved quietly through the trees, about to call his
name, when she came upon the second horse. A very nice-
looking mare Emma hadn't seen before. And there, just
beyond the mare, in a forest clearing, she saw them.

A man and a woman, locked in each other's arms. The
man's jacket and cravat were on the ground, his shirt open
at the neck. The lady's bonnet had fallen to the forest floor,
as had her shawl.

Suddenly, the lady broke free. The man reached for
her, but she pushed him away. She stood with her arms
wrapped tightly around her chest as though to hold herself
together. She was pleading with him, her voice low and
intent, her beautiful face a study in anguish.

And then he spoke. Three words, followed by her name.
Then the same three words again.

A shudder rippled through the woman's slender frame.
Her eyes closed and a tortured sound slipped past her lips.
A battle was raging: the urge to run against the desire to
stay.

Emma knew it well. The wisdom of resisting against
the pleasures of giving in.

Longing versus duty. Obligation versus love.

Suddenly, the woman reached out her hand, tears
streaming down her face, and the next moment they were
in each other's arms. Emma watched as the man lowered
his mouth to her neck, trailing kisses along the smooth

white skin of her throat. He ventured even lower, finally pressing his mouth to the soft swell of her breasts. Wantonly, the lady tipped back her head, a low moan escaping her throat as she drew his head closer, their bodies pressed intimately together in a way that left Emma in no doubt as to their intent.

If nothing happened to prevent it, her brother and Lady Glynnis were about to become lovers.

The decision was agonising, the seconds flying by as she watched the pair sink to the ground. Lady Glynnis's arms were still wrapped around Ridley. He broke away only long enough to spread his jacket over the grass before going back to kissing her, his hand replacing his mouth at her breast.

Emma felt her cheeks flame. She had never seen anything so blatantly erotic in her life. That they were deeply in love she had no doubt, but that they were about to make the biggest mistake of their lives was undeniable.

And yet, what right had she to interfere? It was clearly a consensual arrangement. Neither of them was trying to escape. But if they went ahead and did this, they risked destroying themselves and everything they held dear.

Still, it wasn't her decision to make. Ridley and Lady Glynnis were adults. They knew what they were doing. And if they didn't, God help them when they came to their senses and found out.

Emma stepped back, intending to leave quietly, when her foot landed on a small twig and snapped it in half, the sound echoing through the silence like a gunshot.

In an instant, Ridley was on his feet. He glanced with unerring accuracy in Emma's direction, and as their eyes met she saw his face burn with shame, even as his eyes pleaded with her to understand.

Emma swallowed and backed away. She felt like an

intruder, a voyeur into something she had no business witnessing. But they were the ones in the wrong. How could they have been so foolish? So unbelievably careless? What if Alex had been the one to come along and find them rather than she?

Without a word, Emma turned and ran back to her mare. Ridley did not follow. She knew he wouldn't leave Lady Glynnis alone now, but the damage was done, their secret well and truly revealed. Ridley and Lady Glynnis were in love—and Glynnis was engaged to marry Alex.

How on earth could matters ever have gone so completely and so utterly wrong?

Ridley came to her room later that evening. Immediately after dinner, Emma pleaded a headache and went upstairs. Her brother had appeared in the doorway a short time later, begging to speak with her.

Reluctantly, Emma let him in, but she had been harsh in her condemnation of his actions.

'Have you lost your mind, Ridley?' she snapped the moment the door closed behind him. 'Have you any idea of the trouble you're in? She is engaged to marry Lord Stewart!'

'You think I don't know that?' Ridley dragged his hand through his hair. 'Do you think I'm happy about what almost happened this morning?'

'Never mind what *almost* happened,' Emma murmured, her face burning. 'What *did* happen was bad enough!' She looked at her brother and sighed. 'Whatever possessed you to do something so reckless? Asking her to meet you like that?'

'I had no choice. I had to know, Emma, once and for all how she felt about me.'

'But why would she agree to such a meeting? Only yesterday she accepted Lord Stewart's proposal.'

'I know.'

'Then why—?'

'Because she wanted to tell me the truth, too. Before it was too late. The truth that…she loves me,' Ridley whispered happily. 'And that she has ever since the early days of sitting for me.'

Feeling her legs give way, Emma sank down on to the edge of the bed. 'But I thought she was angry with you for having shown the painting to Mr Towbridge.'

'She was, but you were right, Emma. I painted a portrait of a woman in *love*,' Ridley said quietly. 'A woman who'd never felt or looked that way before, even when she was with Lord Stewart. And Glynnis was afraid Tom would see that when he looked at it. She was afraid her expression revealed the true extent of her feelings for *me*.'

'So she *knew* the look of love on her face was there… because of you.'

Ridley nodded. 'Had it all been on one side or the other, it might have been all right. But because *she* was looking at me with love, and I was *seeing* her that way, there wasn't a hope that our feelings for one another wouldn't be reflected on the canvas. Glynnis knew that the moment she saw the completed painting. And when she realised how she really felt about me and how much she had inadvertently given away…she panicked. She used my showing the painting to Towbridge as an excuse for being angry with me. She accused me of betraying her trust, but it was actually her own feelings she was finding impossible to deal with.'

'Oh, Ridley,' Emma said with a groan. 'This is insane! She's in love with you—but she's going to marry Lord Stewart.'

'She has no choice. Even if she wasn't engaged to him,

she would never be allowed to marry me. Her father cares even more about class distinction than old Widdicombe does. Nothing less than an earl would do for his Glynnis. In fact, he suggested a match with the Marquess of Stahley's son if Stewart didn't make good on his promise.'

'Oh, that's just wonderful,' Emma said. 'But what kind of life do you think she's going to have with Alex now?'

'I don't—Alex?' Ridley frowned. 'When did you start calling him that?'

'Shortly after Linette and Peter became engaged,' Emma said, too distraught to bother making excuses. 'He said that since we were going to be brother and sister-in-law, it made more sense.'

'Well, yes, I suppose it does. Oh, God, and now Glynnis is going to be *my* sister-in-law,' Ridley said. 'I don't think I can bear it. I'm going to *have* to say something to him.'

'Him?'

'Lord Stewart. You're right, Emma,' Ridley said. 'It's madness for Glynnis to marry him when she loves me. She didn't plan on falling in love with me any more than I planned on falling in love with her, but we did and now we *have* to do something about it.' He took a deep breath and said, 'I'm going to ask Lord Stewart to release Glynnis from her promise.'

'Are you mad?' Emma said in horror. 'You'd be the laughing stock of London. A titled lady can play games if she wishes, but she does *not* back out of a marriage to an earl's son in order to marry an artist. I'm sorry, Ridley, but those are the facts of life!'

'But you just said it's insane that she marry someone else.'

'Of course it is! But going to Alex and expecting him to release her so that she can marry you is equally ludicrous. You just said Lord Leyland is more of a stickler than Alex's father. I guarantee if you go through with this, you *will* find every door in London slammed in your face.'

'Then what would you have me do? Let her go?'

Emma closed her eyes. 'Yes, because you have no other choice. Daughters of earls do *not* marry artists.' *And heirs to earldoms do not marry penniless nonentities.* 'Papa's right. You would have stood a better chance had you stuck it out and become a barrister. At least then you would have been received at Court. You would have had a profession with some degree of respectability.'

'Then I am lost.' Ridley sank down beside Emma on the bed, his expression bleak. 'She will marry Lord Stewart and give him the portrait I painted of her, and I shall never see her again.'

'Unfortunately, you *will* see her.' Emma put her arm around his shoulders. 'At Linette's wedding. At the birth of their first child. And at every family gathering and event that follows. But you will not let on to anyone how devastated you really are because it will gain you nothing. When you go to Linette's wedding—'

'I can't go!'

'When you go to Linette's wedding,' Emma repeated firmly, 'you will greet Lady Glynnis as a friend. Then you will kiss your sister and wish her happy in her new life and only then may you leave. But do not do this other thing, Ridley. You must *not* give Lord Widdicombe any reason to hate you. Because if he finds out about this, he will—and then I doubt very much there will *ever* be a wedding between Linette and Peter.'

The words seemed to shock Ridley awake. 'You think the earl would forbid them from marrying?'

'I'm surprised he didn't do it after the débâcle with Aunt Dorothy. He certainly wouldn't permit it if you were the cause of the break up between his heir and the lady he believes to be perfection in every way.'

The words were as difficult for Emma to say as they were for Ridley to hear, but they were the truth and they both knew it. If Ridley persisted in bringing his relationship with Lady Glynnis out into the open, they would all be ruined.

'Linette would hate me,' Ridley said quietly.

'I don't think Linette is capable of hate, but I know it would break her heart,' Emma said. 'And I think that would bother you far more than if she said she hated you.'

'It would. I can live with my own unhappiness. I couldn't bear knowing I had been the cause of hers.'

'Then it's settled,' Emma said. 'Lady Glynnis will leave with her parents later today and that will be an end of it. She and Al—Lord Stewart will marry. Linette and Mr Taylor will marry. And you and I will make the best of it.'

He glanced at her quizzically. 'You *and* I?'

Emma closed her eyes. 'Yes, Ridley. You *and* I. And if you wish to leave this room with your fingers still capable of holding a paintbrush, I suggest you not ask any more questions.' She sighed. 'There have been more than enough shocking revelations for one day.'

As it turned out, there was still one more shocking revelation in store for Emma. It was just after lunch that the letter was delivered. It was addressed to Emma and the young lad who brought it was told to make sure it was put directly into her hands. Upon breaking the seal, she discovered it was from Lady Glynnis.

Dear Miss Darling,
You will no doubt find the occasion of my writing to you unusual, but given what you witnessed yesterday

morning, I wanted to set matters right between us. I would also beg you to burn this after reading, as what I am about to say could have disastrous consequences if it were to fall into the wrong hands. As it is, I hope you can appreciate the level of trust I place in you by being willing to send such a letter.

It will likely be clear to you now, that your brother and I are in love. I tell you this, because I would hate you to misinterpret what you saw in the forest. You are no doubt aware that I have accepted Lord Stewart's proposal and that we are to be married. I hope you will wish me well, for it was always my intention to marry Alexander. As I told you that day, our friendship goes back a long way and I cannot think of a better or kinder man in all of my acquaintance. But once I met your brother, I realised how shallow my feelings for Alexander were, and how much more there could be between a man and a woman.

My relationship with your brother began soon after I began sitting for him. I found him to be charming, of course, as any woman would, and handsome because it would be silly to call him otherwise. But during our time together I discovered something else about Ridley: a tender and caring side, as well as a compassionate nature that appealed to me very much. And I discovered, for the first time in my life, a side to my own nature that took me completely unawares.

I don't know if you have ever been in love, Miss Darling. Until I met your brother, I had not. I knew attraction and I knew friendship. But I never knew what it was to ache for someone so intensely that to be without them was akin to a physical pain.

That came to me over the days and weeks I sat for your brother; perhaps now, looking back, I can safely say that the reason his portrait captured what it did is because I was willing to show that side of myself to him. I doubt the same results would have been achieved had I hired someone else to do the portrait. However, since it was your brother who drew out that side of me, it should have come as no shock to me that the finished painting would reflect what I felt when I was with him. Regrettably it did and I reacted accordingly.

Having said all that, we must also face the reality of our lives. I have accepted Lord Stewart's proposal because it is the right thing to do. My parents expect it. His parents expect it. And Alexander expects it. And knowing how deeply it would hurt him if were I to break it off now, I have no choice but to go through with it. Also, as my father would never permit me to marry a man like Ridley, there would be nothing to be gained by calling it off.

I hope you can understand this, Miss Darling. If wishes were horses, beggars would ride. An old proverb, perhaps, but significant in its message here. I will never forget Ridley, but I also know that there can never be anything between us. The rules that govern our lives are strict, the punishments for flouting them harsh. Please don't misunderstand me when I say that enough heartache has been caused by Mr Taylor's engagement to your sister. I cannot be the cause of further disruption to everyone's lives.

I hope that you and I can remain friends, and that you will keep secret the contents of this letter. There will be occasions when we are required to see one another and, for everyone's sake, I wish it to be

civil. But in case you have any doubts, I do like you
and your sister very much.
Yours, in friendship,
Glynnis

Emma slowly refolded the letter. It had taken a great
deal of courage for Lady Glynnis to write what she had.
It was an emotional confession, an outpouring of her soul.
And knowing what she risked in sending it, Emma felt a
warm glow of affection for the writer because, like she and
Ridley, Lady Glynnis had also found love with the wrong
person. And because of her awareness of her duties and
obligations, she had cast it aside to do what was right.

If wishes were horses, beggars would ride.

Emma tipped back her head and stared at the ceiling.
How appropriate the lady's choice of proverb. One needn't
be rich to have wishes. Even the most simple of men and
women had dreams. Unattainable, perhaps, but dreams
none the less. It was what kept people going and gave hope
to their lives. It offered something to aspire to. Except in
her case, it was a dream that could never be realised.

There wasn't a horse in the world that could carry
Emma to the place she so desperately wanted to go.

The day hadn't been much better for Alex. He had
hoped, after having offered his proposal to Glynnis, that
his life would magically fall into place. That with luck,
the confusion he'd felt until this moment would vanish
and leave everything remarkably clear. If anything, matters only became darker and more murky. While his head
knew he was doing the right thing, his heart screamed that
he was not. And as a man who had spent his entire life
listening to his head, this sudden, unexpected voice was
decidedly unwelcome.

He had gone for a long ride in the afternoon, refusing Peter's offer of companionship as gently as he could. There was no easy way of telling his brother how hard it was to spend time in his company now. Childish as it was, Alex knew himself well enough to know that every time he saw his sibling, he would be faced with the knowledge that while he would get the title and the estate, Peter would live happily with the woman he loved. And the woman Alex loved would likely end up becoming the vicar's wife.

He couldn't bear thinking about that either. Emma deserved so much more than John Tufton. A clergyman needed a woman without goals or opinions of her own. One who was content to live in his shadow and who would mould her life around his. That was what Emma's life would be like married to the clergyman and Alex couldn't think of a worse fate for a woman of her vivacious and creative nature.

Consequently, by the time he got back from his ride, his mood was even blacker than when he'd set out. He walked into the house and stood for a moment in the hall, trying to think what he might do for the rest of the day. Then, deciding a few hours with a book was as good a way as any to pass the time, he turned and headed in the direction of the library.

It was as he was approaching one of the smaller saloons that he heard a conversation taking place between his mother and father. Their voices were raised, and though he would normally have walked on, the anger in his father's voice prompted him to stop. Fearing that something untoward had happened, he paused by the open door to listen.

'—won't have it, Sarah. He should *never* have asked!'

'But why would he not ask, Richard?' his mother said.

'You have always given Peter an allowance. Why should you not increase it now that he is about to be married?'

'Because he is not marrying the woman I wish him to!' his father said peevishly. 'He is determined to marry that Darling chit, and do not think I fail to recognise the idiocy in having to say that! Silly name, Darling,' he muttered.

'You cannot blame the child for her name,' his mother said in a tone of mild reproach. 'She had nothing to do with that.'

'No, but she has everything to do with what's happened since. And if Peter thinks I'm going to increase his allowance in order to provide enough money for the two of them to live in luxury, he's got another thing coming. In fact, it's time I put an end to this once and for all.'

There was a slight, tense pause. 'What do you mean?'

'I mean that, if he insists on going through with this marriage, I will cut him off.'

Alex caught his breath, astonished that his father would even think of such a thing.

It was clear his mother was equally nonplussed. 'Richard, you can't!'

'Yes, I can. The money is mine to do with as I please. If it pleases me to cut my youngest son off without a penny, that is exactly what I shall do.'

'But how will they survive?'

'He can apply to the church for a living. That's respectable enough. They'll provide him with a house and a wage and Linette can become a parson's wife, as her sister no doubt will.'

There was another brief pause. 'You think Emma Darling has hopes of marrying the vicar?'

'Why not? I've seen the way he looks at her,' the earl said in a disparaging tone. 'No doubt he thinks to marry her and to improve *his* lot in life through her sister's connection to us.'

'Oh, Richard, I really think you're taking this too far. If Peter and Linette truly are in love, why not just accept it and let them marry?'

'Because love, my dear, is for peasants and stable boys. Not for those of our class. We marry for the good of our families.'

'I didn't marry you for the good of the family,' his mother pointed out. 'I married you because I fell in love with you.'

'You were the daughter of an earl, like Lady Glynnis,' the earl said, his voice softening. 'I did not flaunt my father's wishes and run off with a dairy maid.'

'Perhaps because you never fell in love with a dairy maid.'

Alex managed a smile at the teasing note in his mother's voice, but it was clear from his father's reply that he was not amused. 'Of course not, because I would never have lowered myself to associate with one. But I've had quite enough of Peter flouting my authority. He should be more like Alex. You don't see him acting like an irresponsible fool. He's marrying as he should, to a woman as noble as himself.'

'But have you ever heard Alex say that he's in love with Glynnis?' his mother asked. 'Do you think he genuinely cares for her?'

'What does it matter if he cares for her? If he decides she's not the one he wants to spend his nights with after they're wed, he can find himself a mistress and take his pleasures there. Once he's secured an heir, they can each go their separate ways, as long as they do it discreetly. But at least Alex is doing what society expects of him. What *I* expect of the man who will one day take my place!'

Standing by the door, Alex felt the beginnings of a slow, simmering anger. His father certainly wasn't painting a very flattering picture of his life with Glynnis, and, given the way his father felt about Glynnis, Alex would have thought him reluctant to see either of them seek out other partners. But it seemed his only concern was that Alex marry well and produce the required number of children. It didn't matter what happened between him and Glynnis once the requisite heir had been birthed. They could each go their own separate ways and take pleasure in the arms of another if that's what they wanted. After all, that was the way society did it.

'—never gave a damn about his obligation to me and this just proves it,' his father was saying. 'Well, we'll see who has the last laugh. When he's living with her and not able to scrape together money enough to buy food, we'll see if he thinks love is worth the trouble. I'll have Sufferton draw up new papers as soon as we get back to London.'

'Oh, Richard! Surely you would not be so cruel!'

'Sometimes it is necessary to be cruel, my dear. A son has to learn obedience to his father. Loyalty to his family name. If he doesn't, how will he ever be able to pass those qualities on to his sons? Who, by the way, will also be shunned by good society through the thoughtlessness of this marriage.'

Alex backed away from the door, having heard more than enough. He couldn't believe his father would go to such lengths. To cut off his own son without a penny just to prove a point was the height of cruel and heartless treatment. No, it wasn't required that a father give an allowance to his second son, but that was always the way it had been done in their family. The earls of Widdicombe were known for their generosity towards their children. Even daughters were permitted liberal inheritances as long as they married men of whom the family approved.

Of course, the sons in the line had always done as their fathers expected as well. But now, one of them had dared to step out of line, and his father had made it very clear that he was *not* the title holder to do that with.

In his room, Alex paced the floor, wondering what he could do. There was no point in trying to persuade his father to change his way of thinking. His mind was clearly made up. Peter's asking for an increase in his allowance to cover the costs of his new life with Linette had obviously been the last straw. But if Peter went ahead with his marriage, he *would* be cut off, and possibly disowned.

At one time, Alex wouldn't have believed his father capable of taking such a hard line, but given what he'd heard today, he knew better. And that left him very little in the way of options. In fact, it left only one. If he could not persuade his father to change his mind, or Peter to break off his engagement, there was only one other avenue he could pursue.

Linette. He would appeal to her sense of fairness and family loyalty, and pray that she would be willing to listen. If she loved Peter as much as Alex believed she did, she would do anything to prevent seeing him cut off from his family. Given that the ties to her own were so strong, she would surely wish to see him remain close in the arms of those who loved him.

And there was only one way that was going to happen. Peter might hate him when he found out what he'd done, but if there was any chance of salvaging his brother's relationship with his father—and possibly his very standing in society—Alex was willing to give it a try. He was doing what he had to for the good of the family.

Hopefully other people would be able to see it that way, and be called upon to do the same.

Emma was just getting up from the dinner table when the letter was delivered.

'What's that, Jenks?' Mr Darling enquired.

'A letter from Ellingsworth, sir. For Miss Linette.'

'No doubt a love letter from her devoted swain,' Ridley remarked without enthusiasm.

'Don't be a tease, Ridley,' Linette said, holding her hand out for it. 'May I be excused, Papa?'

'Of course, my dear. Reading like that is best done away from such mundane matters as family and sustenance.'

Emma smiled as Linette scampered off to read her letter. At least one member of the family was happy. Ridley had been noticeably withdrawn since Lady Glynnis's departure, and she oft-times found it an effort to smile in response to her father's quips. He had asked her, more than once, if something was amiss, to which she had promptly and emphatically replied that everything was fine.

Fine. Such a pathetic word, Emma thought as she made her way to the drawing room. It was neither descriptive nor emotive and communicated nothing about the way one truly felt. The weather was fine, but did that mean it was excellent or simply not bad? Fine really said nothing at all…and it described her mood perfectly.

Fifteen minutes on, the clock on the mantel chimed the hour. Emma lifted her head from her embroidery and glanced around the room. Strange, her sister hadn't come back downstairs. Linette liked to finish her day with some quiet reading by the fire, but tonight she had taken her letter upstairs and not returned.

Emma set her tambour aside and started for the stairs. She couldn't explain why, but she had a bad feeling that refused to be shaken. It was as though something unpleasant was about to happen. As though something over which she had no control was going to cause serious harm to those she cared the most about.

She reached her sister's room and knocked lightly on the door. 'Linette, are you coming back downstairs?'

When there was no answer, Emma pressed her ear to the door—and her suspicions were confirmed. The sobs were muffled, but her sister was definitely crying. 'Linette, what's wrong?'

The sobs came to abrupt end. 'Nothing! I'm f-fine.'

'You're not fine, dearest. Can I come in?'

'No. Go away, Emma. Please, just…go away.'

Go away? Linette had never told her to go away before. What could possibly have been in that letter that would make her ask such a thing now? Emma tentatively opened the door and saw her sister sitting on the edge of the bed, the letter lying on the floor at her feet. 'Linette, whatever is the matter?'

Her sister was too upset to speak. Her eyes were red and swollen, her lips compressed as though to keep from bursting into tears again.

Emma closed the door behind her. 'Has this something to do with the letter from Peter?'

'The letter wasn't from…P-Peter,' Linette stuttered. 'It was from…Lord Stewart.'

Alex? Emma glanced at the discarded piece of parchment. Why on earth would Alex be writing to Linette? 'What does it say?'

The younger girl closed her eyes, a shimmer of fresh tears on her lashes. 'Read it. I can't bear to look at it again.'

Quite sure it could contain nothing of a personal nature,

Emma picked it up. The writing was bold and slanted, as though written in a hurry. She could almost see his arm sweeping across the page.

Dear Miss Linette,

This letter will not make you happy and I pray you will find it in your heart to forgive me one day, but know that what I am about to say cannot be delayed. You are aware, I'm sure, that my father has not reconciled himself to your marriage to my brother. I had hoped that in doing what was expected of me, he would feel more lenient towards Peter, but it seems that is not the case.

My father has made it very clear that if you and Peter wed, he will cut my brother off without a penny. In short, he will disown him and I think you can understand the consequences of such an action. You will both be denied access to good society and my brother will be forced to vacate Ellingsworth Hall and look for accommodation of a far more humble nature. This will likely lead to his seeking employment within the church, as this manner of occupation does provide somewhere in which to live.

This might be something you could both bear and I have no doubt that the strength of your love would enable you to endure this. But there is another consideration. If my father disowns Peter, he effectively disowns any children resulting from the marriage. Therefore, I am asking you to do what must be done because you are the only one who can.

I am asking you to release my brother from his promise. A harsh request, I know, and one that will cause you deep pain. But I can assure you that nothing else will restore Peter to his father's good

graces. A father who, I regret to tell you, is not currently enjoying the best of health…

Emma let the letter fall. There was no need to read on.
Everything she needed to know had been said in those four
paragraphs. Alex wanted Linette to break off her engagement to Peter. He was asking her to 'do the right thing'
by appealing to her sense of goodness and love. It was
horrible! After everything they had been through, after
everything that had happened, Alex clearly felt no differently about the matter than he had on the day when he had
asked her to persuade Linette to break off her engagement.
The only difference was that now he had bypassed her and
gone directly to Linette in his desire to achieve his goal.

'He wants m-me to b-break it off,' Linette sobbed. 'He
says I have to…for the good of our children. What am I
going to d-do, Emma? I love Peter so much! How can I
ever let him go?'

Emma had no idea what to say to console the weeping girl. She pulled her sister into her arms and held her
close, even as her heart hardened against the men who
had done this. Dear Lord, was there no end to the misery
that dreadful family was willing to inflict? No pain they
would spare? She was beginning to curse the day she'd
ever heard of Peter Taylor and certainly rued the day Alex
had walked into her life.

Well, it was time to take a stand. No one had the right
to meddle in someone else's personal affairs—Alex certainly had no right to meddle in Linette's. Or to shatter the
poor girl's dreams. She was the least capable of dealing
with emotional heartache. Emma, at least, was older and
strong enough to deal with her own disappointment, as

was Ridley. But she would *not* allow Alex to destroy the happiness of someone as innocent and trusting as Linette. Not as long as she had breath enough to say it!

Chapter Thirteen

It was probably just as well the letter had arrived at the
end of the day, Emma thought as she prepared to set off
the next morning. Had it come earlier, she would probably
have marched off to Ellingsworth at once, demanding to
see Alex and confronting him without having taken the
time to think through what she wanted to say. She would
have flown at him like a mother hen at a fox, her only
thought being to protect her chick, even though both she
and Linette would likely have suffered as a result.

Instead, she had lain awake through the long hours of
the night, reviewing everything that had happened and
trying to come up with a logical argument. If she did not,
she feared she would arrive at the front door of Ellingsworth, angry and emotional, and stumble and stutter her
way through her tirade and, in doing so, forget the most
important things she needed to say.

She couldn't allow Alex to see her that way. She had to
be cool and rational. She needed him to listen to what she
had to say and to present her arguments in such a manner
that he would be willing to give some credence to her line

of thought, perhaps even be open to working with her to reach some kind of satisfactory conclusion.

She accepted that there would be no resolution to her own problem. Alex was lost to her. There would be no last-minute change of heart. No sudden, unexpected revelation that would allow them to be together. He was engaged to marry Lady Glynnis and nothing was going to change that. All she would ever have was the memory of his kiss.

That would stay with her until the day she died. She would never forget the feeling of his arms holding her close, the tenderness of his mouth as it closed over hers, his lips moving so sensuously over hers. She would cherish that memory for ever, like a jewel in a keepsake box, to be taken out and admired when she was old and alone.

But, hopefully, it wasn't too late for Linette. With luck, Emma would still be able to make Alex see the merit in allowing the marriage to take place. Yes, Peter could apply to the church, if not in Little Moreton, perhaps in a neighbouring parish. Mr Tufton would surely know of something. Or they could live here at Dove's Hollow. Her father would never refuse them a room and then there would be no immediate need for Peter to find employment.

There *were* solutions, Emma told herself as she bent to let her maid set the riding bonnet atop her freshly styled curls. There were ways they could make this work. And by the time she spoke to Alex, she intended to have them memorised and ready to present so that he would find no flaws with her logic.

She took a last look at her reflection in the glass and was satisfied with what she saw. She had decided to ride over to Ellingsworth in her new habit because she knew she looked well in it, and a good appearance gave her confidence. Devoid of excess trimmings, the outfit was elegant simplicity at its best. The jacket was a touch darker than the skirt, both being in her favourite shade of periwinkle blue. Her black, high-brimmed bonnet was trimmed with trailing blue ribbons and sat jauntily on her head.

'Have you been in to see to my sister yet, Jane?'

The little maid shook her head as she picked up the breakfast tray. 'I did, but she was feeling right poorly, miss. Said she was supposed to have gone to see her young man this morning, but given how she was feeling, she had Jenks take a letter over to say she wasn't coming.'

Emma froze. Linette hadn't been planning on going to Ellingsworth this morning. She had been planning to take the trap to visit her friend, Miss Tamblyn. Linette had told her as much only yesterday afternoon. Then why had she sent a letter to Ellingsworth cancelling an appointment that didn't exist? More importantly, to whom had she sent the letter?

Emma swept up her skirts and headed for her sister's room. 'Linette, may I come in?'

After a moment, she heard a faint voice say, 'Come in, Emma.'

She opened the door to see Linette standing in front of her wardrobe, fully dressed and with her travelling bag lying open on the bed. 'Are you going somewhere?'

'Yes.' Linette did not turn around. 'To London.'

'London?'

'To stay with Aunt Dorothy. She told me I was welcome to come whenever I liked.'

Emma walked in and closed the door behind her. 'But why?'

'Because I cannot stay here a moment longer,' Linette said quietly. 'There is nothing for me now but memories that grow more painful by the minute.'

'Linette, dearest, what are you talking about? Your life is here, with Peter.'

'Not any more. I've…broken it off.'

Emma gasped. 'What?' She flew to her sister's side and turned her around. 'Why ever did you do such a thing?'

'Because I had no choice. Don't you see, Emma?' Linette whispered, her face crumpling. 'He would have *disowned* him. His own *son*. How could a father do something like that to his child?'

'I fear it is the way of the aristocracy. Obligation and duty mean more to a man like Lord Widdicombe than the love he feels toward his son,' Emma said. 'But that doesn't matter. If Peter still wishes to marry you, his father cannot stop him from doing so.'

'But at what cost?' Linette shook her head. 'I love him so much, Emma. How could I bear to see him reduced to a man with no status? A man forced to give up everything he is entitled to…everything he is used to…because of me. It is more than I would ask of any man, let alone him.'

'Now you listen to me, Linette Darling,' Emma said in a tone that brooked no argument. 'I have been giving this a great deal of thought and there is absolutely no need for you to do anything so drastic. You and Peter can live here at Dove's Hollow after you're married. You know Papa would agree to that. You can have my room and I could use Ridley's. Then Peter could speak to Mr Tufton about employment within the church. He's sure to know how to go about making that happen. And I can give you money—'

'Oh, Emma, it's not the money or the job, don't you see?' Linette interrupted. 'Lord Widdicombe intends to *disown* Peter if we marry. Do you know what that means? It means our children would have no status in the eyes of society. Their own grandfather would not recognise or receive them. How could I do that to them? I can live with the consequences of my own actions, but to know that I

would be condemning their lives from the very start is
more than I could bear.'

'But you don't *know* he would do such a thing,' Emma
said. 'I've yet to see a man who doesn't fall head over heels
in love with his grandchild the very first time he sees him
or her. Do you really think Lord Widdicombe's heart so
hard that he could shut out the sight of his own grandson?'

'I do not know Lord Widdicombe's heart well enough to
hazard a guess. But based on what I *do* know of him, yes,
I think he would, if only to make a point.' Linette shook
her head. 'I could never hurt a child of mine the way he
has hurt Peter. Never! But at least now, he won't have to.
I sent Peter a note this morning, telling him that I am…
releasing him from his promise.'

Emma gasped. 'Oh Linette, you must not—!'

'It's done. And I have asked that he not to come to see
me because I am going away. It's over, Emma. Lord Widdicombe has won. I am not going to fight any more. I am
going to finish my packing and then get ready to leave.'

'Not if I have anything to say about it.' Emma got up
and headed for the door.

Linette spun around. 'Where are you going?'

'To see Lord Stewart. It's time I gave him a piece of
my mind. Then we'll just see who's won and who's lost!'

Alex was in the library going over some correspondence
when the butler appeared at the door. 'Miss Emma Darling
to see you, my lord.'

Alex put down the letter. Emma was here? 'Show her
in, Houston.'

Moments later, she appeared in the doorway and it was
all Alex could do not to run to her and sweep her up in his
arms. She looked lovelier than ever in a deep-blue riding
habit, her cheeks dusted with pink, her lips the colour of

a newly bloomed rose. But her chin was raised in defiance and her eyes flashed fire. She was upset and deeply so. 'Emma—'

'Are you happy with yourself, Lord Stewart?' she threw at him. 'Are you content now that you have ruined her life?'

Alex stopped. 'I'm not sure I understand—'

'You wrote my sister this letter!' Emma said, waving a piece of parchment in front of his face. 'How could you ask her to break off her engagement? What kind of a man are you?'

At once, the cause of her anger became clear. 'The kind who puts the welfare of his family first. I am sorry to have caused your sister pain, Emma—'

'Miss Darling!'

The coldness of her voice struck him like a blow to the heart. 'Miss Darling. But everything I wrote in that letter is true. My father will disinherit Peter if he marries your sister. I heard it from his own lips. He will cut off Peter's allowance and provide nothing in the way of future income. What do you think that will do to my brother, Miss Darling? How do you think that will make him feel, knowing he would not be able to support his wife and his children?'

'He would not be the first man forced into earning a living,' Emma retorted. 'Your brother is an intelligent man. He can find a living that will provide for all of them. He can approach the church, or teach, as my father did.'

'Oh, yes, the son of the Earl of Widdicombe, tutoring the younger brothers of the boys he went to school with. That's a wonderful thing for a man's pride.'

'Pride be damned!' Emma cried. 'If he loves Linette enough, he will do whatever he has to in order to support her.'

'Yes, he probably would,' Alex said more slowly. '*If* it

was only the two of them. But what about their children? Would you have their lives blighted because of a mistake their father made?'

'Your brother has chosen to stay with Linette in spite of everything that's happened,' Emma said, ignoring his use of the word 'mistake'. 'Up until this point, he has stood by her. Now you have gone behind his back and asked the woman he loves to put an end to their engagement. And she has.'

Alex stared at her. 'She broke it off?'

'You didn't know?'

'I haven't seen my brother this morning.'

'Then you should seek him out, Lord Stewart,' Emma said coldly. 'You should ask him how he feels now that his engagement is at an end. Because I can tell you how Linette feels. She is broken hearted! She is going to stay with my aunt in London because she cannot bear to remain here a moment longer. You have ruined her life, my lord. But I don't suppose that matters to you, does it? Now you can go to your father and tell him the good news. Hoorah, Father, your beloved son is not to marry that wretched young lady.'

'Miss Darling—'

'He is free to marry someone from his own class. Someone as stuck up as you—'

'Emma—!'

'Thank God I managed to save him from himself—!'

The rest of the words were cut off. Alex crossed the room in three strides and pulled her into his arms, silencing her with a kiss. It wasn't meant to be gentle. It was meant to punish and it tore his soul apart. He wanted nothing more than to beg her to forgive him, to forget about the duty that had ruled his life from the moment of his birth and to tell her how much he loved and needed her.

He wanted to cast off responsibility and lead the life he wanted. A life with Emma.

But he wasn't free to do any of those things. He could no more shrug off his obligations than he could his name and he could no more have Emma Darling than he could the stars in the sky. Both blinded him with their beauty and both were for ever unattainable.

He carefully set her away from him, aware that they were both trembling. Emma's face was white, her lips pink from the bruising force of his kiss. 'Forgive me,' he whispered, the words torn from his heart. 'I had no right...'

'No, you had no right,' Emma said in a voice so low he had to strain to hear it. 'No right to kiss me like that. No right to go to my sister and ask her to break off her engagement. No right to meddle in something that doesn't concern you. I will never forgive you for the pain you have caused Linette, my lord. And though I never thought I would hear myself say this, I pity Lady Glynnis. You think she is marrying you for the benefit of you both, but you're wrong. A woman can say what she likes, but in the deepest recesses of her heart, she will always long for love. Especially when she knows how powerful the emotion can be.'

She left him where he stood. Not moving, scarcely breathing, the pain in his chest threatening to tear him apart. He might have stood there for a minute or an hour, the memory of her voice slicing into his heart. She despised him. And she had every right to do so...

'Alex?'

Peter. Alex hadn't heard his brother come in. But looking up, he asked the question, needing to know if it was true. 'Have you heard from Linette this morning?'

There was no need for his brother to speak. A look of

such anguish appeared on his face that Alex knew it would haunt him for the rest of his life. 'You have.'

'She sent me a letter. She has withdrawn her acceptance of my proposal.' There was no inflection in Peter's voice. He could have been an automaton reciting lines. 'She wishes me well and says it is…for the best.'

They stood the length of the room away…and the length of the world apart. 'It *is* for the best, Peter,' Alex said, though even to his own ears the words sounded hollow and trite. 'I overheard Mother and Father talking. He was going to cut you off. To disown you without a penny if you went ahead and married Linette.'

'I know.'

Alex stared. 'You *knew*?'

'Of course. It was the only weapon he had left. He hinted at it when he suggested I make Linette my mistress. He tried to tell me she wouldn't be interested in me if I was nothing but a parish priest, because that's all I would be if I refused to do as he asked. So I told him to go ahead and do it. That I would make the best of it.'

'You *told* him that?'

'What else was I to say?' Peter asked quietly. 'I had no intention of giving Linette up. She was my *life*, Alex. I never knew it could be like that between two people. Never knew how complete a man could feel just by having someone like her by his side. Even when I wasn't with her, I felt…connected to her. The knowledge that she was thinking about me, wherever she was, made me feel whole. I don't expect you to understand. I know your relationship with Lady Glynnis isn't based on love. But mine was. And it truly was the most remarkable thing I have ever experienced. I felt as though I could *do* anything…*be* anything… as long as she was by my side. With her, I could have scaled mountains. Without her, I am…just a man.'

Alex had no idea what to say. What *could* he say to a man who believed he had just lost everything of value in his life? A man whose unhappiness now was as a direct result of his own interference? 'What are you going to do?'

Peter managed a smile, even though he looked close to tears. 'What *can* I do? She has taken the decision out of my hands. She's told me she has no desire to see me again. I've lost her, Alex. And there's not a damn thing I can do about it.'

There was nothing Alex could say. If ever he had seen a man tortured by emotion, it was Peter. The life had gone out of his voice and the spirit out of his heart. His eyes were dead, devoid of the warmth and humour that had always been there. In one fell swoop, Alex had destroyed the gentle man his brother was and alienated Emma—the one woman he had ever truly loved. The woman who had opened his eyes to what love was really about and who had made him feel all the things Peter had just described. Everything he had been willing to give up, all for what he had believed to be the right reasons. 'Have you told Father yet?'

Peter shook his head. 'I'll tell him tonight. I'm not ready to see him gloat. I was on my way to the stables when I saw Miss Darling leave. What did she want, by the way?'

Alex grimaced. 'To tear a strip off me for ruining her sister's life.'

'You didn't ruin it.'

'Yes, Peter, I did.' And with a heavy heart, Alex told his brother about the conversation he'd overheard between his mother and father, and about the letter he had written to Linette as a result.

'I thought I was doing the right thing,' he said, humbly, at the end. 'But now, I realise I was entirely in the wrong.

It wasn't my place to interfere. When I see what it's done to you—'

'You acted the way you did for the right reasons,' Peter said without inflection. 'You were concerned about my future. Maybe I was wrong to say it didn't matter. That I could live without Father's approval. Maybe it would have meant more to me when the invitations stopped coming and Linette and I were turned away from the places I've always been welcome at before. Maybe then I would have believed that he truly had my best interests at heart. But right now, all I can feel is this terrible emptiness. This pain for everything I've lost.' He turned and started towards the door. 'You know, it's funny. Father's approval always meant so much to me. I tried to excel at everything I did so he would be proud of me.'

'He always was,' Alex said.

'Until now.' Peter shrugged again. 'And that's what's funny. I don't care any more. It's as though I'm seeing him clearly for the first time in my life. And for the first time in my life, I'm not sure I like what I see.'

Peter quietly left the room. Alex remained behind, staring at the floor. Emma was right. He had interfered in something he'd had no business interfering in. He had tried to do the best for all concerned; instead, he had just ended up hurting the people he loved most. And for what? His father's happiness? His own sense of having done the right thing? What had he to look forward to for all his efforts? His brother's sad face. His own empty marriage to a woman who probably deserved better.

He thought about what Emma had said. *A woman may say what she likes, but in the deepest recesses of her heart, she will always long for love. Especially when she knows how powerful the emotion can be.*

What had she meant by that? Was she suggesting that

Glynnis knew what she was missing and wanted more? Alex had never stopped to consider how Glynnis felt about their marriage. He'd assumed, as most men did, that having several homes to look after and with every comfort at her disposal, she would be happy. But what if she truly wanted more? What if, under the pretence of practicality, she *did* long for love?

He'd never thought about it for himself. Never dreamt he would find anything missing in his relationship with Glynnis—until he'd met Emma and discovered what love was really all about. It was about two people looking out for each other's welfare and happiness. It was his brother being willing to give up his father's approval, his position in society, even his life as a gentleman, in order to be with the woman he loved. It was Linette Darling, willing to set free the man she loved because she feared what it would cost him if he went ahead with the marriage.

And it was Emma Darling. His Emma. Having the courage to stand up to him and tell him he was wrong. To tell him that Glynnis wanted more and deserved better, and that he had a long and empty life ahead of him.

Why? Because he had done what he'd thought right. He had honoured what he had been taught to honour. Respect what had been taught to respect. The traditions that had become the life and breath of his world.

Suddenly, he realised he couldn't have been more wrong.

He found his brother in the stable, waiting for the groom to finish saddling up.

'Ready Thunder as well, would you, Clarke?' he said to the lad tightening the girth on his brother's saddle.

The young lad nodded. 'Right away, m'lord.'

Alex turned and offered Peter a smile. 'Mind if I join you?'

His brother sighed. 'Actually, I'd prefer some time on my own.'

'I understand that. And I'll give you all the time you want…if you'll give me just a few minutes of your time now. There's something I have to say to you, Peter. Something very important. And it can't wait.'

Peter stared down at the stone floor, then slowly nodded. 'All right.'

They set off for the rolling hills behind Ellingsworth. Alex was aware of an incredible sense of freedom, as though on the verge of doing something he had always wanted to do without even having been aware of wanting to do it. But now he knew what needed to be done, and, once having accepted that he was the only one who could do it, it was almost as though it couldn't happen fast enough.

After a vigorous gallop, they reined in their horses and stood admiring the countryside around them. Everywhere he looked, Alex saw new life springing up. Flowers blooming in the hedgerows. Trees budding into leaf over head. The air was warm and sweet with the scent of growing things. London had never looked or smelled like this, he thought wryly.

'Peter,' he said finally. 'I've been giving this situation with you and Linette a great deal of thought. And I've come to the conclusion that I was wrong to suggest to either of you that you break it off.'

Peter's head slowly came up. 'Why?'

'Because you love Linette Darling and she loves you. You were willing to sacrifice our father's respect and approval, and to be disowned without a penny, rather than lose her, and she has released you from your promise, rather than be the one to cause you to lose everything she thinks you hold dear.'

'Yes. So?'

'So, it makes absolutely no sense that the two of you shouldn't be together. That's why I think you should go to her this very minute and beg her to take you back.'

Peter looked stunned. 'Are you serious?'

'Never more so. It's your life, Peter,' Alex said with quiet intensity. 'Not mine. Not Father's. Yours. Even in the short time I've been here, I've seen how happy Linette makes you and how miserable you are now. And I have no reason to doubt that Miss Darling isn't every bit as unhappy. Her sister informed me that she would be leaving for London as soon as it could be arranged.'

'London!'

'Yes. She said she couldn't stay here a moment longer because the memories of you both here were too painful to be borne.'

'But what about Father?'

'Father will have to accept your decision. You're a grown man, Peter,' Alex said. 'And you're not the first-born son and heir. You have the freedom to live your life as you choose and you have a lady out there who loves you to distraction.'

'But you're right about one thing,' Peter said. 'I'll have no money. How can I support Linette without that? I'll certainly have to let Ellingsworth go.'

'Not necessarily. I've been giving some thought to acquiring a country property and I find I like Ellingsworth very much,' Alex said. 'I could take over the payments on the house and you and Linette could reside there until you found something that would provide you with an income. I'm sure Mr Tufton could be applied to for information. Perhaps he knows of a living that might be available in the area. In the interim, I will pay your expenses and provide for the two of you—'

'No! It is too much, Alex!'

'It is not too much. You are my brother and I love you. Consider it a wedding present, if you like. But I want to do this for you and Linette.'

'But what if Father threatens to disinherit *you*?'

'He can't. I am his legitimate heir. He would hardly disinherit me over my efforts at helping my brother.' He might for the other thing he intended to do, Alex thought narrowly, but he couldn't worry about that yet. 'However, if it makes you feel any better, I will do everything I can to make Father see that this *is* the right thing to do. I know Mother will back me up and hopefully between the two of us we can bring him around.'

'And if you can't?'

'We'll cross that bridge when we come to it. For now, go and find Linette and tell her the two of you are going to be married. Just don't mention anything to Father yet.'

'But I don't see how—'

'Trust me, Peter,' Alex said. 'I'll be returning to London today as well. There are a few other things I need to take care of. But believe me when I say that I am doing what needs to be done and that, by the time the dust clears, matters will have been settled for the best.'

Chapter Fourteen

Alex had visited the stately home of the Earl and Countess of Leyland and their daughter many times in the past, but never had he expected to be paying a call of this nature. Within minutes of arriving, he was shown into the music room where Glynnis was practising the piano. 'Alex!' She rose immediately to greet him. 'I didn't know you were back in London.'

'I've only just arrived.' He crossed the room to kiss her cheek, then stood back to look at her through the eyes of a man newly awakened to the subtleties of love. She was as beautiful as ever, but for the first time, he saw the shadow across her smile and realised her eyes were curiously flat. 'How have you been?'

'Well. Mama has been keeping me very busy with plans for the wedding.' She bid him sit down. 'Shall I ring for refreshments?'

'No, I won't stay long. I've come to talk to you, Glyn. There's something I have to say.'

Her smile was uncertain. 'It sounds serious.'

'It is. Come, sit down beside me.'

She settled herself on the loveseat by his side and, for a moment, he just looked at her, seeing in her face that of the girl he had grown up with. He remembered laughing with her in the past, the joy in her eyes so apparent, so fresh. He hadn't seen that joy once during their time together at Ellingsworth. Not even when he had asked her to marry him.

How close they had come to making a dreadful mistake by going ahead with a marriage to which neither of them was emotionally committed. 'Glyn, there's something I have to tell you,' he began, 'and it's not going to be easy—'

'Say what you must, Alex,' Glynnis interrupted. 'You and I have always been honest with one another.'

'Have we?'

He knew the question caught her off guard. He saw the blood rush to her cheeks and watched her eyes fall. 'Well, as honest as two people can be, I suppose.'

He shook his head and, reaching over, took hold of both of her hands. 'We haven't been honest at all, Glyn. And I think…no, I know that it's *imperative* that we be honest with each other now. Before we go any further down this road.'

A tiny line appeared between her brows. 'I'm not sure I understand.'

'Glynnis, do you love me?'

Her eyes widened in surprise. 'Surely you know the answer to that.'

'I'm not sure I do. And until this moment, I'm not sure it mattered. But it matters now and I need you to be completely honest with me.' When she still said nothing, Alex sighed. 'Would it make it easier if I told you…I wasn't in love with you?'

It was a harsh thing to say and the last thing he wanted to do was hurt her. But he owed it to both of them to be brutally honest. Especially in light of what he was about to tell her. 'Well?'

Slowly, Glynnis pulled her hands free. She stood up and walked back towards the piano. 'Why are you telling me this now? We are…engaged to be married.'

'Yes, we are. But we aren't married yet. And given the events of the last few weeks—'

'Events?' She glanced at him over her shoulder. 'What events?'

'My brother's engagement to Linette Darling. Our meeting the rest of her family.'

Falling in love with Emma…

Glynnis turned, and for a moment, he saw a flicker of alarm in her eyes. 'What has meeting the rest of her family to do with anything?'

Alex's gaze narrowed. Was it just his imagination or did her reaction to that one remark seem a little out of keeping with the importance of the comment? 'It has a lot to do with everything.' He slowly stood up and went to stand beside her. 'Because as hard as it is for me to say this, it's only fair that we both face the fact that…my brother is not the only one to have fallen in love with a member of the Darling family.'

Her face went white, her gasp echoing around the room. 'Oh, Alex, I'm so sorry. I never meant to hurt you. Truly. I never even meant that you should find out. It just happened. I was s-sitting for the portrait and we began talking and—'

'The portrait,' Alex said, grasping hold of something that might explain what she was talking about. 'Towbridge mentioned something about a portrait.'

Her eyes opened wide. 'He did?'

'Yes. He said if ever he'd seen a picture of a woman in love—'

'Oh God, he said that? Then you've known all along!' Glynnis said miserably. 'I was stupid to think word wouldn't get around.'

And then to his astonishment, she burst into tears.

Alex was dumbfounded. He had never seen Glynnis cry before. Except that one time when she had fallen out of a tree and broken her arm. Other than that, she had always been one of the most stoic and controlled women of his acquaintance. And yet here she was, weeping as though her heart were breaking. Had he truly misread the situation so badly? Was she so deeply in love with him that the thought of losing him to Emma truly had broken her heart...'Glynnis, I—'

And then just as abruptly, he remembered something else she had said. *I never even meant that you should find out...*

'Glynnis, what *exactly* are you trying to tell me?'

For a moment, she gazed at him, her lips pressed tightly together as though afraid to say the words. Then, shaking her head, she sighed. 'I'm sorry, Alex. I never meant to fall in love with him. But as the days passed and I came to know him better, I realised I had feelings for him that went far beyond anything I should have felt for him, and, well, one thing led to another and before I knew it, it was... too late.'

Alex was very nearly speechless. She had fallen in love...with another man? 'Glynnis, I'm sorry, but I honestly don't know who or what you're talking about.'

'But you just said Tom told you about the painting. And that...you knew I was...in love with a member of the Darling family,' she whispered.

'No. I said *someone* was in love with a member of the Darling family,' Alex said. 'I didn't say or suggest it was you.'

She blanched. 'You didn't?'

'No. I was trying to tell you that it was me. *I* fell in love,' he said quietly. 'With Emma Darling.'

'Emma!' Glynnis whispered. 'You're in love…with Emma Darling?'

'That's what I've been trying to tell you.'

And then, to his astonishment, her expression altered and she actually started to laugh. 'Oh, Alex, this is truly madness! We are both beyond help, do you know that?' She wiped her eyes, took a moment to recover herself, and then said sadly, 'Then you really didn't know.'

'Know what?'

'That I am in love, too. With Ridley Darling.'

Ridley Darling. It took a moment for the words to sink in. 'You're in love…with Emma's *brother*?'

She nodded.

'The painter?'

She nodded again. 'Idiotic, isn't it?'

'I don't know whether to be shocked or relieved,' he said. 'I don't suppose you have any brandy in here.'

'As a matter of fact…' Glynnis started towards a small cabinet in the corner and, opening the door, drew out a decanter and two glasses. She tried to pull out the stopper, but her hand was shaking so badly that Alex had to take over.

'I think you'd best leave that to me. I hate to see even a drop of good brandy wasted.' He filled the two glasses and handed her one. 'But we both need a bit of a bracer. Cheers.'

'Cheers.' They downed the brandy, after which Glynnis pressed a hand to her heart. 'Goodness! That certainly clears the mind.'

'Excellent shock therapy,' Alex agreed, refilling his

glass. He held up the decanter, but Glynnis quickly shook her head.

'Another one of those and I won't have my wits about me. And I think I need to know exactly what we are both saying.'

They were silent, gazing at one another as though seeing each other for the first time. 'You're in love with Emma Darling?' Glynnis said finally. 'Truly?'

'That's what I came here to tell you,' Alex said softly. Then he laughed. 'I thought it was going to be a shattering revelation. As it turns out, it is only one of many.'

Glynnis bit her lip. 'Oh, Alex, I cannot believe this has happened to *us* of all people. You and I have always believed in the sensible approach to marriage. We both agreed that to make such an important decision based on sentiment was the height of stupidity. And yet, look what's happened. We were each promised to the right person, only to fall in love with the wrong one.' She stared at him in bewilderment. 'How could we possibly have been so mistaken?'

'Because we didn't know any better,' Alex said. 'Neither of us ever expected to fall in love.'

'Does she know?'

Alex shook his head. 'I haven't told her in so many words,' he admitted. 'And given what I did just before I left, it may not matter.' In a few words, he told Glynnis of the letter he had written to Linette, of Linette's reaction to it, and of Emma's response to him as a result.

'But never mind me,' he said. 'What about Ridley Darling? Does he know how you feel about him? More importantly, does he feel the same way about you?' Glynnis blushed, but Alex saw the happiness in her eyes. 'I see that he does.'

'I'm sorry, Alex. I still feel so strange talking to you

about this, but…yes, he loves me. I didn't know for certain until the day I was leaving Ellingsworth. We'd had a terrible fight in London. Over the painting. That's why it was so difficult for us when we met at the ball. I'm sure you noticed.'

'I was aware of a certain tension between you,' Alex admitted. 'But we were all a little on edge that night. I put it down to the meeting between Father and Linette.'

'That didn't help,' Glynnis acknowledged, 'but that was entirely separate from what Ridley and I were going through. You see, that was the first time we had seen each other since we parted in London.'

And then she told him what had happened with regard to the painting and to her relationship with Ridley as a result.

'So you thought it was Tom Towbridge who had exposed you.'

'I could think of no other way you would find out. He was the only one who saw the painting and I was sure he recognised the expression of love on my face,' Glynnis said simply. 'Naturally, my guilty conscience led me to believe he would put it down to my feelings for Ridley and tell you the same.'

'He did nothing of the kind,' Alex said. 'He simply said he hoped he would be lucky enough to meet a woman one day who loved him as much as you obviously loved me. So he did recognise the expression on your face, Glynnis. He simply attributed the reason for it being there to me.'

'Oh, Alex. This a fine mess we've landed ourselves in,' Glynnis murmured. 'What *are* we going to do about it?'

'Well, we are going to start by releasing each other from our promises,' Alex said, taking her hand and leading her back to the loveseat. 'And then you are going to tell Ridley

Darling that you love him and that he has to marry you. Or he will have me to answer to.'

But Glynnis was already shaking her head. 'There's no point. Father won't allow me to marry Ridley. He's more of a stickler for propriety than your father. He would never allow me to marry so far beneath me. And if I don't marry you, he'll only push me in the direction of someone else with a title as good as or better than yours.'

'But you're in *love* with Ridley,' Alex said softly.

'Yes, and you're in love with Emma. But you haven't said you're going to ride back to Little Moreton and ask her to marry you.'

'I'm not even sure she would have me.'

'You'll never know if you don't ask.'

Alex looked at her and, for the first time, felt a fleeting moment of regret that he hadn't been able to feel more than friendship for her. 'You are a very special lady, Glynnis. Darling's a lucky man.'

She reached out her hand and gently caressed his cheek. 'I think the problem with us, Alex, was that we were always such good friends. You looked out for me and I did my best to protect you from the girls who were after you for all the wrong reasons. Somehow in the midst of all that, we developed feelings for one another that were anything but romantic. You are truly the best of men and I admire you tremendously, but…'

'You don't love me,' Alex finished softly.

She shook her head. 'Not in the way a woman should love the man who would be her husband. I didn't have the courage to tell you that before. And I would have married you, rather than disappoint everyone else. I thought perhaps you did care for me, in that way. But it would have been like marrying my brother.'

He snorted. 'That would have made lovemaking decidedly uncomfortable.'

'Oh, Lord!' Her cheeks flushed crimson, but then she started to laugh. 'Yes, it would, wouldn't it.' And then they laughed together as the truth of the situation hit them both. 'So, what do we do now?' she asked.

Alex got up and said nothing for a moment. He hadn't expected any of this, but now that they had cleared the air, the answers suddenly seemed obvious. 'Glyn, would you consider leaving London if it meant you could be with Ridley Darling?'

She looked up at him with an expression of surprise. 'Probably, but Father would never approve—'

'I didn't say anything about your father approving. I asked if you would be willing to live somewhere other than London if it meant you could be Ridley's wife.'

She gazed at him in silence for a few minutes. Then, slowly, she nodded. 'Yes, I would.'

'Then that is what you must do.' He walked back to where she sat and drew her to her feet. 'You must contact Ridley and tell him that I have released you from your promise and that you and he must make plans to marry as soon as possible.'

'But how—?'

'You are both of age. I will make arrangements for a special licence and will be present at the marriage to witness that everything is done legally and above board. Then you and Ridley can return to London as man and wife and present yourselves to your parents. Based on what your father says, you will go from there.'

'What if he tells me to get out?' Glynnis asked.

'Then you will have to decide where you want to live,' Alex said. 'You have, I believe, an inheritance from your mother's parents?'

'Yes! I'd almost forgotten. Papa has always been so generous with my allowance, I've never had to draw upon it.'

'And I believe Mr Darling has money of his own. From all I've heard, he is making quite a name for himself as a portraitist; once the scandal of this dies down, he will be in demand again. You, however, may have to reconcile yourself to the fact that you will never be received by good society again, especially if your father chooses not to recognise your marriage. But outside of London, there's no reason why you can't lead a very happy and fulfilled life. Most importantly, you will be with the man you love and I wager your father will eventually come round.'

'I'm not so sure.'

'I am. Your father adores you. He would cut out his heart rather than see you walk out of his life altogether. And I will do all I can to facilitate his acceptance. After all, he will blame me for it happening. Not you.'

'But I do not wish him to have the wrong opinion of you, Alex,' Glynnis said. 'It is only fair that he knows I fell in love with someone else, too.'

'Will that matter to him?'

She slowly began to smile. 'It may not matter to him, but it will to Mama. She turned down a duke's proposal to marry my father, because she loved him and not the duke. She often tells me the story. I think, in her heart, she was always a little sad that you and I weren't marrying for love.'

'Then it sounds as though you're already halfway there,' Alex said. 'Between your mother and myself, I'm sure we'll be able to bring your father around. Especially once he meets Ridley. The man's a charming rogue, but he's likeable all the same.'

Glynnis sighed. 'He is much more than that.'

'Yes, I'm sure he is.' Alex smiled and bent down to kiss the top of her head. 'Or you wouldn't have fallen in love with him.'

'And what about you? How are you going to resolve your situation with Miss Darling? And with your father? He won't be pleased when he learns about this. You saw how he reacted to Peter's engagement to Linette. He will be furious when he hears that his heir has decided to cast aside discretion and follow his heart.'

Yes, he would, Alex acknowledged. But right now, that wasn't his biggest concern. His biggest concern was in finding out if Emma still wanted him. Once he knew the answer to that, there would be plenty of time to decide how he would deal with everything else.

Two days later, Emma sat in front of her easel, trying to muster the enthusiasm to continue with her painting. Ever since Alex had gone back to London, it was as though a light had gone out in her world, immersing her in a Stygian darkness from which there was no escape. She wouldn't have believed it possible to miss a man so much, to feel as though even the effort of living wasn't worth the trouble, but, clearly, that's what losing love was all about.

She gazed at the stone angel in front of her and sighed. 'I would trade places with you if I could,' she murmured, dipping her brush into a pot of paint. 'Stone angels don't have hearts that can be broken.'

'Are you sure?' a man said quietly. 'Have you ever considered that someone did break her heart and maybe that's why she's not smiling?'

Emma stiffened. *It couldn't be.* He had no reason to come back to Dove's Hollow. And why had he come back now? This was the *worst* possible time for him to be here. She wasn't strong enough to see him. She couldn't talk to him rationally when it was as much as she could do just to breathe.

She stretched out her arm and carefully touched the flat side of the brush to the canvas. 'Angels don't fall in love. They live in heaven where all is bliss and harmony. Love is part of this world. Or of hell.'

'It doesn't have to be.'

'Sadly, it is. At least for this family,' Emma said, feeling the onset of unwelcome tears. Oh, yes, that was perfect. Now she was crying. Why couldn't he have just stayed in London and left her alone? 'What do you want, Alex? I thought you had gone back to London for good.'

'No.' She heard the crunch of his boots on the gravel path. 'I went back to London because there was something I had to do. Someone I had to see.'

He stepped into her peripheral vision. Emma turned her face away so he wouldn't be able to see her tears. 'Am I supposed to know who you're talking about or are you going to make me guess?'

'You probably already know.'

'Lady Glynnis.'

'Yes.'

Emma stabbed paint against the angel's wing. 'Have you set a date for the wedding?'

'There isn't going to be a wedding,' he said, forcing her to draw back her arm as he moved to stand between her and the canvas. 'At least, not between Lady Glynnis and myself.'

Emma's gaze flew up to his. 'But…you are engaged!'

'Not any more. We talked about it when I was in London and we both agreed it wasn't going to work.'

Wasn't going to work? Emma thought her heart had been pounding before. It was close to exploding now. 'I don't understand. You asked her…to marry you. She said yes. It was a long-standing arrangement.'

'Yes, it was. But I asked her *before* I knew she was in love with another man. But you knew that, didn't you, Emma?' he said gently. 'You knew all about the relationship between Glynnis and your brother.'

Emma jumped up, knocking over the water jar. 'How did you find out?'

'Glynnis told me. Why didn't you?'

'Because it wasn't my place to say anything,' Emma said, flustered. 'It wasn't my secret to reveal.'

'Maybe not, but surely I deserved to know that the woman I was marrying was in love with someone else.'

'Of course you did, but Glynnis asked me not to say anything. She asked that it be our secret.'

'How fortunate for all of us then, that it isn't a secret any more.'

Emma looked at him. Was he furious—or devastated? He didn't appear to be either, but a man like Alex was good at hiding what he was truly feeling. He only let a person see what he wanted them to. 'You don't seem overly upset,' she said cautiously.

'That's because I'm not upset. I am *delighted* to know she is going to marry the man she loves.'

'Marry!" Emma gasped. 'Lady Glynnis is going to *marry* Ridley?'

'That was her intention when I left London.'

'But…what will her parents say? What will society say? He is an artist. She is the daughter of an earl!'

'Yes, but she is also a woman in love. And now that she is free to be with the man she loves, nothing is going to stand in her way. Very determined is Lady Glynnis when she sets her mind to something.'

'She must be,' Emma said in bewilderment. Because

she would be going against the tide of popular opinion; doing something frowned upon by society and likely by everyone else she knew. All because she wasn't willing to live without the man she loved.

And then, an even more daunting thought occurred to Emma. 'What is your father going to say when he hears about this? He adores Lady Glynnis.'

'Yes, he does. And I hope that when he realises how much she loves Ridley, he will be able to find it in his heart to wish her well and to forgive me.'

Emma bit her lip. 'What do you think the chances of that are?'

'Realistically? Not good,' Alex admitted with a shrug. 'But he will have no choice. Unless your brother changes his mind, he and Glynnis *are* going to be married. They probably won't end up living in London, but I don't think either of them cares about that. Ridley will find work elsewhere and, knowing society the way I do, this notoriety will only add to his cachet and people will seek him out even more. Glynnis's only concern is that they be together.'

Emma looked up at him, struggling to grasp everything he was saying. 'Is this what you came to tell me?'

'One of the things.'

'There's more?' she squeaked.

'Yes. The other reason I went to London was to tell Glynnis I could not marry her.'

'Yes, I know. Because she was in love with Ridley.'

'But I didn't know that when I went there, did I?'

'Then why...?'

His smile had a slightly wicked edge...and suddenly, there wasn't enough air in Emma's lungs to finish the sentence. Her mouth opened, but the words didn't come.

Alex just smiled. 'I did a lot of thinking after our last conversation, Emma. And I realised you were right. I had no right to interfere in Peter and Linette's relationship. Your sister is a sweet, gentle woman and she is marrying my brother because she loves him. And he loves her. I don't think I realised how much until I saw his face after he received her letter breaking off their engagement.'

'But they aren't getting married,' Emma whispered. 'Linette is in London with Aunt Dorothy.'

'Yes, I know. I thought Peter would have gone to see Linette before she left, but apparently he went to see Mr Tufton instead to ask him about employment within the church. But Peter is in London now, intent on trying to change your sister's mind.'

'*What?* But you said they should not—'

'I know what I said and I was wrong. I told Peter as much, too,' Alex said. 'I told him to go after Linette and beg her to marry him because I couldn't bear knowing that I was the one who had caused those two dear people so much heartache.'

Emma had no idea what to say. She was hard pressed to believe what Alex was telling her; though she was delighted for her sister and Peter, she couldn't believe that Alex would change his mind so completely, even to allowing Ridley and Lady Glynnis to marry.

If only…

No, that was asking too much. Cupid had only so many arrows in his quiver and he had already expended more on her siblings than any one family had a right to expect.

'To say I'm happy would be putting it mildly,' she said finally. 'I never thought it possible that matters would turn out like this. I had hoped Linette and your brother might have an opportunity at finding happiness together, but I never dreamt there was a chance for Ridley and Lady Glynnis as well.'

'We don't ask to fall in love with the people we do,

Emma,' Alex said quietly. 'Sometimes it's the last person in the world we expect to fall in love with; sometimes it is the last person we *should* fall in love with. But none of that matters because when you find that person and when you know it's right, you'll move heaven and earth to try to be with them. You will defy your family and fly in the face of society because all that really matters is being with that person.

'Sometimes, it doesn't work out,' he said. 'Sometimes, no matter how hard we try, the odds are too great and the sacrifices too high. But I have come to believe that if the love between two people is strong enough, they *will* find a way. A piece of iron only becomes stronger the more time it rests in the fire. I think that's true for relationships. When put to the test, love either gets stronger or melts away entirely.'

Emma nodded blindly. Tears were filling her eyes as fresh pain welled in her heart. She had never loved this man more than she did at this moment. He had done everything he could to facilitate the relationships between Linette and Peter, and Ridley and Lady Glynnis. He had swept aside duty and obligation to help them be with the people they loved and he had done so without thought or consideration for himself. She had no doubt he would receive a chilly reception from his father and from society for the part he had played in bringing those two couples together.

'And what will you do now, my lord?' Emma asked softly. 'You will find things very difficult in London for a time, I think.'

'Perhaps, but it has been on my mind to leave London for a bit,' Alex said. 'I told Peter I would take over the lease of Ellingsworth Hall, and that he and Linette could live there until they are able to make arrangements for a place of their own.'

'You would do that for them?'

'Of course. He is my brother. I would do all that I could.'

'But…what will your father say?'

'I don't know, but, whatever it is, he will have to resign himself to the situation. I dare say when he sees his first grandchild, those resentments will fall away, as they should.'

'What about the state of his health? This might be more than he can tolerate.'

Alex smiled. 'I am convinced he will outlast us all. I told Mother as much and I stand by my claim. But I'll speak to the doctor once I return to London and find out exactly how things stand.'

'Then, you will be living here. In the area,' Emma said, wondering how she would bear it.

'Yes. I find I rather like Little Moreton. It has a charm I didn't expect, but then I suspect that has much to do with the people who live here. Especially with the Darling family, who seem to have made such a lasting impression on every member of my family. By the way, I never did tell you what I wanted you to paint for me.'

The abrupt change of subject left Emma frowning. 'I was hoping you had forgotten all about it.'

'I haven't. Fortunately, the picture is almost completed, so you can finish it for me now.'

'Finish it?' Emma said. 'I haven't even started it.'

'Yes, you have. It's right there in front of you.'

Emma stared wide-eyed at the painting. 'The stone angel?'

'Yes. I've grown rather fond of this particular angel,' Alex said, looking down at the canvas. 'But there is one thing I would like you to add. One word. But only the right word will do. Otherwise, I don't want it.'

Emma gazed at him in bewilderment. 'You want me to paint a word. On this painting.'

'That's right.'

'Why would you want a painting with writing on it?'

'As a memento of the day.'

'Why? Is today special?'

'I'm hoping it will turn out to be, yes.'

'And what is the word?'

'You will have to be the one to tell *me* that, Miss Darling.'

'I cannot read your mind, my lord.'

'You won't have to. Now, if you wouldn't mind sitting down again.'

Emma frowned, but resumed her seat in front of the easel. Alex picked up her brush, dipped it in a bright blue blob of paint and handed it to her. 'Now, somewhere on the painting, I would like you to write the answer to a question.'

'I still don't understand.'

'You haven't heard the question yet.'

'Oh, very well.' Emma turned to look at the painting. 'What is your question?'

'Just this. Emma Darling.' He slowly dropped to one knee on the ground beside her and said, 'Darling Emma, will you marry me?'

She dropped the brush.

Patiently, he picked it up, wiped the gravel off the bristles and, dipping it in the blue paint again, handed it back to her. 'Would you like me to repeat the question?'

'No…yes, that is, I heard the question. I just don't understand—'

'I shall explain later. Just paint your answer.'

Emma faced the canvas. This was impossible. It couldn't be happening. He wasn't really asking her to marry him, was he? She turned back to look at him, but he sat without moving. Waiting.

She glanced back to the canvas. He *was* asking her to marry him. He was waiting for her to write her answer, yes or no, on the painting of the angel. He wasn't teasing her. He was very serious.

And ever so slowly, Emma began to smile. She smiled until she thought her face would split. So, this was how it felt. This was how you knew when it was right. When the world seemed a brighter place and no problem seemed insurmountable. This was how you knew you were in love.

She took a long, deep breath and slowly pressed her brush to the canvas. He had given her paint enough for one short word. And there, right where the stone angel's heart would be, she carefully, and lovingly, painted the word *'yes'*.

Beside her, Alex made a sound. It might have been a murmur of joy, or relief, or a combination of the two. But whatever it was, Emma knew she had given him the answer he wanted.

'I love you, Emma.' He slowly got to his feet and drew her up with him. 'You know that, don't you?'

'I do now.' Aware that she was still holding on to the brush, she set it down, and then looked up into the face of the man with whom she would be spending the rest of her life and whispered, 'I love you too, Alex. With all my heart.'

His mouth covered hers hungrily, demanding a response, and willingly Emma gave it to him. She held nothing back, kissing him with a passion that surprised her and a depth of sincerity that could leave him in no doubt as to her feelings. A passion that was echoed deep within her soul.

Yes, there would be challenges. Their life together would not be as easy as some. But as long as Alex loved her, Emma knew she would be able to face whatever came her way.

'There might be one small problem,' Alex said when he finally, reluctantly set her away.

'Other than your father and most of society, you mean?'

'Yes. Do you think your Mr Tufton will agree to marry us?'

Emma blushed and laughed softly. 'He is not *my* Mr Tufton.'

'Of course he is! He's besotted with you.'

'Really? Then why did he ask Miss Cynthia Brown to marry him last Tuesday?'

'He did?'

'So Mrs Connelly informed us. And if Mrs Connelly says it's true, it must be.'

Alex smiled. 'Perhaps he did that because he knew you were mine.'

'You did a very good of keeping *that* a secret, my lord.'

'Only from you. I'm sure Mr Tufton knew exactly how I felt. But it is just as well. At least now I won't feel the need to glare at him as he pronounces us husband and wife.'

Emma tutted. 'There would never have been the need for that. You are the *only* man I have ever cared about, Alex. You must have known I was falling in love with you?'

Alex bent his head to kiss her one more time. 'I didn't. But I shall never get tired of hearing you say it. Now, shall we go and tell your father the good news?'

Emma nodded and, with Alex's arm tucked around her waist and the other holding his newly acquired painting, they walked back to Dove's Hollow as the real stone angel smiled her crooked smile and the warm spring rain gently began to fall.

Epilogue

Ellingsworth Hall—September, five years on...

It was a happy crowd that gathered to celebrate the fourth birthday of Michael Richard Percy Taylor, son and heir of Lord and Lady Stewart, and grandson of the Earl and Countess of Widdicombe. Peter and Linette arrived first, bringing with them their three-and-a-half-year-old daughter, Mary, followed by Ridley and Lady Glynnis, the latter suffering through the early stages of her pregnancy, but joyous nonetheless.

Next came the grandparents: Lord and Lady Widdicombe, the Earl and Countess of Leyland, and Emma's father, who had become even closer to Emma during the weeks and months following Michael's birth. Only the two aunts were missing, Aunt Dorothy having written to say that she and Augusta were travelling in Switzerland as they had reconciled in the weeks following Augusta's separation from her husband.

A tent had been set up on the grounds of Ellingsworth Hall to offer protection in case of rain, but as the day had dawned clear and bright, no one sought to use it—except to procure refreshments from the magnificently laden tables set out within. Emma fondly watched her husband prepare a meal for her, smiling when she saw him place an extra piece of chicken on an already heaping plate.

'I shall not fit into any of my gowns if you keep on feeding me like that,' she complained good naturedly.

'Ah, but you're eating for two again, my love,' Alex said, adding a spoonful of potatoes, a helping of roast parsnips and a generous portion of Cook's excellent bread stuffing. 'And I would not wish to see my lady go hungry.'

Emma sighed as she eyed the plate, knowing that despite her protestations, she would most likely finish off every delicious bite. 'I wasn't this hungry when I was carrying Michael. I must be having twins.'

'Or a girl. Remember how ravenous Linette was when she was carrying Mary? I swear Peter had to bring her food at all hours of the day and night. Made it devilishly hard for him to finish his sermons.'

Emma laughed. Oh, yes, she remembered well her tiny sister's unusual preoccupation with food. Once she had recovered from her initial bout of morning illness, Linette had gained a very healthy appetite and six months later had been delivered of a beautiful baby girl: a pink-and-white angel who charmed everyone she met, including, and most particularly, her two doting grandfathers.

'Would you mind if this baby was a girl, Alex?' Emma asked as they left the tent and strolled out into the golden autumn sunshine.

'I would be delighted if it was a girl, but would be equally pleased if it were another boy.' He glanced down at her, his eyes darkening as they lingered on the lush fullness of her breasts. 'Knowing how much you want a daughter would give me an excuse to keep on making love to you.'

Emma blushed at his blatantly sensual tone. 'You hardly need an excuse for that, my lord. Given the frequency of our lovemaking, I'm surprised it took as long as it did for me to conceive again. It took so little with Michael.'

'Ah, yes, but I had all those weeks of pent-up longing and frustration to get out of my system.' Alex leaned over to nuzzle a kiss into his wife's neck. 'The first time we made love was *very* powerful.'

Emma felt the familiar sense of urgency, aware that the memory of their first night together still had the power to move her. The intensity of their passion had caught both of them unawares and Emma still blushed when she thought about all they had done and how wantonly she had responded to her new husband's caresses.

She blushed even more when, upon approaching the group seated on chairs in the shade of the big elm tree, she caught Linette watching her and saw her begin to smile.

'I swear Linette had developed the ability to read minds since becoming a mother,' Emma murmured. 'She always starts to smile whenever I'm thinking about you.'

'Then she must be smiling all the time.'

'Odious man. Are you insinuating you are all I think about?'

'Of course.' He stopped and drew her against him, mindful of the well-laden plate he was still carrying. 'God knows, you are all *I* ever think about.'

'All right, you two,' Ridley drawled. 'Need I remind you that there *are* others present, including two young and highly impressionable children.'

'You need remind me of nothing, brother-in-law.' Alex kissed his wife soundly on the lips, then turned to grin at

Ridley. 'I just wanted to make sure no one questioned the depth of my love for this woman.'

'I doubt there's *ever* been any question on that score,' Lord Widdicombe said drily. He was bouncing his grand-daughter on his knee, but turned to glance fondly at his younger son. 'Or on your brother's.'

Peter smiled, looking completely relaxed and at ease as he stood behind Linette's chair, gently rubbing her shoul-ders. He was now the vicar of St Anne's in the neighbour-ing parish and it was clear from the look on his face that church life suited him. He and Mr Tufton had become fast friends and Linette had taken to her role as a clergyman's wife like a duck to water. They had set up housekeeping in the old manse, a lovely stone house reminiscent of Dove's Hollow, and were already well loved by their parishioners.

'Thank you, Father,' Peter said now. 'I am the first to admit that I've never been happier and that it is all due to Linette being my wife.'

'And what more could a father ask than to see both of his sons so happy?' Lady Widdicombe commented with a smile.

'I venture to say your sons' choices have made you a happy man as well, Widdicombe,' Lord Leyland observed. 'You're in far better health than you were when they met and not nearly as cantankerous. You haven't stopped grin-ning since the day Michael was born.'

'Don't forget that Mary has him wrapped around her pretty little finger,' Lady Widdicombe added.

'Guilty as charged,' the earl said. 'But wait until it's your turn, Leyland. You have no idea what holding your first grandchild in your arms is going to do to you. I cer-tainly didn't.'

'Well, I'm definitely looking forward to finding out,'

Lady Glynnis said weakly. 'Given the way I'm feeling today, it cannot come soon enough.'

'Never mind, dearest,' her mother murmured. 'Like you, I suffered dreadfully in the early days of my pregnancies, but it does eventually pass. It just means everything is proceeding as it should.'

Emma's heart went out to her sister-in-law. Glynnis and Ridley had been forced to endure much more in the early days of their marriage than either she and Alex or Linette and Peter had, and when Glynnis had miscarried in the early weeks of her first pregnancy, no one had been overly surprised. So when Ridley made the announcement a little over four months ago that his wife was pregnant again, the news had been received with great joy and quiet prayers that all would be well. Emma knew how anxious they were to start a family.

'Uncle Ridley,' Michael said, abruptly getting to his feet after obviously having had enough of adult conversation. 'Have you brought me a present?'

'Michael!' Emma gasped. 'It's not polite to ask people if they've brought you something.'

'Why not? I did it all the time,' Ridley said, ruffling his nephew's blonde curls. 'And of course I've brought you something. In fact, if you ask your grandfathers nicely, they might just take you down to the stables and show it to you.'

'The stables!' The little boy gasped. 'You bought me a *pony*?'

'I didn't say that.'

'But you said my gift was in the stables! That must mean it's a pony!'

Mr Darling got to his feet and reached for his grandson's hand. 'Well then, young man, I suppose we had best take a walk down there and see if you're right.'

'You come too, Grandfather Widdy,' Michael said. 'And you, Mary.'

Lord Widdicombe, who seemed not to mind that his revered name had been shortened in such an unseemly fashion, gently set Mary on her feet and then stood up to take her hand. 'Come along, my dears. Let's go see what all the excitement is about.'

As the two men and their grandchildren started in the direction of the stables, Emma glanced at her brother with an expression of mingled affection and annoyance. 'Have you really bought him a pony, Ridley?'

'I have. In fact, I've bought ponies for *each* of them.'

'What?' Linette squeaked. 'For Mary as well?'

'Well, I wasn't here for her birthday in April and when I was down at Tat's and saw these two little gems, I knew they would be perfect. And I did clear it with your respective husbands first.'

'That doesn't justify your continuing to spoil them,' Emma said.

'Of course it does. Spoiling is the prerogative of uncles and grandparents,' Ridley said. 'Besides, given that I'm such a rich and successful artist now, I can well afford it.'

That was another unexpectedly happy conclusion to a situation about which Emma had harboured serious doubts. After Ridley and Lady Glynnis's secret marriage in the neighbouring parish, one arranged by special licence and witnessed by Alex and Emma, the pair had returned to London, only to be met by the stony disapproval of Glynnis's father. Alex had done his best to try to smooth things over, but the earl had been intractable, refusing to acknowledge the marriage or even to receive the pair in his house.

It had been a heart-wrenching time for all of them and

a situation for which Emma had seen no hope of a happy resolution.

Until Lady Leyland had taken the matter into her own hands. Daughter of a marchioness, she had refused to be denied access to her own daughter and, secretly delighting in the news that Glynnis had married for love, she had set about re-establishing the pair in society. She had called together several of her closest friends, all of whom were very highly placed and all of whom had married for love, and told them the truth of Glynnis and Ridley's situation by also telling them of Alex and Emma's.

She had explained that it was Alex who had released Glynnis from her promise because he was in love with another woman, only to discover that *she* was in love with another man. The countess had also stressed that no improprieties had taken place and that surely four such good-natured and well-intentioned people should not be cut off from the company of others, simply because they had chosen to follow their hearts and marry for love rather than obligation.

Her strategy had worked. Doors that had been closed in the newlyweds' faces slowly began to open and the invitations had started arriving again. At that point, the countess had turned her attention to her husband, knowing that his approval mattered far more to Glynnis than society's ever could. And using every stratagem she could think of, the countess had slowly begun to chip away at his anger.

Naturally, there had been resistance. Even when society had begun to welcome Glynnis and Ridley back, the earl had refused to back down. But when his wife had gone to him with the tragic news of Glynnis's miscarriage, concern for his daughter had driven all other thoughts from the earl's mind and he had immediately gone to see her. In the following days, all had been forgiven, the marriage had been accepted and, as a result, Ridley's popularity as an artist had soared.

'Speaking of gifts, there's something in the house for you, Emma,' Ridley said casually. 'You might like to take a look at it before the grand unveiling after dinner this evening.'

'Before the *what*?'

Emma looked to her husband for an explanation, but he only smiled and drew her up out of her chair. 'I think that's an excellent idea, Ridley. You don't mind if we leave all of you for a few minutes, I trust.'

'Not at all. Just don't forget to come back,' Ridley warned. 'I don't want to be the one to explain to Michael why you're not here when he gets back from his visit to the stables. Or for some time after that!'

Her gift was hanging on the drawing room wall. It was a large canvas, beautifully framed, and the moment Emma saw it she knew how special it was. 'Oh, Alex!'

It was her stone angel, even to the smudge of blue over her heart. But it was a painting within a painting. Arranged around the stone angel was a portrait of her new family. Alex standing tall and proud, dressed as he had been on their wedding day and gazing at her with so much love that anyone looking at the painting would have to be able to see it. Emma was standing next to him, wearing the gown she'd worn the night the two of them had met, and she was holding Alex's hand. And there in front of them was Michael, his bright blonde curls reflecting the warmth of a late afternoon sun. It was an incredibly moving portrait of a family bound together by love.

'Oh, Alex, it's beautiful!' Emma whispered, touched beyond words by what her brother had done.

'Happy birthday, darling,' Alex said, drawing her into the circle of his arms. 'I knew you would like it.'

She looked at him in wonder. Her *birthday*? But of course! In all the preparations for Michael's birthday, including the week-long visit of Ridley and Glynnis and all the grandparents, Emma had completely forgotten that it was her birthday as well. She turned back to stare at the painting in wonder. 'You asked Ridley to do this for me?'

'Yes. He's been working on it for quite some time.'

'He must have been.' Emma moved closer to the painting, lightly touching the canvas. It was truly remarkable the way Ridley had combined her painting into his so that it was almost impossible to see where one canvas had ended and the other began. 'I don't know how he did this,' she murmured, 'but I can see why he's gained such a reputation for brilliance. He has managed to incorporate my painting of the stone angel perfectly into his own.'

'Yes, because the painting wouldn't have meant nearly as much to either of us if Ridley had painted a new angel. It would have been…imperfect.'

'Imperfect?' Emma glanced back at the painting. 'Ridley would have painted the statue a hundred times better than I ever could.'

'Exactly. Your flawed stone angel means more to me than…than a flock of perfectly painted angels ever could. And you know why.'

She turned her head to meet his gaze and felt the familiar longing begin. 'Yes, I know.' Her voice grew husky as she stepped back into the warmth of his arms. 'Because only our angel knows how much we went through to be together.'

The kiss was slow and thoughtful and when at last Alex raised his head, his eyes were dark with desire. 'I love you, Emma. You know that, don't you?'

'Yes, and I love you. But…I'm not sure you can refer to a group of angels as a flock, my lord,' she whispered against his throat. 'It makes them sound like sheep. Or pigeons.'

'Then what do you call a gathering of angels, beautiful lady?'

'Perfection.' Emma closed her eyes and felt the thrum of desire as his lips brushed over hers again. 'Exactly like my life here with you.'

* * * * *